HO   **WHERE HE WAS**
NL

Continuing along the block, he looked for familiar faces. He found them sitting at the window table of Brooks Restaurant. Dell Schroeder, wearing his stained Pioneer Seeds cap, sipping a cup of coffee and sharing a story with stubble-faced John Wilson. Frozen there on the sidewalk, Wallace was bombarded by memories.

The glass separating Wallace from the two men saved him from blurting out a greeting. As it was, he stared long enough to draw their glances.

Wallace forced himself to turn away. It was becoming harder to maintain his balance. It was time to finish what he had come here for. He had to face his own life.

I can't do it. I can't face him.

How can I deal with it when *he* looks at me like a stranger? How can I keep from blurting out, "Dad, you're looking good, I haven't seen you in two years. I came the long way home . . ."

DON'T MISS *THE TRIGON DISUNITY—EMPRISE, ENIGMA*
AND *EMPERY*—
ALSO BY MICHAEL P. KUBE-McDOWELL . . .

"As fascinating as it is ambitious!" —*Locus*

"Reminiscent of Arthur C. Clarke at his best."
—*Newsday*

ALTERNITIES

MICHAEL P. KUBE-McDOWELL

ACE BOOKS, NEW YORK

ALTERNITIES

An Ace Book/published by arrangement with
the author

PRINTING HISTORY
Ace edition/October 1988

ISBN: 0-441-01774-6

Ace Books are published by The Berkley Publishing Group,
200 Madison Avenue, New York, New York 10016.
The name "ACE" and the "A" logo
are trademarks belonging to Charter Communications, Inc.

PRINTED IN THE UNITED STATES OF AMERICA

10 9 8 7 6 5 4 3 2 1

ACKNOWLEDGMENTS

Marin Paul, for legwork in Boston; Doug Houseman, for lending his expertise and pieces of his library; L. P. Feist-Deich, for legwork in Philadelphia and a thousand clippings; my father, for sharing his memories and fielding odd questions at odd hours; Marc Satterwhite, for scouting Bloomington; the staff of the State Library of Michigan, for eternal patience. Any errors or amendments of the facts are my responsibility, not theirs.

For Eleanor Mavor and Melissa Singer,
who opened doors

And for Russ Galen,
who now guards them

CONTENTS

I pray Heaven to Bestow The Best of Blessings on This House and All that shall hereafter Inhabit it. May none but Honest and Wise Men ever rule under this Roof.

—President John Adams

You think that if we are victorious, I shall not know when to stop. You are wrong. I shall know.

—Josef Stalin to Anthony Eden, 1941

PRELUDE

Little enough good news, Walter Endicott thought as he skimmed the headlines of the Philadelphia *Bulletin* he had just purchased in the hotel shop. Little enough to make me want to avoid newspapers these days.

The King of Egypt in Washington, begging President Humphrey for more American aid to prop up his tottering regime. A third outbreak of the mysterious waterborne flu in Chicago, two hundred hospitalized. Another lynching in Mississippi—that made three this week, or was it four? And the Indians' losing streak had stretched to six, with hated Detroit threatening to lock up the league crown by Labor Day.

A bell chimed and the door to the elevator behind Endicott opened. Moving toward it, he tucked the paper under his arm and dropped the change from its purchase into a pocket of his tan overcoat. As he entered the car, the elevator guard offered a quiet "Good evening, sir."

"Six," Endicott said, settling against the back railing.

"Yes, sir."

At least in the smaller circle of his life there was order. The streets outside were quiet, the police much in evidence, enough so that he had felt comfortable walking the few blocks to the restaurant. Bookbinder's had lived up to its reputation; the dinner of stuffed crab and boiled shrimp was enjoyable despite having been taken alone. And the old Bellevue Stratford was well air-conditioned against the August heat, which was

1

almost as important as its staff being accommodating about his needs.

Endicott nodded to the guard as he left the elevator. There was no urgency in Endicott's pace as he walked down the well-lit hallway, feeling for the key among the change in his pocket. He had that comfortable full-bellied feeling and nearly an hour to enjoy it before the woman would arrive. One appetite sated, another just starting to build.

Letting himself into his room, Endicott dropped the newspaper on the cherrywood dresser and the overcoat on the foot of the bed—already turned down by the maid, he noted approvingly. There would be no interruptions.

He brushed his teeth with a brisk efficiency, splashed hot water on his face and rubbed the oils away. As he dried his hands, he studied the reflection in the mirror. He carried a dozen pounds more than he had as a twenty-one-year-old Navy enlistee, but he carried them well. The close-cropped hair was almost pure white now, but still thick and full, the hairline showing no signs of receding. His features were clean and masculine, his wrinkles few.

I look my age, he thought. Forty-six. No reason I should want to look any different.

He stood in the bathroom doorway for a long moment, his hands steepled and pressed against his mouth, as he considered carefully whether there were any further preparations to make. The contents of the small black case tucked between the bed and nightstand—there was no reason to hide them any longer. The woman would have been told what he expected.

But neither was there any reason to lay them out like some ten-year-old displaying a prized collection of shells and stones. When he had need of something from the bag, he would have the woman retrieve it. That was the best way, always.

He coaxed music—a Schumann symphony, pleasant enough and undemanding—from the radio in the sitting room and settled in a comfortable chair. The newspaper was within reach, but he let it lie undisturbed and allowed himself to wonder briefly what she would be like.

It was important that she not be too slender. The underfed, coltish look which was so fashionable offered Endicott little. Such were too fragile, too boyish. The essential feminine character, the blossoming of female sensuality, required a softer roundness in hip and breast, Rubenesque, callipygian. Such women moved well, in and out of bed. Such women knew how to give, and accept, the fullest range of pleasures their bodies offered.

With luck, he was waiting for a woman of that kind.

Endicott reached for the newspaper and opened it to the business section. The agate type of the market listings offered happier news than the front page—four of his five major investments were up for the week.

Packard Motors was the only dog, down on reports that its new line-leading Atlantic was languishing on dealer floors. Wags were already calling it the Packard Titanic, and predicting that within six months the company would be too weak to fight off a takeover. Wolves with names like Ford and Leyland were already circling.

Endicott shrugged off the news. He had kept the Packard stock largely out of sentiment. His father had worked for the firm in Connorsville for seventeen years and faithfully plowed a share of his earnings back into his employer, determined to build a family fortune. And the first car Endicott had bought when he turned in his Navy uniform in 1945 was an eight-year-old Packard 120 that looked like junk but kept running on love and mercifully little money for three more years.

Three long years, still vivid two decades later. Him pursuing a GI Bill diploma from Michigan State and Grace trying to make a home out of the awful Quonset-hut married housing on the East Lansing campus. The car had saved their sanity more than once, carrying them on innumerable weekend sojourns to the Lake Michigan shore. They had sold it, with regret, when he took that first real job in Cleveland. No car had ever meant more to him.

Especially not that dog of a Kaiser-Frazer we bought next—

At that moment, the lights flickered once, then failed, plunging the suite into darkness. At the same instant there was a crackle of static from the radio, and the music died a dozen bars from the piece's climax.

"What in hell—" Endicott exclaimed.

An eerie faint greenish glow marked the face of the alarm clock, which Endicott saw double, reflected in the dressing-table mirror. Except for that, the blackness was total and unrelieved. Frowning, he folded the newspaper as best he could, set it aside, and sat back in the chair to wait.

A minute passed, and the lights remained off. Annoyed, Endicott rose to his feet and felt his way to the phone, meaning to call the front desk. But the instrument was as inert as a child's toy.

Moving like a caricature of the newly blind, Endicott found the door to the suite and cracked it open. He looked left, toward the elevators. His night vision was excellent, and yet he could see nothing, sense nothing. It was like looking into a vat of black paint.

He looked to the right. There was a faint glow at the end of the hallway, though the end seemed much farther away than he had remembered it being. The glow seemed to pulse and flicker. An emergency light with a sick battery, or the flashlight of a bellman, he thought. Or a fire.

Except there were no emergency lights in the halls, no side corridors where the bellman could be standing, no hint of smoke in the air. Closing the door behind him, Endicott started down the hallway, the fingertips of his right hand grazing the fabric wallcovering to guide his steps.

The glow did not grow perceptibly brighter as he neared it. He could not even be sure that he was getting closer. Nor did the source of the light reveal itself. It seemed as though the corridor itself was glowing, walls and floor and ceiling lit somehow from within with a light that blurred all detail into an undifferentiated halo. The strangeness of it slowed his steps, but curiosity drew him ever closer.

Then suddenly every square inch of his skin was seized by a crawling sensation, as though he were naked and had walked into a giant spiderweb. There was a resistance pushing back against him, and he strained to continue forward. A moment of tension, then the resistance broke and the sensation passed.

But when it did, Endicott found himself surrounded on all sides by the pulsing glow, now a dozen times brighter. The floor beneath his feet, the ceiling over his head, the walls on either side were all consumed with energy. In fact, it was impossible to say that walls and ceiling and floor still existed.

He spun around and looked back the way he had come. There was nothing to see but the omnipresent dazzle of light. What was behind him was what was before him. It was as though he had come through a doorway that no longer existed.

Endicott did not waste a moment wondering if what he was experiencing was real. His was an orderly world. He trusted it to behave, trusted his senses to be reliable and true. If what his senses told him about the world seemed inexplicable, it could only be because he did not yet know enough about what he was seeing.

Squinting and shielding his eyes with one hand, he reached out to his right. The wall was not there. But *something* was. He felt something liquid wrap around his fingertips and slide off, as though he were adrift in a canoe, his hand trailing in the water. He found the same phenomenon to his left.

Experimentally, he took a step. And another. And another. He was braced for resistance, prepared for the clammy-clingy feeling of the phantom spiderweb. In time—five hundred steps? a thousand?—he found both. Pushed forward, straining, struggling, against a force far more powerful than the one which had impeded his entry into this place. With steady pressure he broke through, and his next step carried him into a room his eyes embraced with relief.

But if he was still in the Bellevue Stratford, he had wandered into a section ordinarily closed to guests. It felt as though he were somewhere else entirely. The great room looked like a ballroom or dance floor, but it was cluttered with racks filled with cardboard boxes and huge wooden tables covered with dust.

He wondered if he were sick, if the seafood could have poisoned him enough to make him dizzy and disoriented. Clearly he had been wandering for some time. The power was back on. But more than that, it was morning, sunlight streaming in the eight closely spaced windows along the long wall to his right.

The evening's pleasures were lost, but he had other reasons for being in Philadelphia, other appointments to keep. There was a stairway a few steps from where he stood, and he started down. The next level was small rooms, closed doors, and narrow corridors, none of it familiar. He continued his descent—three floors, five, nine.

He reached the ground floor a puzzled man. He could not be in the Bellevue Stratford. It was all wrong, the appointments too shabby, the darkness of the corridors a mark of decrepitude rather than taste. Just how far had he wandered in the dark?

At the end of the high-ceilinged main corridor, a street exit beckoned, and he headed in that direction. Outside, Endicott turned and looked back at the building from which he had just emerged.

Lost, he thought. Completely lost.

Above the door was a stone entablature with the legend 483 THE CAMBRIDGE 483 appearing in relief. The building was ten stories of red brick and white stone, like a layer cake, decorated with black wrought-iron balconies and topped by a greenish mansard roof perforated by dozens of windows. Endicott had never seen it before.

Where the hell am I?

He looked both ways down the wide street. There were no cars parked along the curbs, save for one streamlined oddity half a block away. There were no trolley tracks. A panel truck with a

5

squashed, bulldoglike cab trundled past on a side street, its exhaust a mixture of sweet and foul.

Everything looked wrong. Endicott did not know Philadelphia well. But he did not think this could be Philadelphia, even though it was impossible to think it could be anything else. Where was the burned-out half-collapsed shell of City Hall, its walls braced by yellow scaffolds while the plebians debated restoration? Where was the Ritz-Carlton, the mansarded Union League, the massive Academy of Music, or any of the Broad Street landmarks?

Tentatively, he started walking toward the corner. The street signs at the corner said MASSACHUSETTS AVE and MARLBOROUGH ST. When he looked north, he saw a long, low bridge spanning a broad, smooth-surfaced river. The Delaware? Could he have wandered that far? What had happened last night?

Belatedly, he noticed the bright yellow box chained to the lamp post across the street. He hastened across, but stopped short when he was close enough to read the decal atop the newspaper vending machine. THE MORNING GLOBE, it said. THE BEST OF BOSTON.

He denied the sight at first, then busied himself trying to manufacture explanations for the box being in Philadelphia. Even explanations for his being somewhere other than Philadelphia. Even for being in Boston. Until he looked closer and saw something which made a joke of any explanation he could hope to create.

Endicott sank to his knees on the sidewalk, clutching the top edge of the box with both hands for support. There were no coins in his pocket, but he did not need them. He stared through the scratched glass at the front page of the Boston *Globe* for Monday, August 22, 1966, stared with disbelief at the small headline tucked in a box at the top:

Sports: BOSOX LOSE IN 10th,

INDIANS SWEEP YANKS . . . 1C

He was not in Philadelphia. He was not even in what he would have called Boston. He was somewhere that could not be, where things that he knew to be false were apparently true. And for the first time in his life he felt the horrible touch of desperate insecurity that comes from questioning whether there really were any rules to the game.

RS: Why didn't you come back then? Why'd
you try to make the delivery anyway?

WALLACE: Cause that's what you sent me there
to do. Because the drop point was only six
blocks from the gate house. Come on, Charlie.
What's the problem? You got three agents
under the sheets already and everybody else
locked up tight because of the new blow. Did
you really want me to turn around and
come back with the A.V.'s still on my hip?

RS: Were you briefed on the contents of the
[courier] bag?

WALLACE: Shit, you don't have to be a genius
to know that when they shoot you up before
sending you out that there's bugs in the air.
Come on, Charlie, you know how dirty it is
over there. Half the runs we make we're
carrying blood or bugs or drugs. Why do you
think the moles call the gate house the
Pharmacy? I don't know why you're giving
me such a hard time about this. There wasn't
any exposure.

RS: You let a badge grab you. You brought
a hostile into the maze. That's not exactly a
hundred-grade first-class clean run.

WALLACE: I handled it.

RS: And now I've got to handle the mess
you left when you were done. I don't want
to burn you, Rayne. But this is serious.

WALLACE: For crying out loud, I didn't break
any rules. There aren't any rules for what I
walked into. That's a fact.

RS: You're a runner, Rayne, not a mole.
You're not supposed to get creative. Next time
stay put and let us handle the problem.

CHAPTER 1

The Runner Stumbles

Philadelphia, Alternity Red

The moment Rayne Wallace passed through the Philadelphia gate, he knew something was wrong. The station staff should have been expecting him, should have had the maze of corridors and rooms which was the gate house fully lit.

But the space Wallace emerged into was in total darkness. His senses jangling, he dropped into a crouch, clutched his courier pouches tightly, and froze there, waiting for the gate to return and the ethereal light it radiated to show him where he was. There must have been a focus shift, he thought. This isn't the Burgundy Theater. The floor's carpeted and the room feels too small.

Minutes later—excruciating, interminable minutes—the gate reappeared. By its cold fire he saw that the focus had shifted to the bedroom of what had once been, according to the numerals stenciled in black on the flocked wallpaper, Suite 1232. Still in the hotel, he thought. Okay.

The suite was empty of furniture, deserted, silent. The door to the cavelike corridor stood permanently open, bolted to the wall with a metal strap. Moving lightly, Wallace glided out into the gloom. He did not need light to find his way down to the field station on the first floor—he knew the old hotel by heart, every turn and doorway, every stairwell and guideplate.

He knew it better than anyone except another runner would, and only runners belonged in the gate house. If someone else was there, something would have to be done to remove them.

There was a small chance that the lights being off was an innocent accident, a matter of carelessness or mistiming. But there had been enough trouble in Red over the last year that Wallace thought otherwise. Something was seriously wrong.

He hesitated, unsure of what was expected of him. The gate was open, the disruption of his passage past. He could go back the way he had come, back to Home and the Tower, and report the focus shift, the anomalous transit.

For a brief moment, he considered doing exactly that. But he had never missed a delivery in nearly two years as a runner, and the two courier pouches he carried—an endomorphic one slung over his left shoulder and a thinner version strapped to his belly—tugged at his sense of pride.

The first was full of documents and interrogatories intended for the station staff. The other contained a dozen or more vials of vaccine intended for a team of moles working the Washington-Boston axis, protection against the latest round of viral terrorism by Les Miserables.

Besides, he thought as he continued on, *what the hell could I tell the Section now? I've got to go downstairs, at least, and find out what I can.*

The hallway was as dark and deserted as the suite had been, carrying forward the illusion of a bankrupt hotel sitting empty while its owners tried to find some way to get it out of receivership and finance remodeling into office space.

It was an illusion which suited the Guard's modest operation in Red, and which dovetailed nicely with the depressed financial climate of the downtown area. And if increased gate traffic or an improving economy some day stretched the credibility of the cover story, Red Section staffers were prepared to convert the Bellevue Stratford into a members-only club.

Wallace took the back way down, twenty-four flights of concrete and steel stairs descending into a black pit. Fingers gliding lightly on the handrail, he took the steps as quickly as he could in silence. After a few flights, his breathing was louder in the confined space than the sounds made by his foam-soled shoes.

When he reached the final landing and the solid wood door which led to the field station offices, Wallace hesitated, wishing he were armed. Though he was qualified with the Guard's basic .25 caliber automatic, he did not have one with him. It was impossible to bring a metal object of any size through the gate, as the energy flux had a nasty habit of grounding itself through the metal, with spectacular but unpleasant results.

But there's nothing to do about it, Wallace thought as he pushed the door open, so no point to wishing—

There was no gate monitor at the desk, but by then Wallace would have been surprised if there had been. He worked his way cautiously toward the front of the building, passed through a second door marked EMPLOYEES ONLY, and came out in the high-ceilinged, Greek-columned lobby.

A few steps away was the entrance to the research annex, formerly the Hunt Room restaurant. There should have been a dozen analysts in the annex, slaving over tables filled with newspapers and books being screened before being taken through the gate. The books and papers were there, but the analysts were not.

Nor could Wallace find any sign of the stationmaster or his staff in the complex of field offices. The entire station seemed deserted, but, curiously, not abandoned. There was no more than the usual disorder, most of which was purposeful camouflage anyway. It looked for all the world that everyone had simply decided not to come to work that day.

Except that a gate house was never, ever, left unattended.

Checking the Broad Street entrance, Wallace found the doors locked securely. He could see what seemed to be a paper sticker plastered across the crack between the doors on the street side, like a butterfly bandage across a laceration. He could not have opened the doors without tearing it. The building had been sealed. Emptied and locked up.

What's the matter, Joel? he asked the stationmaster in absentia. *Forget to pay the taxes?*

Whatever the reason, Wallace was determined not to let it stop him. Though he hadn't been directly briefed, he knew the importance of the drugs he was carrying. Three North Coast agents had already come down with the Widowmaker virus, and two were near death. Everyone else in the dirty zone was in hiding, breathing triple-filtered air in safe houses, waiting out the bug's three-week viability.

There was precious little the local medical community could do to protect the healthy or ease the pain of those already infected. That was why the biological terrorism of the nihilists who called themselves Les Miserables was so effective.

Bastards! The Soviets have got to be supplying them—and sitting back and laughing—

But the Rho 7 antiviral reagent Wallace carried could do much. A gift from the advanced medicine of Alternity Yellow, at worst Rho 7 would put the Guard's agents back in the field. At best it might clean out Barnes and Nilsson before their lungs were so severely damaged that death seemed the better choice.

No, he had to complete the run. He could not miss the contact. If he couldn't find another way out, he'd just have to break one of the seals and risk whatever fallout that act engendered.

Leaving the station pouch in one of the safe deposit boxes behind the front desk, Wallace went looking for a way out. The street entrances to the one-time pub in the basement were locked up tight, and the hotel's service and delivery doors were sealed as well. Every possible exit on the ground level was stickered, locked, or both.

But when he climbed the stairs to the second floor, Wallace found an escape. In a room overlooking the cantilevered hotel marquee, Wallace removed a tight-fitting sheet of black-painted plywood from the window frame and found only a few jagged fragments of glass poised to keep him from leaving.

He also found a street unnaturally quiet. No trolleys crawled along the tracks down the center of Broad Street. There was no traffic on either sidewalk as far as City Hall Square, no doorman across the street at the Gentlemen's Cafe, no purring cab at the Ritz-Carlton's taxi stand.

Odd as that was, it was a relief to Wallace. It meant that what happened had been citywide, that the gate house hadn't been singled out. And the most obvious answer to what had happened was something Wallace could deal with: the Brats bringing the terror to yet another city.

If they had blown a bomb here, it would be the first for Philadelphia. There had been numerous threats, most of them bluffs, a few real but thwarted by the hard-nosed city police— who were good enough at their business to have forced the Guard to take extra precautions with operations here.

An evacuation was the only answer that made sense, though it didn't explain why someone hadn't come through the gate to Home with word—even the fastest evacuation would have to take hours. But that puzzle could be worked out later. For now, there was a pouch of antivirals that needed delivering, all the more so if Wallace's call was right.

Mindful of the razor-edged glass, Wallace eased himself out onto the stone sill and then down to the marquee, which groaned distressingly when his weight was added to its load. Crouching, he paused to scan once more for unwelcome witnesses.

None were obvious, though that was far from saying none were present. It's hard to hide in an empty city, Wallace thought, swinging his legs over the edge and dropping to the sidewalk a dozen feet below. Best to get this done fast.

Terry's Spirit World was a curiosity, even a miracle—a direct successor, one of few, of the thousands of nineteenth-century wood-shack saloons which once dotted Philadelphia street corners. It had survived three fires, two neighborhood renewals, a bankruptcy, and Prohibition. A dozen names had appeared above its doors: Honagan's Licensed Tavern, Mario's, and The Iron Mug, among the most enduring. But for all its history, Terry's Spirit World was now nothing more than a quiet drinkery occupying the ground floor of a three-story brick Colonial revival.

A few tourists occasionally tottered in to see the collection of antique and foreign liquor bottles which gave it its name or to taste a cheese steak off the time-seasoned iron griddle. But for the most part, Terry's served a neighborhood clientele of sedate middle-aged men who complained into their whiskey about life but otherwise minded their own business.

Wallace had been in Terry's several times before, as part of the process runners called softening—making their face well enough known to be ignored. But he did not expect to see the inside of the bar today. En route from the hotel, he had experimented with one of the police stickers to see if they could be removed intact.

The answer was no. Worse, through some sort of chemical trickery, seconds after the paper tore the entire sticker changed color from pale blue to a dramatic red to announce the tampering.

No, his contact would be in the streets somewhere—a roof, an alley, a shadowed doorway—waiting and hoping. Not that the streets were any safer. In the time it had taken to cover a dozen blocks, Wallace had hidden from three patrolling police jeeps and heard, but not seen, a helicopter skimming low over the rooftops.

As he neared his destination, Wallace slowed from his trot to a more deliberate pace. The tavern was dark, the front door sealed. Cupping his hands around his eyes, he peered through the lightest pane of the stained-glass window.

He glimpsed a shadowy human shape, an ominous motion. Reflexively he flinched, turning and scrambling away. A fraction of a second later there was a muffled roar, and the heart of the door blasted outward, glass and wood splinters scattering over the sidewalk and beyond into the street. Wallace was caught by the fringe of the technicolor shower, but with no bare skin exposed to its assault.

12

"How do you like that?" demanded a voice from inside the bar. "Come on, try again and get some more!"

The voice was familiar to Wallace, and not at all threatening, despite its owner's best intentions.

"O'Brien, you are one jumpy son of a bitch," Wallace bellowed back, letting the tension go in a rush. "You goddamn bastard, you can fuckin' forget a tip from now on."

Long-necked and slender, like one of the bottles displayed on walls of his tavern, Terry O'Brien advanced out of the shadows to the shattered door, shotgun hanging limply in his hands. He looked hard at Wallace, then swallowed just as hard.

"Sorry," he said, then caught himself. "Say, you shouldn't be here. It's not my fault—"

"Not your fault? You're the one holding the artillery," Wallace said pointedly. "What the hell are *you* doing here?"

"Three times in a month I've been broken into," O'Brien said, examining the wreckage. "They said we might be out for forty-eight hours. I wasn't going to leave it and come back to nothing."

"No, you'd rather break it up yourself," Wallace said. He stole a quick glance down both side streets and a peek back over his shoulder. There was no movement, no sign that the shotgun blast had been heard. "Since you're open for business, how about pouring me one to help me settle the nerves you jangled?"

O'Brien nodded sheepishly and unlocked what was left of the door.

"Listen, Terry," Wallace said, following him to the bar. "I was sleeping one off in my hotel room, and when I woke up everybody'd gone into hiding. You're the first person I've seen all afternoon. What's going on? Where is everybody?"

"The mayor closed down center-city this morning," O'Brien said, reaching for a glass. "Black Label, isn't it?"

"Make it a shot and a chaser."

"Right. Anyway, I guess the barricades went up at five this morning. They kept all the commuters out and then chased out the night owls and the locals, checking cards on everyone at the barricades. I guess Rizzo's boys did a pretty good job—you're the first person I've seen all day, except for the boys in the jeeps."

A worried look crossed O'Brien's face. "I don't know what I'm going to do now," he added, scratching his chin. A large dragon ring on his left hand glinted in the light. "If they come through and see that mess, they'll know I'm here. They're going to give me a hard time, I know it. You, too."

"You didn't say what this is all about," Wallace said. "Is it the Brats?"

O'Brien nodded. "I saw the mayor on TV an hour ago. He said that they'd caught three of them and were looking for more. They were going to blow a bugbomb from the clock tower at the Reading Terminal. Can you imagine what that would have done, with the traffic through that station, all those commuters carrying it back out into the suburbs? Sick, sick, sick—"

That settled it. The drop was dead. His contact had either been unable to enter the city or been thrown out with the rest. Nothing to do but return to the gate house and leave the drugs there. Someone else could complete the delivery when the restrictions were lifted.

"I guess I'd better go on back to the hotel," Wallace said, draining the beer glass. "Doing business here is hard enough. I don't want any trouble."

"Why don't you stay?" O'Brien said, anxiously twisting his ring. "I'll feed you on the house."

Wallace demurred with a shake of his head. "I'd better go."

"I'd better put this away," O'Brien said, reaching for the shotgun.

Both decisions were right decisions, but both were made too late. As Wallace slipped down off his stool, a shadow flashed across the side windows and brakes screeched. Cursing silently, he dove to the floor as the police came fast through the door.

But O'Brien stood frozen behind the bar, shotgun half-raised, earnest words of explanation dying in his throat. The badges did not wait for explanations. The first through had a pistol in hand and opened fire. His partner, hard on his heels, joined in when he had a clear line. O'Brien wobbled in place, his blood spattering as the bottles on the wall behind him shattered. Then his knees buckled and he collapsed out of sight behind the bar.

Shit shit shit shit shit, Wallace cursed as he cowered, eyes squeezed shut against sights he did not care to see, on the tavern floor. *Just what I needed—to be grabbed in the middle of a Brat roast with a bag of glass bullets under my shirt—you might as well just shoot me now—*

On the day that Wallace qualified as a runner, Jason March—then an acquaintance, now a friend—had straight-facedly handed him a small blue-covered booklet bearing the title THE 1-A's HANDBOOK. The booklet contained a single page bearing two rules. The first was, *Don't Get Caught*. The second was, *See Rule #1.*

No official document put it that bluntly, but the truth was that the Guard expected its runners to slip in and out from Home to their destinations and back with minimum exposure. Most of the danger to runners was considered to be in the maze itself, where haste or carelessness or, sometimes, simple bad luck could make yours the one in every two hundred or so transits that came up on the board as OVERDUE, RU (Reason Unknown).

Beyond that, there was exposure on any run that went beyond the gate-house walls, and Wallace had a cover in all three alternities for which he was qualified. In Red Philadelphia, he was Robert Wallace, a salesman for an out-of-town food distributor. In Yellow Britain, he carried credentials as a construction inspector for the City of London. In Blue Indianapolis, he passed as a legal courier—on those rare occasions when he was allowed outside the gate house.

But unlike what the Guard set up for a full-time mole, Wallace's covers were tissue-thin, consisting of little more than the contents of his wallet. It was Wallace who had to make the cover real, to give it dimension. Only by projecting credibility could he head off the telephoned query, prevent the background check. He was the first and only line of defense, and the papers he carried were mere props.

He had gotten good advice on covers, thankyouverymuchJason. Every time he came to Red, every minute spent softening, he was Robert Wallace. He knew him, knew that young, glib, hard-drinking salesman well enough to know that he would be terrified by the violence, intimidated by the brush with Authority.

"Jesus Christ, sweet Jesus Christ," he began to babble as he lay on the floor. "What's going on? You shot Terry. I don't understand what's happening—"

As he spoke, the first officer, a hard-faced white man with thinning black hair, was moving cautiously around the end of the bar to make certain that O'Brien was no longer a threat.

"Shut up, you," the second officer snapped.

Twisting his head toward the voice, Wallace received a jolt. Advancing on him was the boogeyman from an Indiana boy's nightmare—a nigger with a gun. The officer was short for a badge but well-muscled, a charcoal troll in uniform. The namestrip above his pocket read CHAMBERS.

Wallace had seen the mixed couples passing unnoticed in Yellow London, knew that in Red something called an equal access law was eliminating the Negro schools, had heard that in Blue the Indianapolis hospitals allowed Negro doctors to treat patients of any race. Far more important, he understood from talking with Jason, who had made some thirty runs to Alternity White, that it was the closed doors of racism which had turned America's major cities into war zones and brought General Betts' martial-law government to power.

But Wallace had also grown up with a mother who explained to her son that there were no blacks in town "because they wouldn't be happy here," with a father who worried aloud about the wisdom of teaching black soldiers to kill and then letting them loose in society. The mixed signals—new and old, information and programming—had left him not knowing what he thought was right, and preserved childhood fears intact.

"ID and pass," Chambers demanded. "Where are they?"

"In—in my wallet." Wallace's voice was trembling; the line between feigned terror and the genuine article had blurred. "In my pants pocket. On the left."

"This one's dead," announced the first officer.

Chambers grunted in answer. Letting Wallace look down the barrel of his pistol close enough to catch the stink, Chambers fumbled for the leatherette wallet and extracted the Guard-manufactured identity card and travel pass.

Those ought to buy me about four minutes, Wallace thought, watching the policeman's face. *Food jobber from Mercer, hah.*

But the questions Wallace was expecting didn't come. "Arms behind your back, Mr. Wallace," Chambers said. A moment later, a plastic strap was tight around Wallace's wrists, the meek little ratcheting sound of the catch a misleading measure of the quickcuff's strength.

Some protest seemed in order, even if it was guaranteed to have no good effect. "I don't understand what I did wrong—"

"Up, Mr. Wallace," Chambers said. "You're going for a ride."

What had saved him so far, Wallace thought as he tried to keep his balance on the narrow seat in the back of the speeding jeep, was that his captors weren't detectives. They were foot soldiers in an urban war, trained more for obedience and rote thoroughness than curiosity.

But the questions they hadn't asked would be asked eventually. The courier pouch was still strapped to his midriff. They would find it, and they would defeat its lock and open it. There was no chance of it going undiscovered until the six-hour chemical timer ran down and reduced the contents of the bag to dust.

And then they would draw the obvious, completely wrong, conclusion that he was one of the Brats.

Which was fine as far as the Guard was concerned, but less promising for Wallace. True, Rizzo didn't have quite enough of a free hand to carry out his oft-stated solution to the terrorism problem—which would involve disemboweling Wallace with a power drill and then mounting his head on a spike outside police headquarters.

But if Wallace's future wasn't completely black, it was certainly bleak. The Guard had rescued more than one runner from an ordinary criminal offense, paying the bail in manufactured money so that he could escape to Home. But there would be no bail for a Brat terrorist.

The jeep took another hard, high-speed turn, and Wallace slid clumsily sideways on the seat until he was directly behind the driver. As he squirmed back into an upright posture, he concluded that getting out of the jeep would be no problem. Chambers was dutifully keeping an eye on him from the front passenger seat, but Wallace was confident he could throw himself over the side of the vehicle at any time.

But that was no answer. They'd either end up scraping him up off the pavement or shooting him down in the street. Only marginally better outcomes than ending up in Rizzo's little Home for the Criminally Suspicious—Short-Term Boarders Only. He had to get the jeep stopped and the two badges distracted.

Wallace had archived one idea when they put him in the jeep, under "There's Gotta Be a Better Way, But . . ." With each passing block, every foot farther from the gate house and closer to police headquarters, it seemed more and more certain that better ways were in short supply.

Roll the dice, Wallace thought.

The jeep was slowing to round a corner, and Chambers was looking away as he reached for the radio. Now—

In one quick motion, Wallace pulled his knees up to his chest, then drove his feet against the back of the driver's seat. The hinged seat back pitched forward, jamming the badge hard against the steering wheel.

The jeep, already turning, lurched sharply left as the driver fought to free himself. The struggle pitted the strength of the driver's arms against the power in Wallace's legs. Chambers was not a factor. The black was fighting his own battle—against inertia, against being catapulted from the vehicle.

Wallace had the edge, but even more, he knew both the rules and objectives of the contest. For two long seconds, he held the

17

badge helpless against the wheel as the jeep continued to turn, curling left toward a solid barrier of storefronts. Then, with a massive jolt, the jeep struck the curb and leapfrogged it, front wheels wobbling in midair.

The shock separated both Chambers and Wallace from their perches. Wallace tried to transform his graceless jouncing exit into a controlled backflip, but he had lost his leverage too soon. He came down awkwardly, twisting his right ankle and falling hard to his knees and then his side. A moment later, its driver still frozen behind the wheel, the jeep drove itself self-destructively into the wall, metal screeching, masonry cracking, glass tinkling.

Rolling over, Wallace struggled to his feet and ran. He felt painfully slow, naked to the bullet he was sure was coming, awkward and helpless with his hands bound behind him. But he ran without looking back, his mouth set in a tight line, his thoughts an evolving refrain: *one more step, one more step—one more block—one more chance—*

Though Wallace's heart was racing, his steps felt leaden, as though his feet were churning through mud. The distance between his hunched shoulders was a hundred yards, a target any junior marksman could hit. The city blocks grew longer even as he ran them.

Following the dictates of his paranoia, he zig-zagged across the city, up this street, down that alley. Every corner he turned gave him a few moments of safety, a brick and steel shield for his back. Yet every corner he turned held the threat of encountering another police patrol.

Five blocks from the wreck, hurrying down a narrow canyonlike alley, Wallace slipped on the trail of slime leaking from an overloaded trash dumpster. With no hands to break his fall, he sprawled headlong, his right shoulder taking the brunt of collision with the oil-stained gravel-strewn pavement. He skidded to a stop on a cushion of torn clothing and bloody, abraded skin.

Twisting around, he looked back the way he had come. There was no one else in the alley. He had lost his pursuers.

Or his pursuers hadn't found him yet. Chambers was back at the wreck, tending to his partner. Why chase a fugitive alone on foot when the radio could bring a dozen jeeps screaming into the area?

With a painful effort, Wallace sat up. Or maybe Chambers was hurt, too. No pursuit. No radio alert. And no reason except his own recklessness and panic that could keep him from reaching the gate house safely.

A razor-sharp rusted edge on the dumpster obligingly sliced through both the plastic handcuffs and the heel of one hand. Still no pursuit.

New strategy, he thought, trying to staunch the free-flowing blood as he started down the alley at a trot. *In this one, I use my head, and get there alive.*

Wallace edged up to the southeast corner of Broad and Sansom with triumph already in his heart. Hugging the wall, he peeked around the corner at the old Bellevue Stratford a block away. The wide boulevard was still deserted. There was no sign that the gate house had drawn any special attention in his absence or that a reception was waiting for him there.

Then a bullet licked off the concrete facing just above Wallace's ear. He jumped as though he had grabbed an electric wire. Ducking his head, he plunged around the corner and headed on a line for the hotel. Ten flying steps and he was off the curb and into the street. Fifty carried him halfway down the block and halfway across the street, to the trolley tracks which bisected it. He ran mouthing heartfelt half-formed prayers for deliverance.

There had been no more shots, but he did not make the mistake of thinking his prayers had been granted. He knew that when the badge rounded the corner where Wallace had been standing moments before, he would again be a target. The question was whether he would reach the hotel before that happened.

Each step was a discrete victory, an increment of hope. Wallace searched frantically for the quickest way back in, knowing that he could never retrace his marquee escape in time. He thought about breaking a window, and wondered what he would break it with.

Then a thought hit him which nearly stopped him in midstride, midstreet. Idiot—why don't you lead them back to the one place they can't be made curious about. You can't go back inside at all, he scolded himself. You lost. Almost doesn't count.

Then bullets were flying again, whining hornets in the air, and Wallace's feet carried him forward without instructions from his conscience-bound consciousness. Crossing Walnut Street, Wallace narrowed his focus to a pair of stairwells tucked against the front face of the gate house and leading down below street level.

The first, closest to the corner, was the entrance to the Broad Street subway. On any other day, the subway would have been an ideal place to lose or waylay his pursuers. But today it promised him nothing, for below he would find no trains, no crowds—only locked gates.

The second stairwell was the wrought-iron-ringed street entrance to the former Irish pub in the basement of the gate house. He angled toward it and hurled himself over the edge recklessly, saving himself from broken bones by snatching a handhold on the brass railings on the way down. Then he crept back up the crumbling concrete stairs for a glimpse of his adversary.

It was Chambers. The officer was a hundred feet away, dragging his right leg as he walked steadily toward where Wallace hid. Chambers, stalking him with grim confidence of vindication. Chambers, determined to erase an error. He did not even waste a bullet firing at Wallace's head, knowing that, momentarily, he would have a much easier shot.

There were only two choices, Wallace realized, both with little appeal: compromising the gate house, or dying where he was.

He stole another look over the edge. Chambers was just sixty feet away, close enough for Wallace to read both pain and cold-eyed purposefulness on his face. But this time, Wallace saw something else: Chambers was alone, with no radio visible on his hip. Which meant that no one knew where he was, even if he had been able to call in an alarm before leaving the jeep.

And Wallace knew then what he had to do. Seizing two loose fist-sized fragments of concrete, he hurled the smaller blindly up and out in an arc toward Chambers. He leaped to the bottom of the stairwell and used the larger to shatter the small window in the pub's wooden door. Reaching through the opening, he frantically clawed at the locks, knowing that the sound of breaking glass would pull Chambers in like a magnet.

The door fell open at last, and Wallace dove inside. But instead of fleeing, he lingered in the pub, crouching behind a half-wall near the inside entrance until he saw Chambers' shadow in the stairwell. The badge was moving more slowly now, and Wallace realized there was a danger he would grow too cautious and decide to wait for support. That could not be allowed to happen.

"Hey, nigger-boy!" Wallace called out. "How's your buddy, huh?"

Chambers' only answer was to keep coming down the stairs, the barrel of his revolver leading the way.

"Fuckin' black monkey, you're too dumb to live," Wallace taunted. "You're never going to catch me."

This time the answer was a bullet fired through the doorway.

It thudded into the half-wall where Wallace had been hiding and exploded through the other side in a shower of wood splinters and plaster bits. But by then Wallace was already on the move.

Playing a deadly game of hide-and-seek, Wallace led the badge higher and higher in the building, careful not to let Chambers too close, careful not to draw too far ahead. There was a noisy race in the stairwell, third floor, fourth, fifth. Wallace kept up the taunts to keep Chambers coming, exploiting the badge's single-mindedness and his wounded pride, his pain and his hate.

All the time, Wallace was feeling for the gate, for the faint touch of its energies. Like all experienced runners, Wallace had learned to read the shivery sensation in his body and to follow it to its source. With a call as clear as a siren song, the gate guided Wallace through the midnight maze of the hotel.

Finally, at the end of a long hallway, he saw the telltale glow, spilling out through one of the open doorways and splashing across the facing wall. He ran toward it, knowing that Chambers was close behind him, showing Chambers his fleeing silhouette. He plunged through the doorway just as the barking report of the revolver sounded in the corridor.

The gate was there, shimmering, open. But Wallace balled himself in a back corner of the closet, out of sight of the door, and waited.

He did not have to wait long. Chambers had to be sensing the end of the chase, confident beyond certainty that his quarry was unarmed, believing that his perseverance was about to be rewarded. Suddenly he was there in the doorway, revolver secured in its holster as a precaution. He was ready to finish the job with his powerful hands.

But he could not have known what he would see, could not have guessed that the source of the cold yellow light would be an oval of bare wall wider than his outstretched arms. Forgetting Wallace for a moment, he stepped toward the gate uncertainly, raised a hand to try to touch it.

And as he did, Wallace rose up from where he crouched and flung himself at Chambers from behind. As he wrapped his arms around the bewildered officer, the force of the collision and Wallace's driving legs carried them both forward—toward the wall and through the gate.

Once through, Wallace barely had time to release his grip before the white fire lashed out. A wave of pressure drove him inexorably away as, in silence but with terrifying intensity, the

21

energies inside the gate discharged through the dozens of metal objects which Chambers wore and carried.

One second crawled into the next. Chambers became the heart of a man-sized ball of dancing lightning. The dazzle was so intense that Wallace had to look away, and for one long moment he felt regret, empathy. He had lost friends between the gates, and dreamed at times of dying there, and in neither case had he conceived of a death this cold and final.

Then the light was extinguished, and Chambers was gone, consumed. The seething energies of the gate quieted, and Wallace suppressed his qualms. He had done what was necessary. He was a member of the Tower Guard, and he had protected his Home. His victim had only been a shadow, an unreality from an unreal world.

Except that it was the first time he had killed for the Guard, and the shadow had worn the face of a man.

Downham House
Knight's Bridge Road
Essex

November 14, 1975

Dear Gregory,

... There is a bit of a chill here already, and once again this year we are facing a terrible problem with rodents looking to come inside. After much persuasion, the landlord has agreed to release some weasels—or to look the other way while I do—in the hope that the rodent invasion can be blunted. The problem is that weasels are proscribed and it may be difficult, tho not impossible, to bring them into the country. Please ask your father if he knows any dealers, or whether any trappers there might be willing to take on the job. The expense and responsibility on this end will be mine ...

With affection,

Robbie

. . . .

GLAVNOYE RAZVEDYVATELNOYE UPRAVLENIYE INTERCEPT

. . . .

Sender identity: Robert Halcomb Taskins, United States Ambassador to Great Britain
Recipient identity: Gregory O'Neill, United States Secretary of Defense
Evaluation: Imputed relationship verified, files. Complaint verified, local interviews. GRU New England verifies that John O'Neill, father of Gregory, owns small farm outside Derry, Massachusetts.
Conclusion: Personal communication.
Delete from alert list: WEASEL, LANDLORD.

Vladimir Orens, GRU London

CHAPTER 2

Wolf May Come,
Sky May Fall

Essex, England, The Home Alternity

That was the damnable thing about dealing with parliamentary governments, Robert Taskins thought as he hurriedly dressed. You never could be sure whom you would be dealing with one year to the next.

The summons had come early, delivered in person by a fresh-faced aide from the new Prime Minister's office. And summons was the only word for it: "I wish to speak with you at once. Come to the Admiralty." It was signed D. Somerset, PM, as if it were still necessary for him to politely remind people who he was.

To be sure, there were still many questions about David Somerset. No one had expected the fall of McLeod's Conservative government, and certainly not over such a question as the reorganization of British Rail.

In retrospect, it was easy to see that the vote had reflected Conservative factionalism, not Labour strength. The CP was full of frustrated ambition, middle-aged pols with their own power bases who were watching their prime years slip away while McLeod's team kept them on the fringe. Their expectations had been raised by nineteen years of Conservative dominance, and they had broken ranks to warn McLeod, not to unseat him.

So thought the rebels, and so thought Taskins. Almost no one in the U.S. legation had predicted that Labour would muster enough seats to end McLeod's personal nine-year reign. The few who had were the embassy's new gurus, and were now leading the scramble to come up with useful answers to the question, "What will Somerset do?"

Taskins had his own questions and problems. There had already been two exchanges of dispatches—handcarried because of the gravity of the matter—between Washington and London, and yet Taskins was still without instructions. Three years of careful work was at risk, both from the new players brought in by the upset and from the loose ends represented by the vanquished.

But absent guidance from President Robinson or the CIA, he could do nothing about either danger.

Taskins had waltzed gracefully through the official ceremonies accompanying the change of government, carefully avoiding any substantive conversations with Somerset or his advisors. Better to be elusive than to christen the new relationship with lies. Easy enough to maintain the routine Home Office contacts, let Somerset see to a new Cabinet and the vagaries of settling in.

A month would be soon enough to call on the PM personally. A month would be time enough for Robinson to decide.

But Somerset, making a habit of the unexpected, clearly thought it more urgent than Taskins did that they meet. So they would. And the preeminent question now was not what would Somerset do, but what did he know.

The embassy car was waiting at the end of the walk, motor purring, tiny American flag fluttering from the fender. Taskins settled in the back, clutching his leather case on his lap, and nodded to the driver.

"The Admiralty," he said hoarsely.

Throughout the fifteen-minute drive, he gazed trancelike out the side window as the myriad dimensions of the dilemma arranged and rearranged themselves in his head. Stony faces and stone figures flashed by equally unnoticed.

Taskins was met at the curb by a young lieutenant, who caught the car door and then ushered him inside with brisk efficiency. They moved past the security post unchallenged, then entered an empty lift. The lieutenant's bronze key passed them through to the third floor.

"This way, sir," the lieutenant said with a gesture.

"Where are we? Whose offices are these?" Taskins said, following.

"Admiralty offices, sir," was the unilluminating reply. "Here we are, sir."

• • •

The unlabeled door opened to a dark-paneled room which he would have called a study had he found it in a private home. There were three men in the room. The only one Taskins knew by sight was Somerset.

The Prime Minister was standing by the heavily draped window, arms crossed over his chest, the ash from the cigarette in his left hand threatening to drop to the thick carpeting. He had the workingman's build, the masculine good looks of a cinematic union leader or infantry first sergeant.

Somerset turned as Taskins entered. "Thank you, Robert," he said, walking two steps to a pedestal ashtray and crushing out his cigarette. "My Home Secretary, Benjamin Caulton," he said, nodding toward a man seated a few feet away in a high-back leather chair.

Caulton had a pillowlike belly and a round, perpetually flushed face, but his eyes were steel-blue and catlike. The third man, slender and hawk-faced, seated in one of the dim corners of the room, went unintroduced. Taskins assumed him to be a functionary, most likely there to take notes, and ignored him.

"Of course," Taskins said. "What can I do for you, Mr. Somerset?"

"I wonder if you would answer a question."

"Certainly, if I can."

Somerset waited until he had performed the minor ritual of retrieving and lighting another cigarette before continuing. "Does your government have nuclear warheads in the British Isles?"

His tone was casual, but the question rocked Taskins back on his heels. Indecision made him hesitate, and when he did, Somerset went on.

"I hardly expected a direct answer. Let me attempt to discourage any evasions by telling you about a most interesting report I received yesterday afternoon from MI-5. Four times in the last year, it seems, various of our agents have made reports suggesting that American agents might be trying to smuggle some sort of nuclear armaments into the country."

"Mr. Somerset, I—"

"The most interesting part of this is that K was instructed by the Home Secretary to seal the reports and not pursue the matter," Somerset continued. "I assume that this was done with the PM's knowledge and consent—"

Taskins stared at the man in the corner with new realization. The director of MI-5, the British Security Service, had gone by the code name "K" for more than sixty years. But the changing

26

faces that went with that name had always been hidden behind a high wall of secrecy.

"—so tell me, Mr. Ambassador, if you will: Did you have an arrangement with my predecessor that he would look the other way while you brought nuclear weapons into the British Isles? Or to put it plainly, what the hell is going on?"

Instructions be damned.

"Yes," Taskins said, meeting Somerset's direct gaze. "Yes to both. We had such an agreement. And there are nuclear weapons in the British Isles."

Caulton grunted in surprise and stirred in his seat. K did not react at all.

"You see, Bennie, they *are* that untrustworthy," Somerset said casually. He flicked the ash from his cigarette into the bowl, then looked back to Taskins. "How many, and what type?"

Swallowing hard, the Ambassador forced himself to answer. "Ten at the moment, with five more to come. Weasels." When Somerset's face showed no flicker of recognition, he went on. "Thirty-four-foot solid-fuel intermediate range missiles, on mobile carriers. They have a maximum range of fifteen hundred miles—just enough to reach Moscow."

Somerset was still unreadable, his questions measured, his demeanor calm. But Caulton was growing more agitated with every word.

"Let me understand this," Caulton sputtered. "You're not talking about bombs that can be carried by our Hawkers or missiles for the Vigilance frigates. You're talking about a guerrilla nuclear force owned and controlled by the American military but hiding on British soil."

"Not hiding. Granted shelter," Taskins said.

"Madness! Not only do you take it on yourself to violate our treaties with the Soviet Union, but instead of doing it in a way that provides us with strength in times of crisis, you embark on . . . on rocket terrorism. Have you no respect for us, for our sovereign rights, for our historic partnership—"

"Enough, Bennie," Somerset said calmly. "Where are the missiles, Ambassador?"

Taskins regarded Somerset with curiosity. There was something going on here that he, Taskins, did not grasp. But the cues he was receiving as the discussion progressed were beginning to dissipate his alarm.

"I don't know the specifics, and in any event, they're always changing," he said. "They're mobile, after all. But I believe that most of them are somewhere along the eastern coast—

Bridlington, Lowestoft, smaller coastal towns. They're camouflaged as heavy-haul tractor-trailers—lorries."

"What is their strategic purpose? Why did McLeod allow them in?"

Taskins took a moment to find a chair while he composed an answer. "Mr. Somerset, I'm the Ambassador to the U.K., not the national security advisor or President Robinson, and I don't know that I have either the knowledge or the right to speak for them. But if I can remind you that there's Communist missiles in Guiana, six minutes away from American soil—"

"What is that to us?" Caulton interrupted caustically.

Determinedly, Taskins continued. "Moscow has us on a very short leash. If we can adjust the balance by putting a few kilotons on *their* doorstep, I say it's a good thing to do. I'm sure Prime Minister McLeod recognized that and did as much as he felt he could to aid us."

"Does Moscow *know* what's on their doorstep?"

"Not yet."

"Do you intend to tell them?" Caulton asked. "Or just start a war without warning?"

"Hold on to reality, Bennie," Somerset said gently. "No American President is mad enough to invite a thrashing from the Red Bear."

"They're of no value unless the Russians know they're there," Taskins said. "Of course we'd tell Moscow. But not until the Weasels are all in place. And not unless the British government is prepared to take the heat and let them stay."

Extinguishing what was left of the second cigarette, Somerset walked to the window. "It seems to me that the French are as shaky now as the West Germans were in 'fifty-three. It must look very tempting to Secretary Kondratyeva. Especially when they're certain that we Brits won't intervene because of promises made two decades ago."

"Their Parliament is forty percent Communist already," Taskins said, wondering at the change of focus. "I don't think there'd be much point to fighting over France."

"Perhaps not. But if Paris becomes another Red capital, John Bull is going to start wondering where it ends. I can hear the screaming in Parliament already. They'll expect some strong action, some unambiguous warning to the Soviets to leave us be." Somerset paused to blow a perfect smoke ring, then turned to face Taskins. "Very well. I have a message for you to relay to Washington. Tell Peter I like his style. The Weasels can stay."

Taskins released an audible sigh of relief. "I—"

"In fact, I think we want more than the numbers you talked about. Squadron strength, perhaps. I'll get back to you on that. And we must discuss operational control," Somerset said. "But the most important thing is that this has to be absolutely quiet."

"Understood."

"I don't know if you do understand. K, what about using MI-5 as a—what's the word I want, a test, to measure how sharp the Yank security is."

"Tiger team," K said.

"Right. A tiger team. I'd like to think we can spot leaks before the GRU can, give you a chance to recover. I do believe that our boys are sharper than theirs. It is still our country, after all."

"I think that would be a valuable check," Taskins said.

"But, Robbie—understand that we won't take your punishment for you. If we're caught at this, I intend to blame McLeod as loudly as I can, and I'll expect you to pull the Weasels out of the country as fast as you can. I want your missiles in my pocket. I don't want them thrown in my face."

Taskins gathered his feet under him and stood. "I understand," he said.

Somerset touched a flaming match to a new cigarette. "It doesn't matter that you understand," he said. "See that Robinson understands."

South-West Africa, The Home Alternity

The small twin-engined cargo plane had been flying low over the empty lands for nearly four hours. Taking off from the tiny airfield at Baia dos Tigres, at first it had followed the Atlantic coastline south, passing Cape Fria and skimming the desolate salt pans, dunes, and bare rock of western Etosha.

Presently the spectacular eight-thousand foot mass of the Brandberg, thrust upward out of the plain like a granite invader from a world below, slid past out the left-hand windows. Then it was dead east by compass across the Namib Desert, to avoid the South African enclave at Walvis Bay and the string of tiny towns along the railroad which ran northeast into Damarland.

West of Okombahe, the Angolan pilot took his plane off the deck, climbing a thousand feet above the hardveld until he had spotted the dry bed of the Omaruru River. For nearly five minutes, they were on the radar at Rooikop Airfield, and possibly at Windhoek as well.

That was the most nervous time for the lone passenger, a moustachioed white man who wore khaki shorts like a tourist and never initiated a conversation except with an order. The name he used was Kendrew, though it was understood that it was not his real name. Real names were for realities which contained morning newspapers and traffic jams.

Kendrew knew that there were no military aircraft based at either field and that the plane would not linger long enough for the supersonic interceptors from Cape Town to hunt it down. But still, he worried. It was exposure, and Kendrew hated exposure like a finicky housewife hates water spots on the crystal. Even when the flaw went unnoticed, it irked him that he had not found a way to eliminate it.

Suddenly there was the truck, sitting square in the middle of the riverbed less than a mile ahead. A half-dozen Freedom Now soldiers milled about near it. One of them would be Xhumo.

The pilot buzzed the truck playfully, dipping down until the plane roared by a mere dozen feet above the canvas canopy. Then he brought the high-wing Fokker around in a tight turn, scanning for the markers the guerrillas had laid out across the ground for him. The landing seemed to take forever, the Fokker floating down, crabbing in a crosswind, flaring.

Then the wheels touched, the cabin bounced, and the drone of the engines waned for the first time since Baia dos Tigres. It was replaced by the noise of the FN truck roaring up out of the wash to chase down and draw alongside the plane.

Kendrew bounded out of the cabin, but neither Xhumo nor his men needed direction. The plane's crowded cargo area was unloaded with brisk efficiency: eight long boxes containing French automatic rifles, twenty cases of ammunition, and the treasure—three crates containing a dozen American-made shoulder-launched antiarmor rockets.

The Buzzsaw launchers had been a special request, with a special target—South Africa's deep-water port facilities at Walvis Bay. Loss of the port would add to the pressure already created by raids on the Luderitz–Port Elizabeth railway and Upington road. Already sentiment was growing in Johannesburg for abandoning the half-century trusteeship of the old German protectorate. Let them go, went the thinking. There's nothing there worth this much fighting. Let them have it.

When that happened—and Kendrew thought inevitably it must—the FN could focus their efforts on the real prize, toppling the Soviet-backed white government of South Africa. For the black majority it was a war of liberation. For the United States it was a chance to regain access to the awesome mineral resources capricious Nature had hidden in the tip of the African continent.

"You understand that you have to crack the storage tank," Kendrew said to Xhumo when the unloading was done, "or the fuel won't burn. Go for the kerosene first. HE, HE, then incendiary. Save the antiarmor rounds for the motor pool."

"Many thanks. Soon we give a party in Walvisbaai," Xhumo said, his smile a yellow crease across his face. "You tell President Robinson he is invited."

Kendrew grunted. "You throw a party in Johannesburg, and I promise you he'll come."

Washington, D.C., The Home Alternity

Peter Arnold Robinson was a congenital early riser. Though his family had moved off their Hazelhurst farm when he was twelve, his father trading the tractor for a wartime assembly line in Rockford, the habit had stayed with him. A reliable internal alarm usually woke Robinson within a few minutes of five A.M.—winter or summer, White House bedroom or Minnesota lake retreat.

He awoke nôt only early, but clear-headed and energetic. Unfortunately, most of the rest of the Washington world did not, including his wife Janice. It was the one serious mismatch in their natures, intruding as it did on the more intimate parts of their lives. He would gladly have traded their late-night "sleep-making" for a morning tumble with the sheets warm and the fire high.

On rare occasions, wakened by a dream or his movements in bed, she would turn to him in the early hours. And from time to time, if the hunger stayed with him, he would keep his first appointment of the day, then excuse himself to return to bed and Janice nearer her natural waking time. From time to time, and time and again. In college, his sexual appetites had earned him the hated nickname Peter Rabbit. In his five years in the White House, those appetites had made his "9:00 A.M. conferences" an insider's knowing joke.

But most mornings, he would lie quietly beside his wife's sleeping form. Staring at the ceiling with folded hands tucked behind his head, he would compose his plans for the day, his remarks for an appearance, his thoughts about an unresolved problem.

Some mornings, like this one, he would lie there and simply enjoy looking at her.

It was a tribute to his own appeal that he had been able to overcome the liability of an attractive wife in a national election, where the well-kept but mature look was ever synonymous with responsibility and respectability. At forty, Janice still had real beauty, the kind that survives the removal of makeup and morning-after touseledness. *Not like the plastic beauty so many Washington wives sport, whale-oil and flower-squeezings pasted half an inch thick—*

A mercy, considering his drives, that she still excited him. A mercy, considering his position, that he could satisfy so much of his need at home. Opportunities and alternatives were there for a President as they had been for a Congressman. But the back-door romance that had destroyed the Vandenberg administration was too fresh a memory for Robinson to give himself permission to indulge.

At six o'clock, he left the bed to soak the knotted muscles of his neck and his eternally stiff right knee—blown out ten years ago during a family softball game—in a long, near-scalding shower. He reached the private dining room a minute before his breakfast of scrapple and French toast did.

A single place had been set, and his short stack of newspapers was already there, carefully culled of those sections Robinson had no interest in reading. There was that morning's *New York Times*, defiant leader of the eight or ten rebellious dailies not subscribing to the Federal News Service. And the Washington *Post*, flagship of the FNS and, in Robinson's mind, symbol of what responsible journalism was all about. And on top, yesterday's Chicago *Tribune*, to which he turned first, eager to measure his own thoughts against its sports columnists. Trade talk was in the air in the wake of the Bears' fourth straight loss, and Piccolo was clinging to the coaching job by his teeth. *At the very least, he has to give the kid quarterback from Stanford a shot—*

Robinson expected to finish both his breakfast and his reading without interruption. It was understood by family and staff alike that this time, this room, belonged to him. So when the knock came halfway through, Robinson knew that it foretold something serious.

"Come in," he called out, folding his paper and setting it aside.

The door opened to admit William Rodman, Robinson's bald-headed White House chief of staff.

"Good morning, Peter. Sorry to disturb you—"

"That's all right," Robinson said graciously. "What's happening this morning, Bill?"

"There's been another submarine contact off New York harbor. I thought you'd want to know."

"When?"

"Within the half-hour, just after dawn. The ship involved is the freighter *Castle Point*, American registry."

Robinson folded his hands, elbows resting on the table. "Any details?"

"She was outbound in the Ambrose Channel. The captain reports a Soviet submarine surfaced a hundred meters to port and ran with them for five minutes. They counted five tubes, which sounds like a Horizon-class boat. We won't know for sure until the Coast Guard retrieves the film one of the crewman shot. A copter is on the way to pick it up now."

"Was that the only shooting?"

"Yes, thank Heaven."

"And the *Castle Point*. Was she inside or outside the line?" Robinson asked lightly.

"Inside. No question about it."

Robinson nodded, retrieved his fork, and speared another bite of scrapple. "Thank you, Bill. I'll be down in a little while," he said, and engulfed the meat with a quick bite.

"Anything you want me to do?"

Signalling for patience with his fork, Robinson waited until he had swallowed to answer. "O'Neill already knows about it, I presume. Still no answer on the last protest we filed?"

"No."

"Then there's no sense drafting another one. Just add it to the gripe file. There's nothing we can do about it now."

Rodman nodded and removed himself.

Nothing we can do about it. The admission ate at Robinson all through the rest of his breakfast. Nothing we can do about a Russian submarine playing tag with the shipping coming out of our most important port—

He stopped eating and stared out the window at the trees, remembering a letter he had received in the first year of his first term.

The letter was from a Michael Gaston. a worker in the Philadelphia Navy Yard. He had taken his family on a three-day summer expedition to Wildwood, New Jersey. The last day, while they were sunning and playing on the sand, a Soviet submarine had surfaced out past the breakers and cruised briefly along the shore.

"My boy was so excited," the man wrote, "to see a warship out where it belonged, in the sea. He said it looked like a great

33

big gray shark and kept asking, 'Did you work on that sub, Daddy?' I couldn't bear to tell him it wasn't one of ours.

"Why does this have to be, Mr. President? Why should my son and the thousand other kids that were there that day have to suffer the humiliation of watching a Russian submarine cruising unmolested off an American beach? Maybe we can't rid the ocean of Soviet sharks. But I'm sick at heart to think that we can't even drive the monsters back to deep water where they belong. Something has to be done."

Slowly, almost mechanically, Robinson finished off his breakfast, collecting the last of the syrup with the last of the French toast. He glanced at his watch. Seven-thirty. Rodman would be waiting for him in the Roosevelt Room.

Nothing we can do about it, Mr. Gaston—still, he thought as he rose from the table. *But something is being done. Because it doesn't have to be that way. And I swear that when I leave this drafty old mansion, it won't be that way any longer.*

EXECUTIVE ORDER 75-05
Supplemental to EO 68-09, NSC 68-31, EO 72-14
February 16, 1975

TO: Albert Tackett, Director
    National Resource Center

The NRC is directed to make a priority mission of
the following:

1. To investigate known alternities for potential
   use by Alpha list personnel as an alternative
   to the Boyne Mountain shelter in the event
   of a national crisis.
2. To evaluate known alternities for potential
   use by Alpha list personnel as a permanent
   relocation site in the event of a nuclear
   exchange.
3. To develop and carry out operations both
   domestically and in the appropriate alternities
   to facilitate the availability of the above
   options.

The director is instructed to:

1. Report to the President within sixty days on
   the feasibility of option 1 above.
2. Report on a continuing basis to the President
   on the status of option 2 above.

Interagency support:

1. No interagency support is authorized, including
   DIA, CIA, NSA, G-2, INR, and AEC. No interagency contacts are authorized, including blind
   assists. All operations are to be handled internal
   to the NRC.

Security:

1. Preemptive detainment and execution is
   authorized in the event of Official Secrets Act
   violations.
2. Code name for this mission shall be RATHOLE.

CHAPTER 3

The Cornucopia

Boston, The Home Alternity

Albert Tackett's suite on the thirty-sixth floor of the National Resource Center offered every comfort and convenience he could think to ask for. He had the huge desk and fine furniture which were traditional corporate status symbols; a bank of terminals and phones providing unrestricted access to Defnet, USIA, and the White House; and a personal staff of three to relieve him of the more routine labors of his office.

Few government servants, even in Washington, enjoyed comparable accommodations.

But to Tackett's mind, one of the office's most attractive features was what lay outside it. The Tower, as the NRC's silver and black monolith was commonly called, stood at the intersection of Massachusetts Avenue and Marlborough Street, on the south shore of the Charles. Being a corner room on the top floor, his office boasted the panoramic perspective of both north- and east-facing windows.

Tackett was forever taking issue with visitors who found the Boston cityscape a monotonous, monochromatic expanse of over-crowded real estate. There were many worthy sights that could be seen from his eyrie, even without the aid of the fine Swiss-made 7x50 binoculars he kept at his desk.

To the northeast was the broad, tranquil expanse of the river, now dotted with small sailing craft taking advantage of Indian summer breezes. In the afternoon, the long, slender shadow of the Tower swept across the river surface, the building serving as the gnomon in a twentieth-century sundial. At night, four-car elevated trains crawled across the Longfellow Bridge in the distance, their lighted windows transforming them into strings of pearls.

Due east, the green stripe of Commonwealth Avenue pointed the way toward the parklike Boston Commons. But his was the least attractive vista from which to view the regal four-story red-brick homes which lined both sides of the avenue. From above, the view was of flat tar-paper roofs and a forest of chimneys, not the bay windows, turrets, and wrought iron which gave the street its charm. Beyond the Commons lay the heart of the city with its hundred Colonial treasures, the wonderful restaurants of Winter Place and Hanover Street, the stone churches.

True, there were blots on the landscape as well, such as the somber institutional housing development sprawled across former railroad land west of the Navy base. Officially, it was known as the Fort Point Federal Housing Center, but the broad expanses of unadorned, windowless concrete had earned it a simpler and more descriptive name—South Block.

But Tackett was forgiving, even of such blight. He knew so many special places hidden in the confusion of streets which made up the old city that his affection for Boston could not be dimmed.

There was one sight visible from Tackett's office that could be seen from no other vantage point in the city except the Tower, through windows which faced inward rather than out. For the Tower was built around a great central atrium and within the atrium was nestled a piece of the past—the nineteenth-century Cambridge Hotel, gate house to the alternities.

The Tower's architecture was a practical one, designed to enclose, secure, and protect the precious gate house. But the design was also appropriately symbolic, for the gate house was the focus of everything that went on in the Tower. The Cambridge was the pipeline through which flowed the knowledge the nation needed to revitalize its moribund economy and tip an unfavorable balance of power.

It was astonishing what the NRC had already brought back—secrets of computer chips equal to the best the Germans were providing the Soviet bloc. Maps of undiscovered oil deposits exact to the best location for the wellheads. Plans for superconducting electronic circuits which virtually powered themselves.

The gleanings were beginning to pile up, in fact, faster than they could be absorbed by NRC experts and injected into the body economic. Though only four years new, the Technology

Transfer Division occupied ten floors of the Tower and claimed nearly half the agency's employees. So many Transfer agents were in the field that, despite pointed requests for discretion, they had already created a potent societal mythos.

There were a hundred versions of the same story: the man in the three-piece suit, the man with the black briefcase, the stranger who knows your own business better than you do. He comes to a defense contractor, an engineering office, a mining co-op. He is from Washington, from Boston, from a think-tank named the NRC. He gives them a gadget, a plan, an idea, and a promise that if they'll only try it, they'll see that it's a better way.

And the promise always comes true.

The nickname bestowed on the Transfer agents was as inevitable as it was undignified. It was the same in Topeka and Trenton, San Francisco and Shreveport—a spontaneous linguistic acclamation. What else could you call them but Santa's elves?

Vandenberg had built the Tower and created the Guard when the mystery was new and the benefits to be gained only a dream. It was an act of boldness and vision, the invisible crowning achievement of what most considered a failed presidency.

The sheltering walls of the base section had risen in just sixteen months, cannibalizing a church, several dozen homes, and pieces of three streets. Tackett had built the organization even faster, from fifty to five hundred to more than five thousand employees.

It was almost too big now, almost too much for Tackett to see clearly and direct wisely. He saw Section chiefs and second-hand reports exclusively, spent almost as much time holding hands in Washington as he did looking over shoulders in the Tower.

And when Tackett was in Boston, the growing demands of coordinating Rathole gobbled more and more of his time. It was the one task he could not delegate; the one mission on which Robinson expected him to be dirty to the elbows. Day-to-day supervision of the rest of NRC's operation had gone by default to the deputy director and his staff.

But the old street spook in him refused to let go completely, insisting that no Executive Operational Order go downstairs without his informed signature. With ExOps averaging a dozen a week, that insistence sentenced him to enough long days in the office that the nighttime cityscape was rapidly becoming as familiar as the daytime.

Marian complained, and justly. She filled her days well enough with her clubs and friends, but with the boys gone the house on

Nahant was a tomb, a beautiful prison, and nights alone were hard. She couldn't understand why someone in Tackett's position had to work so hard—wasn't leisure one of the privileges of power?

He could not explain without violating security, and she could not have understood without violating her view of the world. The Tower Guard was his—his creation, his responsibility. It bore the stamp of his personality: hardworking, pragmatic, fiercely loyal, committed. And its success was his gift to the old friend, now disgraced, who had lifted him out of the morass of the CIA and entrusted to him the mystery of the gate.

As Tackett watched from on high, a lone runner emerged from the Cambridge and crossed the hundred-foot-wide buffer strip to the gate control complex. Another transit completed. The sight reminded him that there was work that needed doing, and he had been away from his desk longer than conscience would allow.

But it was envy, not guilt, that stayed with Tackett as he turned from the window. Envy of the runners, the moles, anyone for whom the gate made the unreality of an alternity a tangible world, anyone taking part in the adventure of the millennium.

For Tackett had never made a transit of the gate, and barring disaster never would. It was his own ExOp that shut him out, as it shut out all those born too soon. He belonged to the Common World, the history the alternities all shared. An Albert Tackett was alive in every alternity, each living its own life, following its own path. And there was no room for another, even as a visitor.

Because it was his own decision, he knew it was a good one. The danger to the Guard was too great even to consider a self-indulgent one-time exception. The maze and the worlds beyond it belonged to the children.

But he could not stop wishing that he was young enough to make a transit of his own to Blue or Yellow, and, just once, see the world as it might have been.

Wallace's appearance at the gate control complex caused a sensation.

"Red Section, this is gate control," the gate monitor was saying into his telephone as Wallace came through the double doors. "Your lost sheep is back. Right. I'll tell him."

Replacing the phone, the monitor stared quizzically at Wallace. "Jesus Christ, Rayne, what happened to you? Looks like you were the runt in a dogfight."

"Make it a gunfight, and you've about got it. Want to log me in?"

"Already logged."

"Then I'm on my way upstairs for some body work," Wallace said, displaying the still-oozing laceration on the heel of his hand. "Tell Red I'll be over for a debrief as soon as I get sewed up."

"Sorry," the monitor said. "They already want you in D-8."

Wallace flashed an annoyed expression. "All right. Could you—"

"Done." As Wallace moved past the gate control station, the monitor pushed another button on his phone. "Medical Services, this is gate control. Runner needs a house call at Debrief 8."

There were two men waiting for Wallace in D-8—Charles Adams, his Red Section supervisor, and an Ops Division referee Wallace had seen occasionally but did not know. It was hard to say which of them looked more unhappy.

Adams gestured at a chair, then switched on a recorder. "Transit summary, please."

Wallace's concern deepened. The usual opening was a more casual, "What happened?" or "How'd it go?" The referee's presence made a difference, of course, but there was more than that in Adams' voice.

"I found the gate house abandoned and sealed. When I tried to complete the run, I found that there was a general evacuation because of the Brats. Before I could get back to the gate house, I was picked up. I escaped, taking out the patrol that picked me up."

"So they made you."

"No. If they made me as anything, it was as a Brat who got away. Which reminds me," Wallace added, unbuttoning his shirt to expose the pouch. "The clock's got about an hour to run on this, so we can save the AVs." But as he removed the pouch, there was the telltale grating sound of a broken vial. "Some of them, anyway," he said apologetically.

"When you came up overdue, I sent Volcker across," Adams said stiffly. "He saw that the station had been evacuated, retrieved the station log, and came back. Which is what you should have done. Why didn't you?"

"That's not my job," Wallace said defensively. "I don't even know where to look for the station log."

"In the pickup locker. That's where Volcker found it."

"Is that procedure?" He looked to the referee. "I never heard of that."

The referee said nothing.

"I had a pouch to deliver," Wallace continued. "And I thought you'd want to know what was going on."

"The station logs told us," Adams said.

Wallace's brow furrowed. "They did?"

"Why so puzzled?"

"If they had time to update the logs, they'd have had time to send back an alert."

"They tried," the referee said, breaking his silence. "Apparently she didn't get through."

Another name for the engraver—

"She who?"

"Brenda Hilley."

"She wasn't a runner," Wallace said with a flash of anger. Station staff were almost always delivered to their assignments by ferrymen, rather than being trained as runners themselves. It was simple economy of resources, good runners were too valuable to tie down in a field station. "She had no business trying a transit."

"No one there was a runner," the referee said. "Somebody had to try."

"Is that procedure, too?"

At that moment the doctor arrived. He clucked and fussed over the seeping laceration on Wallace's hand, frowned at the abrasions and bruises on Wallace's torso, the tenderness in the abused shoulder.

"This man should come upstairs with me right now," he pronounced. "He needs stitches, X-rays, a full exam, and, I would guess, a good night's sleep. You can have him back in the morning."

"We're not finished here," Adams protested.

"I see no notable head injuries," the doctor said dryly. "And looking at him, I find it hard to believe that he's going to forget what happened."

Adams opened his mouth to argue, but the referee stayed him with a touch on the arm. "Do what needs doing, Dr. Glass. And assign him a room for overnight. But Charlie or I'll want to talk to him again yet tonight."

Glass frowned, then nodded. "All right. I'll call you when I'm done with him."

He motioned, and Wallace followed. They made the trip through the busy corridors to the infirmary in silence. But after

41

the door to the treatment room closed out the rest of the world, Glass turned a quizzical grin on his patient.

"I can guess how you got beat up. What'd you do to get on the hot seat?"

Sitting bare-chested on the edge of the examining table, Wallace shook his head in frustration. "Hell if I know. Who was that with Adams, anyway?"

An eyebrow climbed skyward in surprise. "Ron Hastings. Section liaison for the director. Troubleshooter. You didn't know?"

"No," he said glumly. "And I wish I still didn't. How about some aspirin?"

"About six?"

"That'll do for a start."

Sewed up, shot up, scrubbed down, and changed out of the shreds of his Red Section clothes, Wallace felt almost human. He could tell that his shoulder, already stiff and balloonlike with swelling, was going to get worse before it got better. But the rest of his injuries were easily shrugged off.

It wasn't as easy to shrug off the feeling that he was in deep trouble with Adams, who had reappeared with his typewriter-sized tape recorder within minutes of being called. By then Wallace had had a chance to rerun the transit in his head. He reached the same conclusion this time as he had before—he hadn't done anything wrong.

But Adams was snapping and snarling from the first word, as he had been downstairs even before Wallace began his report. It was as though he'd brought some standing grievance into the room with him, one he could only work out by nailing Wallace to the wall.

Every question was an accusation. Wallace had violated transit rules. When Wallace pointed out there were no rules covering the situation he had found, Adams declared he had violated "accepted procedure." When Wallace argued that he had *followed* accepted procedure, Adams pronounced that he had failed to use "commonsense good judgment."

He could not win. Adams was not debriefing him—he was building a case against him, before he'd even heard the whole story. But the tenor got worse, not better, after the whole story was told. When Adams heard about O'Brien, he raged over losing one of three fully softened drops in the city. When he heard about Chambers, it became almost impossible to talk to him.

After an hour of it, it dawned on Wallace that Adams wasn't

really talking to him at all. He was performing for the tape recorder, doing everything possible to color in his favor the impression anyone who reviewed a transcript would form.

That made a little more sense, but not enough. Finally Wallace reached out and switched off the recorder. "What's with you, Charlie? I've never seen you like this before."

"I've never had a runner do this to me before."

"Come off it. The only sweetheart runs are the ones that don't leave the gate house," he said, thinking of the work of the low-status ferrymen, who backpacked documents forty pounds at a time between the outstations and home. "What's really going on here? Are you up for review or something?"

Adams stared coldly at Wallace. "For your information, Ops is thinking about closing down Red Section."

"Because of my run?"

"No," Adams said, relaxing fractionally. "I was told two days ago. They've sent a proposal upstairs to the director. They don't think they're getting enough out of Red for the trouble and manpower. There's a lot of talk about it being too dangerous."

"So that's why Hastings was there. Well, I know a lot of people who wouldn't cry if they did close Red."

"Including yourself, I take it."

"It *is* a mess over there."

"So you can be proud when it happens. We'll get you a T-shirt that says 'I killed Red Section.' "

"Charlie, are you worried about your job?"

"Damn right I am."

"Well, hell, Charlie, don't take it out on me. Anyway, they'll find a place for you."

"A place at the bottom of somebody else's pecking order."

Wallace sighed. "You know, if you'd just said something up front, I could have helped. I don't suppose you want to spin those reels backward and start over?"

"No," Adams said, reaching for the machine. "Next time stay put and let us handle the problem."

Ruthann Wallace surveyed the living room in dismay. It was impossible to impose order on a house containing a three-year-old. Eventually she would believe that firmly enough to stop trying.

At least there was some point to cleaning here in the Block, she thought as she started gathering up Katie's detritus. She had lived in more than one home where all you could accomplish by

43

keeping the contents tidy was reveal the fundamental shabbiness of the surroundings.

She remembered all too vividly the last place she and Rayne had lived—a second-floor apartment over a family laundry in Bentonville, Indiana. The rickety wooden stairs out back. The canted, weatherworn balcony that scared guests back inside. The humpback ridge down the middle of the kitchen floor where one stalwart beam had resisted sagging.

There had been a hot spot in the middle of the living room floor from a dryer duct somewhere below, usually marked by the curled-up yellow form of Rayne's cat, Rufus. When they came home each night, they had to throw the windows open to rid the apartment of the smell of bleach, soap, and solvents.

Medford Federal Housing Center—better known as North Block—was a different story. Just five years old, it contained three floors of neat, well-maintained apartments. True, the apartments were small, and the Wallaces occupied one of the smallest— they actually had less space here than above the laundry.

But the layout was intelligent enough that Ruthann barely noticed. And there were amenities. Three rooms had carpeted floors, there was a recirculating air system almost as good as air-conditioning, and they rarely heard their neighbors on either side or above.

None of those features accounted for a waiting list which was, in light of the rate that vacancies were appearing, three years long. For the building was in fact a shelter, the topmost floor fifteen feet underground. The central access core with the community rooms, clinic, and food caches was topped by a six-foot-thick cap of reinforced concrete, angled and sculpted to deflect and diffuse the shock waves of a nuclear air burst as near as a quarter-mile away.

It was a good place to live, friendly, safe. Security was good enough upstairs that most people left their doors unlocked, or even open. The children in a given nexus treated the whole corridor as their playground, and Ruthann had made friends among the mothers in hers.

But sometimes she wished for a window—just a little window, to catch a fresh breeze from, to let in the warmth of the afternoon sun. A window to stand at when Rayne was late and she was bustling about the apartment after Katie could no longer occupy her mind—

In the morning, Wallace was obliged to repeat parts of his story for an audience consisting of Charlie Adams, Ron Hastings, and the Red Section chief, an old-line CIA man named Gradison. The place was a Red Section conference room, and this time it was Gradison who led the questioning.

"All right," Gradison said finally, nearly three hours after they had begun. "I think we have the picture. Wait here, would you, Rayne?"

They left him alone in the room for several minutes, and when the door opened again it was Gradison alone who reappeared.

"Rayne, I'm afraid I'm going to have to lift your Red certification," Gradison said. "But I want you to know this is not punitive. I'm trying to protect you and our operation there. We don't know how aware the Philadelphia police are about what happened or how hard they're going to be looking for you. If it turns out you're right, that you covered your exposure, then maybe a month from now I'll be able to bring you back."

A month from now there may not be a Red Section, Wallace thought glumly. "Do I stay Grade 3, sir?"

"Worried about your checks?"

"My wife will be."

"All right, I'll tell you what I'm going to do. I'll suspend your papers instead of lifting them. That'll keep you at G3, at least until we review your case a month from now," Gradison said, resting his folded hands across his round belly. "But you might want to use that time to work on your certification for one of the other alternities, just in case."

Sure, Wallace thought. All I have to do is get a tan and learn Arabic for White, or lose five inches and turn slope-eye for Green. "Thank you, sir."

Gradison grunted. "Just trying to be fair. What happened to you wasn't your fault."

It was a grudging vindication, little more than politeness, but Wallace seized on it gladly. "That's how I see it. I was beginning to wonder if I'd get anyone to agree."

Gradison grunted again, reaching for the doorknob with sausagelike fingers. "Anyway, you're released. Call me in a month and I'll tell you where you stand."

The Guard's training and administration center occupied more than half of the Tower's base section, including all of floors three through ten. With more than three hundred runners, sixty crackers, and twenty instructors on the roster, they needed that much space and more. Compared to the tranquility which ruled above the fifteenth floor, the hallways in Guard country bustled like downtown sidewalks.

Which meant that there was no way for Wallace to get from the Red Section offices to the runners' change-out room without crossing paths with any number of fellow Guardsmen. Not eager to talk to anyone, Wallace fended off greetings with nods and the lifted hand.

But in the change-out room, he encountered a face for which different rules applied. "Hey, Jason."

Jet-haired and lithe, Jason March was unembarrassedly sitting naked on the bench by his gray steel lockerlike wardrobe, polishing a wing-tip shoe. March was the first friend Wallace had made in the Guard. He had been a G2 when Wallace was a trainee. Thrown together by the soon-to-be-abandoned mentor system, they found themselves united by their love of combo music and dark beer and their virulent hatred for the Boston Celtics.

March was G5 now, and his growing command of Russian and Arabic kept his schedule full with Black and White Section assignments. That meant that Wallace crossed paths with him less often, mostly in the change-out room, and one or the other of them seemed to miss their Thursday night Notes Club "date" about half the time. But friends they still were.

"Hey, Rayne," March called back, looking up from his labors. "I heard you came back from your run in several pieces."

"I came back in one piece," Wallace said, spinning the dial on his closet. "But I felt a bit subdivided when Adams got done with me."

March chuckled. "My informant must have confused the two."

"You inbound or out?"

"Out."

"I guess I can't interest you in a beer at Reggie's."

Shaking his head, March said, "Too early, anyway."

Wallace checked the watch he had just retrieved from the smallest of the three compartments inside his locker. "A little, maybe. Where to?"

"Yellow. Domestic drop."

While he slipped his wedding ring back on his finger, Wallace took a second look at the clothes hanging from March's valet. Jacket and tie, pale blue dress shirt—that almost always meant a Yellow puddle-jump.

The Alternity Yellow gate house was abandoned Dunstanburgh Castle in Northumberland, on the North Sea. For obvious reasons of logistics the field station had to be elsewhere. For less obvious reasons it was in lower Manhattan, though the Guard did operate a small substation in London.

46

To get from the gate house to the field station meant a five-hour flight on one of the needle-nose Lockheed screamers, and a runner had to look the part of someone who could afford the trip. March wouldn't even have to wear a pouch on this run—Yellow Section would have a leather briefcase waiting for him.

"I guess that means scratch Thursday."

" 'Fraid so. I left a message for you upstairs. But let's do something this weekend, huh? How about Saturday?"

"Sure," Wallace said, closing his wardrobe. "I'll look at the papers. Somebody worth hearing ought to be playing." He edged away, feeling vaguely dissatisfied. "Have a good run."

He took the long way out, past the door to the chute and the oak-backed brass plaque that hung on beside it. The plaque called him back, and he paused in front of it to scan the single column of names.

There could be no monuments to fallen Guardsmen outside the walls of the Tower, so they remembered their own inside them. The Guard had neither seal nor motto, and so the plaque carried a legend only: "In Memory Always With Us." Mawkish and uninspired, and yet somehow enough to stab straight through to the place where disquieting emotions lived.

Thirty-one names, but room enough left for twice that number. Which made the plaque not only a memorial, but also a warning. It was the last thing the runners saw before starting down the chute, the direct corridor to gate control. Even those who chose not to look at it saw it in their mind's eye in the process.

Thirty-one names, soon to be thirty-two. He remembered Brenda Hilley as a plumpish girl given to white turtleneck sweaters and silver and turquoise Indian jewelry. Pleasant smile. A screening analyst, he seemed to remember. He wondered if she'd volunteered for the transit or been volunteered by the stationmaster. Wondered if it mattered.

Thirty-one names. He ran a fingertip across the metal where Brenda's name would be added, leaving a faint chromatic streak of body oil on the gleaming brass. It seemed a desecration, and he hastily rubbed the streak away with the sleeve of his shirt.

"In Memory Always With Us," it said, but that was a lie. No one talked about the lost, even those who'd known them. It was considered bad form, maybe even bad luck. The people whose names appeared on the plaque lived on only as an uncomfortable reminder that the maze killed.

For, except for the odd mole or two killed in a random traffic accident or caught up in a riot, everyone on the list had disappeared between gates. Crackers lost probing the maze, runners who never completed a routine transit, ferrymen who failed to deliver themselves and their packages to the other side. *Gee, R.W., you could have been one of the exceptions—*

Wallace shivered and tore himself away before his imagination put his own name on the plaque. "Ready for the engraver." That was the Guard's joking euphemism for death. It was an honor he had come close to earning himself, an honor he could do without.

For more than twelve hours, the suggestion that he had screwed up had been eating at Wallace. As he left the change-out room, the only way he could think to rid himself of the bilious taste of that thought was to get a good run under his belt, as soon as possible.

The dispatcher on duty behind the assignment desk was Deborah King, a familiar if not friendly face. More than a year ago Wallace had made the mistake of innocently flirting her up with his wedding ring resting in his locker. The scolding she had given him when she discovered he was married had been hot enough that his ears still burned when he thought about it.

It had been impossible, then or since, to persuade her that he had not been looking to cheat on his wife. Worse, at a yard party a few weeks later at Jason's, Deborah had made a point of seeking out and befriending Ruthann. Seeing them sitting together, but not knowing what they were talking about, had made for a miserable afternoon.

Which was exactly what Deborah intended. "I didn't tell her anything," she had said just before leaving. "I just thought you needed to squirm a little." The only comfort Wallace could take was that her ferocious reaction meant that she might have said yes if the proposition had come. And there was at least some balm for the ego in that.

" 'Lo, Deb," he said, approaching the desk. "21618—Red released me. Mark me clear and tell me what you have."

"Some kind of release. Your Red certification's been suspended."

"I know. It's protective, not punitive. I'm still okay on Blue and Yellow. What's the rotation look like?"

"Normal. Eight or ten names ahead of you on each. Not that—"

Eight or ten names was a two-hour wait, at least. "I can do ferry runs."

"Not that it matters," she repeated. "You also have a three-day medical hold from Dr. Glass."

"What?"

She reached for a clipboard and showed him the order.

"So what does this mean?" he asked, glancing at the paper and looking up. *Nice eyes—*

"It means you're going home. Did you even call your wife last night?"

"No," he admitted, realizing.

"Figures. Well, you've got a couple of days to make it up to her. Give the little one a hug for me."

That was the most annoying fallout of all, Deborah King's self-appointed, proprietary interest in the happiness of the Wallace household. But this time Wallace barely noticed, realizing for the first time how close he had come to never seeing his daughter Katie again.

"Yeah," he said with a crooked smile. "I'll try to work an extra one in."

ANOMALY REPORT 23

Transit Log Number: 61
Transit Date: March 18, 1968
Transit Agent: Donald Freepace

Abstracted from Transit Report 031868-5

Who else was out there? Were you running
some sort of test? ... I wasn't alone, that's
what I mean. Yes, on the return. I was
right in the channel, locked on the gate, and
all of a sudden there was something between
me and the gate. I could feel it. I could feel
the break. No, I didn't see anything. A
shadow, the most it was was a shadow. How
could I describe it anyway? It's not normal
sight. It's not the kind of seeing we do out
here. Not like you standing between me and
the door. I see you instead of the door. This
was different. Just—a break. I stopped ...
I don't know, five minutes. It felt like five
minutes.... Of course I was scared. Every
time I go through the gate I get the heebies.
It's so fucking weird, coming out and seeing
streets jammed with big cars.... I don't have
any idea what it was if it wasn't someone
from here. Maybe that's what happens when
you put two of us in the same corridor. But
if it wasn't you, then I don't know. And I
don't want to think about it, either. Maybe
we're not the only ones who know about
this.... No, I don't want to think about that.
Brian's been missing for three weeks. How
could anybody stand to be in there for three
weeks? That's what scares me the most, you
know? Getting lost in there, and never
being able to find my way out. Bad enough
when I think about being alone. I'd be worse
if I had to think I wouldn't be.... Just a
shadow, a break in the corridor. I wish you
could tell me what it was.

Investigator's Report:

No corroboration is available. Stress-induced
psychosis is inferred. (Possible case study for
postulated transit anxiety syndrome.) Non-
punitive transfer to alternative assignment
ordered. Psychological division follow-up
recommended.

Eleanor Emerson

Eleanor Emerson
Staff Operations & Training
NRC 02-243

CHAPTER 4

Alpha List

Bethel, Virginia, The Home Alternity

Even with a steel-chassised gas-burner, it was a tedious forty-minute drive from the Capitol garage to the tree-lined approach to Walter Endicott's rural mansion. But serving in the Senate had conditioned Endicott to the point where his tolerance for tedium was very high, and he was barely aware of the bicycle-snarled approaches to the Potomac bridge or the crawling commuter traffic on the Jefferson-Davis Highway.

It helped that he had nothing to do but ride in the back seat of the Mercedes and read his copy of the day's Cleveland *Plain Dealer*. Endicott rarely left his office until the paper arrived, usually shortly after three. It was a daily ritual now nearly a decade old.

Considering how much trouble was involved in getting him the paper, he wished sometimes that he enjoyed it more. Most Senators received their homestate newspapers by federal mail, three to six days late if from east of the Mississippi, ten days or more if from the West Coast.

Endicott's copy got special handling all the way through—the first of the midnight press run,—it was couriered to Cleveland's interurban train station, shuttled to Pittsburgh, transferred to a Washington-bound train, and picked up at Union Station by a junior staffer from Endicott's office.

All so it could be discarded by the chauffeur when the car was cleaned at the end of day.

For forty minutes was more than enough time to read this

Plain Dealer, and rarely was there anything in it Endicott needed or wanted to read twice. He usually left it behind on the seat of the Mercedes without a thought.

The national section was interchangeable with the national section of any Federal News Service paper. Fair enough—the same could be said of the AP or UPI papers of home. But by comparison with those syndicates, and Endicott had been no great booster of the press, the FNS offered an unpleasant mix of half-truths, studied silence, and propaganda, leavened with what it called "cheer" pieces.

What interested Endicott were the local features, from city government down to the minutia of engagements and obituaries. Through his business connections, his wife's patronage of the arts scene, his friendships high-placed and low, Endicott knew by face and name literally thousands of people in that "other" Cleveland. Hundreds had partied or been overnight guests on the Endicott yacht berthed along the Gold Coast.

It was an irresistible curiosity to Endicott how those same people had fared in this world, a curiosity partly satisfied by scanning the paper for news of them. On any given day, he would find from five to a dozen references, most of them surprises in one way or another.

Sometimes it was startling how little difference there was, like the Northside city councilman who was arrested in both worlds for taking bribes. Sometimes the twists were startling enough to make Endicott laugh out loud, such as when the woman he had known as a call-girl madam turned up as the owner of a chain of upscale bedroom boutiques.

He came by his curiosity honestly. He had spent most of his first three months in this strange twisted reflection of the world studying his own counterpart, at once repelled and fascinated.

In this world, as in his own, he had done well for himself—perhaps even a bit more so here. His alternate was married, as he had been, but to a different woman—curiously, to a woman with whom Endicott had enjoyed a quiet affair half a dozen years back. When he finally gained entrance to his alternate's elegant Gates Mills house, he found a hundred familiar objects and a thousand more that were unfamiliar but pleasing to his tastes and sensibilities.

The truth was that Endicott had not planned at first to kill his alternate and replace him. But here was a power base ready for the taking. And as he thought on it, he saw that it would be easy, an invisible crime. If it even qualified as a crime. He *was* Walter

Endicott. These possessions, this life, belonged to Walter Endicott. To *him*, if he was bold enough to assert the claim.

It was that conviction, as much as need or opportunity, which finally moved him. With each passing day, the existence of his alternate distressed him more. Something which came from deep inside him, from the place where the self fights for recognition, came to find the sight of the other to be intolerable.

He did it by his own hand, at a time of his own choosing. And when it was done, when he had faced himself without flinching and seen himself die without disintegrating, Endicott knew for certain that there were no rules, no cosmic plan, no God. Life truly was a game, and there was nothing to fear in this life but unfriendly Chance and the selfish drives of those more ruthless than himself.

And understanding that, he intended to see that he was not victimized by either.

Washington, D.C., The Home Alternity

Peter Robinson finished scanning the two-page summary of that morning's submarine contact and pushed it back across the nineteenth-century mahogany table toward the Secretary of Defense.

"This will do for the FNS, but it's not enough for me," he said. "A simple answer, please, Gregory. Did we know that sub was sitting in New York harbor? And don't bother to tell me that it wasn't actually in the harbor. You know that's how it's going to read in the damned *Times* tomorrow."

Gregory O'Neill looked pained. He had already endured a minor dressing-down in the Cabinet Room, before a hastily convened meeting of the National Security Council senior membership. Now they were alone in the President's private meeting room, and it could only get worse.

"We knew it was in the area," O'Neill said. "There'd been contacts off and on for the last two days. But no, we weren't on it right at the moment she surfaced."

"And after?"

"We tracked it for twenty-six minutes. She picked up the liner *Kestrel* and ran with her for a while, right under her keel a hundred feet down. Then she turned south and went deep and we lost her."

Robinson leaned back in his chair and toyed with a pencil. "I've given the Navy fifteen billion dollars for Cyclops on the promise that I'd know when a Russian sub had its nose up our ass. What's going on here, Gregory?''

"That's about the busiest waterway we have, sir. I think the boys with the headphones did a good job to stay with it as well as they did.''

"Are you telling me that this is the best I can hope for?''

Conscious of past history, O'Neill hesitated. He had survived longer than either of Robinson's previous Secretaries of Defense, but the common element in their departures had been an attempt to explain to the President why something he had asked for wasn't possible.

Robinson read the hesitation and guessed the reason for it. "Shoot straight, Gregory. You're not in that much trouble with me—yet.''

With a rueful nod, O'Neill complied. "Operationally, we're right there. Communications are first-class. The Bell Labs people have really come through. It's the front end that's weak. We're pushing the limits of this generation of sub detection technology. This isn't news to you.''

"No.''

"The moored sonobuoys are sensitive but not reliable, not as reliable as something that hard to get to needs to be. The look-down rigs in the P-5 planes aren't worth a damn in shallow water. We don't have enough ASW frigates to patrol the whole coastline. On top of which their Horizon-class boats are quiet as a whisper at a hundred paces. So, yes—this is the best you can hope for. For now.''

Robinson mulled that for a moment. "What about our friends in Boston? Is there anything better in the pipeline?''

"Nothing that I'm aware of.''

Idly, Robinson drummed his fingers on the desk. "What's the head count?''

"As of about two hours ago, fifteen subs within the two hundred-mile range of the Javelin batteries.''

"And if I gave the order to take them out, how many would you expect to survive?''

"Under present conditions—with no war alert?''

"Under present conditions. This very moment.''

There was something about the way Robinson had framed the question that disturbed O'Neill, but then the whole Javelin program had never sat well with him. It was hard to see the defensive value of fixed coastal missile batteries against a mobile submarine force, especially when the same money could have bought badly needed patrol boats.

The Javelin batteries had some PR value domestically, that was true. But the only tangible impact of their presence so far was to prompt the Soviet Naval Command to bring in extra deep-water boats on both coasts, presumably to target the batteries. Within ten minutes of the outbreak of war, the batteries would be gone.

The way O'Neill added it up, unless they were used preemptively—an idea which deserved no consideration, in light of the total strategic picture—the Javelins were next to worthless. It didn't much matter how many subs with empty silos the Coast Guard sank. It didn't matter to the Russians, and it didn't matter to the targets of the inbound missiles.

But there was no point in arguing the point. The Coast Guard was delighted with their expanded role, the Navy was officially indifferent, and Javelin was the issue over which Robinson's first Secretary had departed.

"Five," he said curtly. "Minimum. Maybe as many as eight."

"That's not good enough."

"I know. Not when we're targeting boats with a hundred men in them and they're targeting cities of a hundred thousand." *What would you say if I told you we could get them all?* he wondered.

"So what are you going to do about it?"

O'Neill bristled. "We've increased our capability five hundred percent since Cyclops deployment started—"

"It looks like another couple hundred percent is in order."

"With all due respect, sir, you're not making allowance for the difficulty—"

"I make no allowances for people who tell me they can hit a target and then fall short."

"Rayedon Electronics made the promises, sir, not DOD. And I specifically cautioned—"

"Then pull the contract out from under them and give it to someone who can do the job," Robinson said quietly.

"The learning curve on the technology the NRC is fronting to Rayedon—"

At that moment the telephone rang. On the second ring, O'Neill started toward it, but Robinson stopped him.

"Don't. It'll be for me." Just as a playful child might have, Robinson backpedaled from the table in his chair, coasting on silent casters to the corner table where the telephone rested.

"Yes, Walt. How are you? Just a moment." Robinson looked back toward O'Neill. "Push it, Gregory. Find an answer." Then he swiveled a half-turn in his chair, turning his back on O'Neill, dismissing him. "No, I wasn't aware of that—"

The Tower Guard courier was waiting in his usual place, seated on the upholstered bench in the entry foyer. He came to his feet as Endicott came through the front door.

"Good afternoon, Senator."

"Collecting already, Donovan?" Endicott asked lightly. "I thought I already paid you for this month. Well, come on in."

It was an old joke, and the young courier answered it with a polite smile as he fell in behind Endicott. In the courier's brown case was another Cleveland *Plain Dealer*, also bearing that day's date. There the similarity ended.

This was the real paper, the one that described the world Endicott had left behind. This one was feisty, opinionated, defiantly liberal. This one was important enough to justify the trouble involved in getting it into his hands. And this one could not be casually discarded. Donovan would wait until Endicott was finished reading, then take it away again to wherever the Guard filed or destroyed outworld originals.

At first it had annoyed Endicott that Tackett refused to trust him with permanent custody of so much as a photograph clipped from the social pages. Who did the bastard think he was going to betray the secret to? The house was safe. Divorce was unaccountably difficult in this world, but Grace had effected an equivalent separation by staying behind in Cleveland. Endicott lived alone, and his one live-in servant had long since proven his discretion concerning matters easily as sensitive.

But his annoyance had fallen on paranoia-deafened ears, and Endicott had fallen into the habit of reading the papers back to back just to be rid of the courier's presence as quickly as possible. Sometimes, just to twit the courier, he would leave them both lying on the table side-by-side when he was done, both tangibly real, and yet both completely contradictory.

Invariably, the courier would gather up that which he had brought with barely a glance at the other. It seemed sometimes to Endicott that the Guard selected for a lack of curiosity. Even its leadership was painfully parochial. Their world was real—the others were false, mutants, shadows.

Well, he had lived in one of those shadows and knew better. It was this world, with history books full of Presidents named Vandenberg and Stevenson, where Tennessee Williams never wrote *A Morning of Mourning*, where a Triple–Crown-winning horse named Stalwart had turned the memory of Citation to a yes–but—it was this world that was hard to take seriously.

Donovan followed him into the study, politely closed the door behind them, and spun the dial on the pouch's combination lock. "Here you go, sir," he said a moment later, handing the paper over.

"You keep on hitting the flowerbeds, there'll be no tip for you," Endicott said with mock gruffness.

Donovan grinned; that was a new variation, and welcome for its novelty. "I don't know how many more of them there'll be," he volunteered, retreating to his chair by the door. "The director is talking about shutting down operations in Red."

"I'd be sorry to hear that," Endicott said lightly, settling in an armchair which caught the afternoon sun from the sheer-draped windows.

He said nothing more, but the comment opened a second channel in his thoughts which remained busy until after Donovan was gone. Then he moved to the telephone and dialed a number from memory, a number the very possession of which denoted power.

"Peter, this is Walter. Yes. I won't keep you long, Peter. I understand that the Guard is considering terminating its operation in Alternity Red. That's right. Well, then Albert isn't doing his job. I want you to know that I wouldn't be pleased by that. I wouldn't be pleased by that at all—"

Boston, The Home Alternity

Rayne Wallace stood at the pickup chute outside the Tower's west entrance shivering in the wind. The temperature was just above freezing, a record cold for Boston on that date, thanks to a front which had moved down from Canada overnight, surprising everyone, Wallace most of all. When he last left home two days ago, it had been sixty degrees and Indian summer was in the air. Time to get the heavy coat out of the box.

Predictably, two smoke-belching flesh-haulers stopped before the company van appeared, one for the Dorchester route, the other headed for Arlington. They swept up most of those waiting with Wallace, leaving him feeling not only cold but abandoned. Wallace accepted it fatalistically. Riding the company van was considered a privilege, but sometimes the advantages were more perceived than real.

He advanced to curbside and stood there with arms crossed over his chest, looking hopefully down Marlborough toward the mouth of the garage. A few moments later, another of the waiting joined him there, a hook-nosed man with hair the color of his gray tweed coat.

"You run today?"

Wallace took a second glance at the man. Ops. Or Tech Transfer. Too old for the Guard, anyway. "Yeah."

"Where to?"

"Red."

The man shook his head. "It's getting nasty over there."

"I know," Wallace said, looking back down the street. "From what I hear, we won't be there long."

"Yeah." The man hesitated. "Listen, do you ever get over to Yellow?"

Wallace knew what was coming—he had heard it at least twenty times before. "I've got papers."

"They have a perfume there that just drives me crazy. Fire and Ice—from Revlon. I guess it's in all the stores. My wife got some from a friend about six months ago, and I tell you, friend, it made her feel like—you know how some women change when they put on a slinky dress or climb into a nice pair of heels? That's what it was like—"

Amused, Wallace let the man chatter on, careful not to give him any of the standard cues that said he was interested. Officially, runners were sternly forbidden to bring any alternity-specific materials back through the gate or any unscreened materials from Home through the other way.

But enforcement was more a matter of honor than strict gate security, and there existed a minor black market in outworld commodities. From what little Wallace knew of it, perfumes from Yellow were a popular item, along with fine stone jewelry from White and pornography from Green. Wallace had also heard of an avid philatelist, supposedly a Tower executive, who had posted a standing offer of $40 for any post-1950 mint U.S. stamp from beyond the gate.

The bootleggers were tempted by the lure of pure profit, since in most alternities their stock could be purchased with "funny money"—the Guard's perfectly authentic Home-minted counterfeit currency, issued freely to runners and moles for their expenses. Wallace was not tempted, especially not today. The security his family enjoyed because of his Guard appointment was too valuable to risk. He had enough cause for worry already on account of the fiasco in Red.

But the hopeful buyer prattled on, his voice showing a touch of nervousness over Wallace's continued silence. "The damn thing is that it was just a half-ounce bottle and it's just about gone. I wrote to Revlon and they said they had a perfume by that name thirty years ago, but they stopped making it. Can you imagine that? The most intoxicating scent I've ever found on a woman and they stopped making it! I told them I'd pay a hundred dollars to get hold of some more—''

"Sorry," Wallace said finally, as a blue-gray twelve-seat van nosed out of the Tower garage and headed their way. "I can't help you."

"Oh, I'd never ask anyone to bootleg some," the man said, back-pedaling quickly. "I was just talking to pass the time. About time the damn van came, eh? Cold enough today to turn a man soprano—''

"Katie-cat!" Wallace called as he opened the door to apartment 2E-16. He whistled. "Where's my Katie-cat?" There were two new cats in the nexus within the last month, and Katie had taken to crawling around on the back of the couch and meowing endearingly.

But the answering voice was mature and edgy, not childlike and joyful. "She's next door with Christa," Ruthann said, appearing at the bedroom door. "Where have you been, Rayne?"

"Working." He took in her rumpled hair and reddened eyes. "Where've *you* been? You look like hell, honey," he said, scooting forward for a quick hug and a forehead kiss. "Be back in a minute."

His daughter was seated crosslegged on the Watkins' living room floor, intently coloring a tree bright purple while Christa attacked a sheet of paper with blunt-tipped scissors. Katie threw down the crayon when she saw him. "Daddy, I knew you would be home," she said, running toward him.

Answering her delighted smile with a grin, he squatted on his heels to receive her. "Give me a knock-down hug," he called.

She threw himself into his arms, and he toppled backward until he was lying flat on the carpet with Katie on his chest.

"Now a smackeroo," he urged, and tiny arms pulled her face close to his for a loud kiss on the tip of his nose. He clambered to his feet with Katie still clinging to his neck. "Woof, you're getting heavy."

"Can I have a cookie?"

"Well, let's go see about that," he said, shifting her to a more stable perch on his arm. "You going to say good-bye to your friend?"

Katie freed one arm to wave. " 'Bye, Christa."

"Good-bye, Christa," Wallace echoed, and turned away, heading for the door. "It's sure good to see you, my little Katie-cat."

She giggled, then meowed twice.

"Does that mean you're glad to see me, too?"

Holding character, she bobbed her head solemnly.

"I'm glad. Let's go try to find that cookie. Do cats like cookies?"

Bethel, Virginia, The Home Alternity

"I'm going downstairs, Evan," Endicott called to his house man. "Will you watch for the others?"

"Yes, sir."

Though hardly a mansion, the place was more house than Endicott really needed, especially with Grace in Ohio. It was a party-giver's house, with its triple-oven kitchen, huge south-facing brick patio, and manicured grounds. Grace would have filled it with friends and socialites. But Endicott preferred to treat it as a retreat, and there were few invited guests.

It was the basement that had sold Endicott on the purchase. Unlike in so many houses, even pricey ones, the architect had not sacrificed headroom to ductwork and plumbing. The ceilings in the sprawling basement were a generous nine feet high.

The former owner, a du Pont executive, had made full use of it. On the east side, he had had the earth excavated to provide full-length windows and a French-door walkout for a guest room featuring a huge platform bed. He had walled off the northwest corner for a thousand-bottle wine cellar, sealing it off behind a huge vaultlike oaken door taken from a bankrupt French winery. And in between, he had created an L-shaped party room reminiscent of a private club bar, with soft lighting, comfortable chairs, and hardwood paneling.

Endicott had made his own modifications. The wine racks were moved out, a discreet carpenter and a bemused blacksmith called in, and the basement transformed into something more in keeping with Endicott's particular self-indulgences.

Flipping on the Tiffany lamps in the central lounge, he crossed the room to an antique walnut armoire and opened it. He took a moment to survey the implements arrayed within, making sure that all was in order. Then he moved to the vault door and threw back the locking bolt.

As the door swung open, the girl's head jerked up. A pair of haunted eyes looked at him.

"Hello, little one," Endicott said, moving closer to the wall where she was chained. "I hope you're well rested. There's going to be a small party here tonight, and you're the star attraction.''

Her gag precluded any answer, but he was disappointed not to see a stronger reaction in her eyes. It was time to think about replacing her. She had been in the house six weeks, and her spirit was almost broken. All that was left was a spark of hope that someone was looking for her, that the next time the door opened it would be a rescuer. But no one in this world even knew her name.

Endicott crouched before her and reached out to brush the hair back from her cheek. She knew better than to flinch, and endured the unwelcome touch.

Yes, almost finished with you, he thought with regret as he stood. But there was a certain freedom that went with that knowledge. *It should be an interesting evening.*

Boston, The Home Alternity

Ruthann Wallace lay wide-awake in bed beside her sleeping husband, too full of bitterness and despair to sleep. The eighteen inches between them seemed like a hundred miles.

She had spent two days worrying over him, only to have his first words to her be a cruel slap. But instead of rebelling, she had instantly accepted the blame, bathing herself in self-hate for disappointing him, for failing him.

There was nothing she could do about the eyes, red from crying. But in the few minutes he was gone getting Katie, she had brushed desperately at her hair and changed out of her well-worn slacks into a skirt and sandals, a look she knew he liked.

But he had hardly noticed. He spent the first half of the evening on the floor with Katie. When it was time for her to put the child to bed, he stretched out on the sofa in front of the television. By the time she returned from the baby's room, he was watching *The Nation Tonight* on TV-1 and looking very much like someone who didn't want to talk.

She left him there and changed again, this time into her one bedroom luxury, a slinky white synthetic robe with a neckline that drew the eye downward and showed her legs off well if she sat just right. She sat where he could see her and waited for the news to end.

"I was worried about you," she said as he rose to change the channel.

61

He looked at her curiously—not at all the kind of look she had hoped to elicit from him. "The Guard would tell you if something happened to me."

"Did it?"

The television had most of his attention. "What?"

"Did something happen to you? Those stitches on your hand—"

He shrugged and retreated to the couch. "I got a few bumps. I'm okay."

"Where were you?" she blurted out.

"I can't talk about it, Annie. You know that."

That was when she had lashed out. "You leave me here all alone—you can't tell me what you do—you don't come home and then when you do come home you're hurt. What am I supposed to do, Rayne? How am I supposed to help you? How can I be a wife to you when I can't even talk to you?"

But his face had just gone cold. He gave no answer, staring at the television screen. A few minutes later, he got up and grunted something about going to bed. She followed him in, still hopeful. He liked the way she moved in the robe. If only he'd look up and notice her, *really* notice her—

She saw the bruises when he undressed and wanted to touch him, cried inside at the sight of that beautiful body so shockingly battered. She wanted to know why, but knew better than to ask.

Still hoping, she sat on the edge of the bed while he disappeared behind the toilet screen. When he returned, he asked her to give him a chance to fall asleep before she came to bed.

"It's hard for me to fall asleep, the way you spin like a top before you get settled," he had said, the words a knife in her chest.

She left as he asked, because she did not want to show him her tears, to let him know that he had hurt her. When the crying was done, she came back and quietly slipped into bed.

And now she lay there, unable to sleep, listening to his breathing, feeling his warmth in the bed. Wondering why he was angry, and what she could do to make them whole again.

Federal News Service
International Bureau
Washington, D.C. A2058

FNS NEWS:

News Media Contact:
Phil Madison 202/555 5806

FOR IMMEDIATE RELEASE
October 14, 1977

FALLOUT CONFIRMS
JAPAN NUCLEAR TEST

Airborne radioactivity, presumably from
a Japanese nuclear explosion, has been reported
by the U.S. Atomic Energy Detection System this
morning. The radioactivity is concentrated in
a diffuse cloud of dust three hundred miles wide
and circling the earth at high altitude.

The cloud was detected by Air Force
reconnaisance aircraft during routine patrols
west of Baja, California. Little fallout is expected.

Intelligence experts indicate that the
cloud was most likely produced by an explosion
which took place 1:00 A.M., EDT, October 10,
1977, at Minami-Tori-shima in the West Pacific
Basin Test Area. Seismic signals consistent
with a 60-kiloton test were recorded at that
time.

Ernest Clifton, Secretary of State, issued
a statement which said in part, "We continue
to view with alarm what appears to be an
accelerated program of weapons development
by the People's Republic of Japan. In the
current international climate, such a program
is not only unnecessary, but unwise."

Speaking to reporters, Clifton reiterated
the U.S.'s standing offer to host a six-power
summit to discuss reducing nuclear weapons
worldwide.

—FNS—

R-77-1032

CHAPTER 5

None
But the Honest and Wise

Washington, D.C., The Home Alternity

It was drizzling in the capital, a cold rain falling out of sluggish gray clouds. Another six weeks and the same sort of clouds would have Washington residents cursing sloppy wet snow and street-freezing sleet.

As the Oldsmobile limousine coasted to a stop in the West Executive Drive, Tackett ducked out, shrank into his raincoat and hurried up the steps to the north portico. Just inside the West Wing doors, a white-uniformed White House guard waited impassively at the security station.

"Albert Tackett to see the President," Tackett said, slipping the coat off and folding the damp surface inside.

"Good morning, Mr. Tackett," the guard said, scanning the appointments list. "If you don't mind, would you please tell me the date and place of your birth?"

Tackett did not mind. The token check was by now a familiar routine. "October 1, 1920. Wichita Falls, Texas."

"Thank you, sir. I have a message that the President would like to see you upstairs before the meeting begins. You can go right on back."

Tackett experienced a momentary flare of annoyance. He knew the way to the family quarters on the second floor well enough, but it was a longish walk, and there were closer entrances he could have used had he known. And though he could leave his coat with the porter, the heavy briefcase had to stay with him.

But he could hardly say no. With a wordless nod of acknowledgment to the guard, he started off down the corridor toward the White House proper, passing the Oval Office on the way. Farther on, a maintenance crew was skimming and scrubbing the pool. There was a sharp smell of chlorine in the connecting breezeways.

By the time he reached the elevator to the family quarters, Tackett's heart was racing and his breath coming in open-mouthed pants.

Got to get more exercise, he thought as the elevator doors closed. *Always too much else to do.*

He found Robinson in his dressing room, finishing off a Windsor knot on a navy blue presidential tie.

Nine A.M. conference, Tackett thought. "Good morning, Mr. President."

"Hello, Albert," Robinson said, turning from the mirror and flashing a smile. "Thanks for coming up. Walk with me, will you?"

Groaning silently, Tackett fell in beside the President as they started back the way he had come. "There's something I wanted to get settled before we sat down with the others," Robinson began as they boarded the elevator.

"Of course," Tackett said.

"I've been told that you're considering closing up operations in Alternity Red."

Tackett responded to the statement with irritation. *How did you hear that? Hell of a secret agency we've got—*

"There's a proposal to that effect under review right now," he said. "We do weighted ratings of the data retrieved from each of our field stations every sixty days. Red has finished last for six months running. It's not a viable candidate for Rathole. And in terms of cost per unit, it's easily our most expensive operation."

"Something has to be, doesn't it?" Robinson said as they exited the elevator on the ground floor and turned right down the arch-segmented corridor. "I want you to reject that proposal, Albert."

It's my proposal, you son of a bitch—

"You're not running a profit center up there," Robinson continued. "I don't want us turning our noses up at any of the resources the Tower makes available to us. You never know what will turn up where."

Let me do my job, goddammit!

"There are other considerations," Tackett said. "It's become extremely dangerous for our agents over there. This week alone we've lost two moles to Brat bugs and nearly lost a runner to local security."

"That's unfortunate," Robinson said, pausing in the middle of the west sitting room. "But we don't close up shop in Moscow or the German Republic when we lose an agent or two. Two kids died in training at Fort Dix the other day. O'Neill isn't going to come to me and say 'shut it down, Pete.' I thought your people were ready to pay that kind of price if they had to."

"They are. But I thought I had the right to decide whether what we were getting was worth the price."

"I want Red kept open, Albert."

"Is it that important to Endicott?"

"Senator E isn't asking you, Albert. I am. And you still haven't said yes."

Tackett nodded reluctantly. "As you wish."

"Good," Robinson said, his face thawing around a hundred-watt smile. He clapped Tackett on the shoulder and inclined his head toward the door. "Then let's go join the roundtable, and you can show us what you've got in that mobile file cabinet of yours."

Boston, The Home Alternity

Wallace was struggling to understand. It seemed as though Ruthann were angry with him, even though he could not think of a reason why she should be.

His first day of medical leave had been a confusion of crossed signals. She had carried on as though he wasn't there, rising early even though they had a chance to sleep in, taking Katie in the wagon to go shopping in the morning, leaving Katie in the nexus and disappearing downstairs to visit one of her friends in the afternoon.

Yet in the evening, when he shaved and changed before heading out for a few hours at the Lakeview Lounge up on Fellsway West, she accused him of abandoning her and then broke into tears. As if just because Jason was away, he should pass up spending time with his other friends. She knew not to expect him to stay in Thursday nights. Or should have known.

Mason thought he understood. "Tears. That's how women manipulate us," he had said over the rim of his beer mug. "She's trying to tame you, Rayne, make you safe."

"I *am* safe."

"Nonsense. None of us are, and all of them know it. She

66

doesn't know what goes on up here. Probably afraid you're fucking the bargirls.''

Wallace had cast a lazy glance across the room at Jean, the thick-thighed baby-cheeked waitress who seemed to be on duty seven days a week at the Lakeview. "No danger of that. Besides, she used to hang out at the same clubs down in Randolph before we were married. She knows I'm no good at grab-and-go.''

"No killer instinct.''

"Something.''

It had been a slow night at the Lakeview, with the television broken and only Mason and one other of the Thursday regulars there. He had lost five straight dollar-a-game eight-ball contests to Mason, then come back to the Block early, before eleven.

But Ruthann was already asleep, curled on her side on the far edge of the bed, her back to him, the edge of the sheet drawn up to her neck and held fast in a tangle of knotted fingers. He had sat Indian-style on the floor beside the bed for several minutes, hoping that she would sense his presence and awaken. Finally, he gently brushed a lock of hair back from her cheek, kissed her on the newly bared skin, and retreated to his own side of the bed.

His confusion notwithstanding, morning offered a second chance to mend fences. He had awakened before she did, a rare event. Now, at the first sound from Katie, he slipped carefully out of bed, filled a bowl with cereal for her, and parked her in front of the television with the sound on low. Then he returned to bed and Annie, eager to erase the distance between them the best way he knew how.

She was lying on her back now, the sheet down around her waist, revealing part of a cotton nightdress covered with pale blue flowers. Bending over the bed, he teased the sheet down by increments until it was no longer an obstacle. As though responding to the exposure, she turned sleepily on her side and curled up, her back to him.

Still careful not to wake her, Rayne slipped into bed beside his wife, drawing close enough for wayward strands of her hair to tickle his face. Propping his head on one hand so he could watch her, he boldly rested his other hand on her rounded hip, feeling the warmth of her body through the thin cotton fabric.

With a light touch, fingertips just grazing the nightdress, he explored the roller-coaster undulations from waist to mid-thigh. She shivered slightly and squirmed down into her pillow, turning her buttocks upward.

He accepted the silent invitation and caressed the pleasantly full roundness there, traced the crease between the cheeks. He tried to tug the hem of the nightdress upward, seeking bare skin, but the garment was held too firmly beneath her.

Edging closer, he kissed a bare shoulder. His free arm snaked around her waist and found the buttons at the bodice. Patient fingers released one, two, three buttons, and then sought her right breast, cupping its softness, teasing the nipple to crinkly firmness. He hoped she was dreaming, hoped that she would awaken from pleasant fantasy to even more pleasant reality. She had once given him that experience, his mind soaring through trancelike erotic vignettes as her mouth and hands pleasured him.

With her eyes still closed and a drugged slowness to her movements, she snuggled back against him until his erection was pressed flat against her buttocks, the nightdress still intervening between his skin and hers. He planted nibbling kisses along a line from her shoulder to her neck, gently blew a tangle of hair away, and continued the kisses up to her earlobe.

A hint of a smile appeared on her lips, and she turned lazily onto her back, consciously or unconsciously allowing him freer access to her body. He seized the collar of the nightdress in his teeth and pulled it back, baring her right breast. His mouth sought her nipple. He nibbled it tantalizingly with his bared teeth, teased it with his dancing tongue.

His hand moved down slowly across her belly until it rested lightly above the apex of her thighs. Fingers walked the fabric of the nightdress upward, upward, until the hem reached her hips, revealing her thighs and silken mound. He touched her there and her legs parted for him, her wetness betraying her desire. She made a happy cooing noise deep in her throat as his fingertips found the swollen bud of her clitoris.

Then she seemed to come fully awake, and everything changed. She had been moving easily with his touch, creating an intimate rhythm together. Then she seemed to go rigid, not with pleasure but with resistance. She pushed his hand away and pulled him atop of her, guiding his hardness between her thighs and deep inside her.

But her motive seemed not to be desire, but impatience. When she moved, there was something false about it, as though she were trying to hurry him to his orgasm. Half-asleep, she had been there with him, sharing, the distance between them zero. Awake, the chasm opened again. She was submitting to him, enduring rather than enjoying. He was doing to, instead of doing with.

The change of tenor robbed Wallace of much of his own

desire, though pride would not let him acknowledge it. He moved against her dutifully at first, then with increasing anger, as though anger could replace the urgency lost with the disappearance of passion. Fighting to maintain his erection, Wallace simplified his thoughts, chasing away demons of doubt, trying to call down the memories of other couplings, of fantasies yet untested.

Suddenly there was a thump and a cry from beyond the bedroom door. "It's Katie," Ruthann said, pushing him roughly away and rolling out of bed. The nightdress fell back to its normal below-knee length as she moved toward the door. It seemed to Wallace an exclamation mark on her declaration of indifference, a visual denial that she had been locked in a sexual embrace with him.

He waited, wondering if she would come back, wondering if he wanted her to. Experience had taught them to treat Katie's interruptions as a game, a challenge to desire rather than an obstacle. They hid under the covers when she came uninvited into their bedroom, giggled together and started again when she was gone.

But this was different. And before long, the sound of running water and dishes clanging in the kitchen sink made it clear she wasn't coming back. Wallace decided in the moment of realization that he was glad. And as he showered, the good intentions of the morning, abraded by the frustrating encounter, hardened over into a callus.

He saw what was happening. She accepted his caresses without answering them, absorbed the energy he focused on her without returning any of her own, and in doing so somehow managed to make him feel as though he were the one being unfair. More of it would only make him feel worse, not better.

It would be up to her to initiate from now on; he would not volunteer for such treatment again.

Washington, D.C., The Home Alternity

Tackett wished Robinson had chosen another room. This was a meeting better suited to dark alleys, candle-lit catacombs, the back seats of black cars with tinted windows. The West Wing was too public, the Cabinet Room too proper. From above the fireplace mantelpiece, Thomas Jefferson stared down at them. At the other end of the room, American and presidential flags kept each other company.

They had met here instead of the Oval Office because of the contents of his briefcase, because they would need the conference table's several square yards of leatherette and fine wood. But the table was *too* large. There were fourteen places along its racetrack perimeter, fourteen leather-covered armchairs with brass plates on the back denoting their "owners." The empty seats made Tackett pointedly aware of who was not there.

The Vice-President was conspicuous by his absence. Tackett did not wonder at that; Jessie Barstow had been forced on Robinson by the party, and he had repaid the party by making Barstow an outsider, a smiling ribbon-cutter so far separated from the real power that not even Barstow himself could pretend he mattered.

But there was no one from the congressional leadership, not even from Robinson's own party. No one from NSA. No one from the Justice Department, not even the Attorney General. Only two of ten Cabinet members. Closely held indeed. Everyone would take their own notes today.

The five men who were at the table constituted Alpha Prime, Robinson's new inner circle. Endicott, the NRC's diligent friend on the hill, there because he knew too much. O'Neill, who knew everything about the threat and nothing about the promise. The Secretary of State and the CIA director, both largely in the dark. And Rodman, Robinson's loyal lieutenant, a brooding man who made a point of knowing everything.

Five men, and two of them already on the inside.

They had gathered at the far end of the table, ignoring the nameplates, oblivious to Jefferson's stare. "Hello, gentlemen," Robinson called out to them, angling for an empty chair. "Hope you all have your thinking caps on today."

While further pleasantries were exchanged, Tackett took a seat across the table from the President, pushing aside the ashtray and pad of paper to make room for his briefcase. By the time he ran the combination and checked the contents, Robinson was looking expectantly in his direction.

"I'm ready whenever," Tackett said.

Robinson nodded. "Fine." He shifted in his seat so that he faced the others. "I asked each of you here individually, without telling you who else would be here or why I wanted to see you. And now that you know the who, you may still be wondering about the why.

"Well, if you look around this table, you'll see the six men that I trust the most. Of all those who serve or claim to serve this country, you are the six men whose loyalty I know I need not question. And you are the men I'm counting on the most to help put things right, to restore this country to its proper place on the world stage.

"I won't give you a lecture in balance-of-power politics. I don't need to. You know all the mistakes of the fifties, from the Korean sell-out to the surrender of Berlin. I want to focus on where we are now."

Robinson was rolling now, and Tackett had to smile to himself. Was there ever a President who worked an audience better, who mixed praise, patriotism, and old-fashioned town-hall persuasion with such irresistible effect? Watching it was like watching a master stage magician perform.

"I don't like saying it, but I've got to be honest. The Soviets have so little fear of us that their submarine commanders feel safe playing tag with freighters inside our territorial waters. No wonder that countries that once were our allies have so little confidence in us. It's a miracle that Canada and Mexico have held as firm as they have.

"We're under siege, gentlemen, and the kids now in high school can't remember it ever being different. We saved the free world in the forties, and then turned our backs on it. A penny-pinching isolationist government—yes, a Republican one, more to our shame—and a public who just couldn't see the point to American boys dying in Seoul or Manila. That's what cost us the chance to shape a world to our liking.

"It's gotten a little better these last five years. We've made a difference. But not enough. My father was a plain speaker, and I know how he'd have said it: We're still up shit creek. We've been there so long the color of the water's starting to look good to us.

"But by God, we've finally got us a paddle. And we didn't have to break up the boat to make it." He gestured toward Tackett. "You all know Albert. You know that the National Resource Center has been a big part of the recovery we're seeing domestically. But most of you are still in the dark about what's really going on up there in Boston, and just how much it means to us.

"At least, I hope you are. Because what's really going on up there makes the Manhattan Project look like . . . like a bunch of Boy Scouts building crystal radios."

His tone became less convivial. "You're going to hear some things today that would be hard to credit if you heard them anywhere other than here or from anyone other than Albert and me. I expect you to deal with your doubts and get past them without a lot of hand-holding.''

He looked hard into their eyes for confirmation of their understanding. Finding it, he turned to Tackett. "Albert?"

Tackett nodded and leaned forward. "Santa and his elves," he said with no trace of a smile. "I know that's what you call us. The question is, where do the toys come from? I can guess what you think—that we've got a bunch of pampered geniuses up there turning out ideas as fast as hens lay eggs."

There were chuckles from Robinson and Endicott, and an uncertain smile on the face of Dennis Madison, the CIA director.

"I hate to shatter illusions," Tackett said. "But the truth is, we don't make our toys. We steal them."

Ignoring the explosion of puzzled expressions, Tackett reached into the briefcase and retrieved an oversized hardback book with a familiar burgundy-colored binding. Keeping the spine turned away from the group, he reached out and dropped it in the middle of the table with a thump.

"When I was a kid and I wanted to know something, I'd walk down to the little branch library above the five-and-dime and look it up in the Encyclopaedia Britannica," Tackett continued, retrieving a sheaf of paper from his briefcase. "It represented absolute authority as far as I was concerned. I bought one for my kids years before they could read well enough to use it."

"I thought I was the only one who'd done that," O'Neill said with a friendly smile.

Tackett dealt them each a single piece of paper from the top of his stack. "That's a copy of a page from the Chronology section of a 1976 Britannica yearbook, specifically November—"

Secretary of State Ernest Clifton had been the first to receive the paper. As he scanned it, he abruptly started laughing.

"Problem?"

"What is this, Albert? 'In the closest popular vote in American history, National party candidate Daniel Brandenburg narrowly defeated Republican incumbent Roland Maxwell,' " he read. "Shoot, even I wouldn't vote for Rollie. But who the hell is Brandenburg?"

Robinson sat back in his chair and folded his hands in his lap. "As the paper says, he's President of the United States."

Grinning stupidly, the Secretary of State looked to Robinson. "You mean you're not?"

"Not where that book came from," Robinson said quietly.

Clifton's grin widened momentarily, then collapsed as he took in Robinson's meaning. "Look, there's only one President of the United States—"

"There are at least six," Tackett said, "not including General Betts, a military dictator who sometimes claims the title."

The Secretary of State's mouth worked as his thoughts spun. "Well, all right, sure, there's probably a hundred people who think they're President. Like they think they're God or Napoleon. But there's only one United States—"

"There are at least seven," Tackett said, "counting our own. There may be more."

Clifton had reached a point of total cognitive block. He blinked as though there were something in his eye, shook his head, and looked for help to the others.

"I warned you," Robinson said bemusedly.

"You understand what he's talking about?" Madison demanded of Robinson.

Robinson nodded. "Yes."

The Secretary of State had found his voice. "Where exactly are these other United States supposed to be?"

"I'm going to try to tell you," Tackett said calmly. "Please, E.C., Dennis, everyone, relax. I know it's hard, but sit on your questions for a little while. We're not crazy. The truth is, the world's a little crazy. We were just a little late discovering it."

The props helped. They always did. The Guard had learned that lesson early: Things were more real than words. You could bounce words off someone's forehead for hours and still not put a dent in their denial. But give them something tangible to hold in their hands, and more often than not their self-assurance dissolved like sugar in hot water. And then you could talk to them.

For the Secretary of State, it was the currency kit—three green Washingtons with slightly different designs and very different signatures, one green Eagle, one oversized red-white-and-blue sheet that looked more like a baby stock certificate than money, and a square silver coin the size of a quarter. All dated 1977, all with a face value of one dollar.

He spread the samples out on the table in front of him, stared, rearranged them. He talked to himself, held the bills up to the light, grunted, frowned. He borrowed a "real" dollar bill from Endicott and compared it with each of its kin.

For O'Neill, it was the yearbook. He rested it at an angle against the edge of the table while he paged slowly through it, like a guilty student trying to hide forbidden reading material in his lap. His expression never wavered—somber, even troubled, from title page through to the index. "Left at the first star, and straight on till morning," he murmured at one point.

For Madison, it was a glossy catalog of small aircraft for sport and pleasure flying—high-wing float planes, aerobatic biplanes, swept-wing canards, fragile-looking gliders. He studied each photograph with the critical eye of an intelligence expert, the knowledge of a former Army pilot, and the heart of a boy who had dreamed of flights to the moon.

Tackett gave them time, but not too much time. Wait too long and resistance would start to build again, he knew. Tackett was a veteran of what the Guard called the cold shock interview. While they were grasping for answers, he supplied them, explaining Endicott's role and his presence, describing concisely the general state of the world lying beyond each of the six known gates, providing a simple understanding of the functioning of the gate.

And by the time he was done, he knew that they believed.

"If I can have those things back, we have other matters to talk about," Tackett said.

A thoroughly chastened Ernest Clifton gratefully slid the currency along the table, glad to be rid of its disturbing presence. By contrast, O'Neill was reluctant to surrender the book. Only the CIA director seemed to have found equilibrium.

"There's nothing you've shown us that couldn't be a fraud," Madison said, handing the catalog across the table.

"That's true," Tackett said. "Does that mean you think they are frauds?"

Madison frowned dourly. "Truth is, I'd really like to believe that. I've sat here trying to figure out what your game was, and how you'd conned the President."

"I don't con easily, Dennis," Robinson said.

"I know, sir. So maybe the world is a little crazy." He hesitated, frowning. "Do you seriously think you can keep this a secret?"

"We have so far, including from your people," Robinson said. "Is there someone at the table you don't think can be trusted?"

The director scowled. "No, of course not. But what about when more people know? And how do you know what the Russians know?"

"The cover is solid," Tackett said. "There have been four-teen attempted penetrations of the Tower by the KGB. We intercepted most and steered the rest into a controlled environment. As far as the Soviets are concerned, the Tower is a think-tank, plain and simple."

"Thank you, Albert. I'll take it from here," Robinson said. He pushed back his chair and ambled to the other end of the room, stopping before the flag to study it. "When we started a couple of hours ago, I said I wanted to restore this country to its proper place. You all knew what I meant by that.

"When I was in my twenties, ours was the greatest nation on this earth. Our Navy had friendly ports around the globe. Our soldiers were the heroes of Europe. Our products were in demand the world over. An American citizen could go damned near anywhere and know that his passport protected him. We had power, and we had respect."

He turned to face them. "What we've lost has become even more clear to me from reviewing NRC reports on the various alternities. Somehow, in some of those Americas, we capitalized on opportunities that we forfeited here.

"This is the world we made, and we have to live in it. But we don't have to accept it the way it is. Because new opportunities are always coming along, and this time we're going to make the most of them.

"The Soviet Union is an old alley cat that's grown fat and lazy sleeping in the sun. They still think they're champion of the street, when the truth is that they're a couple of steps from the pet cemetery. Whereas we're the tame little kitten that grew up lean and mean while no one was looking. And the street is going to belong to us.

"But we have to stop thinking like a kitten to make it happen. We have to take chances. We have to assert ourselves. We have to make our claim, and then we have to make it stick.

"That's a dangerous business. Maybe we'll get what we want without having to fight for it. More likely we won't. Change costs, and sometimes you have to pay in pain."

He paused, letting that sink in. "I don't want war. But war is always a possibility. If they push us, we'll fight for what we believe in. We'll fight for what belongs to us. We'll fight, and we'll hurt them, and we'll win. But only if we're prepared.

"You all know what the Alpha List Crisis Evacuation Plan is all about. Most of you have taken part in at least one rehearsal—"

Not me, Tackett thought. Living in Boston shut him out of the primary evacuation plan. But he knew how ambitious the flash evacuation programs were—sixteen helicopters from Andrews Air Force Base descending on preset pickup points around Washington to snatch upwards of a hundred key officials and their families and whisk them to the five shelters scattered along the eastern Appalachians.

After he began to spend so much time in Washington, he had driven up to Boyne Mountain on his own to see the primary shelter. It was civilized, though hardly luxurious. And it felt solid, safe. Fifteen hundred feet of rock was immeasurably more reassuring than the eggshell dome of the South Block, his family's designated alternate.

"—so you know what the shelters are like. I'm glad we have them. But the truth is that they're not good enough. The Russians know where they are. You can bet that they're all targets, along with Washington. And even if they weren't, shelters won't be much help if the Russians fight dirty, with bugs or ground-burst bombs."

Robinson pushed aside a chair and lighted on the edge of the table. "That's why I asked Albert to help me find a better answer, a better hole to hide in. One that would assure our families a decent life even if the worst came to pass. You've probably guessed where this is leading."

"The alternities," the Secretary of State said, looking pleased for a change.

Robinson nodded. "The plan is called Rathole. I'm reviewing some more detailed information about the various options. I intend to make a final decision this weekend. Within sixty days, Rathole will be a mature option. It will be there for us if we need it."

"Rathole," O'Neill echoed. "Lovely name."

"What happens to your gate if the Russians drop the Super on Boston?" Madison asked skeptically.

That one was Tackett's to field. "We don't know," he said evenly. "We've taken pains not to disturb the gate house even in small ways. There's no way to tell what happens if it's destroyed."

The director grunted. "I'll tell you what happens—we don't come back. Have you thought about that?"

"If a submarine missile buries Boyne Mountain in its own rock, we don't come back either," Robinson said with sudden sharpness. "Do you have an objection to survivors having a chance to live decent lives? Does everyone have to suffer?"

"No—"

"Because if you have a problem, it'd be just as easy to strike you and your family from the Alpha List. You can stay here in Washington and paint a fucking bull's-eye on the roof of your house."

There was some uneasy laughter. Tackett did not join in.

"I'm not that eager to die," the CIA chief said. "I was just wondering if you'd thought through to the end."

"We have," Robinson said. "Dennis, I'd like to be able to protect everyone. I'd like to be able to go on the air and say, we're going to war, but don't worry, nobody's going to die. But we can only protect a few. And it makes sense to me to protect the most valuable members of our government. We embraced that principle when we adopted ALCEP."

"Keeping the government intact is the key to postwar reconstruction," the Secretary of State volunteered. "I don't have any problem with this."

"We've dedicated our lives to our country," Robinson said. "We don't have to sacrifice them, as well."

The CIA chief was still wearing a mystified frown. "Why tell us this?"

"What do you mean?"

"You haven't asked us for input, for a decision. You haven't asked us for anything. It's almost as though you told us as a favor. But you don't use state secrets as favors. You could have changed ALCEP, had everyone on Alpha List put on a train and shipped to Boston without saying word one about why."

O'Neill answered. "Can't you read between the lines, Dennis? Look who's here. State—Defense—CIA. We're the face the country shows to the rest of the world." He turned a hard gaze on Robinson. "That's it, isn't it? That's what this meeting is about. Sixty days' lead time before the rules change. Sixty days to stop thinking like a kitten."

Looking pleased, Robinson met O'Neill's gaze. "Yes, Gregory. That's what it's about. I want to turn up the heat on that old alley cat. I want his place in the sun."

EYEWITNESS RECOUNTS TRAGEDY IN GERMANY

"Something's Wrong . . ."

By JOHN RASTEN

Special to the *New York Times*

MANNHEIM, Jan. 17, 1951—This was not the story I drove 171 miles to write.

This was to be a story about the return of the liberator of Europe to the nation he had vanquished. This was to be a story about the North Atlantic Treaty Organization and what it would mean to the free peoples here, now looking east at Red Russian tanks and learning that fear has survived the fall of the Nazi empire.

Three hours ago my photographer and I were standing on the airport apron at Mannheim, sharing the company of an Air Force crew chief and scanning the gray skies for Dwight Eisenhower's military transport plane. A bitter wind was blowing across the dry, brown expanse of the field.

The press attache had told us to expect the plane to be on the ground by 1:00 P.M. At 1:10, he came out of the terminal building to advise us the plane had been late leaving Paris. There was no cause for worry, we were assured.

We did not worry. We passed the time by complaining about the cold and the indignities of our respective professions.

At 1:40 P.M., the silver four-engined C-72 carrying the General and his new NATO command staff appeared as a silent speck in the western sky. Hardened to the comings and goings of aircraft, the crew chief offered me his binoculars. I watched as the plane, nicknamed *America*, bore in straight toward the field, five hundred feet in the air.

To this untrained eye, it seemed that the pilot intended to pass over the field before circling to land. I was about to ask the crew chief for his opinion when the plane abruptly nosed over and began a steep descent.

We watched together for one long second as the plane dropped, like a dart bumped off a table. "Something's wrong," the crew chief said, and ran for his vehicle.

The roar of the engines filled the air. They whined, bit at the air, seemingly dragging the aircraft down toward the earth. Somehow in the last instant, the pilot managed to bring the nose up.

It was too late. Directly in front of where we stood, the fragile-bodied transport slammed into the ground with a sickening jolt. Wings shaking and fuselage flexing, *America* rose a dozen feet into the air before settling back to slide out of control along the hard-frozen runway in a cloud of fine brown dust.

The landing gear snapped like toothpicks. One huge tire bounced and rolled crazily alongside the plane like a small dog chasing a car.

Still there was no fire, and observers only just realizing what had happened allowed themselves to think that somehow those aboard might yet survive. Then the plane slewed sideways and skidded off the runway. A wing tip caught the ground and the wing folded, fuel spilling from broken tanks.

In an instant, a gout of bright orange flame enveloped the doomed aircraft. A deep-throated explosion rattled the terminal windows. Black oily smoke climbed skyward in a funereal signature. To those of us who were there to see the twisted, blackened metal left when the fire was quenched, the survival of radio engineer Walter Gropius is nothing short of a miracle.

But for all of the free world, Eisenhower's death in that blazing cabin is a tragedy far outweighing the miracle. The architect of D-Day—the conqueror of Hitler—the eloquent spokesman for American values—he of the benevolent smile and pragmatic mind—is gone.

CHAPTER 6

'Twixt Scylla
and Charybdis

Washington, D.C., The Home Alternity

Part of the power of the presidency, Tackett thought as he repacked the briefcase, is that you can always get the last word. With a simple, "Thank you, everyone," you can end discussion whenever you choose.

Madison had been entirely right—Robinson hadn't called them in to ask their advice. And when it began to look like he was going to get an unsolicited contribution from O'Neill, Robinson had simply thanked them and excused himself, ending the meeting.

There was not much conversation in the wake of his departure. A tradition of etiquette—or was it paranoia?—called for any postmortems to be conducted away from the West Wing, in the privacy of a car or the inner sanctum of an Executive Office Building suite. While on the President's turf, the staff tended to keep its own counsel. But watching them scatter, Tackett knew that this time more than etiquette was at work.

Rodman followed on Robinson's heels, and the CIA chief was almost as fast out the door. Probably going out to Langley to scream at his people for not keeping him informed, Tackett thought, spinning the locks on his case. The Secretary of State glanced at his watch, said something about a hearing on the Hill, and backed out the door. O'Neill left without moving; he sat in his chair and stared at his own folded hands, which were perched on the edge of the table.

Endicott was the exception. He circled the table to where Tackett stood and peered curiously into the briefcase. "Hell of a road show you've got, Al," he said. "It's like having a patent on the funniest joke ever told."

"I guess it is at that." Tackett picked up the heavy case and started for the door.

To his annoyance, Endicott followed, inviting himself into Tackett's company. With a will, Tackett stilled the queasy feeling Endicott evoked in him. The President was expecting both of them in the Oval Office. He would have to endure it a while longer.

Several paces down the hall, the Senator touched him on the arm. "If I could slow you down just a moment, Al—"

"Something wrong?"

"Nothing wrong. Just a little request."

Save your breath, Tackett thought. The President's already scratched your back for you. "What is it?"

But Endicott's interest was more personal than an objection to disbanding Red Section. "A few weeks back you procured a . . . ah, package for me. I'm sure you remember."

Procured. That's the right word, all right. "I remember."

"I have need of another, same specifications."

Another? Tackett was incredulous. It's not like you can use them up—"Something wrong with the girl?"

"No. Nothing wrong. I just have need of another. You do remember?"

"I think so." Tackett remembered. White. Female. Long hair, chestnut preferred. Well fed, but not fat. Young, but not too young. A one-man operation, nothing on paper. Tackett had selected and instructed the iceman personally. No one else knew.

The Guard's icemen had carried out more than a hundred snatches in the last five years, some of them involving different "versions" of the same person. They had brought back aircraft designers, electronics and computer engineers, guidance and propulsion experts, crack cryptologists, weapons specialists.

Each snatch required its own ExOps, a clear prior justification. Often Tackett said no. The risks were substantial at both ends. The disappearance of prominent or talented people drew unwelcome attention. And a clean snatch did not guarantee success. Several early targets had never found a reason to work productively for the Guard. Two had managed to commit suicide.

Tackett had become more selective, narrowing the candidates he would consider to those technical specialists whose special knowledge could be put to immediate practical use. Otherwise worthy candidates that he rejected went onto lists for reconsideration when either the risks or the pressure to produce were reduced.

But Endicott's package had been procured outside the rules. There was no ExOps anywhere in the files on the woman, for the only justification Tackett could offer was that he had been ordered to have it done. Which was not nearly enough to keep the whole business from setting his teeth on edge.

Endicott was holding Tackett in an expectant gaze. "I trust you'll be able to take care of it, then," he said.

Tackett answered with a hard, cold stare. *Giving me orders, you bastard? I'll take care of it, all right. I'll keep it to myself and pretend you never said anything. That'll take care of it.* "I'll look into it," he said. "No promises."

He turned away and moved on down the corridor before the Senator could say any more. The President apparently liked and trusted Endicott. Tackett was not obliged to feel the same way, and he didn't. Endicott's real usefulness had ended when he surrendered the secret of the Cambridge to Vandenberg; Robinson had other friends who could chair the Intelligence Committee. If it had been his call to make, Endicott would have quietly disappeared long ago.

Never too late, he thought, raising a hand to the President's appointments secretary as he passed through to the Oval Office. *That would really take care of it—*

Robinson settled back into the white and red claw-footed armchair by the fireplace and invited his guests onto the facing couch with a gesture. "Let's see the dossiers."

With a nod, Tackett pulled the briefcase to his lap and attacked the locks. Beside him, Endicott stretched out his legs and snuggled down into the corner in search of a comfortable position.

The contrast amused Robinson. The two looked for all the world like the loyal eldest son and the carefree black sheep from an episode of *Sins of the Wealthy. And I love 'em both,* he thought. *Need them both. Even if they can't stand each other.*

"From what Al said down the hall, the only real choices are Yellow, Green, and Blue," the Senator offered, peering sideways into the briefcase.

"I have profiles for the both of you on your counterparts in every alternity except for White, which I think we're all agreed General Betts can keep with our blessing," Tackett said, handing a black-covered report an inch thick across to Robinson and a slightly thinner version to Endicott. "I think you'll find all the fundamental questions answered there," he added.

The fundamental questions: Who am I? Who's in charge? How much distance is there between the two?

"I'd guess so," Robinson said, hefting the dossier. "You *have* been working hard."

"And I thought the Guard was padding that line-item for typing paper," Endicott said. "Jesus, Al, I'm going to have to skip meals to get this read in a week."

"I wanted the President to have the detail he needed to make an informed decision," Tackett said stiffly. "He asked that you be provided equivalent detail."

"Thanks a lot, Peter," Endicott said wryly, flipping through the first few pages. "Remind me to send you a thank-you present—a couple of new puppies with diarrhea, maybe, or an eager little trixie with the clap."

That brought a chuckle from Robinson. Skimming the contents of his own copy, he asked, "What's your projection, Albert? Where should we go?"

"Sir, that's not my decision to make."

"I don't want a decision, just an opinion. Did you do run-ups on yourself, by the way?"

"No, Mr. President."

"Even better. It'll be an unbiased opinion. What do you say?"

"We've had several of the analysts score the options," Tackett said. "The majority came up for Alternity Yellow. We'd have the option there of staying in England, which would almost assure that all the Common Worlders on the list wouldn't draw attention to themselves. And it's a comfortable place, on the whole."

"Looks like I'm missing my Yellow bio here," Robinson said, frowning at the page before him.

"No, sir. Your counterpart in Yellow is dead."

"Really," he said lightly. "How did I die? Anything dramatic?"

Tackett shook his head. "A car crash on National Highway 5, coming back in a freezing rain from a party in Chicago. December 24, 1971."

"Rather ordinary, if you ask me," Endicott observed. "Unless it's your name the stonecutter has to spell right. What about me? Where am I dead? Besides Red."

"In Alternity White. You were shot by your wife's lover, May of 1965," Tackett said with evident satisfaction.

"So young. I hope they at least fried the bastard."

Tackett smiled. "Your wife hired him a first-class lawyer—

possibly bought a judge, too. He served sixty days probation for involuntary manslaughter."

"The bitch."

"You don't even know her," Robinson said, bemused.

"How much more do I need to know?" Endicott said gruffly. "Well, needless to say I'm not interested in going there. Or to Red, of course."

"I don't think you understand what's planned," Tackett said sharply. "The public profile of the Alpha List member counterparts and the internal security of the particular society are the top considerations. We're not crossing over to take over—we're crossing over to protect our families and preserve our government. We're crossing over hoping to come back."

"Yes," Robinson affirmed.

"In point of fact, counterparts for several members of Alpha List are dead in every alternity," Tackett continued. "That hardly matters—we can't go there as ourselves. We have to go there prepared to deny who we are, to keep out of the way, to hide if necessary."

"We'll have the gate, the Station's financial resources, and friends," Endicott said. "I see no reason to condemn us to poverty and obscurity."

"You can always go back to Red," Tackett said, poker-faced. "You aren't dead there, only missing-and-presumed."

"Lovely place, my old home," the senator grunted. "Brats and bugbombs and other brands of unpleasantness. A business friend of mine was taken hostage and murdered just last week. Thank you, no. I think I can do better."

"I think we can all do better," Robinson said. "I don't think any of us can see taking a family to Red."

"No," Tackett agreed. "But Blue, Green and Yellow are all excellent candidates for a quiet refuge, temporary or permanent. And we have well-established stations in all three that can provide transition support."

Barely aware he was doing so, Robinson made a wet sucking noise by drawing a breath with his teeth pressed against his lower lip. An aide had once pointed out the idiosyncrasy in a critique of a press conference, and Robinson had demanded corroboration from a half-dozen other staffers before he was convinced it was real. "I thought Green was where the mob owned Washington."

"It is," Tackett said. "It makes less difference than you might think."

"I'm poor there," Endicott said, reading from his binder. "Heaven forfend."

"I'd hope that the choice of destination for Rathole would turn on those conditions that affect everyone on Alpha List," Tackett said coldly.

"Of course it will, Albert," Robinson said reassuringly. "You have to understand that what catches our eye the first time through the material is the personal dimension. It's a natural bias."

"I understand that, sir—"

At that moment, there was the sound of raised voices beyond the Oval Office door. The three all turned their focus that way in time to see Gregory O'Neill burst through the doorway, with the red-faced appointments secretary following on his heels. They spoke at once, O'Neill insistent, the secretary apologetic.

"President Robinson, I have to talk to you—"

"President Robinson, I told Mr. O'Neill that you—"

"—and Albert about this business—"

"—and Mr. Tackett and the Senator had business—"

"It's all right, Donald," Robinson said easily. "Come on in, Gregory. Go on, Donald, leave us. Gregory, find a chair and join us."

But O'Neill was too agitated to sit. "This has been going around in my head all morning," he said. His hands moved jerkily in the air, a silent stutter that underlined his distress. "I don't understand why in God's name these alternities exist. What's the purpose? Albert, you're living right on top of this thing. What have your people found out? Have you done anything at all to figure out the reason?"

"We have a research section looking at that issue—" Tackett began.

"What do they tell you?"

"They tell me what I told you in the Cabinet Room. Everyone accepts that the alternities are real, but no one can explain them. Frankly, we're more interested in the 'what' than the 'why'—we have our hands full trying to understand how to best make use of the gates."

Robinson was watching O'Neill closely and not liking what he saw. "Perhaps you could outline what you *are* doing, Albert."

His face wrinkling up in a scowl, Tackett complied. "Well— the research section is working with our crackers, trying to gather more data about the maze itself. We close down the maze to everyone but the crackers for six hours out of every twenty-four."

"That's a start," O'Neill said.

"But that's a means to an end—several ends: finding any other exits that might be there, cutting down on our runner losses, finding a way to bring metallic objects through. There are a hundred inventions we could make immediate use of if we could simply buy them there and bring them through. As it is, we have to acquire designs and plans and try to recreate them here, a much slower process."

"That's a philosophical question you're asking, Gregory," Robinson said easily. "You're asking why the world is the way it is."

"I know that, but isn't it worth asking? Don't you realize what we're sitting on? How this changes everything? My God, when I think of the revolutions in human thought—the Copernican revolution only changed where we are in the universe. This changes *what* we are. And the questions for theology, philosophy— how can one soul be split among seven bodies?"

O'Neill was looking fragile and lost, a condition without precedent in Robinson's dealings with him.

" 'Other sheep I have, which are not of this fold,' " Robinson quoted. "Gregory, we each have to wrestle with that one on our own. It's not a matter of state interest. It's a question of private conscience. Albert never promised you wouldn't have a few sleepless nights about this. God knows I did."

"I don't know that we have the right to keep this to ourselves," O'Neill said, shaking his head. "I don't know that we have the right to exploit it this way. This is a . . . a revelation. It belongs to everyone."

"Including General Secretary Kondratyeva?" Endicott asked. "Would you like to see it shared with him? I'm sure you don't mean that."

Some of the rigidness left O'Neill's body, and he seemed to settle back onto his heels. "No. I don't mean that."

"Then you understand that this is being handled the only way it can be handled," Robinson suggested.

"I don't know." O'Neill turned on Tackett. "But you've got to put this higher on your list of priorities," he said, the edge returning to his voice. "You've got to see that 'why' gets the attention it deserves. You're the only one who can. What you've been doing is dangerous, like a kid who's never seen a gun playing with a new toy he found in his father's dresser drawer."

"Secretary O'Neill, I take this responsibility more seriously than you know," Tackett said coldly. "No one knows better than I what a queer business this is. I confront it every hour of every day."

"But your people don't. You can't tell me if this gate is natural or artificial—"

"How could it be anything but natural?" Endicott scoffed. "For the love of mother, grab your ears and pull your head back on. Copernicus didn't move the Earth. He just rewrote its biography."

"—or why the worlds are so much alike," O'Neill plunged on, insensible to interruption. "That bothers me. If they're so similar, why aren't they identical? There're so many questions you haven't even addressed."

"There's a question of resources," Tackett said.

"What about some of these alternities where the geopolitics are more stable? Why can't we approach our counterparts and draw on their resources, attack the problem together?"

Tackett's look of contempt had deepened with every word. "Problem? I don't see a problem. I know which world I live in, and which President I serve. These other realities are our enemies just as much as the Soviet Union is. You're a dreamer if you think contacting them directly would bring anything but trouble."

"They're *us*, if what you say is true. How can they be enemies?"

"They're *not* us," Endicott said with unexpected forcefulness. "Not on any level. Don't make that mistake, Gregory. Even when they look like us, they're not us. They have their own lives, and that's what they care about. Just like we have to care about ours. Albert is right. To protect ourselves, we have to control the maze. That's Job One. Job Two is to use this resource to our best advantage. That's what the Guard is there for. Not to provide employment for every crackpot physicist and would-be philosopher."

"How can we use it wisely when we don't understand it?" O'Neill turned to Robinson. "I don't see any choice but to back off, go slow. Whatever the answer, this can't exist for such a shallow purpose as giving us a hiding place from a shooting war."

Enough. Robinson rose up out of his chair. "Gregory, I think you need to take your own advice," he said, taking the Secretary by the elbow and guiding him toward the door. "Back off—go slow. You're trying to swallow this whole and it's about to choke you. Break it up into pieces. Digest it. Fit it together with

86

what you already know. Then it'll be time to wrestle with some of the implications."

O'Neill took a deep breath, sighed, and nodded. "You're right. I'm sorry. It was eating me up. I had to come talk to you. It's not as though I can go discuss it with my priest."

"No, let's not do that," Robinson said with an easy smile, pulling up a step short of the door. "It's a jolt, Gregory. It is for everybody. But you'll get on top of it."

"It's hard to see how."

"It was hard for me, too," he said soothingly.

O'Neill was hesitating, reluctant to take his cue to leave. "I wouldn't have interrupted—"

"My door's open to you, Gregory. You know that."

Still O'Neill hesitated.

"We'll talk later, Gregory," Robinson said, reaching for the handle and pulling the door open.

That cue O'Neill could not ignore. His expression still troubled, he reluctantly exited the room.

The instant the door closed behind him, Robinson's expression changed. "Arrogant son of a bitch," he muttered under his breath. "He'd better get his head on straight before he comes in here the next time or I'm going to be looking for another Secretary of Defense."

"He's fighting himself," Tackett said sympathetically.

"He can damn well do it in his own office," Robinson said, turning back to his visitors. "Where were we, Albert?"

"You were asking my opinion on the site selection for Rathole."

"And you were doing your best not to give one. All right. We'll do it your way. I'll review the report and let you know my decision within a couple of days."

Tackett looked unhappily at Endicott. "I would rather this material not have that kind of exposure—"

"If you expected to take an answer back with you, you should have made the dossier short enough to read in one sitting," he said curtly.

"Yes, sir," Tackett said, chastened. "Would you like me to remain in Washington?"

"I don't think that's necessary. You can send someone around to collect the binders. Walter, you've got the skinny one. Can you call me by Saturday night with your comments?"

"I can."

"Good. That will do it for now, then. I thank you both."

When they were gone, Robinson sat for a moment in the chair, the heavy black book resting on his knee. I should have known, he thought. Reflective type. No sense about what questions aren't worth answering. What's the mystery, Gregory? God has been generous. He's giving us a second chance. And getting lost in philosophy is a good way to box it.

Precautions. O'Neill would settle down, almost certainly. But if he didn't, Robinson had to know. He walked to the desk, dossier tucked under one arm, and pushed a button on the phone. "Get me Westheim at the NSA."

There was a brief pause, and then the connection was live. "This is the President."

"I recognize your voice, sir."

"Step up the monitoring on Secretary O'Neill. Blanket him. I want to know when he hiccups and how many times he brushes his teeth at night. I want to know who he sleeps with and what he says in his sleep. Can do?"

"Can do, sir. I'll activate the in-place coverage immediately. And we'll have someone with him within the hour."

Boston, The Home Alternity

There were times that Ruthann Wallace did not understand her own perversity. Hurts were to be shrugged off, not carried forward. Swallow them, bury them, cast them aside—do anything but let them collect in the subconscious to breed more hurt.

She knew that, and yet sometimes she watched herself do just the opposite. It was easy to turn the hurt to anger, anger that caromed around inside her like a trapped wasp until it found an opening and arrowed straight for a soft spot in Rayne's ego. And then, warmed by the glow of her vindication, she was ready to be generous. Except then it was too late, the wheel having taken another turn.

"I could have forgiven him, except he didn't ask," she had explained to Rebecca on the phone. No, not explained—complained. "I could even have enjoyed this morning, except he didn't ask about that, either. He was just all over me before I was even awake. And then when Katie fell and cut her forehead on the coffee table, I actually think he blamed me. There's blood on Katie and milk all over the living room, and I think he expected me to satisfy him before I cleaned up."

"Even Rayne couldn't be that much of a jerk."

"Don't bet on it."

"Honey, you two are just out of sync. Sounds like you're taking turns being jerks. Nothing personal."

Except because it was true, it *was* personal. "He deserved it," she said, masking guilt with indignation. "Besides, he's left me on the edge often enough. It'll do him good to find out what it's like."

"Honey, it never does any good to leave a man to finish by himself," Rebecca said with sad-voiced sagacity. "One of you is going to have to break the cycle, or you're going to turn into one of those women with a regular Monday appointment at the lip-and-shiner clinic."

Ruthann did not think Rayne would ever hit her. But there were enough other ugly pictures of the future that were all too believable. Jenny, who'd lived with her husband in the other apartment over the laundry, confessing over coffee to dozens of affairs and a cold technical marriage. Donna, just east in the locus, battered into timidity by her mate's endless criticism and disapproval. Her own mother, endlessly compromising with her silent, life-embittered father in the name of peace.

She was too young to resign herself to any of those fates. There were too many years ahead to accept that they had to be unhappy ones. *We were happy in Indiana. We can be happy here, if only I'd stop making stupid mistakes—*

In midmorning, Rayne had gone up to the exercise room in the central core. It was past noon now, and Katie was fed and napping. She listened for his return as she sorted through the clutter of a kitchen drawer, a task she could leave in the time it took to push the drawer closed.

"Katie-cat?"

She jumped up from her stool and hurried toward the living room. His hair was wet and two shades blacker than usual, the skin bared by the cream-colored sleeveless shirt glowing with a reddish flush. *Beautiful,* she thought. *He really is beautiful.*

"She's napping, sweetheart. Work-out feel good?"

"Mostly," he said, moving his right arm gingerly in a circle.

"Can I give you a massage? It might help keep you from stiffening up."

He looked at her with surprise. "Sure. That'd be nice."

While he stripped off his shirt, she spread the soft comforter being used as a throw on the back of the couch on the floor. "On your tummy," she said, patting the comforter, and he stretched out obediently beside her.

She straddled his body, one knee on either side of his waist, and centered her attention on his back. As her touch evolved from silky stroking with fingertips to working the deep muscles with the heel of her hand, she could feel him relaxing, accepting her touch, surrendering control to her. At the same time she could feel herself responding to his nearness, to the fresh-sweat fragrance of his body, the radiant heat of his skin against hers.

"I was talking to Elaine this morning. She says that there's still a lot of fall color out beyond Sterling, around Mount Wachusett."

"Mmm," Rayne said into the comforter.

"Since tomorrow is our day with the car, I was thinking that it would be nice to take the family out that way for the day. Maybe if it's warm enough we could even have kind of a Good-bye-to-Fall last-of-the-season picnic."

"Won't be warm enough. And I'm going downtown to see Jason."

Just like that. A flat refusal, as thoughtlessly casual as could be. She quelled the impulse to rip gobbets of flesh from his back with her nails. "All day?"

"Uh-um. Going to pick him up around six. Could you get the left shoulder? Gently."

She leaned forward and began to work the shoulder. "That's okay, then. We'll still have time for the outing. If we left by ten, we'd be back in plenty of time without having to rush."

"That feels wonderful," he said. "The Indiana-Purdue game is tomorrow. Besides, I really don't want to be on the run all day. It could be a late night."

Break the cycle, she ordered herself as she felt her body start to go rigid. Don't answer in kind. "Then I guess Katie and I will go by ourselves. I really want to see the colors before they're gone. We can collect some leaves to press."

"Ouch," he said. "Easy there."

"Sorry." Her hands walked to his neck and began to work the muscles there.

"I don't know about you going all the way out to Sterling," he said. "I've been meaning to talk to you about the mileage on the Spirit. We've been one of the top two or three shares in the club two months running. I don't know where you've been taking it when I'm not around, but we can't keep going overbudget on the fuel allowance."

With an effort, she sat up straight and tucked her trembling hands under her arms, a precaution akin to sheathing a weapon. "I go visiting. I go shopping. Sometimes I just like to go driving. I take Katie up to Marblehead or Rockport to look at the ocean. Are you telling me I can't, that I have to stay home?"

He tried to look back over his shoulder at her. "I'm just asking you to watch the miles. We're budgeted for fifteen percent of the monthly allowance card. If we keep going over, I don't know where the money's going to come from.''

Retreating still further, she stood up. "Then what did we buy into the club for?" she demanded. "If we can't afford to drive a car, why did we want to own a piece of one?"

"Hey," he said, starting to turn over. "I didn't say—"

The temptation he was about to present her with would be too much to resist, and she made herself back away. "That's fine," she said bitingly, unable to silence herself. "You go where you want and do what you want to. If you ever get tired of running all over, maybe you can look around and see if I'm still here."

It was more than she should have said, and less than she wanted to. The urge to hurt him and the impulse to hide her own hurt collided, and she succeeded at neither. Angry tears rising, she fled out the front door, knowing as she did that it was an empty gesture.

For he would be there every day of the rest of her life, the same as she saw him now. And knowing that, she saw that her life was one with Jenny's and Donna's and her mother's—a curse to be endured, a sentence to be served alone in a place that Rayne could neither visit nor cared to share.

from WORTHY WORDS: The Art of Oratory
in the Twentieth Century

President Robert A. Taft, Inaugural Speech,
January 2, 1952

". . . Throughout this campaign I made clear what I believed was the best path. With a deep sense of responsibility, I accept the judgment of the electorate and vow to you today to lead us down that path. It is time for America to put America first.

"We have seen in Korea the folly of trying to achieve political goals through military means. Where next would the internationalists try to entangle us? Palestine? Greece? China? Berlin?

"What would it take to satisfy them? Thirty billion dollars and three million men in uniform? The forced conversion of our veterans to reservists? Universal military training?

"Yes, yes, and yes—that is what it would take. And that is the future which the American people have wisely rejected. Before one more American family learns of a son killed in a faraway land. Before the collectivists have stolen traditional American independence. Before we have sabotaged European self-reliance with an overlapping encumbrance of inflexible promises and short-sighted treaties.

"I do not mean for one minute that this nation can dare turn its back on the real dangers of Soviet communism. I am as committed to this nation's defense as any citizen past or present. A standing defense establishment of one million men, well trained and well equipped, will be this nation's shield. A modern bomber force, carrying the awesome power of the atomic bomb, will be our strong right arm. No nation anywhere will dare attack us.

"We will be strong. We will be safe. We will build for ourselves a Fortress America. And within its walls we will enjoy the richness of our land and our people, the luxury that our industry and ingenuity will bring, the precious blessings of our democratic heritage.

"We will become, once again, a nation dedicated to liberty. The God-given liberty of an individual to think his own thoughts and live his own life as he desires to think and live. The liberty of a man to choose his own occupation and run his own business. The liberty of a man to rise on his merits and enjoy the fruits of his labors.

"Together we will found an American Golden Age. With prudence and wisdom, we will know a safe and prosperous world, and secure a bright future for our heirs. The path lies before us. Today, together, let us take the first step."

CHAPTER 7

Memento Mori

Northumberland, England, Alternity Yellow

Dunstanburgh Castle at dawn was a spectacle Jason March had long ago come to love. The gaunt ruins of the thirteenth-century fortress overlooked the choppy North Sea from a desolate clifftop eyrie. The cold morning sunlight fired a diamondlike sparkle in the slick coating of sea dew which decorated leaf and stone alike.

Thickly matted green creepers covered many of the crumbling remains of the enceinte and barbican, invading even the inner courts of the donjon. It seemed to March as though the earth herself was grasping at the castle, seeking to pull down the walls and return the stone building blocks to the natural storehouse from which they had been drawn.

Part of that impression came from the isolation. Dunstanburgh Castle seemed to belong to the earth by default, abandoned even by the tourists, who would sooner continue up the coast to the restored showplaces at Bamburgh and Berwick-upon-Tweed than fight the rutted dirt lane that led to the squat age-battered shell.

When the station car that had ferried March up from Alswick had bumped its way back to the main road, the illusion was complete. The castle belonged to the earth and the sea. He was merely a trespasser in Time.

As he picked his way into the central bailey, he felt the first faint tug of the gate. Using a broken wall as a makeshift stair-case, he followed the call up to the tunnel-like archers' gallery, high in the battlements. The darkness of the gallery was broken at intervals by light streaming in the loopholes where soldiers had once stood to defend the approach to their liege's home. But the scant sunlight was inadequate to offer relief from the bone-numbing chill of the damp stone passageway.

The gate was close now. A side passage brought March into a darker and colder place, a chamber in the heart of the armored gate house. He brought out his transit light and banished the darkness, homing on the gate by the jangling of his nerves. His entire skin was an antenna for its energies. If he closed his eyes, he could see the dancing lights which betrayed the gate's proximity.

It was there in the chamber below, pulsing faintly, its pale light suffusing the dank enclosure.

How many ghost stories have you inspired, March wondered with a faint smile. *How many demon nightmares have you starred in?* Hooking his thumbs under the straps of his backpack to pull it snug against him, he lowered his head and plunged through.

The Yellow node was uphill from the gate. He climbed, dragging himself forward on the invisible substance of the maze, boots slipping, hands clawing. March had once heard a runner compare moving though the maze to climbing a taffy mountain in the dark. It was an apt enough description.

When he reached the node, he expected to sense three chan-nels, geometrically spaced like the spread fingers of a hand. One led to Home. One, perversely, a long way around to itself. The third led to points unknown, having taken two skilled crackers without giving up its secrets.

But, to his sudden and acute distress, March realized he could see-sense only two channels at the node, and it was the channel to Home which was gone. He knew where it should be, and yet it was not there. He knew the shape of the maze at that point, and yet found it different.

Where the channel should be was a blank spot—no, a blind spot in his perceptions. It was as though he were touching something with a nerve-deadened hand. Something was interfer-ing with his sight, preventing him from seeing what, despite the evidence of his senses, he knew had to be there.

He stood frozen in the node, trying to understand the anoma-lous reports from his senses. It was as though a door had come down, a giant's shadow fallen across the unreal world. Suddenly March knew real fear, a white knot of terror uncurling in his stomach like a spitting firework snake. His skin crawled with the nearness of something—

—Something so cold that it seemed to draw the heat from his body and sap the fundamental energy of the maze.

—Something so alien that to let it touch him would mean a screaming death in the silence of the maze.

Curiosity fled. Courage fled. And March fled, clawing his way back down toward the Dunstanburgh gate, plunging into a living recreation of the young boy's worst nightmare: being chased by the thing that cannot die.

When at last he reached the end and dove through the gate to find himself lying on the algae-slimed floor of the lower chamber, it was like waking up in a room he no longer knew and being terrorized again by the disorientation. It was not until he stood shaky-legged in the morning sunlight on the topmost wall of the ruined castle that he could begin to believe that he was safe.

Even then, March knew that safety was a fleeting thing. For, as much as he hated the thought in that moment, the maze was the only way Home, and all too soon he would have to return to the gate and try again.

Washington, D.C., The Home Alternity

It was a little church, just off M Street, within shouting distance of Embassy Row. St. Dunstan's Cathedral. O'Neill could not clearly remember who Saint Dunstan was. English, certainly. There was something about Dunstan and a king. Or a king's wife. Was he the patron saint of musicians? Or of blacksmiths? Both seemed right. Maybe it was both. The Church had had its renaissance men, too.

Not that it mattered. St. Dunstan's offered everything he needed. It was unlocked and empty. And unlike at National Cathedral, no one knew him here. There was no one to see and no one to wonder.

He pushed open the oak doors separating the narthex from the nave and walked slowly up the aisle toward the altar. The crucifix hanging in the apse was grotesque, a sort of Swedish-modern–Gothic montrosity in hammered iron. Blacksmiths. Blacksmiths and armorers, he remembered. And musicians, too, for all he knew. It didn't matter. None of it mattered.

Three pews from the front, O'Neill genuflected and sat down. He leaned forward and rested his forearms on the back of the pew in front of him, looked up to see a Daliesque black iron Virgin Mary looking down on him from an alcove. Her metallic features were ambiguous—his mind supplied the detail, interpreting shadow and glistening highlight.

He looked away to the crucifix and saw it with different eyes. There was a rawness, a tortured quality to the very material itself. It vitalized the icon, sweeping away the memory of a thousand tranquil-faced ceramic Saviors rendered in inoffensive pastels. The faintest hint of a pleased expression appeared on O'Neill's face, then disappeared as he lowered his head to pray.

Dear God—

Self-consciousness cut short the orison. Since childhood, a silent prayer had always seemed to O'Neill to somehow be less real than the same prayer spoken. It was cheating somehow, shallow and easy, the unwitnessed thoughts so easily deniable. Hiding behind the skirts of God's omniscience. *Of course He can hear you—*

O'Neill drew a deep breath and began again. "Dear God," he whispered. "I've struggled to find the meaning. I've tried to see the majesty of Your Design in this. I don't think I can do it alone. The thoughts I've had—I wonder if there are many Gods for the many worlds. Like Franklin believed. All the Deists who built this city—this country—a more forgiving way to think. Too easy. Too easy."

Hanging his head, O'Neill squeezed his eyes closed and fought for order and control.

"It's not that I can't believe You can shape Creation this way. I see Your hand in it, the power of a will that shapes the Universe to its bidding. But I can't see the reason why. I've been reading Revelations, wondering. A sign of the endtime. Always the prophets. This week, this year, next year, the millennium. Someday one will be right.

"Or a sign for the age of science. A Gordian knot that no Einstein can unravel, to call the skeptics back to faith. How do You reveal yourself to a world armored against the touch of the divine? A mystery for a time when all mysteries have been unmasked. A challenge to explain the unexplainable.

"Oh, Father, what reason is enough to fill worlds with copies of your children? What am I to them, they to me? Are we reflections, brothers—more than brothers? Nothing to say that each soul must be unique, nothing except the wrongness that fills me when I think that mine is not.

"I've wondered, too, about Your old rival. I never believed, still doubt. To believe in him is to worship him. To believe is to give him power. And this—the teachings say that the Dark Lord's power is to destroy, not to create. How could this be his

96

work? Perhaps his power to deceive could make this real, but to what end? What gain? It's even harder to divine his motive than Yours.

"The thought that comes back again and again is that perhaps this isn't about us at all. I know that You love all Your creatures, and so many have fallen. Perhaps this is neither sign nor temptation, but a judgment on us for our stewardship. Do elephants still walk the plains of other worlds? Do eagles soar in their skies? So many have fallen—

"But most of all I wonder if this was knowledge You never meant for us to have. A secret stolen from You like fire from Olympus, stumbled on in the dark. And that the question 'why?' has no answer with any meaning on our scale."

O'Neill opened his eyes to the dense grain of the wood before him, blinked away a trace of moisture. Pressing his lips into a hard line, he drew a deep breath, fighting the tightness in his chest. Then he closed his eyes, sighed, and slid back against the harsh support of the pew.

It was always hard to gauge the good prayer did. Sometimes, like now, O'Neill felt a measure of inner release when he was done, a touch of quiet at the center of his being. But did that come from outside or from within? There were no new answers offering themselves for his examination, no voices guiding his thoughts. No magic. Was it the act itself which brought the blessing—an exercise of the psyche, with God as psychiatrist? He had never answered the question to his satisfaction.

Opening his eyes, O'Neill looked up at the crucifix. "But then, even You had questions till the end," he said softly, and rose to leave.

On the way out, he wondered how long the man pretending to be asleep in the last pew had been there.

Boston, The Home Alternity

The young saxophonist was blowing hot and sweet, a tumbling cascade of notes that seemed to whirl around the club like chromatic ghosts. Donovan's was not a good place for talking. The owner liked his music loud, and even the piano was double-miked. But even if it had been, the ax man had made clear early that tonight was a night for listening. He ripped off lines so complex that they demanded his audience's full attention, playing loving games with key and interval, stroking the ear with solos as clean as they were electrifying.

Wallace and March had come to the little downtown walk-up to hear Jo-Jo Richards, a refugee from the much-loved but long disbanded Northeast combo Street Heat. But most of the night the headliner had been under siege, hunched over the keys of his upright, hard pressed to match his sideman's energy and altitude. The cellist and drummer had long ago faded into the background, becoming almost more a part of the audience than the performance.

Now, in the last number of the set, Jo-Jo and the kid were coming together on a musical Seventh Circle, flying so high and in such perfect synchrony that Wallace's heart ached to hear them and know that in a few moments it would all end. Every note was charged with the excitement of spontaneous creation, for the two musicians had pushed each other past the safe areas bounded by the limits of rehearsal. The audience sensed it, and seemed to hold its breath as it waited to see if they would rise or fall together.

Trading licks, they created a dialogue between sax and piano, then made them speak together in elegant harmony. What sounded like a closing crescendo mutated into harmonic digression, then became the prologue to an even more subtle and elegant closure, surprising and yet exactly right.

The hundred-odd patrons of the tiny club were on their feet by the last bar, and their cheers and applause drowned out the final notes. "Beautiful," Wallace shouted to Marsh across the little table. "It doesn't get better than that."

March smiled and nodded in agreement.

"And not a recorder in the hall, is the hell of it."

"That's why you've gotta come out," March called. "There's just too much good music that never gets near vinyl."

The musicians were exiting without fanfare, and the bargirls started fanning out to blanket the room during the break. "What do you think about staying for another set?" Wallace asked.

"I think we've heard the best they've got," March said. "Besides, Jo-Jo's going to garrot the kid backstage for stealing the show, and then who'll want to listen?"

As if in reply, the club owner came to the microphone just then and announced, "I've been asked to tell you that in response to your requests, Jo-Jo is going to do a solo set after this break, so don't go away—"

They looked at each other and laughed. "That does it," Wallace said. "We're leaving."

"We won't take a threat like that sitting down," March said, snatching up his glass and draining the long-nursed last ounce of warmish beer.

As they reached the sidewalk, Wallace checked his watch. "Almost eleven. Are we done in?"

"I'm not."

"Good. What about going down to Blue Tony's? There's no cover after eleven, and the band goes 'til one."

March showed a mock shiver. "Two thousand years of ballads. No, thanks. What about Deep Harbor Lounge?"

"Canned music."

"I might want to dance."

"Riding heavy? Well, I don't want to stand in the way of love," Wallace said with a shrug, reaching in his pocket for the keys to the Spirit.

"Let's walk," March suggested. "It's only a few blocks."

Wallace shot him a quizzical look. "Try about eight."

"I've been sitting too long. I need to unwind."

Wallace shrugged and fell in beside March as they started down the sidewalk. "Ruthann'd have a fit if she saw this."

"Why?"

"Oh, we had a fight about the car. She wanted to go out sightseeing with it this afternoon and I had to point out how much all her extra driving was costing."

"Who won? Did she go?"

"No. She stayed around the house and sulked all day until I wished she had gone, damn the cost. Which I guess means she won. I swear to God, though, someday I'm going to own more than an eighth part of a three-wheeled plastic roller skate."

"Owning a fourth part in a flex club isn't much better," March said. "You still can't count on having it when it's convenient. Like when a shopping trip pans out and you can't take her home the next morning because you can't have the damn car two days in a row."

"Not quite the same taking her home in a flesh-hauler."

"I think I'm going to buy a tandem bike. Ought to be able to get a good hi-howdy line out of it."

"Something like, 'Hey, sweet-eyes, how'd you like something hard, black, and leather between your legs?' "

March grimaced. "Or maybe not."

A doe-eyed brunette emerged from the club, and both men followed her with their eyes as she retreated down the sidewalk.

"I'm not buying, but passing the bakery window sure can make my mouth water," Wallace said wistfully.

March laughed. "I'll tell you what I really want. One of those

Ford Montanas from Green. Steel body, eight cylinders—it looks like a yacht with wheels, moving through the streets—"

"I've seen pictures."

"And a back seat big enough to hold a party in. Want one? We can get a volume discount."

"I'm past that stage of my life, remember? I just want to cruise my old neighborhood and watch the eyes pop."

"And of course, there's no old flame that you'd want to have see what she gave up."

"Well—maybe one."

"I thought so." March was silent, but it was a silence which suggested he was lost in thought. "I think I'm about ready to get past that stage of my life, too."

Wallace grabbed for the lamp post he was just passing and clutched it in an exaggerated display of fear. "Did you feel the earth tremble? I'm sure I felt the earth tremble. Take it back, Jase, quick. You can't violate the natural order of things that way. Jason March married? The skies will fall."

March turned back toward Wallace wearing a lopsided smile. "The natural order can take it."

"You're serious?" Wallace asked, releasing his anchor. "Who's hooked you?"

They started down the street again. "Nobody. I just . . . ah, I've just decided to shop for something that'll wear a little longer."

"Going to look at the quality merchandise."

"Something like that."

"Then what the hell are we going to the Harbor for?"

"Because I don't want to marry a nun."

"That's all there is to this? You just woke up this morning and decided that you should get married? Just have to work out the details about who you're marrying."

They had reached a corner, and March was silent until they reached the other side. "The truth is, I want to give up running. But you know Ops won't even look at me as a mole unless I'm married-and-child."

"They won't want to, even then. You're top of the list for every Section that uses you."

"Which means I ought to be able to get at least one of them to put in a request to promote me out of the pool."

Wallace stopped short and stared. "So that's the plan, then: to marry someone quick, jumpstart a baby, and say a quiet word to Hubbard or Monaghan about moving you up? What's going on here, Jase?"

March met his stare for several seconds. "We keep stopping like this, the lady of my dreams is going to leave before we get there," he said, and turned away.

"Whoa," Wallace said, hurrying to catch up. "You can't duck me like that. You've been sitting on something all night. Driving down here you hardly said ten words."

"Get off my back, will you? Maybe I just see something in your life that I wish I had. Is that all right?"

"I'd like to hear what it is. Maybe I'd do a better job of appreciating my own if I knew."

March missed the note of self-pity in Wallace's words. "You've got that beautiful kid, somebody to look at and see yourself in," he said, stopping and gesturing angrily. "You've got a great lady to come home to, somebody who worries about you and makes you feel like you were missed. You've got people who care what happens to you. You'd at least leave something behind that says you were here—"

He stopped short, as though he had said more than he wanted to. Wallace saw the agitation in his eyes. "Did something happen on the run today?" he asked quietly.

March frowned, looked down at the sidewalk, spat. "Not officially."

"This is Rayne, remember? Did something happen?"

Raising his head, March allowed Wallace to see the haunted look in his eyes. "Yeah. Something happened," he said slowly. "I got chased back through the Dunstanburgh gate by something Ops says doesn't exist."

Feeling a sudden chill, Wallace gestured toward the empty bench at the shuttle stop a few yards away, in that one motion offering to listen and assuring in advance his support and sympathy. "I think the lady of your dreams can wait a while longer."

Bethel, Virginia, The Home Alternity

Walter Endicott closed the black binder and set it gently on the small cherrywood table beside his bed. He glanced at the clock on the fireplace mantel opposite where he lay. It was late, later than he had realized.

The dossier had been difficult reading. Four biographies. Four lives he hadn't lived but could have. Four glimpses into the hidden self. Four variations on a pattern of self-indulgence and self-interest. The dossier was written in a bluntly objective style which made no judgments itself, but laid them out clearly for others to make.

For him to make. Endicott had been forced at first to ask himself *Am I like that?* The ultimate answer to the question "Who am I"—draw out the common threads in five different lives, like finding the average of five rolls of the dice. The results had been discomfiting. Who am I? A thrice-married failure. A man with power friends and money friends but no real friends. Even a convicted rapist.

He had escaped the *Christmas Carol* nightmare by forcing himself to remember that these were other people. They had his name, but each also had at least a quarter-century of unique experiences and stresses.

To underline the point, he gave them new first names and made himself think of them as brothers. Kin, yes—but distinct individuals. He was not responsible for what they were or did. They were the product of random forces, their actions the consequences of chance. And in the end, the one conclusion he could draw was that he had been unlucky in more than one world.

With a promise to keep, he reached for the phone. "This is Senator Endicott. Please put me through to the President."

"The President has retired, Senator—"

"Who is this? Krysta?"

"Jolynn, sir."

Ah—a new one. "Well, Jolynn, they must be breaking you in on the weekend shift. Pull your book and look at the A list. And when you've finished blushing, you can put me through."

There was a moment's pause. "I'm sorry, Senator. I'll ring the family quarters."

"Thank you."

Shortly, Robinson came on the line. "Another nightowl, I see."

"Afraid so. I certainly hope I'm interrupting something—"

"I wish I could say you were. Janice turned in an hour ago. I've just been seeing to a few minor things here. I take it you've finished looking at the material?"

"Only just."

"And?"

"I think you know that my criteria are different than yours. Certainly they're different from Albert's. I've been through this once, and I can tell you that I don't intend to live a quiet life on what amounts to welfare from the Guard—"

"Understood, Walter."

"I don't know if you do understand," Endicott said sharply.

"You could go to the richest alternity and still have been better off dying here if none of it belongs to you."

"Are you saying it's better to reign in hell?"

"I'm saying that if you don't plan to be someone, to have something, then giving up what you are here is going to suck out your insides like a ten-pound tapeworm."

"We're looking ahead very carefully, Walter," Robinson said. "I hope you can see that."

"I hope you are."

"It's late, Walter. Don't lecture me," Robinson said, with a hint of impatience. "You called to tell me where you hoped to see us go. Please do—with the understanding that your preference is only one factor in a very complex equation."

"Yes," Endicott said. "Understood. Well, it's very simple. I see the most opportunity in Alernity Yellow. I'd be very unhappy to see us end up anywhere else."

"That's a problem for me, Walter."

"I know. But do we need to restrict ourselves to one destination? We might be safer and happier dispersed among several alternities."

"We need to retain a sense of community, Walter," Robinson said firmly. "We'll need the strength that comes with unity. That's what will keep us whole inside."

"Perhaps," Endicott said. "It is late—I won't keep you from your work any longer. You'll keep me posted?"

"I will."

Endicott hung up and contemplated the prospect of a new start, of moving on once more. He had made mistakes here. He had been too impatient, too quick to give away his secret. In that first moment of looking at himself dead on the lawn behind his counterpart's house, he had panicked. He had wrongly believed that if he did not use the corpse to make believers and allies, he would always be alone with the secret.

Irreversible mistakes. He should never have surrendered control of the gate. He could have made better use of it, profited far more from his discovery, by waiting until he could buy the Cambridge himself. All he got now were the leavings, token acknowledgments of what they owed him. And Tackett begrudged him even those.

No, it would not be such a terrible thing to move on. And if Robinson chose a destination not to his liking, that didn't mean that Endicott had to join him there. He had made one transit of the maze unassisted. Making a second one was surely not beyond him.

Washington, D.C., The Home Alternity

Peter Robinson replaced the receiver slowly and looked across the study to where William Rodman sat wrapped in a comfortable chair. "Walter wants to go to Yellow," Robinson said.

"I'm not surprised," Rodman said, folding his hands in his lap. "I wouldn't mind owning a company with a couple billion dollars in fighter turbofan contracts myself."

"I'm sure you wouldn't," Robinson said, reaching for the brandy snifter on the side table. "Myself, I don't much fancy being dead."

"I'm not surprised by that, either."

Robinson smiled over the lip of the glass before sipping a swallow. "Well, Bill—where shall we go?"

"That depends on what you want," Rodman said. "What *do* you want, Peter?"

Gesturing with both hands in a sweeping motion that took in the whole room and everything that surrounded it, Robinson said, "I don't want to give this up. I want to come back here. I suppose that's no surprise, either."

"No," Rodman said with a wry smile.

"Look at me, Bill," Robinson said, coming to his feet. "Have I lost one step? Do I look one day older than when we walked in here five years ago?"

"You know you don't."

"This place turned Rockefeller into a hollow shell. It killed Bob Taft. But I've never felt stronger. Stevenson called his second term a curse. My curse is that they won't let me have more than two. When you're in the middle of the game, it all comes to you. What else could you want, once you know what it's like? How could anyone walk away?"

Boston, The Home Alternity

As late as it was, the bench had offered more than enough privacy. With the shuttles off the roads by ten, the only interruptions came when a late-night stroller wandered too near. Wallace listened thoughtfully, saying little, until March's story was done.

"Did you put any of this in your transit report?"

March shook his head. "I wasn't going to give them a chance to pull my papers. And you know they would."

"I know that Ops doesn't believe there's anything in the maze. I remember back in training, when they made a point of telling us we'd hear rumors and denying them in advance. But I have to think that they'd listen to you—"

"No, they wouldn't. And I'll tell you why. They have to deny that there's something in the maze, even if they know different. They probably *do* know different. Because they have to keep the operation going, even if it costs them a few Guard grunts. Except I don't want to be one of them."

"You don't really know if you were in any danger—"

"Don't take their side, Rayne. I don't need that."

"I didn't mean—"

"You've never seen what I saw. I hope to God you never do. But if you do, you'll know just like I did that everything you are is hanging by a thread. It's like waking up and seeing Death standing at the foot of your bed. You know what it means."

"So you're going to get married."

"To the first woman who looks fertile and says yes," he said firmly. "I'm not going to disappear without leaving a piece of me behind. I'll still do the job for the old man. But I've had enough of runner's roulette."

"You sure know how to make a fellow love his work. Here I am, worrying that they *won't* let me run anymore. Maybe I ought to be worrying that they will."

March smiled in sympathy. "I'm sorry if this is hard for you. But it's more than just needing somebody to talk this out with. I thought you had a right to know."

"I'm glad you told me," Wallace said. He was almost sure he meant it.

Nahant, Massachusetts, The Home Alternity

Albert Tackett took the call from the President on the sea-facing sunporch of his elegant home. A light but steady Sunday morning drizzle had kept him off the putting green behind the house, a customary self-indulgence while Marian was at church.

Instead, he turned to an alternate indulgence, also best enjoyed when Marian was out of the house. First, he cranked open the windows at opposite ends of the porch to create a crossbreeze. Then, settling in a redwood rocker on the porch, he filled his favorite briarwood pipe with a select Turkish tobacco of considerable reputation and even greater bite.

The little brown and yellow pouch had been sent back to him as a gift by the stationmaster of the Blue Section gate. Tackett was doubly grateful for the gift, since Turkish tobaccos—of any grade—were impossible to get locally.

He set the pipe aside when the phone rang. "Good morning, sir. I should advise you before you say anything that this line is no longer scrambled, though it is shielded. Marian was having trouble dealing with the scrambler."

"That should be fine for our purposes, Albert. I hope you're enjoying your life of leisure, up there on that seaside estate of yours."

"I do what I can."

The President chuckled. "You work too hard, Albert. But since you're working for me, I'm not going to tell you that."

"Mum's the word. Have you made a decision, Mr. President?"

"Yes. It's Alternity Blue. For logistical reasons, I wanted to stay with a domestic gate. Blue was by far the better of the two options."

Blue—the Indianapolis gate. "I think that's a reasonable choice, sir. We should be able to control the environment there."

"What is your station strength in Blue?"

"Eighty-five people. It's our second-largest station."

"I don't see how that can possibly be adequate to the demands of moving more than a hundred Alpha List personnel across and servicing their needs."

"It'll stress our financial resources more than our personnel resources. We're going to have to pump more money across. Which means Treasury will have to increase either the size or the frequency of those currency 'test' runs."

"If so, it'll be taken care of. But we're going to need more bodies. I want a commitment from you to double the size of the Blue staff in the shortest possible time."

"Double—"

"As an initial step. If time allows, we'll build from there."

"I can't qualify another eighty-five people for the Guard in anything less than three months. Not on top of our need to replace losses and program our current growth plan. And even three months won't qualify them as moles."

"Then borrow them internally, from the other Sections. This has first priority, Albert. You've got fifty-one hundred people on payroll. If you can't find eighty-five that are being underused where they are—"

"Most of those fifty-one hundred are working on this side of the gate. Technology Transfer. Ops. Analysis. Not covert agents. And an awful lot of them are just plain too old. We can't send

Common World people across, no matter how great the need. Alpha List poses enough problems for us."

"Albert, I don't understand your resistance."

"Sir, this has the potential to disrupt operations in every Section. We're going to have to hit the runner pool, hard. Probably pull people in from everywhere, and you've already told me I can't close Red Section. We're going to be green all over once the Chinese fire drill is done."

"Are you saying you can't do it?"

"No, sir. I'm saying I think it doesn't need doing."

"Noted. I want it done anyway. You're going to need a lot of horses just to pull detailed bios on the full Alpha list."

"I didn't realize that would be necessary."

"It is. Find the extra bodies, Albert. Clear?"

"Clear, sir." Tackett hesitated. "Can I ask you about another matter, sir?"

"Of course."

"Senator Endicott has asked me to have another woman snatched outworld and turned over to him—"

"Problem?"

"Do we have to do this? It seems to me that there should be some limit—"

"Do it," Robinson said simply.

"He presumes a lot on your friendship."

"He's drawing on an account. We owe him."

Tackett sighed. "One way and another, I'd have thought we'd already paid him ten times over for what little service he did us."

"What yardstick are you using? Everything the Tower's given us—you know the list better than anyone—we owe to him."

We earned that ourselves, Tackett fumed silently. The kids downstairs bought it for us. All Endicott did was giftwrap a white elephant. It wasn't worth a damn until he gave it to us.

"What's he do with them, anyway?"

"Do I have to tell you at your age what a man does with a woman?" The President chuckled.

Tackett was not amused. "Men I understand. Leeches are another matter. I wish you'd cut him loose."

"A convenient brain tumor, perhaps, and a quiet death in Walter Reed?" Robinson chuckled again. "It's a little thing, Albert, what he asks. Hold your nose and do it. Save your worrying for the big problems. Like putting things in order in Blue. Your personal attention, now, understand? Rathole is one piece in a bigger picture. I want it there when everything comes together.''

''Understood, sir.''

After he hung up, Tackett sat in the chair scowling for long minutes. The pipe was cold, but he did not bother to relight it. The aftertaste had already turned acid in his mouth. Finally he reached for the phone.

''Bret, this is the old man,'' he said with a touch of weariness. ''Director's briefing in one hour. Call in the team. We've got work to do.''

Meeting notes – 10/16/77

Needed : ALPHA LIST ORIENTATION PACKET
   FOR BLUE
→ HOLD FOR ACTIVATION OF RATHOLE ←

Briefing Outline
   phase 1 : En route — Guard reps on
   each train, no disclosure
   phase 2 : Staged to Tower — minimal disclosure
   phase 3 : Crossgate — adaptive disclosure

• What do we tell them about the gate?
   (look at Guard briefing materials for
   guidelines)

• Consideration : protecting security of Tower Rec —
   blacked out word on trains and vans.
   Can we take them through blind?

Gate City : Indianapolis Ind.
Gate House and Field Station : Scottish Rite
   Cathedral, Meridian St.

NATIONAL :
Federal Government : Pres Daniel Brandenburg,
state sens. (How much do the locals know?)

- Social Control: Identity cards N.R. Relocation permits N.R. No local travel restrictions in effect. (Talk to Martin about setting up "house rules" for A's — local regs too permissive.). Domestic police forces have national information exchange but no federal mandate for internal security (need to minimize exposure to civic violations).

- Media: Wide open. High priority → censor/limit access.

LOCAL:

- Safe houses: Several small (distributed), or buy apartment house? (N. Meridian has possibles) $ $ $

- Glossary: get station staff to abstract from Guard masterlist.

Needs:
clothing, covers, cash, trans., housing. secure communications, extra security staff, ded. ferrymen, etc. etc—

?? Whose idea was this anyway?

CHAPTER 8

What Begins in Fear

Boston, The Home Alternity

Even at 7:00 A.M., the Medford-City Center flesh-hauler was full. Full of people trying hard not to look at each other. Full of people withdrawn inside cocoons of myopic blindness.

Pairs of strangers shared benches, each pretending they were alone. They studied their reflections in the window, scrutinized the papers on their laps, glanced up at the advertisements on the ceiling—anything but look at each other with more than a furtive, suspicious glance.

Wallace was the exception. Spoiled by the company vans, he wanted to share a joke, a grin, a few words of idle chatter. He wanted the dark-haired woman across the aisle and two rows back to look up from her poem cards, bright rectangles of floral color, so he could tell her in a moment of eyes meeting how attractive he thought she was.

Most of all he wanted something to keep his mind off the double-edged anxiety that went with returning to work. His own problems had been bad enough; what Jason told him Saturday night was worse.

But the bus was full of strangers. Even those that had gotten on with him at the Block had been strangers—science faculty from MIT and Harvard, execs from the Navy shipyard, junior surgeons from Chelsea and Memorial. Neighbors, but strangers, belonging to circles which had no intersection with his own, their faces as cold as the rest. Even after two years, it had the power to make Wallace feel like a new and not particularly welcome arrival to the city.

But the fact that he was feeling that way this morning was his own doing. He could have lingered at home and taken the company van at his scheduled time. But troubled dreams had opened his eyes a dozen times through the night and finally driven him from bed before even Katie was stirring. Thinking about them when awake, sitting alone in the kitchen, only gave them more power. Talking about them to Ruthann was impossible.

But then, talking to Ruthann had not been an option for a long time. They had come to Boston united, three as one, and silence had divided them. Silence promised with an oath and bought with pale blue checks drawn on the U.S. Treasury.

He shared nothing of his time away, not trivia, not triumph, not fear, not failure. Ruthann and Katie lived in one world, and he moved back and forth between it and his own, the maze of the city linking and dividing them, an ironic echo of the task which took him away from them. The secrets weighed heavy, the silence thundered in his ears. It was easier now to be away.

Work was the antidote. Four days away from the Tower was three too many. A sweetheart run to a downhill gate, that's what I need, he thought as the tandem bus bumped and swayed its way along Mystic Valley Parkway past anonymous plants and warehouses labeled only with large black numerals. It's Jason's boogeyman, not mine.

Except that in his dreams, Jason's shadow had been a Philadelphia cop named Chambers, and it was Wallace he was looking for.

Ordinarily, there was no special rush at the assignment desk on Monday morning. Continuous operations and overlapping duty shifts served to spread the constant parade of runners and ferrymen through the regular Guard's eighteen-hour operational day.

But when Wallace reached the duty room just before eight, he found the desk triple-staffed, with a line waiting for each dispatcher. The room was almost as full of rumors as people. By the time he made it to the front of the line, Wallace had heard several: that Red Section was closed, that Red Section was being expanded, that the Guard was being cut back, that Security was going to rescreen everyone from Tackett on down.

"Wallace, Rayne. 21618," he said. "Any of what's buzzing true, Bo?"

Declining the chance to serve as a rumor clearinghouse, the

dispatcher ignored the question. "Wallace, Rayne," he repeated, scanning down his list. "You're out of the rotation."

"What?"

"You're to report to the clinic first thing to get your medical release. Then you're scheduled to see the deputy director at 10:10. Do you know where his office is?"

"See Monaghan?"

"That's right."

"Uh—somewhere up in Ops, I suppose."

"Take any of the east elevators to the twenty-sixth floor. Turn right and check in with the receptionist at the end of the hall. Got it?"

"Got it—"

The dispatcher was already looking past him to the next runner. *Out of the rotation—what does that mean? God, don't let it mean they've pulled my papers. Not now. I'd never get back on Annie's good side. Damn it, I didn't do anything wrong!*

Deputy Director Bret Monaghan was a whippet of a man, looking out at Wallace with squinty eyes from behind wire-frame glasses. His jacket was already on the back of his chair, and his shirt sleeves were rolled up one turn, revealing a few inches of freckled forearm and a black-banded watch with a badly scarred crystal.

To Monaghan's right, on one corner of the desk, a neglected cigarette consumed itself silently in an ashtray, tiny smoke tracings climbing skyward until the current from the vent scattered them. Behind him on the wall, a reproduction of Diego's stark "Cape Prince of Wales, Twenty-Four Degrees Below Zero" reflected as glare the light from Monaghan's desk lamp.

Wallace waited as patiently as he could while Monaghan made notes on a tablet, most likely about his last visitor. Monaghan's schedule was so tight that Wallace had shared the waiting area with two other runners, so tight that the cushion of the one spare chair in Monaghan's office had been warm when Wallace settled on it.

While he waited, he wrestled with problems to come. *So I lose my Red papers, drop to Grade 2. Probably won't have to leave the Block. Have to sell our share of the Spirit. Shouldn't be hard, in the Block. No new couch. Annie won't like that. Won't like any of it. Won't understand and I can't tell her. Goddamn it all.*

At long last, Monaghan tucked the sheet of paper inside a file and relegated the file to the credenza behind him. With the

113

veined hands of someone twenty years older, the deputy director slowly shuffled through his papers to find the folder with Wallace's name on it.

"Doctor blue-stamp you?" Monaghan said at last, without looking up.

"Yes, sir."

"Looks like you had yourself quite a time over in Red last week."

Wallace did not know whether to minimize it or brag, so he said nothing.

"You all right between the ears?"

"Sir?"

"How do you feel about running?"

"I'm ready to get back in the chute. More than ready."

"You like it?"

Casually as they were being asked, the questions were throwing Wallace off-balance. "It's an honor to serve in the Guard, sir. I'm glad to be here."

Monaghan looked up from his paper, his eyes seeking Wallace's like a marksman sighting on a target. "So you don't like it."

Why is everyone trying to trap me in my own words? Wallace thought desperately. "I didn't say that. I like it. It needs doing. I want to make a contribution."

"You do?"

"Yes, sir." He hesitated, then plunged on. "There aren't many chances to do that back in Indiana, where I'm from. My older brother works track gang for a National Rail maintenance crew. That's about the closest any of the family got."

"I see you were in the Youth Defense Reserve in school. Why didn't you go on into the service? Lose your taste for it?"

After all the interviews Wallace had endured during the selection process, it was a familiar question. He'd learned quickly that the real answer was too complicated.

The query assumed that he had joined the YDR by choice. He hadn't. As a fourteen-year-old with no clearly expressed goals of his own, he was programmed into it by a quota-conscious ninth-grade advisor. He had found more there to like than he expected— trips to Wright-Patterson and Fort Benjamin Harrison, firepower displays at Jefferson Proving Ground, a phys ed program which offered something more interesting than endless pick-up basketball games.

YDR, summer camps at Atterbury, ROTC at Purdue, then the Army and a Monroe Line assignment in the Canal Zone or the

114

Alaskan Territory. Like the leather-faced soldier in Diego's painting, looking out through a tunnel of fur across the Bering Strait at Russia, holding a frost-coated rifle in gloved hands. That was how it was supposed to go.

But it hadn't. One summer camp missed due to his father's heart attack, a year's delay when his application to Purdue was rejected, and suddenly he had found that he had wandered off course with no idea how to get back on.

"Truthfully, our unit wasn't very sharp," he lied. "I don't know how much of a taste of it I really got. But that wasn't why. I got . . . sidetracked." When no understanding appeared on Monaghan's face, he added quickly, "By Annie. Ruthann."

"I see. You've been married—"

"Almost five years."

"Happily?"

Why do you care? he thought hotly. But he hid his indignation. "Well—sure. As much as anybody. I mean, everybody has rough spots now and then, right? But Ruthann's prime." His face creased in a half-smile. "My friends are jealous." One of them, anyway.

"And you have a child?"

The smile widened into a happy grin. "Katie. A sweetheart. Prime."

Monaghan nodded, shuffling a page to the back of the folder. Expressionless, he scanned the new top sheet slowly.

"Sir—about that business in Red. I know it was a little messy, but I don't think I did anything wrong—"

"I'm not concerned about that," Monaghan said, closing the file. "You showed a bit of resourcefulness. And results matter."

"Then what's this about, sir? If you can tell me."

The deputy director sat back in his chair. "We need to expand Blue Section. Ops is setting up an accelerated qualification program for field agents. You were recommended as a candidate. This was your screening interview."

"Recommended?"

"Maybe I should say your name came to our attention."

That goes down easier, Wallace thought. "I understand."

"Your Indiana background is a plus. Everything is going to happen very quickly, Rayne. We need people who can keep up with the pace."

"I just want to make sure I understand: Do you want me for this side of the gate? Or the other side?"

"The other side. Is that a problem?"

Problem? You offer to solve all my problems and you ask if

it's a problem? Jason, my friend, I hope they're calling your number, too. "I don't think—"

"Because it's refusable. You know that. Mole assignments always are. But if I were you, I'd be feeling lucky. You're going to lose your Red papers for sure, and there's enough bad talk about you downstairs that I wouldn't be surprised to see you eased all the way out. You got your high profile the wrong way, you know?"

Swallowing hard at the reproof, Wallace nodded. "What's this going to mean? I mean, to my ticket?"

"Standard," Monaghan said with a disinterested shrug. "Push to Grade 4—Grade 5 when you clear probationary. Release time depends on assignment. I can almost promise you'll be on a six-five schedule for the forseeable future." He dropped the folder on the desktop. "So what are you going to do?"

Six weeks in, five days out—a pay grade he'd never reach as a runner. Wallace did not hesitate. "I'm in."

With a lazy motion, Monaghan reached at last for the red-eyed stub of the cigarette. "Stop by Blue Section to draw your training materials, then clean out your locker," he said. "And catch lunch. In the next ninety minutes. The Section supervisor wants all of you in Aud 5 at noon to get things started."

Washington, D.C., The Home Alternity

The head of the CIA plans division handled the new NSC directive gingerly, as though wary of it. He read it through, looked across the table at Dennis Madison with a deeply troubled expression on his face, then looked down at the document again.

"Is this for real?"

"Absolutely."

"And it means what I think it means?"

"It does."

"You're not just teasing me."

"Never," the director said. "Put on a happy face, Wally. You're back in business."

"All right," the plans chief said fervently. "About damn time."

"How long will it take you to pick a few well-ripened notions out of your if-only box? I'd like to get back to the President with something before the services can. He's going to have to pick and choose, and it won't hurt to be first in line."

"What does Robinson really want? Where are we trying to get to?"

The CIA director idly spun a pencil on the gleaming wood tabletop. "I think you have a full range of objectives from a nettle in the Bear's breakfast to mounting the trophy head on the Oval Office wall."

An eager light came into the plans chief's eyes as he leaned forward in his chair. "How spooky do you want me to get?"

"Don't limit yourself, Wally. I'll prescreen before we walk it downtown. You have something particular in mind?"

"There's a . . . ah, a kind of a neat idea one of my people came up with a year or so back. Very off-the-wall. Very ambitious."

"Want to give me the skeleton?"

"Now?"

"Why not?"

"Well—sure. It was a juxtaposition of numbers that got us thinking. The blast radius of a Mark XII Super at a thousand feet is fifteen miles. The primary international airport for Moscow— that's Sheremetyova—is fifteen miles from the Kremlin."

Madison gave the pencil another spin as he played with the implications. "I see where it goes, but I don't think too much of the margins. If you're going to burn out a bunch of hornets, you've got to hit the nest square the first time."

"Another number or two, then. The ground speed of an Aeroflot Tu-85 is 550 miles per hour. That puts Sheremetyova about two minutes away. Say you're the air controller at Vnukovo. A flight from London aborts a landing because of gear failure and overshoots the airport. How eager would you be to order one of your own airliners shot down? How long would it take you to make that decision?"

"A goddamned Q-plane," Madison mused.

"That would be one way to think of it. I remember reading when I was a kid about the Q-ships during the Second World War, disguising frigates as helpless merchantmen to bring German subs to the surface."

The director shook his head. "You're right, Wally. Very ambitious."

"Too ambitious," the plans chief projected, enthusiasm dimming as he tried to gauge his superior's reaction. "I'll leave that one in the bag."

"I didn't say that," the director said. "I'm right with you. It *is* a neat idea. Work it up. If you can wrinkle-proof it, I'll pass it along."

The plans chief beamed in delight. "Can I have ten days?"

"Knowing how the wheels turn at the Pentagon, you could

probably have ten weeks," the CIA director said with contempt. "No, ten days is fine. But, Wally, let's consider that little trick the upper limit, all right? Give me a package that includes some ideas that won't raise the hair on everybody's neck."

The Secretary of State sat in his padded swivel chair and stared up at the huge Mercator projection of the world on the wall of the conference room. So hard to think boldly. The many years of being painfully cautious stunted the imagination. Where are the opportunities? Where can we push? How hard? How openly? Where is there ferment? Where are there friends?

North America was the fortress, and it was sound. From the Arctic Circle to the Isthmus of Panama, from the Alaskan Territory to the island states of Cuba and Caribbea, all were friends and allies. All save French Canada, which was an exception of no consequence.

Yes, the department could be satisfied with its work close to home. Greater Canada and Mexico saw their destinies were one with the United States'. Honduras and Guatemala were happy enough in their phantom independence, standing under the American umbrella while proclaiming they were unafraid of the rain. More enlightened governments in the Pacific Coast nations worked hand in glove with Washington. Panama, its vulnerability more acutely obvious than some, had begun a consideration of the merits of territorial status. And statehood for the islands had been a coup.

No, all the trouble areas lay outside the Monroe Line. And there were few enough of them. It was a quiet world, the silence of the enslaved. There was little fighting, and less revolutionary fervor. Counting the hot spots did not take long. South Africa. India. Malaya. France.

It was too late for France, had become too late the moment Prime Minister Somerset spelled out the conditions under which the Weasels could remain in England. There was a bloc in Congress ignorantly bleating for aid to Paris; they would never know that France's fall to communism would do more for the democratic cause.

State's hands were tied in Africa until the FN achieved working control of at least part of South-West Africa, or Namibia as they chose to call it. There had to be something resembling a government to recognize.

There was little to choose between in the ten-year-old Indian civil war, as demonstrated by the fact that neither Russia nor China had elected to favor one side over the other in all that time. The fabric of that many-faced society was in tatters, and it seemed unlikely that there would be peace there until the last Hindu slaughtered the last Muslim, or vice versa.

But Malaya was another story. Malaya was the cork in the bottle protecting Indonesia and Australia from the ambitions of the Chinese Communists for an empire of their own. There had been fierce fighting in the jungle forests of the Kra Peninsula for nearly a year.

Troops from the Chinese client-states in Burma and Thailand were supporting the native Chinese minority in a reprise of the post war struggles between the Malayan Communist Party and the British-backed Malay majority. And the MCP had had a disquieting degree of success. Twice Chief Minister Tan Siew Rahman's government had been forced to flee the capital for Singapore when guerrilla advances began to threaten the graceful Moorish buildings of Kuala Lumpur.

Here alone was a place where American involvement could make a difference. Economic aid for Rahman's government, inducements for Australia to increase its aid, a treaty that would open the American armory to both nations, perhaps even the symbolic reappearance of American warships in the South China Sea—all were worth considering.

Pulling a tablet onto his lap, the Secretary of State began to make notes in the pidgin shorthand he had developed as a corporate lawyer in Chicago two decades ago. Malaya was the place. It did not matter that their opponent there was Beijing and not Moscow. Moscow would get the message, all the same.

Moscow, The Home Alternity

The room was far too large to be an office. Though poorly lit and dominated by muted colors, the room suggested courtly excess, evoked the great hall of a czar. The footsteps of visitors echoed off the walls and high arched ceiling as they approached the desk.

Spotlit by sunlight from the rank of tall windows at the south end of the room, the desk occupied an island of carpeting in an ocean of hardwood floor. It was the one warm spot in a cool cavern of a room. In the mind of the desk's owner, the "office" ended at the perimeter of the dark-hued carpet. All that lay beyond was superfluous, immaterial.

General Secretary Aleksandr Kondratyeva had always liked the sun. Summers at his grandmother's in Rybakovka, near

Odessa on the Black Sea, had sealed his fondness. Those pre-war summers of swimming and riding and playing on the postage-stamp shell beaches with cousins from Char'kov and Doneck were the strongest memories of a childhood abbreviated by Hitler's armies.

His Chief of Military Intelligence did not like the sun, but then it was hard to envision Voenushkin as a playful boy. Dough-faced and dour, the head of the GRU was painfully earnest and eternally humorless. He squinted and squirmed in his seat as though the pale October rays were the blinding eye of God Himself.

"Secretary Kondratyeva, I thank you for this chance to speak with you directly," Voenushkin began. "Your generosity—"

"Please, Geidar," Kondratyeva interrupted, "endeavor to use your time more wisely than in thanking me for doing my job."

"Yes, Secretary. I asked to see you because one of our assets in America has produced an intelligence intercept which I felt should be called to your attention."

"You may proceed to do so."

Voenushkin rose half out of his seat to pass a single sheet of brownish-white paper across the desk. The color of the paper announced that it was several hours old, well along toward self-destruction. "This is a transcript of a conversation last Sunday between President Robinson and his spymaster Albert Tackett—"

"I see only Tackett's words."

"That is true, sir. It was a telephone conversation, and the intercept was accomplished with a device that reads the vibrations in a pane of glass. But the references are unambiguous."

"Very well. I will read it." When he was finished, Kondratyeva folded the sheet carefully in quarters and laid it in a large black ashtray. "How do you interpret this intercept?"

"First, it is clear that this National Resource Center is not merely a technical research organization. A significant portion of its employees are involved in espionage. We have suspected this for some time, but without confirmation.

"It is equally clear that the President has asked the NRC to greatly increase its espionage activity to support some unspecified initiative."

"Yes," said Kondratyeva. "I would agree with your conclusions. Do you have any insight into what that initiative might be, or where it might be aimed?"

"No, sir. May I call your attention to several curious items in the transcript? At one point Tackett refers to a 'gate,' at another to 'common world people'—"

"I took those to be errors of collection or translation."

"They are not, Secretary. And they are what concern me."

"Is it not reasonable that they are idiomatic expressions? American English is a forest of idiom."

"We have sought such an explanation in vain."

"Then they are code phrases."

"Perhaps, Secretary Kondratyeva. But my experts tell me that they are more likely slang of unknown reference. The American habit is to use code phrases which have no thread of identity with the object referenced, such as their war plans Chrome and Flying Horse. These phrases—gate, outworld, common world—seem to mean what they mean. It is the reference, not the meaning, which confuses."

As Voenushkin was speaking, the paper lying in the ashtray abruptly darkened to a cocoa brown, then burst into flame with a popping sound. Kondratyeva used the tip of a pencil to keep the burning fragments contained in the ceramic bowl. "This discussion of Senator Endicott—how do you see it?" he asked.

"It is why I wished to see you," the GRU chief said. "It suggests to me that Senator Endicott has both knowledge we desire and a weakness which might be exploited."

"You wish to attempt to compromise a United States Senator? A risky undertaking, Geidar."

"For which I request your authority."

Kondratyeva stood, shaking his head. "Geidar, you must have more courage in your judgment. If this is prudent and necessary, order it done. I welcome the information you have brought. I do not welcome your professional timidity. Exercise the responsibility of your position. Do not hide behind my skirts."

Boston, The Home Alternity

"We have a reservation. The name is Wallace."

"Yes, Mr. Wallace," the hostess said. "It'll be just a few moments."

Arms linked around Wallace's waist, Ruthann snuggled closer and rested her head against his shoulder. "We don't mind," she said. The hostess smiled tolerantly.

Wallace could tell that he had surprised Ruthann, and the knowledge pleased him. It had taken a dozen phone calls to make the arrangements, calls squeezed in during the short breaks that Baker, the Blue Section supervisor, allowed them through the afternoon.

There'd been one call to Rebecca to arrange for Katie to stay the night next door. Five calls at least to track down the delicate yellow-orange day lilies, Annie's favorite. More calls to restaurants near the Block to scout menus and prices for something she would like and he could afford.

And the final call to Annie, proclaiming the kitchen off-limits for her that evening and inviting her to scout her closet for a dress as beautiful as she was.

It seemed like that was the moment they found each other again. He heard the warm smile in her voice when she consented. He noted with pleasure that she did not demand further explanation, but instead indulged his cheerful secretiveness.

"What time?" was all she asked. And she accepted his answer of seven o'clock. Baker's plans for him would allow for nothing earlier without quailing.

When he had arrived home, she was resplendent in a cream-colored cotton knit dress that clung to her curves from shoulder to hips and then became a flirtatious skirt with a profusion of soft pleats. He was not sure he had seen the dress before, but was discreet enough not to ask. The kiss she gave him *was* familiar, the kind of sensuous, unhurried kiss that narrowed the focus of all his senses to her presence.

It had seemed at times in recent months that he had nothing to talk to Ruthann about. His work for the Guard was so much of his life, and he was acutely conscious of what he could not tell her. So much so that sometimes avoiding conversation seemed easier than the mental gymnastics involved in fencing off public thoughts from classified ones.

But walking to the restaurant, they rediscovered how to talk to each other. She had a storehouse of cute-Katie stories to share, he a string of extended jokes ending in painful puns. Then, the nervous cascade of time-filling first-date chatter ended, they rediscovered something more important—not to be afraid of silence. Holding hands as they walked, they let a smile or a squeeze say what needed saying.

The hostess returned and guided them to a small table along one wall. It was away from the first-course common and the traffic it created, but it was also elbow-to-elbow with two other small tables which were already occupied. But Ruthann did not seem to mind.

"What do you think she thought?" Ruthann said as the hostess left them.

"Probably that we're married, but not to each other."

"Really? Do you think so?"

"Sure. Everybody knows that real married people stay home and eat beans and brown bread in front of the news. Only people with something to hide go out in public."

"I didn't know that you were taking me to *that* kind of place," Annie said with a mischievous smile. "We should have been adventurous and taken our rings off."

"We can take them off later—along with everything else."

She averted her eyes coquettishly. "I'm sure I don't know what you mean."

"I'll try to help you remember."

"Just one minute, sir. I have to check the rules. Are old married couples allowed to flirt?"

He reached out and traced a fingertip along the soft skin of her neck. "The hostess will expect it."

"Oh," she said, taking his hand in hers and kissing his knuckles. "I guess it's all right, then."

Wallace had intended to tell her about the promotion over dinner. But somehow the impulse to do so evaded him. Their dinner neighbors were too close for such private matters; he was having no trouble at all eavesdropping on them. The easy flow of the evening was too rare and precious, and he did not want to risk interrupting it.

All excuses, he knew as he paid the check. The truth was that, having discovered he did not need the good news to save the evening, he was saving the news to cap the evening.

The air had turned cool bordering on chill, but they walked unhurriedly arm in arm. "I'd forgotten you could be like this," she said.

He smiled ruefully. "I'd kind of forgotten myself."

"I'm glad you remembered."

"I wanted to do something to celebrate," he said, pulling her closer with an arm around her waist. "But I had such a good time just being with you tonight that it almost doesn't matter."

"Celebrate what? Have you been keeping secrets?"

They had reached the green corridor bordering the elevated train line. He stopped and turned her toward him. "Celebrate good news. Annie, I have something to tell you that's going to put a premium smile on that pretty face."

He saw the hopeful light go on in her eyes. "Tell me."

"I'm going to be promoted to Grade 5. It'll mean another two hundred a week."

"Oh!"

"You're going to be able to drive the Spirit as much as you want, and even order that couch."

"Oh, Rayne!" She smiled cherubically. "If you'd told me sooner I wouldn't have passed over dessert."

"Want to go back?"

"No, silly," she said, and hugged him fiercely. "I'm so proud of you."

"They told me this morning. I've been high all day."

She pulled back from him without breaking the embrace and looked up at him with sober eyes. "But, Rayne, how can they pay you so much? You're jumping over a whole grade. What are they going to want you to do? If it's going to be dangerous—"

"It should be less dangerous than what I'm doing now."

"Then I don't understand—"

"I'm going to have to do some traveling. That's the only difference. I'll be gone a few weeks at a time instead of a few days."

Her expression turned darker still. "How many weeks?"

"Six weeks at the longest."

Her body going stiff, she squirmed out of the embrace. "Bastard—"

"What?"

"You didn't do this to be nice. You did this to manipulate me."

"No!"

"You knew I wouldn't like it. You knew I'd be angry. You just wanted to soften me up with a little phony romance."

"No! I wasn't manipulating you. I don't even understand why you're angry!"

Their voices had risen to the point where they were playing to the full theater of their surroundings.

"Of course not. When you're getting what you want you always ignore my feelings."

"I didn't *ask* for this—"

"Then turn it down. Turn down the promotion."

He held his hands up in a helpless gesture. "I can't."

"You mean you won't."

"I don't understand," he said pleadingly, taking a step toward her. "I love you—"

"No!" she shrieked. "Don't you dare say that!"

He took another step. "But I—"

"Don't you pretend you love me."

"Pretend!"

"When you love somebody, you want to be with them. You don't look for reasons to stay away."

He tried to reach for her. "Annie—"

With an unexpected ferocity, she slapped his hand away. "Don't you touch me. You want to go away, go!" Her hurt began to spill over into tears. "Go! Go right now! Then you won't have to be bothered with me." She planted her palms on his chest and gave him a push that carried him a step backward. "You won't have to look at me, or talk to me, or make love to me. Go away and forget me like you always do. *Just stop trying to make me think you care.*"

Then she ran away into the night, under the elevated and toward the Block.

Wallace stood, stunned, and watched her go. He felt helpless, foolish, abused. And out of his befuddlement rose up a defensive fury. How could she manage to twist something he was doing for her into something he was doing to her? Bitch. Selfish whining cold-souled bitch—

He found himself clenching his fists, weight forward on his feet as though he were about to launch himself in pursuit. Except that he knew that if he chased after her now it would be not to talk to her but to hurt her, and he would not gratify such an impulse. He turned and purposefully walked the other way, away from the Block, away from home.

But still the feeling was there, the screaming need to unleash the teeth-grinding jaw-clamping frustration jangling inside him. His steps turned into strides, his strides into an almost animal stalking. Thought surrendering to impulse, he passed close to one of the biker's rests dotting the elevated corridor, spotting the bench and trash canister resting there in a halo of light.

Seizing the half-full metal cylinder with both hands, he whirled it in a half-circle that intersected the lamp post. The canister crumpled with a metallic groan, folding in half and spitting out part of its contents. The post clanged and vibrated. He hurled the battered canister out into the darkness, and it bounced and rolled across the grass, scattering bottles and wrappers along the way.

That was enough. The boil of his anger was lanced. He stood there for long moments, heart slowly calming, breaths short and hard. The night air seemed suddenly cold, and he wanted to go home. But home meant facing Annie again, and there was too much to risk in that.

Headlights in the distance told him of a shuttle train approaching the Block station, a hundred yards farther along the median. He raced it there, reaching the platform just before the doors closed, and boarded without troubling to ask where it was headed. It would take him away. Whether to end of line in Wakefield or downtown did not matter. Just away, that's all that mattered.

NOVEMBER

1 *Earthquake devastates Guatemala*

A powerful earthquake and several strong aftershocks centered in the province of Huehuetenango caused widespread damage in central Guatemala and Mexico's Yucatan peninsula. The official death toll was more than 2,000, though some experts estimated the actual number of casualties to be twice that. More than two hundred buildings were destroyed in Guatemala City, and damage was reported as far away as Puebla, Mexico. A number of pre-Columbian Mayan temples were badly damaged by the quake, most notably at the Iximiche and Zaculeu archaeological sites. The strongest tremors peaked at 7.9 on the Richter Scale.

3 *Astronauts set endurance record*

UN Space Authority astronauts Robert Lovell (US), Erica Hamilton (UK), Viktor Syedykh (USSR) and Ernhard Schoene (GDR) set a new lunar endurance record, occupying their spartan Galileo Base quarters located on Mare Serenitatis (Sea of Security) for forty-six consecutive days. A fuel-tank leak in the *Delaunay* lunar shuttle had delayed the arrival of a relief crew, originally expected October 18.

7 *Brandenberg elected President, Republicans gain edge in both houses of Congress*

In the closest popular vote in American history, National party candidate Daniel Brandenburg narrowly defeated Republican incumbent Roland Maxwell to become the first member of the new party to achieve national office. Democrat Michael Mansfield finished a distant third in the polling, which appeared to mark the end of national effectiveness for the party of Jefferson and Roosevelt. The Republicans maintained control of the Senate, with 11 of 13 incumbents reelected to give the party 55 seats to the National party's 16 and the Democrats' 31. In the House, Republicans will occupy 200 seats, Nationalists 147, and Democrats 88. A majority of the successful Nationalist candidates were veterans of the Hill who changed allegiance in the wake of the party's rift over U.S. participation in the proposed United Nations Confederation.

CHAPTER 9

The Grave
of Jacob Stalin

Indianapolis, Alternity Blue

The three other new field agents waiting with Wallace in a ground-floor room of the Scottish Rite Cathedral did not look as bored as they had a right to.

Tucked away out of the way by the station staff, they were on hold with nothing to do, not even sightsee. The eight Tudor-arch windows spaced around the hexagonal chamber, the base of one of the cathedral's four main turrets, were filled with a rippled glass which allowed no glimpse of the city outside.

But instead of looking bored, they looked impatient, nervous, or eager—looks that all said "Let's get on with it." It was a sentiment with which Wallace could identify. He and his transit partner, Gary Fowler, had come through near the top of the move, and so had been waiting the better part of two hours.

Fowler had been a stranger, an anonymous face in the new class, until that morning, when Wallace was assigned to bring him through to Blue. Since then, Wallace had collected a few biographical scraps. The son of a Nisei mother and an American father, Fowler had been 1A-certified for the Hirakata gate in Green on the strength of his conversational fluency in Japanese. Fowler's features were essentially Caucasian, but his short stature and slight build betrayed the mixed heritage.

There were footsteps from beyond the open door, and all four looked up hopefully. "Bailey and Scowcroft?" asked the white-haired black man who appeared in the doorway.

"Here," said one of the two, scrambling to his feet.

"Let's be going."

Disappointed, Wallace and Fowler sank back into their chairs. "And then there were two," Fowler said when the others were gone.

"I'm getting used to it."

"You'd better, since we're going to be bunking together. You play cards?"

"Euchre?" Wallace said hopefully.

"Is that a card game?"

"It's kind of like pinochle."

"Oh. No. I meant poker."

"Never really learned the rules. Mom didn't approve. Hearts?"

Fowler shook his head and grunted. "Probably no cards here anyway."

"I never saw any."

"How often have you been here?"

"Thirty, forty times. Only ferry runs, though."

"That's right. This is home for you."

"Sort of. I used to live about fifty miles east of here."

"How do you figure it? It's like they've thrown away the rule book for this project. You never send moles or runners home."

"Or make singles moles," Wallace said, thinking of the half-dozen or so unmarrieds among the new class.

Jason wasn't among them, and by the end of the fourteen-day accelerated training program it had been evident why. The class was not a particularly distinguished group: 1As and 2As, a dozen ferrymen, a number of analysts withdrawn from other stations, even a few desk-types from the Tower. Jason was too valuable as a runner, especially with the ranks of the runners thinned by the mass "promotion."

"And this business this morning," Fowler went on. "Did you ever see gate control such a madhouse? What was that all about? There was no reason for running us through that way."

"I can't figure it either," Wallace said.

There had been a definite air of controlled panic in the Tower that morning. The new class had been sent through the gate like an invading army, two agents at a time every four minutes, just about the minimum clearance required for the gate to reopen between transits. All other traffic had been suspended for the two and a half hours it had taken to get seventy-six agents across. No one Wallace talked to could remember a move on anything approaching that scale.

But the efficiency of the move was deceptive. They had spent three hours being paired off, lined up, briefed and otherwise organized before the first agents started down the chute. Not until nearly the last minute were he and Fowler told who they were supposed to connect with on the other side.

"It felt like some kind of rehearsal," Wallace said. "Like high school graduation, with the people who know what they want done doing their best to keep it from the people who have to do it."

Fowler laughed and gestured at the windows. "You know, I'm taking it on faith that we actually *are* in Indianapolis."

"That much I can vouch for."

"What about this Donald Arens we've been assigned to? Do you know him?"

"I've seen him once or twice, I think. Mole. I don't really know anything else about him."

"Except that he's not a punctual person."

"Punctuality is an overrated virtue," said a new voice from the doorway. "You two ready to go?"

They looked up to find a blond youth leaning against the door jamb, arms crossed over his chest, grinning while they gaped. The minimum age for the Guard was twenty, but Arens did not even look that old. And yet he was a veteran here, three years continuous duty.

"Sure are," Wallace said, standing. "I'm—"

"Wallace. I know. They sent over photos for all us nannies."

"Nannies?" Fowler asked. "Which makes us—"

Arens' smile had a gentle touch of superiority. "Come on, let's get out of here. I haven't seen my apartment for five days, and I've got a date with a cold beer on the balcony," he said. "Besides, I can't wait to see how we're going to divide one bed three ways."

They went out the back way, passing under a tan canvas awning to a navy blue van waiting in the alley behind the cathedral. There was already a driver behind the wheel, and the sliding side door was standing open for them.

In the few seconds and half-dozen steps they were under the open sky, Fowler twisted around for a look at the building they had just left, while Wallace tested the view southward, toward the city center. Then they were inside the van, their vision blocked by metal and painted glass.

"I never saw anything like that on a church before," Fowler said as Arens threw the side door closed and the van lurched forward.

"Like what?" Wallace asked.

"On the awning. There was an emblem, a logo, with two eagles standing on a sword. Something in Latin underneath. Looked sort of Nazi-like."

"*Spes mea in deo est*," Arens said. " 'My hope is in God.' You still haven't seen a church with anything like that. Because this isn't a church. It's a Masonic cathedral."

"I thought it was a church the first time I saw it," Wallace said, coming to Fowler's defense. "I was fourteen, maybe thirteen. Anyway, that cornerstone out front—what's the inscription?"

" 'For the glory of the Grand Architect of the Universe,' " Arens recited.

"That's it. Doesn't that sound religious to you?"

"I said it wasn't a church. I didn't say it wasn't religious. Besides, who else but a Freemason would call God the Grand Architect?" Arens asked rhetorically. "My father belongs to a lodge in Richmond. Pretty silly stuff, if you ask me. Worse than the Elks. Mystic ties and lambskin aprons. Though it's great cover for us here. All we had to do is take the Volume of Sacred Law off the altar and get ourselves kicked out of the state and national associations. We're practically shunned. You couldn't have handpicked a more secure gate house."

Fowler said. "We don't have them in Sacramento, I guess. At least not *my* Sacramento."

"You probably do and just never noticed," Wallace said. "They don't advertise."

Smiling bemusedly, Arens glanced forward over the driver's shoulder. "How about a little side trip to Pickett's, cap'n? My refrigerator's empty and I'm gonna have to feed the kids."

"Forget it," the driver said. "I've been playing taxi for the new class all day. I'm not making any side trips I don't have to."

"Prick," Arens said, sitting back in his seat. "In that case, gentlemen, we'll be home in about two minutes."

The fastest way to find furnished housing for seventy-six new agents had proved to be to drop them like uninvited guests on the doorsteps of the station staff and Indianapolis-based field agents. Many of those staffers, including Arens, lived in a twelve-story apartment house just north of where the gentle flowing Fall Creek passed under Meridian Street.

Built in 1947, the structure was a quickie product of the postwar rush to house veterans and their families. But on the way up to Arens' top-floor apartment, Wallace saw that the second-class construction had been given first-class maintenance. The lobby was spartan but clean, the elevator slow but quiet.

The first glimpse inside the apartment reinforced the impression. The architect had not been generous with space, but there was more than enough for a perfectly satisfactory bachelor's haven. Meridian Arms 12-E featured an L-shaped room of ambiguous purpose wrapped around a small kitchen, a bedroom just large enough for the queen-sized bed shoehorned into it, and a south-facing balcony roughly an armsbreath wide.

The air inside was stuffy, with a faint hint of something spoiling. "I've been up in Chicago doing a job for the Guard," Arens explained as he swept through the apartment, opening windows and inspecting end tables for liquifying food. "Either of you going on the road?"

"I will be," Wallace said. Fowler was silent; he had been assigned to the station as an analyst.

"Anyway, it wasn't something I could leave in the middle, which is why I didn't hit the mark on meeting you two. In fact, I'm going to have to make another trip up there in a couple days as it is."

"You go to Chicago from here?" Fowler asked with surprise, joining the hunt for the offending putrefactant.

"Indy is the base for operations as far east as Pittsburgh, as far west as St. Louis, north to Milwaukee, south to Nashville. You're a half-day's drive from about a dozen major cities," Arens said, peeking in the cabinet under the kitchen sink. "Ecch, here's the problem. Forgot to put the garbage out before I left. I've done that more than once."

"Drive?" Wallace asked, stepping back into the living room to let his host pass.

Arens was carrying what looked like a square galvanized metal tub, extracted from beneath the sink. "Sure. No sense setting up substations all over creation when it's so easy to zip around," he said, heading for the hallway. "None of your 40-mile-per-hour interurban trains. The speed governors on most of the highways are set at 75. You drive?" he asked, pausing in the doorway.

"Yes," said Wallace.

"No," said Fowler at the same time.

"You're going to enjoy this alternity," he said to Wallace. "Back in a minute."

Dinner was more like a lunch, improvised from the contents of Arens' refrigerator and cupboards.

"Did the stationmaster—what's his name?" Fowler asked.

"Kelly. Matt Kelly."

"Right. Did Kelly tell you nannies how long you'd be needed?"

"A few weeks, at least. And Kelly promised us it wouldn't be more than two months. I suppose you're smart enough to figure that not everybody was excited about having company."

Fowler clearly hadn't considered the possibility that they were not welcome. "It's not like anyone has a permanent home here," he said defensively.

"Anyplace you live long enough to hang something of your own on the wall feels permanent," Arens said.

"So you don't want us here."

"I'm not excited about it. But I'm not here all that much, either, so I'll cope. And the subsidy bonus they're giving us for our trouble is sweet enough that you two won't be able to eat it all up," Arens said, chewing. "Anyway, housing is tight, even if you've got deep pockets like the Guard does. The city's been growing. It'll take awhile to line up enough of the right kind of space to break up all the triples."

"What's the 'right kind'?" Fowler wanted to know.

Wallace answered for Arens. "I'd guess the stationmaster's got to be careful not to step on toes by giving us better housing than the people who were already stationed here."

"On target," Arens said, looking down the table toward the serving plate. "You catch on pretty quick for a runner. Now, if you value your life, pass that last bratwurst down to me, and don't let me see you so much as sucking air over it."

London, The Home Alternity

It seemed to Robert Taskins that David Somerset did not belong on 10 Downing Street. It was almost a physical thing—the clash between a tall broad-shouldered man and the modestly dimensioned, densely decorated rooms of the Prime Minister's official residence.

But there was a matter of style as well, discord between Somerset's educated working-class sensibilities and Westminster's expectations, a silent war between a man of Stepney and a house of Stuart. Somerset was not the kind of man who could be happy living in a museum, and Taskins entertained a doleful vision of the Prime Minister ordering the William and Mary restorations and Wedgwood china swept out in favor of plasticine couches and paper plates.

Taskins had been brought in through the Old Treasury, ushered down the connecting corridor from the Cabinet offices located there, and shown into a small study where Somerset waited alone.

"Good morning, Ambassador," the Prime Minister said, raising his eyes from the papers on his lap. "Thank you for coming. This shouldn't take long."

A winged settee was close at hand, and Taskins settled himself on its floral uphostery. "I'm happy to oblige. Though a bit more notice would be of value to me in the future, Mr. Somerset," Taskins said. "I was forced to cancel a staff meeting and a personal appointment to be here at this time."

"I apologize for any inconvenience," Somerset said. "I'm afraid I'm inclined to trample convention when the matter seems important enough. You recall that I promised you that I would have more to say about an expansion of the Weasel rocket program?"

"I do."

"I've been giving this business a great deal of thought," Somerset said. "I believe I can offer you an accommodation which will allow you to more than double the number of weapons sited here while reducing the risk of exposure. After I've explained it to you, I want you to communicate it to President Robinson."

Taskins sat back in the settee, quietly bristling at the man's arrogance. *After you've explained it to me—do you see me as nothing more than a messenger, one of those pink-tailcoated fools wandered over from the Bank of England? Is it impossible to think that you might rather discuss it with me?*

But long years as a diplomat kept any trace of these thoughts from his voice and expression. "By all means," he said. "Please tell me what you propose."

Somerset hauled himself up from his chair and spread a four-leaved map across the flat lid of a massive chest, hiding its splendid walnut marquetry. "BP—British Petroleum—has eleven inactive drilling platforms in the North Sea. Here, and here, and here—you see the marks."

"Inactive—what exactly does that mean in this context? Abandoned?"

Somerset shook his head vigorously. "The platforms are unmanned and, I understand, stripped of much of their drilling gear, but quite sound. It's uneconomic to be at full production just now, what with the export market being monopolized by Saudi oil, and these were the least productive of BP's assets."

"And what have these mothballed oil wells to do with missiles?"

"I would have thought you could guess. I'm prepared to allow you to place two of the launchers on each platform. That would be the ten you have here, and a dozen more. I'm sure you agree that the isolation will provide much better security than trundling them along our public roads, where a traffic accident or a curious thief could unmask the disguise at any time."

Taskins was not at all sure that he agreed, or that Madison, O'Neill & Co. would, either. "It's certainly worth considering," he said, rising from the settee, "and I'm sure that President Robinson will give it his close attention. May I take that map?"

"I had it prepared for just that reason," Somerset said. "It's innocent enough in itself. Please see that the less innocent explanations aren't committed to paper."

"Perhaps you'd prefer to talk directly to the President," Taskins suggested. "I'm certain a secure line could be arranged—or even a state visit."

"No," Somerset said with an understated finality. "It's not yet time for that."

Indianapolis, Alternity Blue

Wallace stood alone on the twelfth-floor balcony of his new home and looked south at the heart of the city. As far as he could tell it was little different from the city he remembered: a few more tall buildings, Meridian Street six lanes instead of four.

He could see the square spire of the cathedral gate house, thought he could make out the slender column of the War Memorial. That had been one of the first field trips he had taken with the Youth Defense Reserve: to Indianapolis to see the Soldiers and Sailors Monument and climb the stairs to the eyrie at the two-hundred foot level.

"Here you are," Arens said from behind, joining him. "I thought you'd disappeared."

"Just sightseeing."

"How's it look?"

"Can't really tell from here," Wallace said.

"I'll tell you what you can't see. A city with no green spaces, no character, and only about eleven women worth chasing. Look—see those grain elevators?" he said, pointing at a file of white concrete columns standing just apart from the city center. "That's three blocks from the state Capitol. The governor can see grain elevators out his office window, can you believe it?"

"So where are you from, Arens?"

"Manhattan. New York City. The best."

"I've never been there."

"Then you probably think this is pretty exciting," Arens said with a friendly grin. "Anyway, I'm going out. This apartment isn't the only thing I've been away from for five days, you know?"

Wallace turned back to the railing. "Okay."

"Problem?"

"Just wishing I could go downtown."

Arens shrugged. "Go."

"What?"

"Just avoid Meridian Street. You're new enough here that most of our people don't know you."

"I thought we were supposed to stay put until our orientation was over."

"You are. But you don't have to."

"Come again?"

Arens flashed a lopsided grin. "First lesson, Wallace. The stationmaster sets down a lot of rules, yeah. But out in the field, we've got our own rules. And the main one is that if you do your job right, the rest is nobody's business but your own."

"But—"

"See, outside the cloister, there's nobody to police us but ourselves. I'll play nanny to the ones that need it, like Fowler in there. But I didn't volunteer to play warden to anybody. So go downtown if that's what you want."

"What about Gary?"

"You want to take him with you?"

"Not really."

"Is he a right guy?"

"I don't know," Wallace said. "I don't know him well enough."

"Then you and I'll leave together. Let him think I'm riding herd on you."

Wallace looked hard at the youth. "You're not setting me up, are you? A little game of let's-burn-the-new-boy?"

"You've got your 'us' and 'them' all confused," Arens said, crossing his arms. "Look, what'd they tell you about fraternizing with locals?"

"Uh—permitted only in the course of official duties. We're supposed to socialize with other people from the station."

"Absolutely right. Except I'm on my way to pin a local girl to her mattress, and if I'm lucky this is going to be the time I catch her fertile as black earth."

"You want—"

"Damn straight I do. So relax. You've got an even bigger secret to tell on me than I have to tell on you. Go downtown and wallow in that homecoming spirit." He winked as he backed away into the apartment. "Just try not to kill any badges while you're out, all right?"

A smile came slowly to Wallace's lips. "You've got it," he said. "Happy fucking."

"That's the best kind."

The city was in fact little different from what he remembered, but Wallace saw it differently now.

He was no longer a wide-eyed fourteen-year-old. He knew a Boston, a Philadelphia, a London. He had a scale of reference against which to measure what had once been the only sizable city in his experience.

And that scale told him that Arens was largely right. He saw Indianapolis now as a generic Tinker-toy scale-model-railroad kind of city, containing all the requisite parts of a metropolis but with the soul of an overgrown small town. Modestly overgrown, at that. It was a ten-minute walk from the White River on the west to the Pennsylvania Railroad tracks on the east, a distance which spanned the entire mercantile, banking, and government complex.

The wide streets were barren of trees, the brick and cinderblock buildings squat and functional, the few modern towers over twenty stories bland and interchangeable. What style and grace Wallace could find was contained in a very few structures: the ornately facaded Publix Theatre, the castlelike Union Station, a copper-spired Catholic church, a turn-of-the-century tobacconist's shop.

But still, it was comforting to be there, walking the almost deserted streets, marking the absence or presence of childhood landmarks. It was not home, but it was familiar, more familiar than foreign.

The six-story Federal Rail warehouse on South Street where his brother had worked was still there, though the sign now said OGIHARA FARM DISTRIBUTORS and the water tower which once sat on its roof was gone. He wandered north of Monument Circle to look on the sprawling Ionic-columned court house, which had so impressed a young Rayne Wallace with its size and classical solidity. It was unchanged and still impressive.

Wallace saved for last a long detour west toward the river and a more personal landmark. He had undergone the first round of competitive screening for the Guard at Oscar C. McCulloch School (No. 5), a grammar school twice the size of the twelve-section consolidated in Hagerstown. He remembered the day and the school vividly, down to the blue and white hemispherical maps of the world which flanked the front entrance.

But No. 5 was a memory only. The site where it had stood was part of the parking lot for a cluster of low-rise apartments under construction. Wallace absorbed that fact with an uncomfortable sense of reality having been violated, and backed away almost superstitiously, retreating mentally and physically to safer havens. As night came to the city skies, he hurried back along quiet side streets to Arens' apartment.

His curiosity had been blunted for the moment, and yet there was a question which nagged at him. *What would my life have been like here,* he wondered. It was a thought the form of which was unfamiliar. Neither Red Philadelphia nor Yellow London had ever stirred such a reflection. He was clearly not of those places.

But this was different. He both belonged, and did not belong. It was home, and not-home. And the conflict between the two brought questions for which he had no answers. "What would my life have been like here?" It was a question which invited him to regret realities which he had accepted, decisions and turnings and events past and better forgotten.

And by the time he returned to the apartment, those thoughts had unsettled him enough that he regretted having left it in the first place.

Port of Indiana, The Home Alternity

There was a stiff breeze coming off the lake, driving small wavelets to slap against the steel hull of the deep-water freighter tied up at Dock 11. She flew the Canadian flag from her stern, and her bow bore the name *Belle Isle.*

Except for those distinguishing marks, she might have been any of a score of nearly identical ships plying the Great Lakes waters. The size of the seaway locks between the lake ports and the Gulf of St. Lawrence had dictated their lines and dimensions, eight hundred feet long and drawing thirty feet of water fully loaded.

Most of *Belle Isle*'s cargo for this voyage was already stowed

137

away belowdecks: refrigerated containers packed with frozen sides of Kansas beef, great rolls of newsprint from Minnesota mills, tanklike shipping casks of agricultural fertilizer.

But the final item on the manifest had been late arriving and was not yet loaded. Six gleaming new candy-red diesel tractors stood lined up on skids on the quay, temporarily separated from their sixty-foot trailers. All six tractors bore the International Harvester logo on their grilles and the Navigator 5000 nameplate on the side of their engine compartments.

By contrast, the silver-white trailers, one of which was at that moment waiting for the bare hook of the tower crane, bore no identifying marks at all. But each was already destined to acquire local coloration soon after their arrival at Glasgow—the royal blue and white of Hampton Transport, the crest and arms of Imperial Tea, and so forth.

The man who called himself Kendrew watched the loading process from the *Belle Isle*'s bridge, high on the sheer face of the aft superstructure. His presence was questioned by neither captain nor bridge crew. The captain, who also held that rank in the Canadian naval reserve, had received his instructions directly from Ottawa. The crew had been told that the harbormaster had asked them to accommodate a "manufacturer's representative" and needed to know no more.

Kendrew waited patiently until the last of the tractors had been lowered into its nesting place amidships. Then as the great loading doors began to close, he left the bridge and went down into the hold to see that they had been satisfactorily secured.

To his pleasure, they had—the loadmaster, like the crane operator, was a member of the Company. Both had been warned that the trailers were more than five times as heavy as their declared weight on the bill of lading and had made the proper allowances.

Walking the deck as the preparations to sail proceeded, the captain met Kendrew at the gangway. "Everything all right?"

"Everything's all right."

"Then see you on the other side of the puddle, eh?"

Kendrew shook his head. "Someone else will take delivery."

"I understand."

By the time Kendrew reached the harbormaster's offices, the lines holding the freighter had been cast off and coiled, and her deep-thrumming engines were edging her away from the dock. On seeing Kendrew, the harbormaster excused himself from his own office, leaving and closing the door behind him.

Kendrew picked up the phone and dialed a number which

appeared in no published directory. When he heard an electronic squeal from the other end, he recited a six-number sequence. A second squeal told him the code and the call had been accepted.

His message was brief. "Mama's bitch has whelped another litter of pups," he said. "Please tell Pa." Then he hung up and moved to the harbormaster's window, allowing himself to linger until the *Belle Isle* passed through the gap in the port's stone breakwater, beginning its two thousand mile journey to the sea.

But Kendrew could not linger too long, for he had a journey of his own to make. Unexpectedly, the reason still unexplained, Madison wanted him in Washington. So for the first time in nearly a year, he was going home.

Indianapolis, Alternity Blue

Wallace found Fowler playing solitaire on the dining room table. "Where's Arens?" the analyst asked, looking up from his game as Wallace entered.

"Still out. He dropped me off."

"Which means we're stuck here."

"I guess."

"They're treating us like prisoners, you know? I didn't think it'd be like this. Blacked-out vans. Everything off-limits except your residence and the gate house. No travel without your monitor. They brought us here to do a job. Why don't they trust us?"

"It'll loosen up."

"It'd better," Fowler said, gathering up his cards. "This guy they've stuck us with—what do you think of him?"

"A little sure of himself, maybe, but all right."

"I don't like his attitude," Fowler griped. "He doesn't take what he's about seriously."

"Maybe he just doesn't take us very seriously."

"He's supposed to be helping us. But here it is, our first night here, and where is he?"

"Working, I guess." *Parting the petals, actually*—

"Is being a field agent a twenty-four-hour job?"

"You do things when they can be done," Wallace said with a shrug. "Did you expect a guided tour of the city?"

"I expected him to put us in the picture."

"Local orientation starts tomorrow down at the cathedral."

"I know that. But with the way they've treated us so far, do you really think they're going to tell us everything?"

Wallace flopped his body into the well-worn club chair near the balcony. "Maybe not."

With a surprisingly agile flourish, Fowler fanned the cards, stacked and cut them one-handed, then set the deck neatly on the table. "Keep a secret?"

Wallace smiled. "I think I can manage."

"While you two were gone, I poked around a little here."

"Not very polite."

"I'm just trying to figure out what they're hiding from us."

"Did you?"

"I found some interesting things. Like last week's television program guide. Did you know that there are fifteen different channels here?"

"I've seen places that have more."

"Not at home."

"No. Not there."

"And a lot of them run through the night. Movies. Music. Sports. And lots of things you never see back home. There's one channel called *Worldview*. Nothing but travelogues—Qatar, the Amazon, and some countries I never heard of. Even one about Azerbaidzhan. That's part of Red Russia. And there's another channel called *Body and Soul* that had a show about anal sex. About how to do it, can you believe that?"

"Too bad there's no TV to go with the guide."

"Oh, but there is—in the bottom drawer of his dresser. I'd have plugged it in, except I didn't know how long you'd be gone, and I didn't want to get caught."

"A television that fits in a drawer? That I have to see," Wallace said, struggling up out of the chair. "Arens will be gone for a while. Show me."

Boston, The Home Alternity

Outside Albert Tackett's windows, the city was a thousand yellow and white stars scattered across a black carpet.

Inside, the chair behind the paper-laden desk stood empty, and the lights over the desk were dark. A few steps away, Tackett and Monaghan occupied opposite ends of a burgundy leather sofa. In Tackett's hand was an oversized mug of coffee, spiked with a generous dollop of Golden Harvest from the bottle in the dry sink. In Monaghan's lap was a clipboard.

"Okay. I'm ready now," Tackett said, sipping. "How bad was it? From what drifted up here, it sounds like the idea of making this into an Alpha simulation wasn't one of my best.''

Monaghan shook his head. "On the contrary, our experience today shows just how badly we needed the practice. We learned a lot about how to handle matters at both ends. We'll be much better prepared if we have to do it for real.''

"Everything back to normal downstairs?''

"We resumed regular operations at 3:20.''

"Against a one o'clock target. Which means the whole operation ran more than two hours over.''

"That's extremely fixable. It was all execution, nothing structural. We were all doing it for the first time.''

"Good. Because that's two hours we can't count on having. How long did the actual move take?''

Monaghan consulted the papers pinned to the clipboard. "Two hours forty-six minutes to move seventy-six people.''

A long sigh escaped Tackett's lips. "Too slow. Alpha List has ballooned to more than a hundred sixty people. We'll still be checking the Ks through when the missiles hit.''

"We can tighten that up a bit, Albert. Toward the end we were clocking about three minutes between transits.''

"We're still going to have to move a lot of them through preemptively. We can't wait for the red ball.''

"No. If only the damned gate would stay open long enough to get three through at once,'' Monaghan said.

"If only Willie's knob-and-switch boys could cook up something to keep it from closing at all,'' Tackett said, referring to the head of the Research Division. He savored a draught of his adulterated brew. "Any feedback from the other side yet?''

"The good news is that everybody came through. But they had some problems, too. Even with the notice, they were man-power short. And they really need to lock up more housing. Even if it's just a big room to throw them all in.''

"I've been promised a two-M supplemental of Blue currency by the end of the month,'' Tackett said. "That ought to be enough for them to put the wheels in motion.''

"Kelly will be glad to see it, that's for certain. Anyway, he'll make adjustments, we'll make adjustments. Like I said, it was a learning experience. The important thing is that the gate handled the traffic without locking up on us. There was only one focus shift at their end, and none at ours.''

Tackett yawned. "Willie can sleep easy tonight.''

"He'll find something else to worry about.''

"Probably,'' Tackett said, another yawn fighting through. "I have to go to Washington next week. Am I going to be able to tell the President that we've got a productive team in place? Or just bodies?''

''I'd stick to bodies,'' Monaghan said with a twisted smile. ''You promised me sixty days, remember?''

''I'm not changing speeds on you,'' Tackett said, setting the mug aside and rising from the sofa. ''I just know he's going to ask. Can you give me an interim report, oh, midday Tuesday before I leave?''

Monaghan joined Tackett standing. ''Will do. By then Kelly will have had a chance to look over what we sent him.''

Nodding, Tackett clapped a hand on Monaghan's shoulder as he passed by en route to the door. ''Good enough. Call it a day, Bret. Let's go home.''

THE JEWELED DAGGER

A film by Stanley Kubrick
Based on the book by Jessame Frank
Reviewed by Richard Barthold

Sixteen years later, "July 3, 1961" and "Norfolk" remain referents which require no explanation, even to those born after the fact. Sixteen years later, the horror is barely diminished, the memories undiluted by time.

One minute, the cluster of communities at the confluence of the James River and Chesapeake Bay were quietly riding out the afternoon rain that was dampening holiday plans. The next minute, 31,000 lay dying, murdered when self-proclaimed peace activists, caught inside the Norfolk naval base, triggered the 20-kiloton warhead they had hoped to "confiscate."

Like Lincoln's assassination and the Japanese attack on Pearl Harbor, Norfolk stands as the signal event of its time, the dividing line between past and future. Norfolk worked irrevocable change on both the nation and the world, and shock waves from the explosion are still rippling through both individual lives and global politics.

The dimensions of the drama have defeated four previous efforts to capture it on film, frustrating directors as able as Herschel Tague (*7-3-61*) and as facile as Byron James (*Rendezvous: Norfolk*). In this, his first film in four years, director Stanley Kubrick has rendered all past and future attempts irrelevant, delivering a cinematic triumph which is at turns brilliant, infuriating, empathic, and prophetic.

As always, Mr. Kubrick takes chances. Unlike in *Algonquin*, the director's labored study of the American muse, *The Jeweled Dagger* profits from all of them. Brilliantly intercutting between the hour after the explosion and the weeks before it, Mr. Kubrick weaves a multibraided story which begins at the end and ends at the beginning. Casting against type, Mr. Kubrick extracts a career-rescuing performance from June
[continued on page C6, col. 2]

[See DAGGER, page C4]
Haver in her startlingly intense portrayal of Earth First organizer Diana Harris.

There is a temptation to enumerate the liberties Mr. Kubrick takes with both Mrs. Frank's narrative and the official record. But Mr. Kubrick's success comes in large part from his ability to see beyond pedestrian details in the pursuit of the essence. The result is a story somehow more compelling than mere truth.

Left untouched and presented with devastating irony is Mrs. Frank's controversial thesis that the Norfolk disaster was not something Harris and her co-conspirators did to us, but something they did for us. There can be no question that the anguish of Norfolk changed attitudes about nuclear weapons worldwide, effectively aborting the arms race and fueling the drive toward internationalism. But can Harris be credited with foreseeing that outcome, and thereby judged a martyr rather than a villain?

Deftly, Mr. Kubrick eschews both sentimentality and propaganda in favor of a Platonic dialogue with the viewer. The contrast between a vast military mindlessly creating weapons it did not want to see used and a small band of idealists purposefully using a weapon they did not want to see created has never been more powerfully presented that in *The Jeweled Dagger*'s closing minutes.

There are a hundred images contained in the film's 142 minutes which vibrate with raw power or reckless pathos. Many are contained in the film's most daring sequence, the seemingly endless parade of faces of Norfolk victims which opens the film. Invading their privacy, the camera shows them crushed, bloody, burned, and yet tranquil in death.

We do not know them, the soundtrack offers only sounds of a sort that can be heard in a dying fire, and yet Mr. Kubrick manages to make us cry for their loss. By the end of the film, when Mr. Kubrick offers the nuclear fireball as a cleansing flame, a crucible for change, it is possible to see those deaths in a different light. It is a stunning reversal, and the capstone of a landmark film which promises to stand as a signal event in its own right. Bravo, Mr. Kubrick. Bravo.

CHAPTER 10

Uncertified Thoughts

Indianapolis, Alternity Blue

It took nine days to get the new class on the streets.

The first five days were consumed by orientation sessions at the satellite station house on South Shelby Street. Wallace faced slanguage drill, law and custom work, and a heavy dose of Kelly's house rules for moles. In the technology lab, better known as the toy shop, he was introduced to coinless phones, filmless cameras, and a tabletop photofax machine which seemed like nothing less than magic in a box.

A few hours were spent in hurried cover construction; he kept his runner name, Ray Wallach, but changed his vocation to commercial safety inspector to conform to the cell to which he had been assigned. Wallace decided to be single (to support the living arrangements), a graduate of Indiana Technical College (one of three institutions where the Guard had an agent who could intercept any inquiries), and a native of Chicago (his real hometown being too nearby and thereby too dangerous to claim).

There was even homework: reading the three Indianapolis newspapers in search of puzzling references. Most of them were in the ads, like the employment classified seeking a "chromatic designer" or the house-for-sale listing promising "green-walling, full interlink, and speed bath."

Throughout the orientation, Wallace felt rushed. It was too much too fast, but at the same time rudimentary—too little for what they were going to be asked to do. Someone was in an awful hurry.

There followed three days of supervised exercises, privately dubbed the dog-and-pony show by the harried agents. Driving a car that ran on a tank of liquid fuel instead of a phased-capacitance battery. Buying food with a transfer card. Shopping without gaping at the plenty like a tourist from India.

The exercises progressed to errand-running, all of which felt manufactured. Did anyone really need flowers delivered to Crown Hill Cemetery? Or photographs of the mayor of Augusta? Or a land survey on a Lynhurst home?

By the morning of the ninth day, Wallace was reading the message clearly. Fowler was right—the stationmaster did not trust the new class, and he was not the only one. There was deep skepticism on the part of the entire Blue team about the quality of agent they had been sent, a suspicion that the newcomers had not been properly vetted.

A suspicion, Wallace had to concede, which was not without foundation. By the ninth day, three prospective moles had already been demoted to the analysts' tank where Fowler and the rest of the newcomers were laboring. And there were several others that Wallace would have recommended without hesitation for the same fate.

Of the three miscreants, one had managed to get a station car stolen by letting it run dry on an errand to Trader's Point and then leaving the keys in the ignition when he went for help. Another had upbraided a local for wearing an American flag patch on his shirt, precipitating a fight that left the mole bloodied and confused. The last, showing true cultural tunnel vision, tried to bribe a city hall clerk to get copies of a public court proceeding.

That morning, the stationmaster himself had come to the satellite station to talk to them. Matt Kelly was a compact, stiff-necked man, older by ten years than anyone else on the staff, a telltale sign that his Blue counterpart was dead. A neatly clipped black beard and large oval glasses minimized the impact of piercing black eyes.

"The Section needs backgrounders on a large number of locals," he told them while an aide passed out small manila envelopes. "I expect each of you to contribute to this work. What we know about your particular subject is in your assignment packet. Track them down and assemble a profile."

For the span of ten seconds, the only sound in the room was of tearing paper. Inside Wallace's envelope was a stiff white card on which was typed:

Barbara J. Haggerty, birthplace St. Francis Hospital, Beech Grove, Indiana, March 2, 1946, no LNA.

Wallace's thoughts raced. Beech Grove was one of the dozens of little villages in danger of being enveloped by a growing Indianapolis. So this was local work. The kind of work that was easiest to get done. Which meant that if they really cared about Barbara Haggerty, someone would have looked her up long ago.

"How much do you want to know?" one innocent asked.

"Everything," Kelly said with withering curtness.

The assignment was a rehearsal for the real thing, a final exam, Wallace realized. Blue Section would never see the reports.

"When do you want it?"

Kelly's tone was chilly. "Yesterday."

Which meant that Haggerty was almost certainly still somewhere in the metropolitan area. Probably alive. Certainly findable. It was a test, not a wild-goose chase.

"In case those answers confused you, I'll spell it out," Kelly was saying. "The perfect report has everything in it that the requestor wants to know, and it's ready the moment he wants to know it. Which means there are no perfect reports. But at least you have something to shoot for."

Wallace looked down at the card again. A tough draw. Women were usually harder to track than men. With a man you could work both forward from the past and backward from the present. But marriage made a woman vanish, her identity submerged in her husband's name. And Haggerty was the right age and era to be married by now.

"Each of you should draw a standard expense advance from the burser before you leave here," Kelly said. "And see the transportation manager if you need a vehicle. But make sure you need a vehicle before you ask for it. Janet guards her budget like a mama lion guards a cub. Questions?"

No questions, Wallace thought. He had been hoping for a chance to show himself the equal of the "regulars," as the station's veterans had begun to refer to themselves. Barbara Haggerty was that chance. *No questions. Just get out of my way and let me to it.*

Washington, The Home Alternity

"My first impression is that it's a bad deal, at least from our end," Gregory O'Neill said. "I would think we'd want to try to make sure that at least those ten stay on British soil. Strategically, it makes no difference whatsoever. But there's some important symbolism there about commitment, about going to the wall if the need arises.''

Peter Robinson nodded, unsurprised. ''That's how I see it, too. The question that concerns me is why Somerset made the offer.''

''It sounds like he's getting nervous, afflicted with a touch of NIMBY syndrome. Or someone in his Cabinet is nervous and managing to make his concerns heard.''

''Bob Taskins' opinion is that very few people in the British government are wise to the Weasels,'' Robinson said.

''There's Home Secretary Caulton. According to Bob's initial report, Caulton didn't exactly leap to embrace the news that the missiles were there. And from their side, the case for relocating the launchers is easy to make. Somerset warned us that if they were discovered, he'd disavow any knowledge.''

''Having them in such an out-of-the way place strengthens that claim.''

''It does.'' O'Neill paused. ''There is something else, though. I didn't see it at first.''

''Which is?''

''My first thought—my very first thought—was something on the order of, 'that s.o.b. wants to have it both ways: He wants our missiles there for show, but he won't risk making the islands a Soviet target.' ''

''Like asking for a watchdog for your house and then keeping it in a storage shed because of the mess.''

''Exactly. Which made me wonder about his commitment, whether he'd ever be willing to see the missiles used. But now it occurs to me I may have had it backward.''

''How so, Gregory?''

''It could be a sign that he *is* committed to the program, that he's thinking ahead to the domestic end of going public. Britain has been nuclear-free for a long time, since we closed our last base there in sixty-six. Having the Weasels off-shore might provide the necessary psychological distance for Parliament to accept them. In any event, Somerset might well think it necessary.''

''Maybe I should talk to Mr. Somerset directly and get this cleared up.''

''That might be wise,'' O'Neill said. ''But even if that is what's on his mind, I still think it's a bad deal for us. Because if we move the launchers to these BP oil platforms, they're not mobile anymore. Once the announcement is made and everyone—including the Soviets—knows where the missiles are, we lose a major strategic advantage.''

"While gaining a lot more firepower. Tough tradeoff."

"True." O'Neill doodled idly on his notepad. "Perhaps Somerset might consider having a few eggs in each basket," he said finally. "He can announce the fixed launchers publicly, and let Moscow know about the others privately. Best of both worlds."

"Interesting. You'll run it past the strategy folks in the Pentagon?"

"I'm going back there directly. I'll take it up with the British action team. Maybe we should bring State in. too."

"I'll worry about that," Robinson said. "Thank you, Gregory. I'll let you go back to whatever it was I stole you from."

"Budget meetings."

"Ah—I did you a favor, then. Oh, and Gregory? I'd like you to come up to Camp David this weekend. Madison has been bugging me to look at some initiatives, and I thought I might as well hear from you and E.C. at the same time. Be ready, will you?"

Indianapolis, Alternity Blue

Profile-building was a game of biographical hide-and-seek, and Wallace had learned how to play before leaving Home. There were a hundred ways to get to a subject. He could play the old friend, the credit investigator, the lawyer seeking an heir. Neighbors talked. Relatives thought they were helping.

The hospital's record of birth gave him a starting point: a yellow frame house on First Avenue, its backyard butting up against a railroad marshaling yard. The Haggertys had long ago left that address, but the elderly woman raking leaves in front of the house next door remembered Barbara had attended Butler University.

Three more links—the Alumni association, another helpful neighbor, and (armed with the new surname) a phone directory—brought him to the duplex Barbara Barrett, nee Haggerty, and her husband called home. That part had taken barely six hours.

The street was quiet, and Wallace was tempted to enter the house. It was the most direct, most efficient source possible, the shortest line between two points. But in midafternoon, with the Barrett family's patterns completely unknown, the risk of being caught was too great.

As though in compensation, the contents of the Barrett mailbox offered several leads, among them a gynecologist's name and address from a bill, and a copy of *Instructor* magazine bearing Barbara's name.

Twenty minutes in a phone booth playing the "May I speak to . . . oh, I must have the wrong number" game produced the name of the intermediate school where his quarry was employed. He went there directly and posed as the parent of a student who would be transferring in. That almost got him in trouble: He had to field questions about his "daughter's" education voucher and other matters on which he was ignorant.

But it also got him not only inside the school, but inside the principal's office, where a lockless file drawer was plainly marked STAFF. He made no move then to riffle it, even when the principal was called out for a moment. It was an older school, minimally secure and isolated in a parklike campus. He would come back.

Midnight found him hiding in the campus's natural area, timing the police patrols. He went in just after 3:00 A.M., hoping he had not overlooked an alarm system.

Haggerty's file was a biographical treasure trove: a personal data sheet, an application for maternity leave at the end of the spring quarter, even her supervisor's annotated evaluations. Wallace used the office's own photofax to copy the documents, and was out in less than fifteen minutes.

"Go where you must, only leave no trail." Wallace had been faithful to the injunction. He had been quiet and quick. The only trace he left was a broken window in the back, something which would be lost in the white noise of random school vandalism.

He read through the file in the morning, his short night abbreviated further by the early rising of his roommates. As he read, Barbara Haggerty slowly became a person. Little by little, she acquired a history. And before long, she would acquire a face.

Wallace had devoted the morning to pursuing some of the many leads offered in the file. The time was profitably spent; he had enough to stop any time. But it was important to see her, to allow her to spring up from the flat, cold file into three-dimensional reality. One glimpse could likely tell him a hundred things he did not yet know.

And so he waited, invisible among the parents, older siblings and contract buses filling the pickup lanes outside the school's main entrance. The building emptied at four, a tidal wave of humanity dispersing itself with remarkable efficiency among the idling vehicles. The staff began to trickle out by ones and twos a short time later. Wallace had suspected they would not linger long on a Friday.

Finally his quarry appeared at the doors, her arms wrapped

around a small stack of books. Even harried and fatigued, she was more attractive than in her resume photo, a halo of soft curls around a dark-eyed oval face, slim legs flashing below the knee-length skirt of her instructor's uniform. For a moment he was tempted to approach her. "Mrs. Bennett, I'm John's father. I wanted to ask you how he's doing—"

Wallace quickly thought better of the idea. He hardly looked old enough to be the father of a fifth grader, much less an eighth grader. "Mrs. Bennett, you probably don't remember me, I was in your class in 1967—" No, that was chancy too. She would be that one teacher who remembered everybody.

He was feeling something he had been warned about by instructors on both sides of the gate—the heady sense of somehow having power over this stranger by what he knew about her. It was as though he were gloating over the one-sided intimacy. *Nah, nah, I have a secret. . . .* The impulse was personal, not professional. And recognizing that helped him to suppress it.

Wallace watched her cross the pavement to her pale blue squareback sedan and deposit her books onto the passenger seat. There was no outward evidence of her pregnancy yet, no telltale roundness that jarred with the rest of her build. Unburdened, she paused for a moment to scan the cloud-studded sky, or perhaps just to enjoy being through for the day.

Impressions cascaded down on him. Hard-working. Hard, too, he guessed. Even though he could see her sitting on the edge of her desk, telling a funny story. Velvet and steel. Unequivocal lines. Her kids liked her, but probably best when they no longer had to answer to her.

Before long, Haggerty roused herself, circled the squareback to the driver's side, and climbed in. A moment later the car was gliding toward where Wallace was parked. He sat calmly watching. As she drove past, she became aware of his eyes on her and raised a hand from the steering wheel to wave to him uncertainly.

He smiled back and reached for his pencil. "Good-bye, Barbara Haggerty," he said aloud, and bowed his head as he started to write.

And when he was done, he drove south, out of the city and into the farmland of Johnson County. He could not bring himself to surrender the car without savoring the pure flying joy of it, power in his hands and the freedom of an open road. It was a senseless, exhilarating self-indulgence, and he reveled in it for more than an hour before duty could call him home.

Peter Robinson hooked his folded hands behind his neck, strained the muscles of his arms and neck against each other, and yawned, an eye-squeezing, jaw-stretching yawn which he made no effort whatsoever to conceal from the others in the room.

It had already been a long meeting, and he had yet to hear from those whose thoughts most interested him. The Secretary of State had insisted on prefacing his proposals with a long-winded explication of his view of current geopolitics and then on spelling out those proposals in painful detail.

Robinson listened patiently to the Secretary natter on for several more sentences about a trilateral pact for the defense of Singapore, then wedged an interruption into a minute pause. "E.C., is this a good place to stop?"

Surprised, the Secretary looked down at his notes. "I have very little more to cover."

Robinson hooked his folded hands over his knee. "Then why don't you go ahead and take a moment to sum up for us, and then we'll all take a break."

The man's anxious eyes showed that he knew he was being cut off. "The key thing to remember is that Malaya is the key to the entire Indonesian archipelago," he said, stiffening in his chair. "By concluding a pact with Singapore, we can make a firm statement without intruding on an issue already joined."

"Seems to me like drawing a line in the sand while the bully is already busy beating up your best friend," the CIA director remarked, *sotto voce*.

The Secretary of State's eyes blazed. "And by funneling arms and assistance through the Australians, we can have an impact on the fighting already underway," he said sharply. "I have every reason to think that Singapore would respond positively to an approach, and the Australians have already expressed interest in acquiring our jungle combat capability—counterinsurgency aircraft and narrow-track armor particularly. I do think this deserves the strongest possible consideration."

You're just not in tune with what I want, E.C., Robinson thought. *Just look at you, starched collar and tie on a flannel-shirt day.* He nodded absently. "Thank you, E.C. Everyone, let's stretch 'em."

"Getting a bit chilly in here," William Rodman said as he rose. "Maybe we could get somebody to come build a fire while we're out draining the dragon?"

"Not with this kind of material scattered around in here,"

Dennis Madison said sharply. "Unless you've got a blind houseboy with A1 clearance."

"The Secret Service—" the Secretary of State began.

"Hell, an old farm blood like me doesn't need hired help to build a fire," Robinson said with a boyish grin. "Contrary to what the Democrats say, I'm not mentally handicapped."

Rodman smiled broadly, and the others laughed. "I'll give a hand," Gregory O'Neill offered.

Eyeing the empty wood box, Robinson said, "Make it two hands, and you can lug a couple three-inch logs in from the porch."

"Done."

Ten minutes later, the fire was crackling briskly, the coffee and doughnuts had been refreshed, and the five had settled back into their chairs.

"Gregory, I'd like to hear from you now," Robinson said. "What do you have to offer up for consideration?"

O'Neill looked into Robinson's eyes with a steady gaze. "I have no new initiatives to propose."

Cocking an eyebrow, Robinson said, "I was hoping for some new thinking about our territorial waters, at the very least."

"There's been no change in our capability. So I can't in conscience propose a change in our posture."

There was suddenly tension in the room, and Robinson was content to let it build. With almost exaggerated slowness, he leaned forward and retrieved a white-frosted French cruller from the tray. "Well, I can't understand that," he said between bites. "Did you read the Friday papers?"

"If you're referring to the Norwegian incident—"

"I am. The Norwegian Navy depth-charged a suspected submarine contact in Trondheim Fjord. The fucking Norwegian Navy, Gregory. They've got nothing bigger than a DE in their whole kid's-toy fleet and they're not afraid to stuff one down the sail of a Red sub."

"If that's what it was," O'Neill said. "There was no sighting, before or after. It was a sonar contact. No screw noises. No oil slick. Not even the head of the Trondheim Fjord monster bobbing to the surface."

Grins and nervous chuckles blossomed, infuriating Robinson.

"I could arrange for one of our ships to hammer a gas bubble or a shipwreck, too," O'Neill went on. "It'd make spectacular copy for the FNS, I agree. But the Soviet naval command will just laugh."

Robinson had heard enough. "I'm not talking about a goddamn public relations stunt," he snapped. "I'm talking about the fact that the Norwegians have got the gumption to draw a line and make it stick. They don't stand for any nonsense inside their twelve-mile limit. Is it just that their captains have bigger balls than ours do? Or is there some other problem—like rules of engagement that've handcuffed our people so long that they aren't worth a damn?"

"Norway is small enough that the Soviet Union can afford to ignore them," O'Neill said in the same even tone. "A flea on a St. Bernard. They wouldn't be as tolerant of us."

"Is that so? Let me tell you how I see it. I think they do it because we let them get away with it. Rockefeller created this problem all by himself the first time he settled for a polite note of protest instead of a nitronyl calling card. How the hell are we ever going to get back to a blue-water strategy, Gregory? Tell me that."

"That Norwegian business caught my eye, too," Madison said, joining the fray. "I'd sure like to see us take a more aggressive approach to coastal defense. Give our skippers the authority to fire on contact. Hell, let them go hunting. And then pin a medal on the first one to come back with his launchers empty. That'll turn things around."

"May I point out that their subs are faster than our destroyer escorts?" O'Neill said. "They can just run away from us. They do it all the time."

"They can't run from a patrol plane, can they?" the CIA director shot back.

"Or from the Javelins," Robinson said quietly.

O'Neill was not dissuaded. "If we go out there head-hunting, we're going to buy a pack of trouble," he warned.

"Which is why I would suggest that this new policy—if adopted—be announced in advance to the United Nations Maritime Commission," Clifton said. "Worded properly, of course, so that it doesn't sound as though we're accusing anyone of anything. Hazard to shipping and that sort of thing. Kondratyeva will have an opportunity to avoid an incident, and we'll be on firmer ground if there are any."

O'Neill looked to Robinson, his expression a mixture of disgust and frustration. "Sir, the cold fact is, it doesn't make a whit of difference strategically whether their subs are sitting two miles offshore or twenty."

"Perhaps not. But it matters, all the same," Robinson said. "Besides, if you're right, don't you think the Reds will loudly deny everything and quietly pull back into international waters?"

"We can't count on that."

"I think we can," Robinson said firmly. "And I think there is plenty of support for that view in this room."

Scanning the faces of the others, O'Neill found unwelcome confirmation of that. "I think they're just as likely to say, 'Well, come on then, boy, let's tussle.' They still have the edge, and they probably think they have a bigger edge than they really do. And it's perceptions, not reality, that drive behavior."

"Noted. If it happens that way, you have my permission to say 'I told you so.'"

"We're talking about the possibility of seeing one of our ships sunk in our own waters."

"I don't think so," Robinson said composedly. "Because Moscow has more to lose by getting in a shooting war with us than they have to gain."

"Moscow won't make the decision. That decision will be made by a single sub captain who's just had his boat rattled in a definitely unfriendly way."

"Their commanders have rules of engagement, too. I'm betting they say withdraw if challenged. And it feels like a very secure bet. End of discussion, Gregory. The decision is made."

O'Neill nodded glumly. "Tell me what you want, then."

"State will draft the policy statement. You sit down with your tactical people and come up with some new rules of engagement for the Coast Guard," Robinson said, licking the icing residue from his fingers. "Get the Joint Chiefs to sign off on them, and then bring them to me."

O'Neill frowned, but acquiesced. "It'll take at least a week."

"That's fine," Robinson said, satisfied. O'Neill was stubborn, but loyal. He knew how to close ranks when the issue was decided. "I'm thinking we'll hold it until after the next incident. I'm sure the Bear will oblige us before too long."

He glanced outside at the already dark sky, then at his watch. CIA would have a long list, and he had hardly seen Janice all day. "That's enough for today, gentlemen. We'll come back to this tomorrow at ten."

Indianapolis, Alternity Blue

"Rayne Andrew Wallace."

"Yes, sir."

"What kind of name is that?"

"Mangled Old German, sir."

155

"Mangled?"

"There should be an *r* on the end—Rayner. It was my great-grandfather's name. Means 'mighty soldier,' or something like that. According to my grandmother, Immigration dropped the *r* and he never realized he could do anything about it."

Matt Kelly smiled and shifted the gum he was chewing to the other side of his mouth. "I'll guess you took some heat about your name as a kid."

"Everybody used to think I was saying Ray," Wallace said with a little shake of the head. "It wasn't until I was sixteen or so that I started to insist they got it right. By then I could take care of myself."

Pursing his lips, Kelly flipped open the cover of the binder in front of him on the desk. "Well, *Rayne* Wallace, this is one fine job you did on Haggerty."

"Thank you, sir."

"Don't get me wrong. I've seen better, and I've seen faster. But I don't remember anything this complete on a forty-eight-hour turnaround from someone as green as you are. How'd you do it?"

"I guess by not trying to decide what's important while I was in the field."

"That's not what I'm talking about. I mean, how'd you do it? You've got her dress size, the due date for her child, college grade-point average. Individually useless, but impressive in the aggregate."

Wallace felt a sudden tremor of uncertainty. Maybe he'd gone too far, crossed the line from dedication to zeal. A break-in, a bribe, three impersonations—maybe Kelly wouldn't be so happy with him after all. "It's out there, all of it," he said evasively. "You just have to be creative about getting it."

Kelly grunted. "Whatever. If you don't want a chance to brag on yourself, I'll let it pass. Just don't forget what worked for you," he said. "Because as of now, I'm releasing you to operations."

Suddenly grinning broadly, Wallace straightened up in his chair. "Thank you, sir."

"You'll be in Donn Frederick's group. Suite 16, the Shelby Street offices."

"Yes, sir," Wallace said, starting to rise.

"Wallace—just don't get *too* creative, do you hear? Your reputation hath preceded you."

Wallace's face fell. "Yes, sir." *Can't get away from it,* he thought resignedly. *It's part of my profile now—*

To Gregory O'Neill's mind, there was a chilling emperor's-new-clothes unreality to the charts the CIA director had brought with him, as though anything committed to print and discussed soberly had to be taken seriously, no matter how absurd.

Madison's words were a cape swirling around the emperor, a noble but vain attempt to mask the nakedness, a skillful effort to disengage the critical faculties of his audience. Astonishment had silenced O'Neill during the first several minutes of the presentation. He stared at the man as though he were staring at a crawling thing, unable to credit what he was hearing:

"The most desirable flight would be an Aeroflot nonstop from a city outside the Soviet bloc. At present, there are three that deserve special consideration: They originate from Madrid, London, and Reykjavik.

"As noted here, using either London and Madrid would require us to take action on the ground, specifically loading the package and replacing the crew. Obviously, that would have to be handled very cleanly and probably would necessitate involving the host country to some degree. Balancing the added risk is the opportunity to use actual Soviet hardware for the penetration.

"The Reykjavik flight is the longest of the three, much of it over water. There are radar dead spots and often long stretches of radio silence. It should be possible to bring down the target airliner over the Norwegian Sea and substitute our own mocked-up Q-plane. The Tu-85s in service on the Reykjavik run and our Boeing-Douglas VC-24 are virtual twins—as they should be, since we cribbed freely from their design. The advantage here is that we can handle it without outside help, since there is no ground interface.

"The choice between the various options would turn on a more careful examination of a detailed action plan, but timing at the other end might become a consideration, too. The optimal trigger windows are the opening session of the twenty-fifth Party Congress, expected sometime next summer, or one of the semi-annual gatherings of the Supreme Soviet. Either one should assure a maximum concentration of the country's top leadership, both civil and Party—"

O'Neill glanced toward Robinson and was horrified to see the President's eyes betraying interest. The sight spurred him to break his benumbed silence. "Mr. President, this is the craziest idea I've ever heard outside of a union bar," O'Neill said sharply. "I'm astonished that Dennis would think something this extreme would get a sympathetic hearing. And frankly, I'm surprised at you for letting him go on as long as you have.''

"This is not something that was hatched overnight," Madison growled, annoyed at the interruption. "Some of my very best people have been working on this for more than a year. I wouldn't bring you something that I wasn't convinced was do-able.''

"I take no comfort whatsoever in that," O'Neill fired back. Bouncing up from his chair, he strode across the room to the chart stand and flung the top chart back, then shuffled roughly through the remaining pages as he continued.

"Where are the charts showing American casualties in the war you've started?" he demanded. "Where are the tables of burn-ward beds for half a million survivors? Did your 'best people' give so much as one minute of that year to thinking about what happens *after* you pull off your coup? Do you think that killing the Minister of Strategic Rocket Forces removes all launch authority from Soviet command and control?''

Madison scowled. "I'm not surprised by this. You swagger and preen with the best sweat-belt generalissimo, but when it comes to actually using it, you can't get it up. You made that plain enough yesterday, when you tried to talk the President into keeping the handcuffs on the Coast Guard. We didn't buy you all that fucking hardware just so you could show it off in parades.''

"An *ad hominem* attack is no substitute for an answer, Dennis," O'Neill said stolidly. "But then you can't answer, because the lie you'd have to tell to keep from admitting I'm right would choke you.''

He turned to Robinson. "This is absolutely reckless, Mr. President. Absolutely and unequivocally reckless. There is no such thing as a one-punch fight. Scorching Moscow isn't going to 'sap their national will.' The Soviet people believe in revenge, Mr. President. And they'll have it.''

Robinson folded his hands over his belt buckle. "Are you so sure of that, Gregory? A people without leaders isn't a nation. It's a rabble.''

"I'm not worried about the Soviet people, Mr. President. It's the captains of the Soviet ballistic missile submarines and the wing commanders of the Soviet bomber squadrons and the generals of the strategic rocket forces that worry me. Turn it around. If Washington were scorched but SAC were still intact, do you think Moscow would be safe?''

"Quite probably," Madison said. "What about all those SAC simulations where you make the boys in the hole think their boards are live when they're not? Half of your missile teams refuse the launch order.''

O'Neill steeled himself not to respond to the implied slur. "We conduct those exercises to weed those people out."

"Which proves that you still haven't managed to figure out who they are before you put them there. Or why they change after you do,'' Madison said, parrying as gracefully as a foil champion. ''Mr. President, take it from a Colorado boy: If you cut a rattlesnake's head off, the body'll thrash around for a little while. But that sucker's dead.''

"Is there something in the water over at Spook Central that encourages this sort of hallucination?'' O'Neill demanded. ''The Soviet Union isn't a goddamned snake. It's not a single mono-lithic organism. It can't be stunned or beheaded. And it isn't going to roll over dead even if this crazy scheme worked and we did manage to atomize the Kremlin.''

"You're the fucking king of *can't* and *don't*, aren't you?'' Madison snarled. ''Why don't you get out of the way and let somebody who's not scared of their shadow get—''

O'Neill was furious enough that his body was trembling with the struggle to contain it, but it was Robinson who interrupted first. ''That's enough of that sort of talk, Dennis. Let's try to keep this professional, can't we?''

Robinson's silence had disturbed O'Neill. Now the President's support emboldened him. ''Mr. President, I can't say it strongly enough,'' he said, turning his back on Madison. ''This nonsense doesn't merit one minute's further consideration. In my judg-ment, the risks of succeeding are even greater than the risks of failing.''

He heard the lecturing tone in his voice, but did not care. ''This whole plan is dishonest, dishonorable, and, I think, funda-mentally disloyal to you, this administration, and this nation. I refuse to have any part in it. If you want to pursue this kind of immorality, you can have my resignation right now.''

He headed for the door without waiting for an answer. It was no dramatic gesture; rather, it was an urgent need to end the conversation before Madison spoke again and sent his anger up past the level where he could control it. He had felt the faint warning touch of the irrational, and he had to back away.

In the seconds it took to reach the door, he heard Madison snicker, Robinson sigh, and E.C. tentatively volunteer, ''If we're taking a break, I need to—''

Whatever the Secretary of State needed was lost in the slam-ming of the solid oak door. He had meant to avoid the cliche exit, but at the touch of the doorknob in his hand his body took over, like electricity discharging through an accidental ground. It was a childish, petulant, meaningless act. And it felt so good that when he left the cabin, O'Neill slammed that door, too.

It was quiet in the grove north of the cabin. The long-needled red pines blanketed sound, while their detritus cushioned the ground under his feet. Beds, O'Neill remembered as he walked. They used to make beds out of pine needles.

He had not expected to be followed, and when he heard the footsteps, he did not expect it would be the Secretary of State who drew up beside him.

"I had to say thank-you," the Secretary said, panting slightly from the exertion of the chase.

"Excuse me?"

"For strangling the baby in the crib."

"Is that what I did?"

"After you left, he said 'Just in case anyone wonders, I'm not letting him resign.' "

"Anything else?"

"That's when I left. But you made yourself clear."

"Why didn't you? Christ, E.C., you left me standing there all by myself."

The Secretary smiled ruefully. "I've been here from the beginning. I learned what subjects he'll listen to me on long before you joined the team. Besides, you didn't need any help."

O'Neill sighed. "I don't need sex, either, but it feels good sometimes anyway."

The Secretary's smile widened, and he clapped O'Neill on the shoulder. "I'm going back. You ought to, too."

"In a little while," O'Neill said. He walked on alone, his steps a little lighter. *I won. Gentle God in Heaven, sometimes You are kind to fools—*

Dennis Madison fussed over his charts, collecting those that had slipped to the floor and then straightening the assembled sheaf. "I didn't know I was going to start a fifteen-rounder," he said, murmuring as though talking to himself. "What got into O'Neill, anyway?"

Robinson waved a hand dismissively. "It happens. There've been a few before, eh, Bill?"

William Rodman turned away from the window from which he had watched O'Neill's retreat into the woods and bared his teeth in a smile that contained no human warmth. "Here and there."

"I did bring some other ideas up with me," Madison said. "Are we going to try to get everyone together again? Or are we done for the day?"

"First things first," Robinson said, raising steepled fingers to his lips. "Can you answer a question?"

"Of course."

"Can we do it without him?"

Madison stopped his housekeeping as though struck. "What do you mean?"

"Can we box him out? Keep it inside the Company and proceed with development work without O'Neill?"

Surprise outweighed triumph on Madison's face. "What about the transfer of the bomb? It was going to come out of Air Force stocks."

"We can go through the Air Force Chief of Staff," Rodman said, moving closer. "Or maybe someone even farther down the line. If the authority comes from Pennsylvania Avenue, no one will question it."

"Then we can do it without him," Madison said. "But why play games? Why not just let him go? He's given you the opening."

Robinson shook his head. "Because he's the best I've had, and I don't want the hassle of breaking in another." He smiled, gave a little shrug, and added, "The devil you know, and all that."

"If that's the way you want it," Madison said. "Are you going to give me an NSC DD on this?"

"Hell, no," Rodman and Robinson said at once.

The CIA director bowed his head gravely. "Okay. I understand the rules now."

"Good." The President stood up from his chair. "Don't fuck up, Dennis."

"I won't."

"Don't be glib with me. Everything's got to be just right, or we fold this up," Robinson warned.

Madison nodded. "It'll be right."

June 28, 1976

The President
The White House
Washington, D.C.

Dear Mr. President,

I am pleased to transmit to you herewith the Research Division's report *The International Balance of Power: Seven Models* in response to your inquiry of May 14, 1976 concerning the U.S. and USSR's relative economic, political, and military strength in the various alternities.

We found this investigation to be most illuminating, and I feel obliged to call to your attention certain conclusions which go beyond the scope of the original inquiry. Specifically, I believe that we have identified a key factor which accounts for the Soviet success in this alternity, the relative prosperity of our Blue and Yellow counterparts in particular, and the delays and difficulties presently being experienced in implementing the NRC's "imported" technologies.

As you know, at the time of the Split we possessed physical and human resources identical to that of any counterpart America and arguably superior to that of the Soviet Union. However, an objective reading of the present balance of power finds us to be at a relative disadvantage to both.

In searching for an explanation for this situation, we examined a host of possible factors, which are detailed in the accompanying supplemental report. It is our firm conclusion that the most significant factor has been the virtual elimination within our society of a free exchange of information in the areas of public policy, economics, and science and technology.

To illustrate: The leading American scientific research journal in Yellow has a circulation of more than 800,000. By contrast, our leading journal has a restricted-distribution designation and reaches no more than 10,000 scientists. Again: The local Soviet Union has 328 independently edited newspapers (up from 59 in

1960), 85 of which are state-subsidized and 24 of which have national distribution. The U.S. has 35 independently edited newspapers (down from 241 in 1960), none of which is state-subsidized and only 3 of which have national distribution. Other examples are included in the supplementary report.

There are many reasons why this free exchange became stifled, including but not limited to the Taft Administration's America-first focus, Attorney General McCarthy's anti-Communist campaign, the 1960 Official Secrets Act, and the creation of the Federal News Service in 1969. Most of the historical factors involve security concerns, but, paradoxically these measures have contributed to making us weaker and more vulnerable.

The relatively free exchange of information and criticism currently enjoyed in the Soviet Union and in our counterpart nations appears to have at least four positive effects:

- it enhances individual creativity by cross-fertilization between otherwise isolated individuals
- it allows us to anticipate and prevent many errors and inefficiencies before the fact
- it provides a mechanism for the correction of errors and inefficiencies after the fact
- as a consequence of the above, it tends to maximize the efficiency with which resources are employed.

A certain amount of what might be called "noise" accompanies this process; free exchange is not tidy, and institutions, like individuals, naturally shy from criticism. But the benefits to the nation as a whole appear to far outweigh the discomforts.

Why are we not stronger? Why are we not richer? The answer seems to be that we have unwittingly chosen to be poor and weak. I urge you to give the highest priority to leading a comprehensive nationwide effort to reopen these closed channels of communication. I am convinced that no goal is more critical to our long-term viability as a nation.

Sincerely,

Devon Mitchell

Devon Mitchell

TOP
SECRET

CHAPTER 11

Obloquy

Near Effingham, Illinois, Alternity Blue

Daddy, are we there yet?

Night was hiding the shabbiness of the flat farmland, dressed only in tattered winter brown. The three-year-old Ford Magic hummed along in the eastbound lane of A-40 at one hundred kilometers per hour, tracking an arrow-straight path along the narrow concrete ribbon. Six carlengths ahead, another car paced the Ford through the night, its interior lights dimmed, its driver asleep behind the wheel.

Rayne Wallace wished that he, too, could sleep. He had eaten breakfast in Indianapolis, lunch in St. Louis, and was looking forward to a late dinner back in Indianapolis again. Seven hours on the road had eroded his enthusiasm, numbed whatever senses took pleasure in speed and sightseeing, and exhausted his patience. All that was left was the nagging suspicion that the car could not be trusted, a suspicion strong enough to keep his eyes open and his hand lightly on the wheel.

"The best AutoMate in America is in the best American automobile," bragged the Magic's brochure. But interurbans broke down, freight trains derailed, the little Spirit stalled unpredictably, and even caliper brakes failed in the rain. How could a little black box in the middle of the dash, an unfathomable marriage of mysterious technologies, be trusted to bring him safely home?

True, he was more trusting now than he had been that morning. For the first hour outbound toward St. Louis, the prospect of letting the car do the driving—at a speed his Spirit couldn't even achieve—nearly doubled Wallace up with gut-knotting fear.

It was like the first time he'd answered a childhood challenge— going down steep Knowles Hill Road on his bike, hands above his heads, the pedals freewheeling below his feet, a truck hard behind him. Except he had been nine then and hardly aware of what death meant.

Seeing the AutoMate system at work had untied most of the knots. A-40 was as much railway as highway, its three lanes crosslinked by switches and sidings to accommodate maintenances, overflow, and emergencies. Driverless freighters bustled along in caravan with "personals" like the Magic and buslike "loungers." Vehicles smoothly joined or left the traffic flow at the interchanges, with never a hesitation. The Magic alerted him and then took the next exit when it ran low on fuel. Most impressive of all, he watched the highway respond to a rain squall by smoothly slowing the line of cars and increasing the spacing between them.

Yes, he was more trusting now, but not trusting enough to sleep.

Yo, Dad— A slight pressure in his bladder made him look at his watch. How much longer? Another hour? He reached out and turned up the volume on the radio, and let his eyes close for just a moment.

> ". . . love that brings warmth to a man's cold heart,
> "Diana,
> "Love that brings light to a life that was dark,
> "Diana . . ."

The radio had saved him from a slow death by boredom. Sound of startling quality poured from the speakers that surrounded him. With his eyes closed, Wallace could imagine himself seated in the audience—club, recital hall, or auditorium, according to the style of music. Instead of coming at him, the sound enveloped him. It was the difference between sitting in the back row at an open-air amphitheater and whistling in the shower.

> ". . . Call down the spirit, the soul of the earth.
> "Join in the gathering, worship and mirth . . ."

There were two dozen stations to choose from, no two duplicating each other. He did not know how such plenty was sustained, any more than he knew how a given station could be received with equal clarity all along the route between St. Louis and Indianapolis or by what sort of trickery the radio's little blue window displayed the names of the song and performer.

> ". . . black light flying high touching deep inside,
> "Time split crying child running try to hide . . ."

But he knew how not to question good fortune. Available at a touch was an almost staggering variety of music, almost all of which was new to his ears—new idioms, new performers, new composers, even a new instrument or two. Not all of them fell pleasingly on his ears, far from it. Rhythms jarred, harmonies clashed. The grating, atonal voice of a vocalist named Xanthe drove Wallace to select a new station. The explicit lyrics of a song titled "Cocktails in the Climatron" elicited embarrassed laughter.

But without his realizing it, the music, too, had been wearing at him. As he listened to song after song which had no emotional context, offered no temporal bearing, Wallace slowly lost the joy of discovery and found instead the pain of separation from all he knew. In time, it all became just so much noise.

Hungry for the familiar, Wallace searched for a channel offering classical music and completed his journey in the company of Vaughn Williams, Franck, and Beethoven. It was not his favorite music, but it had been well represented in his father's eclectic collection, and the melodies were memories of home.

Memories. Lying on his stomach on the oval rag rug reading his assignments while music blared from his father's hi-fi. His father tapping his foot and waggling a forefinger like a tiny conductor's baton. Mother tiptoeing across the springy floorboards as a record played to kiss his father on the forehead. The melodies playing on in his head as he drifted off to sleep on his lumpy hand-me-down mattress, humming silly lyrics along with the Ninth:

"Leibfraumilch und Wiener schnitzel, seig heil uber alles . . ."

Music was more than sound, more even than melody, harmony, and structure. It was an emotional time capsule which could be opened again and again. *I remember that song. It was playing all the time that summer—*

Except that Wallace had had no such summers here, and the songs were empty exercises. In time, some would select themselves to be the memories of this place. But before that could happen, he would have to learn not to hear his own alienness in their unfamiliar words.

Showing a broad, easy grin to the three soldiers accompanying him, Xhumo shouldered the Buzzsaw launcher and sighted the weapon on the steel-gray warship tying up at the south dock.

There had been three primary targets for the Freedom Now raid: the district headquarters of the South African security forces, the transmitter for the Pretoria-controlled radio station, and the prize—the blisterlike tank of the small naval fuel depot on the east shore of the bay.

Xhumo had reserved the fuel tank for himself. It would be a spectacular fire, a freedom flame for the oppressed Bantu townsmen, a funeral pyre for the era of white rule.

But the four-hundred-ton patrol boat *Witbank* was an unexpected prize. It had steamed into the sheltered harbor at sunset, nosing past the tip of Pelican Point while Xhumo and his team were still moving into position. Xhumo exulted. "Today, we will make Pretoria weep," he had told his team.

Now the moment was at hand, the signal bare minutes from sounding. Xhumo and his men were concealed on the bank near a small fishing dock, a few yards from the water's edge. The *Witbank* stood four hundred yards away around the curve of the harbor, pale tendrils of steam still curling up from its single raked stack, its bridge ablaze with light.

Xhumo centered the sight on a spot at the waterline, one third of the way back from the bow. "Be ready," he said to the young soldier who had carried the three extra rockets, each weighing more than thirty pounds, the four miles from where they had left the truck.

"I am ready," the youth said, but his voice betrayed nervousness.

I understand, Xhumo thought. To commit to fight is not the same as to agree to die. The slender-barreled gun turret on the *Witbank*'s foredeck was far more imposing than the pipelike launcher in Xhumo's hands, and the patrol boat boasted several machine guns as well. But Xhumo knew the power he held, and he was not afraid.

"We are the people's courage," Xhumo said. "Be proud."

Just then, the bell in the Dutch Reformed Church began to chime—the signal to the scattered raiders. Xhumo steadied himself, fixed his bearing on the target, and squeezed the trigger.

The rocket leaped from the launcher with a pop and a crackling roar. Showing a bright yellow-white eye to the FN soldiers, the Buzzsaw raced in a shallow arc across the tranquil harbor waters. A fraction of a second later, the rocket struck the *Witbank*'s hull midway between the deck railing and the waterline, blossoming into an orange flower in the night.

There were shouts of alarm from the *Witbank*'s lookouts and from sailors on the quay. But there was no fire aboard, no secondary explosion to rock the steel hull from within, only a rain of casing fragments in the water beside the ship.

Xhumo shook himself, his face suddenly grim. "Load," he barked, and the young soldier hastened to comply. The sounds of explosions and gunfire drifted down from the town, confirming that the other FN teams were at their tasks.

As though prompted by those distant sounds, the two riflemen with Xhumo began to spray bullets wildly in the direction of the ship. A klaxon sounded aboard the *Witbank* and its deck and bridge lights went dark. Sailors, silhouetted against the still-blazing lights on the quay, ran in hunched stances for their gun stations as Xhumo sighted on the shadowy superstructure forward of the stack.

"Load!" he screamed as the second Buzzsaw hurtled toward the ship.

Again, the projectile found its target. Again, there was the blossoming flower, the ringing hammerblow. This time, there were screams as hot, razor-edged shrapnel sprayed the deck and found soft targets crouching in hiding. But the *Witbank* herself remained unharmed.

Xhumo roared in frustration and rage. Sighting on the bridge, now a pale red band across a black tower, he squeezed the firing grip. A moment later he cried out in delight as the rocket knifed through the bridge's shielding and exploded inside, shattering windows and bulging steel plates. Flames and black smoke then owned the bridge.

Sailors ran, abandoning gun positions they had just reached on and near the superstructure. But there were other gunners near the tail, and the fiery trails of the Buzzsaws had shown them their targets. Machine-gun bullets peppered the water in front of Xhumo and his men, then danced up the bank to where they crouched, almost unprotected.

Recklessly, one of the FN guerrillas stood and raised his French-made weapon to his shoulder. An instant later he fell, screaming and clutching at the bloody cavity in his chest. The young soldier who had been loading for Xhumo stared, frozen by the horrible sounds, until a bullet tore through his belly and knocked him backward.

The fourth and final rocket dropped from the young soldier's grasp, rolled beyond Xhumo's reach, and then tumbled down the slope toward the water. Xhumo looked to his right and saw his other rifleman lying on his back, his body jerking in a death dance. All had fallen. All but he who had led them there.

Rage filled Xhumo, and he stood, weaponless, screaming defiance. A hundred guns seemed to be firing on them now, and yet it seemed an eternity until the bullet tunneled through his throat and warm blood filled his mouth. A cry of surprise became a wet choking cough, and he dropped to his knees, then toppled to his side.

Lying there, numbly waiting for the light to fade, Xhumo heard a deep-throated *krumph* from across the harbor, and wondered what it meant. But he could not muster the will or strength to raise his head to see.

May the heart of Pretoria bleed, he thought fiercely. Then he began to pray—not that he would live, but that he would die before anyone from the South African garrison reached him. Not because he feared their revenge or longed for a quiet death. Only so that he could die free.

Indianapolis, Alternity Blue

Rayne Wallace dropped the canvas tray heaped full of mail on the countertop with a thump. "Mission accomplished," he said. "Any reason I shouldn't go back to the apartment?"

The dispatcher hoisted the tray and moved it to a cart standing behind him. "Pull your assignment card from the rack and you'll know," he grunted in reply.

Wallace wandered away in the direction of the assignment rack, which hung on a wall outside Donn Frederick's office. Several of the slots were empty, and most of the others held blue assignment cards. But Wallace's slot held a pale pink card which read: "AEO transit to Home for 48-hour family furlough."

Though it was nearly 10:00 P.M., the light was on in Frederick's office. Wallace knocked and pushed the door open. "Sir?"

Frederick was sitting in the middle of the floor surrounded by paperwork. His folded tie was tucked into the pocket of his shirt, his collar unbuttoned to bare his stubble-shadowed neck. Glancing up briefly, Frederick waved Wallace wordlessly inside.

"Mr. Frederick. I found a pink card in my slot—"

"You're Wallace?"

"Yes."

"Pickup go all right?"

169

"Yes."

"Then what's the problem?"

Wallace flashed the card at shoulder height. "This was—"

"Oh, yes, the pink card. No mistake. It's time for you to cycle home."

"I'd rather stay on the job, if that's possible." *Give me any shit assignment you want, just don't make me go home—*

"You don't want the furlough?"

Hell, no. Would you? "I don't feel any need at this point. Besides, I understood we'd be here five weeks at a stretch."

"You will be, eventually," Frederick said, shifting a page from one pile to another. "God knows there's enough for us all to do."

"Then you'll tear up the card?" Wallace said hopefully.

"Can't and won't," Frederick said with a shake of the head. "Section insists that the new class be cycled home for a visit before they pass out to operations. I bent the rule to send you out on that pickup, but I needed a body. What's the problem, Wallace? Don't you want to see the family?"

"I want to contribute here—"

"You will, Wallace, you will. Take your forty-eight and make the most of it. You'll be hopping when you get back."

"Yes, sir." Wallace hesitated. "Can I at least wait until I've gotten some sleep?"

Frederick considered. "That's fine. The gate's probably scheduled solid right up to the midnight lock-out, anyway," he said, crumpling a sheet of paper and tossing it aside. "Give gate control a call before you go home and ask for the first open slot in the morning."

"Okay."

But Frederick, head down in his paperwork, had already forgotten he was there. Wearing his unhappiness on his face, Wallace withdrew from the room. *Forty-eight hours,* he thought. *If only I could spend them with Katie and not have to see Ruthann at all—*

Wallace and his roommates had settled on the simplest possible system for allocating the sleeping space of the apartment: The last to turn in got the couch. When all three of them were there, most often that meant Fowler turning in early and Wallace ceding the rest of the big bed to Arens later on.

But all three were rarely there. Even when Arens was in town, he was as likely as not to pay an overnight visit to his girlfriend, leaving the apartment and the queen-sized bed to the newcomers.

170

Wallace himself had spent a night away while tracking Barbara Haggerty, and doubtless he would miss more in the weeks ahead.

The only constant was Fowler: home by seven, a meal in front of the television (paroled from its hiding place their second day there), and in bed by ten. He did not go out except to walk to the small grocery three blocks south of the river, a ritual he performed every Monday and Thursday after dinner. Fowler had a fetish for order, and its manifestations had quickly become a source of wink-and-snicker humor for the other two.

It was nearly eleven when Wallace's key penetrated the lock, and so it was no surprise that Fowler was in bed. The surprise was Arens, sitting crosslegged on the couch with a long-necked beer bottle dangling loosely from the fingers of one hand. The television was murmuring words of passionate endearment.

"You're back," Wallace said.

"Chicago paid Indianapolis to take me back," Arens said, looking up from the screen. "I hear you've been on the road yourself."

"That about describes it. I spent eight hours in the car and maybe forty-five minutes in St. Louis."

"Pickups are like that. Everything go okay?"

"Yeah," Wallace said, settling in a chair. "At least the business end of it."

Arens reached forward and turned down the volume on the tiny television. "Meaning?"

"It's nothing," Wallace demurred.

"Shit, that's a queeb's game—drop a teaser and then clam up," Arens said with obvious irritation.

"Look, I didn't mean—"

"You got more friends than you need? That's all right by me."

"It's just a little silly, that's all. I was listening to the radio in the car, going crazy because I didn't know any of the songs. Finally they played 'If I Loved You' from *Carousel* and I just about jumped out of my seat, I was so happy to hear something familiar."

"Nothing silly there. I know the feeling. Except with me it's books. I walk into a bookstore and I feel like Rip Van Winkle."

Wallace nodded eagerly. "One station ran an hour-long biography of this fiver combo named Fresh Air—interviews with the members, a discography, the whole treatment. You could tell they've been as important to music here as the Howlers were back home. But I didn't know any of the members' names, or any of their songs, or any of the other bands they'd played with, or any of *their* songs."

"Some people just don't have any culture," Arens said with a crooked grin.

"I guess that's my problem," Wallace said with an exaggerated sigh. "Anything in the refrigerator that's not a fungal mutant?"

"Try the Chinese stew. Gary made it today."

Nodding, Wallace hauled himself up from the chair.

"Going home?" Arens called after him.

"Hm?"

"The pink card. In your pocket."

"Oh. Yeah. They're making me take a furlough. Tomorrow morning."

"Interesting choice of verbs," Arens drawled, stretching. "But then you haven't said much about your family, have you. What is there to go back and visit?"

"I'm married," Wallace said from the depths of the refrigerator. "With a daughter. The kid is prime, the marriage isn't."

"Don't overwhelm me with rich emotional detail, now."

Wallace peered at Arens over the edge of the refrigerator door. "I don't want to get into it, all right?"

Shrugging, Arens reached for the volume control on the television. "Suit yourself," he said without offense, returning his attention to the screen.

Wallace wished he could have given some other reply, wished he thought there was a reason to talk about it. But what was there to say except that he was trapped in a mistake with a life of its own?

There was nothing Arens could teach him, no answers which talking could reveal. No answers for the man locked in the room without windows except "Be patient. Maybe it won't seem so bad after a few years." No answers at all to why it just didn't work anymore, or to where the love had gone.

Boston, The Home Alternity

The wind blowing through the park was cold enough to turn Katie's breaths to foggy white puffs as she scuffed through the dead leaves. Sitting crosslegged on a nearby bench, Ruthann watched with a mixture of envy and vicarious joy as her daughter discovered the perennial fall pleasures.

"Katie! Time to go in, sweetheart," she called reluctantly,

standing. She shivered as the change in circulation awakened parts of her body that had become numbed to the cold.

After three more kicks delivered to a particularly tempting pile of leaves, Katie came running, cheeks and nose bright red. "Do we have to?"

"We have to," Ruthann said, squatting so she could brush bits of leaf and stem from the child's coat.

"Why?"

"Because I have to start dinner."

Katie wore an exaggerated frown as she reflected on that. "You can do that, and I can play outside," she pronounced at last.

That's how it should be, sweetheart—a backyard with swings for you and a kitchen with a window over the sink for me. A dream for a place you don't even remember. "It's not safe for you to be out here alone, sweetie."

"I'll be careful—"

"We need to go in," Ruthann said firmly, taking her daughter's hand and standing.

Katie pouted, but allowed herself to be led across the outfield grass of the softball diamond toward the entrance to the housing center. Suddenly her eyes lit up, and she pulled at Ruthann's hand like a dog straining at a leash. "Daddy's coming," she said excitedly.

"No, darling," Ruthann said with a sigh. "Daddy's still traveling."

"Daddy's coming!" Katie repeated insistently, pulling away and running ahead.

"Katie—" she began, then looked on past her daughter to the man crossing their path at right angles a hundred feet ahead, moving briskly toward the center entrance on the main walkway. *Rayne*—She stopped and watched as her husband heard Katie's call, caught sight of her, and changed direction to meet her and sweep her up in his arms.

"Katie-cat!" and childish giggles reached Ruthann's ears. Despite wanting to run away, she found herself walking slowly toward them.

"See, Mommy, I was right. It *is* Daddy."

Rayne offered a sheepish smile. "You can join this hug if you want to."

Her own smile felt wan and hollow, but she moved into their embrace, Katie's arms eager and unknowing, Rayne's familiar yet measured. "You could have called and told me you were coming."

"You make it sound like I need permission to be here."

She pulled back. "I didn't mean it like that. How long are you here for?"

"Twenty-four hours," he said. "I'm due back at the Tower tomorrow midnight."

"Will you read me my new book?" Katie interrupted.

"Sure I will," Rayne said. "What's the name of it?"

"*Lady and the Tramp*."

"Oh, boy," he said. "That's a good one."

"I guess we'd better go in, then," Ruthann said. "You haven't very much time."

He looked at her curiously as he shifted Katie to ride on one hip. "Let's go find that book, Katie-cat. Sure is good to see you."

Katie meowed her agreement.

It seemed to Ruthann that so long as Katie was up and about, Rayne was civil to her. He smiled—forced smiles, but better than nothing. Talked to her—about inconsequential matters, but better than nothing. Even touched her—though only to rub her shoulders or kiss the crown of her head, poor substitutes for a truly loving embrace.

But the moment Katie went to bed, Rayne's discomfort at being with her became obvious. She watched him make a beeline for the hi-fi and stack it with records, watched him burrow into week-old papers awaiting disposal, watched him weed his way with painful slowness through the accumulated mail. While so occupied, he barely looked at her. It was as though she had disappeared with Katie.

"Rayne—we have to talk about this," she said finally.

He looked up from the newspaper on his lap. "Seems like all that ever comes from that is yelling or crying or both," he said. "I'm not even sure whose turn it is to storm out of the room."

"I feel like my life is on hold," she said, turning an ottoman into a chair to settle near him. "But I don't even know why I have to wait, or what it is I'm waiting for."

"I don't understand," he said in a tone which suggested he also did not care to understand.

"It's the not knowing that's hard. If I knew—"

"I can't tell you what you're asking."

"Can't you tell me enough to show me it's not always going to be this way? I need a reason to hold on."

He was silent for a moment before answering. "I'm a soldier, more or less. I go where I'm told. I do a job that needs doing. If I do it right, I get to come back.''

Staring, she said, "That's all? That's supposed to give me hope?''

"My Dad was in Europe, with a tank battalion,'' Rayne said, shaking his head. "Mom never knew much about where he was or what he was doing. If he tried to tell her, his letters came censored, marked up with big black lines. It wasn't her place to know. She understood. She just trusted he'd come back. Why can't you do that?''

"At least she knew who he was fighting. She could read about the war in the papers,'' Ruthann snapped.

"I guess not every war makes the papers. You have to figure there's a reason for the ones that don't.''

Frustration cascaded into her voice. "Then tell me something about us, can you? When do we get to be a family?''

"I thought we were one,'' he said, surprised.

"I mean a real family. Look at the way Katie was tonight. She missed you.''

"Did you?''

The question was hurled as a challenge, and Ruthann took a long time answering. "I missed the Rayne I married. I missed the Rayne who took care of me when I was so sick with Katie. I missed the Rayne who makes me laugh and feel like the luckiest woman anywhere.''

His face was softening, but she was not through. "I didn't much miss the Rayne who sulks around here and never talks to me, who resents it when I want some attention from him, who leaves me home alone and never shares what he does or thinks or wants. Which Rayne are you? Tell me and I'll tell you if I missed you.''

His answer was a growl. "You're trying to make me crazy.''

"How?''

He spread his hands in supplication. "Talking like there's two of me. I'm the same person now that I was when we were happy.''

And we aren't happy now. The open acknowledgment of it was a hot needle through the back of her skull, "No, you aren't. Because that Rayne never would have treated me like this.''

"I *am* that person,'' he insisted. "I have all those memories. Sitting with you on your parents' couch while they hid out in the kitchen. Biking up to Limberlost. The train trip here.''

"That's the last good time I can remember. The last time you were really you.''

"Don't do that," he said warningly. "Don't treat me like some sort of . . . some sort of changling. This is me. This is what I am, all of it, the good and the bad."

"Then maybe I just didn't pick very well, did I," she said brittlely. "Because you're perfectly happy with things the way they are, and I'm miserable. You're living your life and I'm waiting for mine to start."

"You *wanted* this. You practically dragged me down to take the Federal exam. You were floating on air when the Guard called me back for an interview—"

"I didn't know it'd end up like this. You don't want anything from me and I need you so badly—"

"I don't know what you want," he said, leaping to his feet and throwing his hands in the air. He retreated a few steps toward the kitchen, muttering as though talking to himself. "I don't know what all this 'waiting for my life to start' is about. We've got more money than we ever had, a nicer home. We've got friends—"

"I hate this place," she blurted out. "I hate being stuck here waiting for you to come home."

He turned and stared.

"It's like a prison, Rayne, it really is. That's why I was driving so much. I just want to run away sometimes. I just want to take Katie and go someplace where you can't hurt me anymore."

Rayne took a step back toward her. "I don't want to hurt you, Annie."

"But you do, every day you're here. Even when you're not." There was nothing to gain from making accusations, but she could not stop herself. "You take me for granted, treat me like all I'm good for is to climb on. You don't take me seriously. You never ask me about anything, you just tell me what you've decided. I'm disappearing, Rayne. I can't see myself. All I see is what you've made me."

She expected denial, rebuttal, indignation. He surprised her. "What is it you want from me?" he asked quietly.

I've been telling you all along, she almost shouted. Do you really want to know? Do you really care?"

"I care."

"Well—I'd like a chance to go out without Katie for a change. I'd like not to have to have her be part of every decision I make. I love her dearly, but it feels sometimes like we're attached with a chain, and she's the one holding the leash."

"I guess I never thought about that."

"And I'd like to have another baby," she said quietly.

The incredulous stare returned.

"I'd like Katie to have a brother or a sister. I think she'd be good with a little one. The way she worries over Kim's new baby. But I don't want to do it if it's all going to fall on me. I need more from you, Rayne. I need you to be a partner. I need you to be a friend, like you were before."

But he was shaking his head even before she finished speaking. "No. We can't manage that," he said firmly.

"That's it? Just no? You selfish—"

As though by mutual consent, both were screaming now.

"What do you want to do to us? Every time I find a way to make a few more dollars, are you going to make them disappear? You've got the easy half of the job, spending it—"

"I didn't ask you for more goddamned money—"

"I've got my own fucking chains, you know. And you're the one holding my leash—"

"Well, why don't you just not come back, then—"

She felt something tug at the back of her slacks and whirled, hand raised. It was Katie, looking up at her with sleep-narrowed eyes. "Was I bad?" she asked in a quavery voice. "Don't be mad, Mommy. I'm sorry—"

Ruthann closed her eyes for a moment and tried to release the massive knot of tension lodged under her ribs. Then she knelt down and swept the child into her arms. "No, sweetheart, you weren't bad, and Mommy's not mad," she said soothingly. "Everything's going to be fine."

"Can I help?" Rayne asked in a chastened voice.

"No," she snapped. "I wouldn't want to get used to you helping, because I know the next time I need you you won't be here."

Gathering Katie close, Ruthann carried her back into her bedroom. She did not look back to see if her words had scored on him. It did not matter. She could no longer permit herself the luxury of worrying about Rayne. It was asking enough to keep herself and Katie whole.

Washington, D.C., The Home Alternity

The room was called the Hatchery, an appropriate nickname for the plans division's project operations suite. The map pinned to the wall bore the legend DOD BEM ET 54. The man studying the map called himself Kendrew.

There was much to take in on the six-foot square map. In a

generous 1:1000000 scale, it spanned an area from Iceland on the west to Norway on the east, from the southern tip of England to the Arctic Circle. It was covered with multicolored circles centered on places with names like Bergen, Durness, and Toshavn. Queer black symbols found in no cartographic guide dotted the landforms and, more sparsely, the wide expanse of the Norwegian Sea.

DOD BEM ET 54 was a battle environment map, the product of the combined efforts of the agency and military intelligence, mostly Air Force. The circles and symbols demarked the special concerns of its creators. Among them: radar sites, with their ranges marked and frequencies noted; air corridors and shipping lanes; airfields and ports, classed by capacity.

Kendrew stood before the map rubbing his tired eyes with the thumb and forefinger of his right hand. The logistics of what the director called "the initiative" were proving to be even stickier than he had thought when first brought in.

As far as the initiative was concerned, there were no friendlies on the map. The British, Norwegian, and Danish installations were as much a threat to security as any Soviet asset, which made finding a hole in the web of listening posts large enough for the switch to take place a challenge.

The whole initiative made Kendrew uncomfortable. There were too many variables, too many elements. How to bring the Q-plane and at least one strike fighter into the area unseen. How to jam the target plane's radio without causing alarm. How to guarantee the kill was swift and sure, and didn't bring a hail of flaming fragments down on a freighter or fishing boat. How to blind or fool the Danish radar station in the Faeroe Islands and the Soviet pickets in the Barents Sea and the British air traffic system—

It was the timing more than the difficulty of any individual element which seemed impossibly daunting. It was as though they were choreographing a ballet knowing that the dancers were clubfooted and the musicians arhythmic.

But the initiative was neither his creation nor his responsibility. He was just part of the team, brought in to give opinions and guidance on ground operations in support of the initiative, not on the merits of the initiative itself. That decision had been made at higher levels, and Kendrew would not question it.

The door to the room opened, and the plans division chief poked his head in. "There you are," he said. "Come on down to the shack. There's some news coming in from Walvis Bay."

There were a half-dozen staff members gathered in the communications center by the time Kendrew reached it. They were listening to an accented English voice on a static-punctuated radio broadcast:

". . . wide divergence on the question of the number of Freedom Now rebels who took part in the raid, as well as the number of casualties . . ."

"Where's this coming from?" Kendrew asked.

"BBC shortwave."

". . . Early this morning, security forces displayed for representatives of the international press eleven bodies of alleged FN soldiers, including one purported to be the rebel leader known as Xhumo . . ."

"Wasn't that our man?"

Kendrew nodded. "This is the third time they've said he was dead."

"So you think—"

"I don't know. Have to be right sometime."

". . . The South African administrator for Walvis Bay claimed that thirty-one residents of South-West Africa's only deep-water port were killed and fifty injured, including eleven children. No evidence was offered for this claim, however, and other sources placed the death toll at less than ten, with most or all of the victims members of the South African police or military . . ."

"Speaking of other sources—what about our own assets?" asked one of the staffers. "Are we getting any humint from the Pretoria cell?"

The plans chief answered. "Too soon for that."

". . . According to South African National Radio, the targets of the raid included schools, the waterworks, and the pilchard and snook canneries which are the mainstay of the local economy. A government spokesman condemned the rebels for a 'reckless disregard for the lives and homes of those who have refused to join in their destructive anti-democratic campaign' . . ."

Do they think we're idiots? Kendrew thought. No popular front would cut itself off from its political base by attacking the people it wants to represent—

". . . independent reports confirm that a fish meal storage building was destroyed during an unsuccessful rocket attack on the South African patrol boat *Witbank*. Reporters were barred from . . ."

"Jesus Christ," Kendrew exclaimed, startled. "He took on a PCE with Buzzsaws? What a goddamned amateur stunt—"

"Hey, the man's dead," someone said. "Maybe."

"He deserves to be. Goddamn amateurs. Tape and twine operations. no discipline, no military sense—"

". . . In a broadcast late this afternoon, Prime Minister Benjamin Fourie accused the United States of supplying arms to the FN rebels. Brandishing an American-made rocket launcher he said had been recovered from the raiding party, Fourie threatened to . . ."

"Did you authorize this operation?" the plans chief asked.

"Hell, no. He was supposed to hit the fuel depot and the security force's motor pool. Son of a bitch. This is three years' work in the crapper. I swear to God, we should have put our Force 40 people there. Amateurs. Goddamned amateurs."

"Are we compromised?"

Kendrew shook his head. "The weapons were clean. It's fully deniable."

"Get me something on paper to pass up the line."

"You'll have it in half an hour."

Indianapolis, Alternity Blue

A familiar-looking oak bed frame lay disassembled in the cargo area of the truck parked in front of the Meridian Arms apartment tower. Upstairs, Wallace found the mattress and box spring standing on edge in the doorway to 12-E, blocking him from entering.

"Yo," Wallace called through the gap.

Arens appeared by the kitchen. "Ray," he said. "Glad to see you. Can you give me a hand with that?"

"Sure."

"We have to go down the service stairs with it. It's too big to fit in the elevator. I guess they didn't make beds playground-sized when this place was built."

"You're moving out?"

"Yep. The place is yours and Gary's as of today. Don't worry, I'm not stripping it to the walls first. The place was furnished. I'm just taking a few things that I bought. Important things, like the bed. I didn't buy it to share with another guy, you know."

"Television going, too?"

"Yeah. It was a blow to Gary when I told him. I think he's going to hit you up to split the cost of a replacement."

"I don't suppose the Guard will pop for a supplemental draw to pay for it."

Arens grinned. "That's how I got mine. 'Tools and supplies' —check? But things have sure tightened up. I think we're spending the green as fast as they can print it. Here, let's get the mattress first. That's the tough one, it's so damned floppy."

"I don't suppose you'd consider dropping it off the balcony."

"The fairy tale involved flying *carpets*."

Wallace crouched and felt for a handle on the bottom edge. "Let's go, then."

The stairwells had been drawn with the same architect's template as the elevators. The only way to make progress proved to be to slide the mattress on edge down each flight of stairs, then flop it over the railing to the next. Surveying the gray-black streaks of grime on the side after the first flight, Arens clucked and shook his head.

"I guess that's why we put sheets on, eh? So we don't have to look at the sweat circles and other assorted stains."

"Sounds good to me," Wallace said with a grunt as he pulled the mattress along. "So, where are you going?"

Flip. "Ah-ah," Arens said as a parent to a child. "You don't want me to break the rules, do you? 'The disposition, residence, and assignment of field agents is restricted on a need-to-know basis.' "

"Moving in with your bedwarmer, aren't you."

Flip. "I'm shocked. What kind of women do you think live here?"

"The kind that sleep with strangers, unless you've just been bragging."

Flip. "Bragging? I thought I'd been very discreet. Tell me my ladyfriend's name. Or if she's tall or short, or anything else about her."

"She fucks."

Flip. "And you think that tells you everything you need to know."

"It tells me a lot."

"Women are different here, Ray. Even classy ones know what they have between their legs." Flip. "Besides, we weren't strangers. I cultivated her for all of a month."

The mattress seemed to be getting heavier and the stairwell air stuffier with each flight of stairs. Beads of perspiration broke out on Wallace's forehead, and he paused to wipe away the moisture on the sleeve of his shirt. "How in the world did you ever get this beast up?"

"Didn't. Bought it from another tenant on the twelfth floor."

"You think if we die in here, anyone will ever find us?"

"Sure—when we get ripe. Come on, the box spring is waiting."

Flip. "You think maybe *it* can fly?" Wallace said with a grunt.

By the time the mattress was secure in the back of the truck both men were flush-faced, panting, and grateful for the bracing air. "You better make sure you have a heaping bowlful of fun on this thing," Wallace said, leaning against the side of the truck.

"I will," Arens said, retrieving a slightly crushed cigarette from a back pocket. He cupped his hands around a match until the cigarette glowed in sympathetic combustion. "So how's the family? Or is that still off-limits."

Wallace shrugged. "We fought again. I just don't know what's going on. I don't understand what she wants."

"Sorry to hear it."

"Aw—" Wallace looked away toward the river. "I guess it just happens. How many really happy couples do you know?"

Arens blew smoke skyward. "Not many. Seems like everybody settles for less than they thought they were going to get."

"I thought we were going to be different."

"Everybody does," Arens said. He took another puff, then dropped the half-consumed cigarette to the sidewalk and ground it out with his foot. "So when are you going to go?"

"Huh?"

"You're ripe for it. That's why we all do it—the what-if game."

"What are you talking about?"

"Going home. To where you grew up. Don't tell me you haven't been thinking about it."

"Did you?"

"Think about it or go?"

"Go."

"That's against the rules, too."

"I thought you were the one who said we make our own rules."

Arens smiled. "Yeah. I went."

"And?"

The other man's face clouded over. "It was worth doing—once."

"That's it?"

"You want me to try to talk you into going? Forget it. I wasn't trying to put ideas in your head. If it matters to you, you'll go. If it doesn't, you won't," Arens said with a shrug.

Wallace pushed himself away from the truck and stood upright. "Well, you're right. I have been thinking about going home," he said. "And it feels—dangerous."

"That's because it is," Arens said. " 'Time turns the old days
derision, our loves into corpses or wives—and marriage and
eath and division make barren our lives.' "

"Is that from something?"

Smiling wryly, Arens clapped Wallace on the shoulder. "From
e heart, my friend. From the heart. You ready to finish this
b?"

"Yah, coach. Let's get 'em."

Washington, D.C., The Home Alternity

'm disappointed," Robinson said shortly, discarding the one-
ge report onto the top of his desk. He folded his hands, elbows
pported by the armrests, and looked up at Rodman. "I want
em to know it, too. Poor judgment, poor planning, poor execu-
n. We look like idiots, again. Ineffectual. *Very* disappointed."

"It's going to be awkward for us now, down there."

"Oh, I don't give a damn about South Africa. I never saw
uch promise there, about as much as throwing a penny in a
ell to make a wish. And we're on a different timetable now.
ut there's something worthwhile that's come out of it, for all
at."

"I don't see it, myself."

Robinson stood. "A lesson, Bill. A lesson about what can
ppen when you trust other people to handle your business,
ople who don't care about it as much as you do. I've made a
cision about the initiative. We're going to do it ourselves and
ep it to ourselves. London and Reykjavik can find out about it
hen Moscow does. I don't want it all coming apart because
me dim-brained bit player fucked up or mouthed off. It's our
ay, and we'll rise or fall with our own people."

"I'll tell Madison," Rodman said with a nod.

"You can tell him something else, too. I don't want anyone
ho had anything to do with that Walvis Bay fiasco working on
ar initative. Incompetence is contagious."

Rodman shook his head. "It's already too late for that, I
ink. Madison said something about Xhumo's controller being
ith the logistics team."

"Tell Madison to lose him," Robinson said coldly. "This is
e endgame, Bill. Red's playing king, queen, and rook against
. We can't afford mistakes."

EX POST FACTO

THE STATE OF THE ADMINISTRATION

As President Brandenburg and his staff head north to their Seneca Lake retreat for the holidays, they leave behind a Washington that is still groping to understand the man whom the American people sent here a year ago to take over the helm of government. Reportedly, a major purpose of this "working vacation" will be to begin drafting Brandenburg's first State of the Union address. We would urge that that be put aside in favor of a hard look at the state of this strange and less-than-wonderful administration.

Beginning with William Wirt and his Anti-Masonic Party in 1832, American politics has endured a parade of one-issue third parties whose entire existence was predicted on virulent negativism: antislavery, anti-immigrant, antiliquor, antitariff, anti-integration, anti-internationalism. Until last year, the American public had never had the occasion to learn the consequences of electing such a candidate.

The lesson has been sobering, at least to veteran Washingtonians. Far beyond the carping about Brandenburg's refusal to aid and abet the traditional orgy of balls, Christmas parties, and greater and lesser revelry are serious questions about Brandenburg's refusal or inability to articulate a clear, positive vision of the future. In blocking (for the moment) natural geopolitical evolution by barring American participation in the United Nations Confederation, Brandenburg and his chimerical National Party seem to have exhausted their fund of ideas.

Though the President continues to wave his campaign flags of "self-reliance" and "independent action," the only reliable feature of his administration to date has been its inaction. Brandenburg has vetoed more bills (and, thanks to a hopelessly divided Congress, sustained more of his vetoes) than any first-year President. The bureaucracy staggers on like a beheaded chicken, its stubborn autonomic functions creating the illusion of life.

Perversely, word of these problems does not seem to have spread beyond the District of Columbia. Eyes still glazed by nationalism, the electorate perceives a dog-jowled sixty-six-year-old divorce as "the nation's most eligible bachelor," credits this grandfatherly man with a wisdom he has not yet demonstrated, and narrowmindedly applauds Brandenburg's defense of yesterday's status quo.

But morning walks through the White House grounds, however homey and picaresque, do not a legislative program make. Does Brandenburg have an agenda? More to the point, does the United States have a President? The chances are that our nation can endure without lasting harm a self-indulgent four-year holiday from grappling with change and responsibility. It remains to be seen whether Brandenburg can muster the vigor and vision to save us from having to find out.

—Editor-in-Chief Malcolm Briss

CHAPTER 12

Tin Roofs
and Porch Swings

East-central Indiana, Alternity Blue

Wallace took the old roads home.

Though the automated highway, A-40 east to Ohio, would have taken him speedily to within a few miles of Hagerstown, the old roads were the roads of his memories. Paper-thin black asphalt ribbons draped across Indiana farmland, they decorated rather than altered its gentle contours.

Narrow gravel shoulders. Faded dividing lines chalking into invisibility. Roads laid out on the section lines of 19th-century county surveys, shaped by the refusal of long-dead farmers to have their fields divided. Roads where lumbering harvesters became the heads of segmented metal worms crawling across the countryside. Roads that swallowed up the beams of headlights in black-night drizzle.

They tunneled through groves of trees, widened to become the main streets of one- and two-stoplight towns, then shrank back to their natural size of two narrow lanes, one coming, one going. Except there had always seemed to be more going than coming, familiar faces that took the roads to Muncie and Richmond and never came back.

He drove past silos standing in ranks of four and across tiny bridges spanning sluggish green-brown rivers. He drove through communities he knew only for the teams their high schools had fielded. The Warrington Blazers. The Ashland Tigers. The Millville Panthers, 1965 Sectional Champions.

And yet he knew them, knew every town he drove through.

There were no surprises a hundred years in any direction. Tin roofs and porch swings, children in mittens and mufflers. With every passing mile, the tightness in his chest and the queasiness in his stomach grew. The deep breaths he took to calm himself threatened to turn into sobs.

It all looked as it should—brown grass and brown earth, fields of corn stubble, sagging wooden fences, roadside farm markets with hand-stenciled signs saying CLOSED FOR THE SEASON. How could it be so much the same and yet not be real, not be the same little circle of the world in which he had spent nearly all of his first twenty years?

Even the signs were the same. The Lions Club and Kiwanis emblems hanging together on the outskirts of town. A placard proclaiming "Trust Deschlingers—Champion SPF Hamps." When Wallace came around the last curve west of Hagerstown and saw Roger Eash's barn it was all he could do to keep the Magic on the road, for the side of the structure bore the same stern reminder:

> Life is short
> Death is sure
> Sin the cause
> Christ the cure

Just like home. The same faded black lettering that he and Donald Eash had plastered with wet snowballs until their ten-year-old arms were tired. The same barn with the same musty-smelling loft full of disintegrating leather tack dating from when the Eashes had plowed with horse or ox instead of a noisy gasoline-burning tractor.

How could there be two of them? Like some sort of county-fair funhouse trickery, making you think you were one place when you were really somewhere else. How could it be so real? Like a stage set for the play of his life. Was there a real Roger Eash inside the farmhouse, round-bellied and bald-headed, his wide-brimmed blue Sheriff's Posse hat hanging on the peg by the kitchen door? How would he like to hear about the son Donald he had never had?

Or maybe there was a Donald Eash, too, a little older or younger, a little more like his gentle mother in the face or a little less like his father in profile. A Donald Eash who would not remember being best friends with a Rayne Wallace in the fifth and sixth grades. *Would not remember a Rayne Wallace at all, because it's me that's not real here.*

187

Suddenly Wallace was afraid to confront the puzzle any more closely, so afraid that the poisonous contents of his stomach threatened a violent upheaval. He slowed the Magic to a crawl as the Hagerstown standpipe and the stiletto steeple of the First Baptist Church came into view ahead, prominent above the stark denuded trees enfolding tin-roofed clapboard houses.

The standpipe. Powerful memories snapped into focus. The night he and three other YDR members had climbed its endless steel ladder to leave their mark in red paint at the top. The way the wind had grabbed at them. The queasy feeling that the steel cylinder was swaying. Jimmy Fox dropping the brush over the side before their message was finished. A crazy stunt. A great coup—

It was not too late to turn back. He could backtrack to Millville and turn south, get on A-40 at New Lisbon and continue on toward Columbus with all thoughts of a nostalgic personal detour firmly banished from his mind. A Christmas present for himself, he had rationalized when the assignment came down. Walk memory lane for a few hours. No one would know.

As no one would know if he fled from an encounter with his own ephemeral reality. This Hagerstown was not his home. And he knew already that his absence here had left no void. Foolish to think it had, *It's a Wonderful Life* notwithstanding—like expecting to see a hole in the lake after you've walked up onto the shore.

Another car roared by on the left, the driver shaking his fist at Wallace for blocking the road. Wallace jumped, and the start derailed his thoughts.

Name the disease. Was that what he was afraid of, the fact of his own nonexistence? As if it meant that he was not real.

But he knew what reality was. He had nothing to fear from this place or the people for whom it truly was home. They could not touch him, could not change him. They would look at him with curiosity, wondering at the stranger—it was always a place that took note of strangers. But because they would not know him, because they would expect nothing from him, he could hide. He did not have to touch them. He did not have to fear them touching him.

Wallace's foot landed lightly on the accelerator, and the Magic eased forward. He would not let himself be afraid.

The new woman's name was Rachel.

Endicott had not asked her name. It was not important to him, as meaningless as any part of her past. She offered it herself, while he was freeing her from the chromed restraints—handcuffs and hobbles—in which she had been delivered.

"Undress," he said.

"What's your name?"

With sudden crackling violence, he slapped her, the stinging blow whipping her face to one side and leaving the red imprint of four fingers on her cheek. "Don't talk." He did not want to be questioned. The last one had always wanted to talk, alternately whining and cursing him, until he had been obliged to gag her to end the noise. He did not like doing that. There were sounds he liked to hear, and he had been harsher with her for denying that to him.

Rachel's response to the slap was unexpected. The last one had gone to her knees in tears. The first one, the young one he had picked up himself on the road near Fairfax so long ago, had lunged for Endicott with clawing hands before he knocked her to the floor.

Hysteria and anger. He had been ready for either. But Rachel showed neither. Her eyes wide and wondering, she obediently began to unbutton her blouse. Obedience, but not surrender. "I haven't really been arrested, have I," she said as she pulled the tail of the garment from the waistband of her pleated slacks.

"No." He should have slapped her again, enforcing the point. But she kept surprising him, breaking the patterns.

The blouse dropped to the floor. "And a man like you doesn't need the money that anyone would pay to have me back," she said, continuing to size up her situation aloud.

"No," Endicott said. "Now shut up."

Naked, her true age showed—thirty, perhaps thirty-two. The extra softness in the hips and slightly rounded belly that the high-waisted slacks had disguised. The first hint of slackness in the muscles of her buttocks and upper arms. Her skin was pale white, with no hint it had ever been tanned—the sign of a woman too busy for vanity. Her breasts were beautiful, lush and round and riding a little low without the bra, the right globe slightly fuller than the left.

Endicott placed her on the platform bed on her back, wrists bound together to the headboard above her head, legs pulled back and tied to the top corners of the headboard so that she was doubled over and exposed. She offered no resistance, and yet her cooperation was measured, calculated, placating, humoring. She would learn.

"Why are you doing this?" Calm, no emotional content at all, like a counselor quizzing a patient.

He ran his fingers lightly along the inside of her calf. "Because there's no reason not to."

"You could be caught—arrested."

A faint smile appeared on his lips, and he shook his head ever so gently. "No."

"How can you be so sure? They'll be looking for me—"

He pinched the inside of her thigh, hard. She jerked, made a noise between a squeal and a grunt, and began to breathe faster. A pink flush blossomed on her thigh where he had pinched her, then as quickly vanished.

"Not here," he said.

She was smart, perhaps too smart. That was something he should have warned Tackett about. Smart women were tricksters, calculating, manipulative, always seeking control, always avoiding conflict. Smart women thought they were better than men, thought they were better men. He had taught more than one the lesson that they were not.

"Are you going to hurt me?" she asked. A hint of a tremor this time.

He ran his fingers through the matted black hair between her legs, fluffing it. The scent of her floated up to his nostrils. "Yes."

"What did I do? What am I that you need to do this?"

"The fact is, this isn't about you at all," he said. "You could have been anyone. Roulette wheel. Wheel of life. Bad luck, Rachel. That's all it is."

"You don't have to hurt me. You can have what you want without hurting me."

"But what I want," he said, caressing a thigh, "is to hurt you."

"Why?"

"Because there's no reason not to."

"That's no answer—"

He brought his hand down hard on her most exposed softness, his calloused hand iron against her. She cried out and raised up off the bed, every muscle rigid, straining futilely to bring her knees together to deny him access.

"It's all the answer you'll get."

The woman forced herself to relax, allowing the ropes to

support her weight. But her breaths remained hot and shallow, her face pale. Fear-scent joined woman-scent in the air.

"Will you kill me?"

Sitting back on his heels, Endicott reached out and opened the lid of a compartment in the platform beside the bed. "That depends," he said, rummaging quietly among the contents of the hidden cache.

"If you're going to kill me, don't you think I at least deserve to know your name?" The words came in a rush, but behind them was that same measured withholding, that same calculating distance.

"No," he said, edging forward to where she could see the black-headed hat pin, its silver shaft nearly three inches long, that he held in his right hand. "You shouldn't be afraid of dying. You aren't even alive."

"I'm as alive as you," she said angrily. "I'm as alive as you and I don't want to die."

With the point of the needle as stylus, he scratched intersecting lines on the delicate skin of her breast. "What, no comforting faith in a life hereafter?" he asked, his tone lightly sarcastic. "Through me you may find heaven."

"I do believe in God, and heaven." Her voice was stronger, defiant. "But I'm not finished living."

"That's up to me to decide," he said, pressing down lightly on the pin, creating a conical indentation at the intersection of the scratches.

"Why are you doing this?" she wailed, her anguish no longer measured.

"Let me tell you about God, Rachel," he said, his voice soft and soothing as a preacher's. "They told me He punishes the wicked. He protects the faithful. Are you faithful, Rachel? Did you go to church on Sunday?"

"Please don't do this—"

He brushed the hair back from her cheek, and she flinched at the touch. "The truth is it's all a joke, all a hoax," he whispered. "I defy your God. He's just a word, a wishful dream. I'm going to hurt you, Rachel. The worst things I can think to do, I'll do to you. There are rules about how you treat women. I'm going to break them. And when I'm tired of you, I'm going to kill you. Don't you think if your God existed, he would stop me? Don't you think he'd stop this?"

A sudden thrust, and the pin pierced deep. She screamed, and in that moment his soul stood naked and hurled the challenge heavenward: *You're nothing! See what I do—I'm free and you're helpless!* And he drew his next breath as easily as his last, untouched by the hand of any power greater than himself.

"This is the lesson," he whispered to her as he withdrew the blood-slick pin. "I am everything there is. The only rules are my rules. The only reality is my reality. She writhed, drawing gasping breaths, as he touched the point to her other breast. "So scream, Rachel. Your pain only matters when *I* feel it. Make me feel it, and for that moment you can be real, too."

He drove the pin deep and felt the familiar surge of defiant self-affirmation. The one thing he could not understand is why, along with the exhultation, he always felt a perverse measure of disappointment at God's silence.

Hagerstown, Indiana, Alternity Blue

There were no longer any tracks on the long wooden railroad trestle spanning the Whitewater River and the narrow flood plains on either bank. Wallace had once played chicken with slow-moving freights here, walked the railing like a tightrope, used it as a diving platform on sweltering summer afternoons.

Now the rails were gone, the trestle had been redecked as a footbridge linking the two halves of a small town park, and the old railroad right of way was marked as a footpath and bicycling trail. Signs at each end of the trestle sternly warned:

NO MOTORIZED VEHICLES

NO FISHING

NO DIVING

No fun, Wallace thought. He kicked a bottle cap off the edge and watched it arc downward to splash in the chilly water, then walked back past the swing sets and picnic tables to where he had parked the car. The chains holding the swings creaked in the breeze.

There were any number of new homes on the outskirts of town, little clusters of pastel look-alikes lining new roads with names like Prospect Place and Cul de Sac Drive. But the heart of town looked very little changed from what Wallace remembered. He drove slowly, pulling to the curb now and then to indulge his curiosity.

Here a familiar old oak tree was missing, there a rambling, turreted turn-of-the-century "mansion" had become a lawyer's office or funeral home. His grandmother's old place on Chestnut had a new garage and an elaborate garden framing the porch. Bobby Frick's house looked spookily the same, down to the toys littering the stoop and postage-stamp front yard. And when he rounded a corner to find a tangle of white paper streamers dangling from a pair of maple trees flanking a driveway, Wallace laughed until he was wet-eyed.

Feeling braver, he headed downtown. He found mercantile Hagerstown the same two blocks of red, white, and whitewashed brick storefronts, dressed up with new streetlamps and concrete sidewalk planters. Parking the Magic, he set out to explore it on foot.

There was a series of little jolts awaiting him. The bank building had expanded, and its parking lot had gobbled up the little appliance repair shop and postal substation which had stood next door. Dave and Dot's, the fountain counter of which had been host to his "first date," was now called Whitewater Gifts, and the old candy case was filled with ceramic cats and dried flowers. He looked for a copy of the weekly newspaper, but there was no dump box bearing its name.

The woman tending the register eyed him surreptitiously, had been since he had entered. *Strangers.* "Do you know where I can get a *Record*?" he asked her.

"There's a music store in the Flatrock Center, over to New Castle."

"The Hagerstown *Record*—the newspaper."

Her brow furrowed. "We get the Richmond paper around noon—"

Further conversation was dangerous. "I must have made a mistake," he said, excusing himself.

Continuing along the block, he looked for familiar faces. He found them sitting at the window table of Brooks Restaurant—older faces, deep-lined faces with deep-rooted names. Dell Schroeder, wearing his stained Pioneer Seeds cap, sipping a cup of coffee and sharing a story with stubble-faced John Wilson, whose yellowed teeth were clamped on the stem of a black-bowled pipe.

Frozen there on the sidewalk, Wallace was bombarded by memories. Schroeder and his antique steam tractor had always headed the Independence Day parade. Wilson's oldest son and Wallace's brother had been friends.

The glass separating Wallace from the two men saved him from blurting out a greeting. As it was, he stared long enough to

193

draw their glances, Schroeder's raised eyebrow, and a comment from Wilson that set them both laughing.

Wallace forced himself to turn away. It was becoming harder to stay here, harder to maintain his balance, even though he had dodged or postponed the most threatening encounters. He could not stay much longer. It was time to finish what he had come here for. He had to face his own life.

But every step closer to the corner was an effort, because around the corner would be the blue and white canvas awning that said WALLACE HARDWARE—FARM AND HOME, jutting out from the two-story brick building which had been a second home to Harry Wallace's sons.

Rayne could close his eyes and remember the stone scrollwork surrounding the "Schrock 1910" which appeared high on the face of the building, the self-memorial of the grocer who had built it. Inside, the narrow aisles, the cupped and time-stained oak floorboards, the wall-filling cabinets of drawers and doors from which his father seemed able to pull any imagined object on request—

Walk!

The store. Think about the store. The dirt basement, how he used to be terrified of it, standing empty and consigned to the spiders and mice who claimed it. The way his brother would threaten to lock him down there, blackmailing him to win his silence. How he finally forced himself to go down there alone, door closed and in the dark, confronting and defanging the monster, taking that weapon from his brother's arsenal.

Better, better—

The maze of second-floor stock rooms, once grocer Schrock's modest walk-up home, with claw-footed bathtub and push-button light switches still in evidence. The mystery of how his father knew what was in every box, just where to find what he needed, just when to order more. His father had kept it all in his head, as if all the bolts and bits and toaster elements and saw blades made one huge clockwork machine which he could look at and see in an instant what was missing or misfiring.

I can't do it. I can't face him.

Deep and dimly apprehended forces tugged at Wallace, alternately urging him forward and staying his steps. It was as though he were in the hands of an apprentice puppeteer, stumbling through his role in the matinee. A shiver rippled through his body, a shiver felt deep inside, the touch of a ghostly hand momentarily disrupting every natural rhythm. The fear that had seized him in the car had returned in full measure.

How can I deal with it when *he* looks at me like a stranger? Or worse, looks at me and gnaws on his lower lip the way he does when he's thinking hard, like he's trying to figure out why I'm familiar? How can I keep from blurting out, "Dad, you're looking good, I haven't seen you in two years. I came the long way home—"

It was a knot Wallace could not unravel. Was there anything closer than a father and a son? Weren't they part of each other? How could his father not recognize him, not know somehow who he was? Like when you swear you've met someone that just walked into your life for the first time.

Jesus, what if that's what's going on? Gates we haven't found, infiltrators we don't know about. Hello, haven't we met? Yes and no, and please don't ask for explanations. You're dead where I come from, and I wanted to spend some more time with you—

Walk!

But he was frozen, a stride or two from the corner. I'll walk by. I'll walk by and look in, but I won't go in, and I won't stop. Just to know he's there. Just to have that one constant. Just to know I might have been.

In that moment he confronted for the first time a terrible truth that he had been hiding from himself. Just as Roger Eash might still have had a son Donald, Harry and Gina Wallace could well have had a Rayne. Second-born, first-born, older, younger, someone who took his name and his place. Life closes round until nothing is missing, all spaces filled.

He barely was aware that his feet were carrying him the other way, back down the block toward the car. The thought of being replaced in his parents' lives by a cipher, a stranger, was more devastating than the thought of never having existed at all. He struggled for a word to describe the feeling. Abandoned. Betrayed. We'd like to trade in our son, please—that one there looks interesting, don't you think, darling?

Mom . . . Dad . . .

He sat in the car for a long minute, running up the engine like some stoplight speedster issuing a challenge. How silly, Wallace thought. How silly to feel threatened. To feel jealous. They would love any child they made. As they loved me there—back Home. How unfair to think they should have somehow saved it for me.

A touch on the gas, a spin of the wheel, and the Magic pulled away from the curb. Before he could manufacture more reasons not to, Wallace let the car carry him to the intersection and past, turning right with deliberate purpose and making himself look.

And there was the store, Schrock 1910, the awning bright yellow—stretched canvas over a ribbed frame, different, eye-catching. But there was something wrong with the printing. ACE HARDWARE. That's all it said, ACE HARDWARE in black letters a foot high across the front. And on the windows the awning shielded, the same mistake.

It was a moment before Wallace realized the mistake was his. He pulled the car into the first available space, blocking an alley, and ran back along the sidewalk.

Even through the windows he could see the changes. Pegboard displays and shrink-wrapped tools. Nuts and screws in little plastic containers, dangling from metal trees. A boy in a bright yellow vest, building a pyramid of paint cans.

Three more steps carried Rayne inside. "Didn't this used to be Wallace Hardware?" he demanded.

The boy looked up. "Geez, I don't know. I've only worked here two months."

"How long have you lived here?"

"Huh?"

"You live in town? Go to school here?"

"Yeah—"

"How long?"

"Uh—three years. No, four."

You sold it. I don't believe it. Why'd you sell, Dad? What else would you do? "You know the owner?"

"I just work here part time."

"You know a man named Harry Wallace? About fifty-five?"

"No."

"Sure you do," Wallace said, voice cracking. "Plays the trumpet for the National Anthem every Memorial Day. At the veterans' monument in the cemetery. The parade. Don't you ever follow the parade?"

The boy's face was drawn up into wrinkled confusion. "Hey, what's your problem?"

Wallace fled, giving no answer. You wouldn't sell it, Dad. You wouldn't, but Mom would. Would have to, to take care of a child or two after you were gone. Goddammit, I didn't come here to find you in a grave—

Isolated in a field a quarter-mile south of the end of the main runway, four oblong grassy mounds each as tall as a man rose from the earth within a fenced compound. From outside, the slope-sided mounds appeared innocuous, yet slightly mysterious, like a pristine Hopewell site sealed off from would-be tomb robbers, or a cluster of land-locked dikes.

But the compound was far from innocuous. For nested within the mounds' cylindrical vaults, like colossal metal pupae, were twelve Mark XII hydrogen bombs, more than two hundred million tons of explosive power contained in a few dozen tons of steel, enriched U-235 and lithium deuteride. Another twelve Mark XIIs were aloft in the bomb bays of some of the wing's swept-wing B-55s, which roared off the main runway in groups of three at two-hour intervals around the clock.

The 397th Squadron prided itself on its trusteeship of the most powerful weapons in the American arsenal. The cartoon emblem of the group, which appeared one day on the bulletin board and had never been removed, was a fierce-faced mosquito with furiously beating wings carrying a gigantic bomb aloft. Underneath, the legend read: 397TH SQUADRON: HOME OF THE BIG SHOTS.

The vaults all faced inward, nominally shielded from the shock of Soviet near-hits by the mass of earth, steel, and reinforced concrete surrounding them. But most of Ordnance Storage Area C's design was directed toward threats on a smaller scale. The double fences were topped by coils of long-barbed hangwire, and the weapons of the two-man guard detail at the gate house were loaded with live ammunition.

Twice each hour, at varying intervals, one of the guards would make a circuit of the compound in the gap between the fences. Automatic rifle in hand, he would "walk the wire," looking for breaches or tampering. None was ever found, but the ritual went on all the same.

For Ben Briggs and Tom Rawley, walking the wire was the most common interruption in a detail marked more by card-playing and coarse talk about women than earnest vigilance. There was little traffic at Ordnance C, little call for the weapons stored there. The Mark XII was a specialized part of the arsenal, carried by less than ten percent of the wing. Usually the aircraft coming off the line for maintenance and the aircraft coming into the rotation balanced, and the ground crews simply swapped out the weapons from one to the other.

But once or twice a week glitches in scheduling would leave

the drones with one more or one less Mark XII on the flight line than was needed. Then a low-slung blue tractor would crawl down the service road from the base, pulling a canvas-draped cylinder on its dolly, or appear with its tow hitch bare to drag a bomb away toward the loading trenches in the flight apron.

Once a week a lieutenant would drive out from base HQ to perform a physical inventory of the arsenal. And once a month or so the base commander would toss them a full-readiness drill, which usually meant a parade of tractors coming out to retrieve bombs for planes not routinely kept full-bellied.

Anything else was an oddity, a curiosity. So when Briggs saw the black sixteen-wheel trailer-truck rolling down the service road toward the gate house, followed by a familiar blue tractor, he threw aside the book he had been reading and jumped to his feet. Rawley was napping in his chair, but a hard push with a booted foot ended that.

"Company," Briggs said, reaching for his rifle.

With groaning brakes, the truck came to a stop at the prescribed mark, and the tractor drew up behind it. A moustachioed colonel, his uniform sharp as his build was trim, hopped lightly down from the cab. Briggs left the gate house and met him at the fence.

"Sir," Briggs said.

The colonel's namestrip read ANDREWS. "Good morning, corporal. I'm Colonel Ken Andrews, from Nawtec. I've got transmittal papers for number 8925. You'll want to call it in." His voice was pleasant, with just a hint of good-humored world-weariness.

Briggs perked up, interested. The National Weapons Testing Center was the umbrella name for a dozen facilities, embracing mock battlefields in Alaska, sprawling proving grounds in the empty spaces of Utah and Mexico, missile test ranges in Nevada and Florida, and the Sea Tactics School in the Gulf.

NWTC served all four services and drew its staff from all their ranks. What with development and qualification tests of new weapons and live readiness firings on weapons drawn at random from the active inventory, NWTC was considered a sexy assignment, with a cachet exceeded only by Edwards or Pax River.

Briggs craved to ask what Nawtec wanted with the bomb, but etiquette prevailed. "Yes, sir," he said. "Please wait here."

He returned to the gate house and the curiosity of his partner. "What's going on?"

"They want an egg for Nawtec," Briggs said, picking up the phone. "Operations desk. This is Air Corporal Briggs at Ordnance C. I have a Colonel Andrews here presenting transmittal papers for a Mark XII, serial number 8925.''

"Give me the sequence number off the TP."

"Alpha three five five edgar zero zero eight."

"One moment. Roger, your sequence number alpha three five five edgar zero zero eight is confirmed. Let 'em have it, Ben. SOP.''

"Whatever you say." He returned to where Andrews stood waiting and let himself out through the smaller gate. "I'm going to need to check the back. If you'll open the trailer, sir.''

"Of course," Andrews said agreeably.

There were no surprises. The trailer was empty except for a small electric winch and the clamps and anchors which would be used to secure the bomb and trolley. "If you'll have the driver pull the truck ahead, past the gate, I'll let the tractor in.''

It took fifteen minutes to pass the tractor through the double gates, open vault 19, and hitch up the bomb-laden dolly. Andrews stayed at Briggs' elbow, showing no special curiosity in the Mark XII and no inclination to idle talk.

"Bet we'll hear that one all the way up here," Briggs ventured at last.

"Excuse me?"

"I was just saying there'll be a hell of a bang when you fry this egg.''

"Um," Andrews said, stepping forward to help line up the dolly with the ramps leading into the back of the truck. Shortly, the tractor rolled away and the winch strained away, inching its burden up the incline.

"How long has it been since we tested a Twelve?"

"Even if I knew, it would be classified," Andrews said, standing back as the blunt nose of the bomb edged into the shadows of the cavernous truck. "You should know that, Corporal.''

Briggs swallowed hard. "Sorry, sir. It's just that I've been on this detail seven months now. I was just curious—''

"Sit on it," Andrews said.

"Yes, sir.''

But Briggs' curiosity persisted after Andrews and the truck were gone, rolling down the road toward the north gate and picking up an escort of two jeeps and a troop carrier. And when Rawley went out to walk the wire, curiosity put him back on the phone to the operations desk.

"Is Jake there?"

"This is me, Ben. Everything all right out there?"

199

"Yeah. Got company?"

"Not at the moment. What's up?"

"Just wondering where they were going with that Twelve—New Mexico or the Aleutians. They'd have to take it to the Aleutians, wouldn't they? It's too big for New Mexico."

"Hmm. Looks like its going to Westover."

"Huh?" Westover was a fighter and transport base near Holyoke, Massachusetts.

"This thing got special handling. I've got a coded 'gram here direct from the Air Force Chief of Staff authorizing the transfer of that Twelve from Racetrack to Slingshot, with the transmittal sequence. We're Racetrack. And I'm pretty sure Westover is Slingshot."

"That's nuts. Nawtec doesn't work out of Westover. And there aren't any B-55s there."

"I'm just telling you what it says."

"Well, what it says is nuts," Briggs insisted.

"Where does Nawtec come in?"

"That's what Andrews said. And his papers said."

"This 'gram doesn't say anything about Nawtec."

Briggs mused. "Maybe I've just been out here too long. Did the base commander know about the transfer?"

"He must have." There was a pause. "But the paperwork doesn't have any place for him to check off on it."

"Maybe you should take it to him."

Jake was not happy with the suggestion. "We're going to look like idiots of the year if it turns out we let go of an egg without proper authority."

"We'll look worse if Andrews trucks that egg into D.C. and fries it on the Mall."

"Yeah." The other man was silent for a long moment. "I'll ask some questions."

"I think that's a good idea."

Hagerstown, Indiana, Alternity Blue

Rayne Wallace sat in the dark in the car and peered up from the street at the lighted windows of his mother's house. His mother's house. Not his house, or his father's house. His mother's house. A little Cape Cod on Lincoln Avenue near the northwest edge of town, just before Lincoln turned into County Road 21. He recognized the curtains hanging in the front windows, the wind chime on the little porch.

He had found his father first, or as much of his father as remained—a rectangular stone in the ground near the Wallace monument in Mare's Wood Cemetery. BELOVED SON HAROLD, d. JAN 8 1961, alongside BELOVED SON THOMAS, d. JAN 8 1927. He had not known that his father's real name was Harold. Everyone had always called him Harry, even Grandmom. And how curious that his father had died on the same date as his stillborn older brother. Coincidence, surely, but somehow unsettling all the same.

Sitting on his heels before the stone, he had cried quietly for his father, but also for himself. His life seemed suddenly tenuous, his visit home having cost him the illusion of his own inevitability. Chance had borne him. The many turnings which followed had been the product of incident and accident as much as choice.

And the consequences of his choices had been hard enough to accept. The what-if game, Arens had called it. There was not much pleasure in the playing.

He knew he would not leave his car. And if he tried, he knew his legs would not carry him, would shield him from his own folly. He sat behind the wheel watching for a shadow against the curtains, a face at the door, any sign of the life within the house.

Intent as he was, he did not notice the state police car when it coasted up behind the Magic. Not until the streetlamp-driven shadow of the trooper fell across the window, and the barrel of his flashlight tapped against the window glass.

Not again—

Quickly, Wallace rolled down the window. "Something wrong, officer?"

"I'd like to see your license, please."

Wallace surrendered it readily.

"Stay in your car, please."

Anxiously, Wallace waited out the long minutes as the officer returned to his cruiser. Presently he returned and handed the card back through the window. "What's your business here, Mr. Wallach?"

"I've been driving all afternoon, down from Fort Wayne, and stopped in town for dinner. You know how a big meal can make you sleepy as a baby," Wallace said, flashing a friendly smile. "I just stopped here for a rest. I didn't think I was doing anything wrong."

"We had a complaint about a stranger in the neighborhood. I guess that'd be you."

"Like I said, I was napping—"

"Where are you bound, Mr. Wallach?"

"Ohio. I've got business in Columbus."

"There's a loitering law in this town, Mr. Wallach. If you're too tired for the road, I'd suggest you stop at the Redwood Motel on State Road 1. Bonnie will be happy for the trade, and you won't be worrying a quiet neighborhood."

"I'm feeling much better," Wallace said. "If it's all right with you, I'll just get on my way."

The officer nodded. "Drive carefully, Mr. Wallach."

Relieved, grateful for a reason to leave, Wallace started the engine and headed south to find A-4O. Strangers, he thought. The village never forgot who they were. You could live there for ten years and still be considered an outsider. "Oh, yes, you're the people living in the Anderson house"—as if it was less yours for having gotten there second.

Hagerstown remembered, because it looked upon outsiders with a jaundiced eye. Outsiders introduced alien ideas, flaunted traditions, broke the unwritten rules. It was a boy from Muncie who had been caught circulating dirty books in a ninth-grade gym class, two transfers from Indianapolis who'd broken into the pharmacy, a girl from Richmond who got herself pregnant and refused to be ashamed.

It wasn't that no one from the town ever stepped over the line, ever trashed a classroom in the wee hours or went driving drunk and killed themselves and two classmates on a lonely moonlit road. But for those who belonged, allowances were made and forgiveness was possible. He goes to my church. He's on my son's Little League team. I went to school with his mom.

Just as Wallace reached the automated, it began to snow, a dusting of tiny icy flakes that gleamed in the beams of the Magic's headlights and swirled in clouds around the streetlamps marking the interchange.

Wallace felt cold inside, cheated. It seemed there should have been something there worth taking away with him, something that was not a weight on his spirits. Some reason for it to be.

Loneliness knotted his heart. The faces stayed in his mind. Weathered, stoic, restful, childish. Not one had opened to welcome him. Not one had seen that he belonged there.

A stranger, like a thousand strangers before. Like all the strangers whose names he had forgotten, who came and a month, a year, two years later were gone again.

And like one he had not forgotten. There was a what-if with a softer edge—

Her name had been Shan, Shan Scott. A unique name, as

202

unique as the spirit within her, a name borrowed like his from an older generation. She would be—what, twenty-six now. Almost twenty-seven. A what-if for sleepless wishing in dark rooms, for dreams that burned. There had been a year of wanting, a summer of talking, and a single kiss.

Shan Scott. Daughter of the new high school principal from Chicago, a senior his junior year. Honey-caramel hair, thick and soft. Laughing, joyful, soulful eyes. She confounded by refusing to play the coquette, alienated by shunning basketball, amazed by talking of books no one else had read. City girl, they had said. Had sneered.

Twenty-seven. Old enough to belong to the Common World. Old enough to be walking this world as well, somewhere.

Feeling as he did, it was a small step from wondering if he could find her to searching for a phone. He found one at the next exit, standing alone at the edge of a diner's parking lot. "Directory assistance for Deerfield."

"Go ahead."

A pilotless trailer roared by on the automated, kicking up a cloud of ice crystals in its wake. "Last name Scott, first name Shan, S-h-a-n." An unusual name. Perhaps he would be lucky.

"I have an S. Scott in Glencoe, an S. Scott in Glenview, and several S. Scotts for Chicago."

Married. Moved. One of the vanished. One in two hundred million, following her own path in her own world. What would she be? Artist? Teacher? She had had ambitions which did not fit neatly into any career. "What about a Franklin Scott?" he asked impulsively.

"I have a Franklin Scott on Wilmot in Deerfield."

Wallace whooped. "That's it." He punched the redirect button, and the phone dialed the number as the operator recited it.

"Scott's," a woman's voice answered, a voice rich as a seasoned violin. Mary Scott, a gentle, generous woman, the anchor of the Scott family.

"Mrs. Scott? I don't know if you remember me. This is Michael." An old Guard trick—everyone knew a Michael or two. It had been among the most popular male names for a quarter-century. "I'm an old schoolmate of your daughter Shan's. I'm in town for a couple of days and I was hoping I could see her. But—"

"Oh, this is such a shame," the woman said. "I'm so sorry, Michael. I know she would have wanted to see you. But she doesn't live in Chicago any more."

"No?"

"She said it was just too hectic for her, Bloomington had spoiled her. She went to school there, you know."

"Bloomington? She's in Bloomington, Indiana?"

"She and some of her friends have a little store. And she's still taking classes. Do you ever get to Bloomington? Or maybe you'd like to write to her. I could give you her address."

"Please," Wallace said.

He scrawled the numbers and words on the back of a dollar bill. His heart was racing.

Bloomington. An hour away from Indy. God—

He thanked Mrs. Scott and politely extracted himself from further conversation. Burying his hands in his pockets, he walked slowly back to the Magic.

What are you thinking, he scolded himself. *This is another alternity. She's not anything like what you remember. She doesn't remember anything you remember. It'd be like starting over.*

But all the scolding notwithstanding, as the Magic edged forward into the snowy night, Wallace found that he could not stop smiling to himself.

For Immediate Release   January 8, 1978

REMARKS BY THE SECRETARY OF STATE
TO THE UNITED NATIONS GENERAL ASSEMBLY
ON THE *MARJORIE* INCIDENT
Wein, Austria

11:00 A.M.

THE SECRETARY: Mr. Secretary, today, the town of Port Charlotte,
Florida, will remember its dead. There can be no burial, for there
are no bodies. But today Port Charlotte will honor and mourn
as best it can five faithful, hardworking men, family men,
fishermen. Let us give them names, that they not be ciphers in
our deliberations:

Daniel Keyes, married, father of two. Alfred Norse, thirty years
a sailor. Edward Janacek, married, father of three. Leon James,
married, father of a one-month-old daughter. Dick Weston, engaged
to be married.

Though any of us may mourn the passing of a fellow human
being, I do not come here to call on you to mourn these five.
We will deal with our grief in our own way.

But I do call on you to condemn their murderers. The sinking
of the *Marjorie* and the death of five of her crew is a tragedy.
But it was no accident. These men died at the hands of the Soviet
Navy.

The facts are not at issue, for a fortunate sixth man, John
Norse, the son of the captain, survived his twelve-hour ordeal to
relate the shocking story. And Dick Weston's camera survived,
the few grainy frames he snapped offering horrifying
corroboration.

The facts are these: A week ago today, a Soviet submarine
rammed and sank the American fishing boat *Marjorie* two miles
off the Florida coast, in the Gulf of Mexico. The submarine then
left the area, left the crew of the *Marjorie* to drown without
so much as sending a distress call on their behalf.

The facts are simple. But many lies have already been told to
obscure them. The Soviet Navy first claimed that the collision
was an accident and that the sub commander did not know of it

until informed by Soviet naval authorities. We exposed this naked lie by releasing yesterday a transcript of the commander's radioed report on the incident, as intercepted by our coastal defense stations.

This morning Pravda released the "official report," and it contains an even bolder lie—that the *Marjorie* was in fact an armed patrol boat and that the collision occurred when the submarine was submerging to escape an unprovoked attack. We are called "provocateurs" and "lawless pirates." You are invited to blame the victims rather than the criminals.

I offer for your consideration a photograph of the *Marjorie* and her captain Alfred Norse, and ask you to picture that "assault." A forty-foot wooden-hulled fishing boat built before the Second World War and armed with a flare pistol and a shark gun, against a modern three-thousand ton, two-hundred-fifty-foot-long steel-hulled missile-firing submarine. It is ludicrous to contemplate.

America is shocked and angry.

We are shocked by the callousness of the Soviet Navy in first striking down and then abandoning these defenseless sailors. Though perhaps we should not be shocked, for callousness is a well-known Soviet trait.

We are angry at the cowardly nature of the attack, angry at the needless loss of our friends and family members, angry at the arrogant violation of American sovereignty and international sea law.

But we are a nation with a respect for law, a tradition of honor. We seek justice, but we will not seek revenge. We must and will respond, but we will not lower ourselves to the level of the sneak attack and the guerrilla war.

Today I place on notice the naval forces of those powers hostile to democracy, the USSR foremost among them. We have not only the means but the will to defend our citizens and our waters.

Beginning today, any military vessel, surface ship or submarine, which intrudes into American coastal waters without prior authorization will be presumed to have a hostile intent. America's coastal defense network is on the highest alert. The commanders of our sub-killer destroyers and antiship missile batteries have full authority to attack and destroy intruders.

I warn the navies of the Communist world and their masters to take heed. The line is drawn. Cross it at your peril.

CHAPTER 13

Triumph of Honor,
Failure of Courage

Moscow, The Home Alternity

The city was firmly in the grip of winter. The Moskva River wore a thick coat of ice, the hurrying pedestrians thick coats of wool and fur. Heads were lowered and faces muffled against the subfreezing wind. The freshest snow, three days old, had been hammered into a lumpy white crust which crunched and squeaked under foot and tire. Sokolniki Park was an arboreal graveyard of bare-limbed trees, the low-hanging sun casting a tangle of long, pale shadows.

Inside a cavernous room, three unsmiling men faced the quiet fury of the General Secretary. "So what is happening?" Kondratyeva asked. "Where is the truth? Geidar says yes, Nikolai says no. Pytor avoids saying anything at all. The Americans call us liars and I am tempted to accept that judgment."

"I believe my captain," Admiral of the Fleet Koldunov said stiffly.

"Do you? Your submarine captain says he was provoked, his boat attacked at close range with automatic weapons, heavy machine guns. Yet the report from Dakar where the submarine is now moored says that these weapons failed to leave their mark anywhere on the hull. Is our armor that impervious, our steel that strong?"

The Minister of Defense rallied to the defense of the Navy commander. "There was damage to the sail from the collision. Enough, perhaps, to conceal evidence to support Captain Avilov's account."

"I trust that our shipwrights in Dakar are competent enough to detect bullet holes even in crushed metal," Kondratyeva said dismissively. "There is no evidence."

"True," Voenushkin agreed. "And yet, I, too, believe Captain Avilov has told the truth. And Avilov's officers are unwavering in their support for him—"

"A conspiracy of the guilty."

"I do not think so, Secretary."

"What explanation have you, then?" Kondratyeva demanded. "That those who wielded the weapons were incompetent?"

"No. I believe that they were most competent."

"Explain."

The Intelligence director sat back in his chair and steepled his hands in his lap. "I have been contemplating the notion that this incident was staged, carefully scripted by the Americans. A fishing boat leaves port and does not return. Who is to say that it is the same boat which faced down the *Nachodka*? Six sailors go out, one comes back, and a town mourns its dead. But there are no bodies, only the tales of one man. Who is to say that they are truly dead?"

"A deception, Geidar?"

"Perhaps. I have examined the photographs released by the Americans. They show only the ocean and our submarine, and a few feet of gunwale that could belong to any boat. No hardworking fishermen. We should watch these 'grieving' families closely. Perhaps, 'heartbroken' or 'destitute,' they will one by one leave their hardworking little town in the next months. With new names in new cities, who will know that this father, that husband, is returned from the dead?"

Kondratyeva clapped his hands together and brought them to his lips. "And the crew of this *Marjorie*—"

"Soldiers, CIA agents, guided toward our submarine by the American Navy. Their purpose from the start to draw an unwary Soviet officer into a foolish act. To create an incident which would fire the American blood fever and provide the context for Secretary Rollins' impassioned performance in Vienna."

The Minister of Defense was nodding, his face wearing a look of wonder. "Yes. Yes," said Medvedev. "No bullets struck because none were fired. Only blank cartridges, empty noise to panic Captain Avilov."

"Who did not panic," Koldunov said quickly.

Voenushkin nodded in agreement. "He submerged, as instructed, as he reported. There was a collision, yes. But Captain Avilov did not ram an American fishing boat. I greatly doubt whether a submarine of *Nachodka*'s class is nimble enough to accomplish the feat unless undetected until the moment of impact. I believe the *Marjorie* sailed deliberately into the submarine's path.''

"Brave men. Loyal men," Kondratyeva mused.

"No doubt. Even if an air-sea rescue helicopter was waiting just over the horizon, they risked death. Some may have lost the risk.''

"How confident are you of this analysis, Geidar?"

"I am always confident of American duplicity."

Kondratyeva turned toward the Admiral. "Nikolai," he said. 'How real is the American threat to our submarines? And do not try to impress me with the skill of your crews and the superiority of your vessels. Impress me with the truth.''

"American detection methods are much improved," the Admiral conceded gruffly. "Their attack submarines are still largely blueprints. Their destroyers and corvettes are a minimal threat. Should they choose to employ their patrol aircraft and missile batteries, the threat would be greater.''

"Do you have any reason to think that they will choose not to employ them?"

"The Javelins are untested against live targets. Perhaps they will fear betraying a weak hand.''

The Minister of Defense spoke up. "I believe the Americans will use all their weapons, or none.''

"As do I," said Kondratyeva. "How much greater a threat, Nikolai?"

The Admiral huffed and squinted. "The continental shelf is broad, especially on their Atlantic coast. There is limited room to maneuver, few usable submarine canyons. True security may be found only off the shelf, where our boats can enjoy a generous canopy of water.''

"You will not guarantee their safety."

"They may be able to find us. I do not think they can reach us, not unless a boat should be caught on the shelf.''

"Which is where they are designed to operate. Where they must go in order to accomplish their mission.''

"Yes."

Kondratyeva turned to the GRU director. "The intelligence these submarines gather—how valuable is it?"

"The value of what we have learned in the past is modest," Voenushkin said. "The value of what we might learn in the future is immeasurable.''

"And how much would be lost if these vessels were with-

drawn past the twelve-mile limit the Americans claim, if they
respected, let us say, a fifteen-mile line?"

"Much. Most."

"And are there no other assets by which we may gather the
same intelligence?"

"There are other assets, each with its strengths and weaknesses.
There is some overlap."

Kondratyeva made a chinrest of his folded hands. "It seems to
me that we could survive the withdrawal of these vessels from
American waters for a time, until the Americans have cooled
their fever and relaxed their vigilance."

"That would be a dangerous—" the Minister of Defense
began.

"To keep the submarines on station is dangerous," Kondratyeva
snapped. "The danger of lost vessels, and dead sailors, and
renewing the flame of America's war passion. The danger of
escalation and miscalculation. We must weigh one against the
other."

"And so we dance to Robinson's tune?" asked the First
Minister, who alone among them could risk such a question.

Sighing, Kondratyeva looked away, out the frost-glazed window. "Sometimes a child must be allowed to have its way."

"And sometimes it must be put in its place."

"It is not the time for that, Pytor," the General Secretary
said. "Nikolai, I wish the submarines withdrawn. Please see to it
immediately, before events overtake us."

The Admiral of the Fleet rose, bowed dutifully, and hastened
from the room.

"Now, my friends," said Kondratyeva softly to the two
who remained. "I have need of seers, not soldiers. Let me
hear your thoughts on the thornier question—to what is this
prologue?"

Bloomington, Indiana, Alternity Blue

Five Friends. Wallace drove past slowly, peering at the handpainted
blue sign above the recessed entrance to the little store. He saw
that lights were on inside, and the sidewalk was freshly swept of
the fat-flaked snow which had been falling since midafternoon.
They have a little store, Mary Scott had said. Almost there.

The odd and the offbeat owned that stretch of Morton Street,
one block toward seediness from the town's main business square.
Next door to Five Friends was The Second Sex, which billed

itself as "A Women's Resource Center" and hid behind windows boarded up with unpainted rough-cut cedar. Across the street in an old freight terminal was The Nine Lives Furniture Reincarnation Co., its huge sign depicting an oak and porcelain Hoosier hutch like the one which had stood in his grandmother's kitchen.

Most improbably, on the corner nearest to where Wallace parked stood something calling itself The Traveler's Club Restaurant and International Tuba Museum. The name tempted Wallace inside, where he found an old-fashioned fountain counter, a menu offering Ethiopian and Turkish dishes as the day's specials, and walls hung with tarnished, placarded bombardons, euphonia, and double-bass saxhorns. He laughed with childlike delight at the sight, and, defying the weather, bought an ice cream cone to take with him.

The cone gave him something to do as he stood in front of Five Friends, summoning the courage to go inside. Behind the many-paned display windows, arrayed on tiers of pale-blue stairlike shelves, was a polyglot of offerings as eclectic as the store's neighbors—album jackets and French-language books, queer kinetic sculptures in metal and fat pillows in the shape of sleeping cats, hammered silver jewelry and earth-toned macrame, raw crystals and polished marble eggs.

Crumpling the sticky napkin and pushing it deep into a pocket, Wallace mounted the single step to the entrance and pushed open the door. A bell jingled, but, contrary to his experience, no clerk came running to pounce on him.

The inside of the store was much like the face it showed to the street—hundreds of items which seemed to have little in common except for the space they shared. But the floorplan was more appropriate to a house than a retail store, with arched doorways leading from the large front room to what appeared to be a maze of smaller rooms in the back.

All in all, Five Friends felt more like a place to visit than a hard-boiled retail establishment. There was even a rocking chair and wicker footstool by one of the bookcases, with a small handlettered sign offering browsers a "simulated hearthside reading environment."

Wallace's eye was caught by a many-hued butterfly hanging from the ceiling, its kite-sized wings made of a luminescent film which shimmered in the backlighting. He was still staring at it when she appeared in one of the archways.

"Hi," she said in a friendly voice, slightly breathless. "I'm Shan. It's been kind of quiet this afternoon, so I've been doing some work out back. If I can help you with anything, just come find me."

Then she was gone, almost before he could realize she had been there, mercifully before the shock could show on his face. Her clothes were like nothing he had ever seen her in—mannish slacks that ended at midcalf, a kimono-sleeved white blouse with contrasting black shoulder lacing that suggested epaulets. The honey-caramel hair was longer, gathered at the back of the neck with a wide wood-and-leather barrette instead of flowing free to frame her face.

But the eyes. The voice. The electricity that surged through him when she was in the room, and drained from him when she vanished. Those were exactly the same. Exactly. And then he heard music from somewhere in the back, a song softly sung in a warm and gentle voice, and followed it without thinking.

He found her two rooms away, sitting crosslegged in the middle of a huge circular rag rug, a book lying open in front of her. A gray-black cat patrolling the perimeter of the room fled at his approach, but Shan seemed not to notice him until he spoke.

"Pretty song," he said.

"One of my favorites," she said, looking up. "Did you find something?"

"Still looking. I've never been in here before," he said. "It seems like a place you need to take some time in."

She smiled. "I'll tell the others. They'll like that."

He crouched down near the doorway. "Then the name does mean something. Five Friends."

"We share the expenses, we share the work. Everything out there is something that one of us loves, that one of us thinks is beautiful or important or special. Some of it we make ourselves. Mark makes the sculptures—he's got a little studio here, in the basement. Diana does the macrame."

"What's your contribution?"

"The books, mostly. Did you look at them?"

"Not really."

"I don't put anything on the shelf that I haven't read. About half the albums are ones I picked. And Patrick is teaching me about crystal and stone."

"Mark—Diana—Patrick—you—and . . . ?"

"Christine. We were all in school together here. All except Mark. This place is a 'someday-we-ought-to' that became real."

"You're lucky. But how did you ever get a license?" he asked, shaking his head.

She gave him a questioning look, and he realized he had

slipped. Here there was no need for the Essential Business Permit, the blue certificate with the federal seal that hung above so many cash registers back home.

"Zoning is the owner's problem," she said. "We just paid the first month's rent and opened the doors."

"I like the idea," he said. "Is it working?"

"I don't think anyone thought we'd get rich," she said cheerfully. "And we haven't."

"Isn't it hard, everything being so personal? What about the people who come in, look around, and leave without buying anything? Doesn't that make you feel rejected?"

"Is that what you're going to do?" she asked, eyes laughing. "No, actually that makes it harder to let them go. Especially the things that are one of a kind. We don't sell very hard, I'm afraid. As you saw."

He pointed toward the book. "Am I keeping you from something?"

"Madama Blavatsky's *Isis Unveiled*," she said, glancing downward. "I'm studying theosophy."

"I don't know what that is."

She laid a silver bookmark in the center of the book and closed it. "Most days I don't feel like I do, either. I can only read it in small doses. A little reading, a lot of thinking."

"Then can I ask you to show me some of the music you recommend? That song you were singing, if you have it."

She cocked her head, surprise parting her lips. "You don't know what it was?"

"I'm afraid not."

"Then you do need my help," she said, uncoiling her legs and rising gracefully to her feet. "I don't think Judy Collins ever recorded a more beautiful song."

"Judy Collins," he repeated. *Here, too. Common World.* "She's a favorite of yours?"

"For years. Oh, I know her kind of music doesn't get much time on satellite radio," she said. "But there's more to life than a Hot List stamp of approval. That's what this store is all about. I wanted to call it Pleasures and Treasures, but I got voted down."

She led him from the room, then paused in midstep and turned to look back at him. "I just realized—you have the advantage of me, sir."

"Hmm?"

"What's *your* name?"

He held her eyes for a moment, weighing the look in them.

213

"Rayne," he said, answering in more than words. "Rayne Wallace. I was named after my great-grandfather."

Her face lit up. "Really? I was named for my mother's older sister—grandmom's first. She was killed by a runaway truck when she was eight."

I know, he thought. "I like your name."

She smiled at him uncertainly, uncomfortably, and turned away. He followed, remembering.

And when strange thoughts come into your head, you wonder if it's little Shan James, fighting for a little more of her life, sending you a message. When you told me that I laughed—I didn't mean to, it was just such a surprise—and you got angry.

Except with what I've seen, I'm never again going to tell anyone what can't be. So don't tell her, little spirit, he thought as he trailed Shan to the album rack. *Please don't tell her that I already want her—unless you see in her that she can love me, too.*

Black Duck Lake, Minnesota, The Home Alternity

The beating of the helicopter blades overhead was a perfect multiple of the throbbing in Gregory O'Neill's temples, making the twenty-minute flight from the small jetport at International Falls into the heart of Superior National Forest an unending torment. Neither aspirin nor massage, both of which he had applied in large quantities, had brought any relief.

Relief, if there was to be any, lay another fifteen wooded miles ahead, at the cabin on the southwest shore of Black Duck Lake. For the torment was only partly physical. O'Neill had thought the cold blind anger was under control, thought he had successfully pushed it down under an insulating layer of rational professional discourse.

But the closer the single-rotor four-place blue and white Boeing Vertol came to where the President was waiting, the harder it was for O'Neill to forget his personal outrage, the sharper and more intemperate became the inner voice rehearsing the encounter. It had been playing in his head for twelve hours, becoming a conversation that would not wait, could not keep until Robinson returned from his vacation.

Lied to me. You lied to me—

The news had come to him late the night before, in a phone call he had taken at home in his quiet, book-lined den. The call was from the SAC commander, a dutiful, unexcitable man O'Neill had known for twenty years, since he was Senator Church's aide and the commander the project leader on the YF-7O interceptor project.

"Gregory, what in the hell does the CIA need with an H-bomb?" he had asked, quietly but quite indignantly. "And why in the hell was I cut out of the procurement process?"

How could he answer? What could he say?—Sorry about that, Blaze. I was cut out, too. How fast would *that* little story spread, destroying his credibility with the Pentagon, crippling his ability to control the men who occupied the Tank, the Joint Chiefs' boardroom enclave off the Bradley Corridor.

Shaken himself, O'Neill had little sympathy to spare, little capacity to soothe someone else's ruffled feathers. "There's nothing I can tell you now," was his blunt reply. "But I'm going to get some answers." It was a weak promise, and the SAC commander was unassuaged. But O'Neill had managed to both hold down his own feelings and hold off his old friend until he could escape from the conversation.

Then he had seized the glow-eyed black-boxed NSA scrambler in both hands and hurled it, broken wires flying out behind, through the den window and into the snowy backyard. Nor was that the worst of it. When his wife came running to see what was wrong, he had barked something about minding her own damn business, and then walked out on her when she refused to take the advice.

O'Neill was not proud of the way he had handled it. But there was no question that the provocation was extreme. He had been fighting against the same kind of loss of control ever since, fighting the impulse to forgo words and express himself by opening up Robinson's skull. *It would be an interesting trial—*

"Pinetree, this is White Rose," the pilot was saying into his radio. "How's the ice on the porch?"

"Twelve inches thick if it's a foot," came the answer. "Bring her on in."

The pilot twisted his head around until he could see O'Neill. "Wally says the lake's solid," he shouted over the rotor noise. "I can put you down right by the front door, if you don't mind a little slipping and sliding. It'll save you that long walk in from the helipad."

O'Neill bobbed his head in agreement, then slid sideways on the seat to peek out through the small side window. The FNS called the Black Duck retreat—a five-room frontier-style log cabin heated with twin wood stoves, the only permanent structure inside a thousand-acre national preserve—the "White House in the Wilds." Taking a more sarcastic turn, the *New York Times* called it Pa Robinson's "Little House in the Big Woods."

As O'Neill watched, the trees suddenly fell away beneath them. The pilot swung the helicopter wide over the lake, then dropped down to within a few feet of the lumpy, snow-drifted lake ice and bore in toward the shoreline where the cabin stood, a hundred feet upslope from a small pier. A man in a long gray coat stood on the end of the pier, watching the chopper's approach.

It had to be Rodman. As much Robinson's friend as his chief of staff, Rodman was the only White House aide allowed to accompany the President on his retreats. And it was Rodman who had answered when O'Neill had called to tell them he was coming. Rodman who had told him flatly to stay in Washington.

"He and Janice are celebrating their twentieth," Rodman had said. "You know that. Let 'em be. We'll all be home Tuesday."

"I'm sorry. This can't wait, Bill."

"If it's important enough to disturb Peter here, then it's important enough for him to come back to the city," Rodman had countered. "Why don't you tell me what the emergency is, so I can tell Peter why he has to cut his second honeymoon short."

At that, O'Neill's veneer of civility had evaporated. "I didn't call to ask permission, particularly not yours. I called to give the President fair warning. I'll be there about two this afternoon."

"Don't do it, O'Neill," Rodman had threatened. O'Neill had not answered. He had simply hung up.

It had to be Rodman waiting, and it was. He pounced on O'Neill as soon as he had disembarked. "You're way out of line on this one, Greg-boy," Rodman said, blocking O'Neill from advancing down the pier.

"Get out of my way, Bill."

The helicopter roared up over the trees toward the helipad, the downdraft creating a brief, furious blizzard. "Goddamned Ivy League faggot," Rodman said. "You know what your problem is, O'Neill? You don't know what it means to be part of a team. I should have told the Secret Service to blow your goddamned chopper out of the sky."

The insulating layer burst, rent through as though slashed by a razor. Without conscious thought, O'Neill took a half-step forward and delivered a savage roundhouse right to Rodman's jaw and throat.

The sound of his gloved fist against Rodman's bare skin was muted, but the power of the blow was not. Rodman's head whipped to the left. He took one, two staggering steps in that direction, half retreat, half quest for balance. The second step found nothing but air beneath it, and Rodman toppled off the pier and crashed heavily to the ice. There was a cracking sound, and the gurgling of water.

Two Secret Service agents in white winter combat suits came running from the woods, one arrowing toward Rodman, one, weapon drawn, toward O'Neill on the pier. Feeling release rather than guilt, O'Neill started toward the cabin. He did not trouble himself to see if Rodman was hurt, or drowning, or both. In that moment, he did not care. With equal disdain, he brushed aside the agent who tried to intercept him.

"O'Neill, Gregory Patrick. January 11, '27, Hempstead, Long Island," he recited without breaking stride. "The President is expecting me."

The cabin was little more than a rectangular box twenty-five feet by sixty, seemingly the product of a box of Lincoln Logs in the hands of an unimaginative child. The logs which formed the heavily-chinked walls were as raw on the inside as the out, and the ceiling overhead was a forest of rafters and roof timbers.

A wall of heavily varnished knotty pine divided a third of the cabin's length off as a bedroom suite. For all practical purposes, the rest of the cabin was a single large room, broken up by a massive stone chimney pillar in the center. The chimney served both a fireplace facing the living room and a wood-burning stove in the kitchen.

From beyond the pine wall, O'Neill heard the sound of running water, and then Robinson's voice: "Make yourself comfortable, Gregory. I'll be out in a few minutes." Faintly, he heard Janice laugh, or more aptly, giggle.

Leaving his coat and gloves on the coat tree by the front door, O'Neill walked to the other end of the cabin and settled in a chair facing the cold hearth. No one else was in the cabin, nor had he expected there would be. This place was all Robinson's. The Secret Service, the command communications staff, and even Rodman were obliged to live in trailers adjacent to the helipad, a quarter-mile away.

Despite their exile, the cabin's rustic atmosphere seemed false and forced. Over the hearth hung a thirty-inch muskellenge mounted on a plaque, its mouth gaping open as though about to take the hook. O'Neill doubted it had been caught in Black Duck Lake, or even by Robinson personally. The muskie's blank staring eye gave the trophy a surreal quality.

Discomfited by the wait—an old trick, making a caller wait—

O'Neill went to the window and looked out toward the lake. There was no one in sight, so presumably Rodman had survived the encounter. O'Neill felt a brief pang of guilt, but it was tempered by the pleasure of discovering that somewhere between the pier and the cabin his headache had vanished.

Turning away, O'Neill looked for something else to divert him. There was not a book, magazine, or newspaper anywhere to be seen. Likewise radio or TV. A victrola stood along one wall, but its record compartment contained only bottles of liquor. No distractions, O'Neill thought. Except Janice.

Somewhere a door opened and closed, and O'Neill looked up to see Robinson approaching, barefoot and wearing an ankle-length burgundy robe.

"Hello, Gregory," Robinson said, his voice and manner relaxed. "Janice and I were out skating just before you got here, all the way to the west end and back. I swear that a hot shower is the only way to really drive the chill out." His smile broadened. "Well—almost the only way. Do you skate?"

"I never learned how."

"I had to teach Janice. But you'd probably be forcing things now to try. It's a skill best learned at a young age, when the bones are forgiving and you don't have so far to fall."

"I'm sure." Was there a second message to that? Robinson was not usually that subtle.

Before O'Neill could decide, the front door opened, and there was the stamping of snow-covered feet. Then Rodman appeared at the end of the little hallway between the chimney and a rank of closets. His cheek was reddened by more than the wind, and his eyes were cold and hard.

"Sorry I'm late, Peter," he said, advancing toward them. His voice had a hoarse rasp to it. "I had to change clothes."

Robinson held up a hand to stop him. "No, Bill. No notes on this one. Leave us alone."

Query, disapproval, and threat passed across Rodman's face, the first two meant for Robinson, the last directed at O'Neill. "I'll be in the trailer," he said gruffly, and retreated.

Robinson turned to O'Neill. "Well, Gregory. You came a long way to get something off your chest. Why don't you do it?"

"You're going ahead with this Q-plane business."

"It has a name now. Mongoose. Yes, I gave Dennis the green light to advance the work on hardware."

"Without telling me."

Robinson lowered himself slowly into an easy chair. "You said that you preferred not to have anything to do with it."

"That's bullshit. You led me to believe this thing was dead."

"I never said anything of the kind."

"You said you wanted me to stay on."

"Yes. To do the things that you do best. Though I assume that one of the reasons you're here is to resign again, and to get it right this time."

"I'm here because this scares the shit out of me, and I'm trying to find out what the hell is going on in your head that it doesn't scare you just as much."

"Why don't you sit down, Gregory?"

"Is it that bad?"

Robinson laughed. "I just thought you might be getting tired of looming over me like a vulture."

Feeling foolish, O'Neill retreated to a chair.

This is starting to get away from me, he thought. *I should never have hit Rodman. I could have used that anger—*

"You know, of course, that I don't have to answer to you," Robinson was saying. "But I don't mind you knowing what's going on in my· head on this, because I know that the logic is very clear. And because you could make a positive contribution to the effort if you came to see that."

"I don't see myself supporting this under any circumstances."

Robinson waved a hand absently. "The world is full of surprises. Wasn't it you that said 'there are no one-punch fights?' Or are you just so fast I didn't see the flurry?

"Yes, I saw, from the bedroom window," he went on, not giving O'Neill a chance to answer. "I'll wager it's been a few years since a Cabinet member laid out his President's chief of staff. I'm going to have to ask the White House historian about that when we get back."

"I don't think Bill considers the fight finished," O'Neill said, flushing. "Which is exactly my point about Mongoose. There are major command and control centers in Kiev, Omsk, and Khabarovsk, manned by generals and admirals who will know exactly what is expected of them when the lines to Moscow all go dead."

"The weakness of strong centralized power, Gregory, is that the satellite regions become dependent on it. It's why dolphins are easier to kill than sharks."

O'Neill shook his head. "Snakes—sharks— this zoo of metaphors you have for the Soviet Union worries me, Mr. President. I worry that they get in the way of seeing the Soviets for what they are.''

''And what is that, exactly, Gregory? What insights do you have that escape the rest of us? Or have you spent so much time in the E-ring that you've been infected by the Pentagon's habits of mind?''

Robinson came up out of his chair and paced in front of the hearth as he continued. ''The Reds are all-powerful. They have tougher tanks, bigger missiles, better soldiers. They have no alcoholic sentries, no careless maintenance techs, no defective build-it-cheap-and-build-it-fast hardware.''

He stopped in midstride and turned to face O'Neill. ''Is that it, Gregory? Is that what I'm supposed to see?'' he demanded, gesturing angrily. ''Am I supposed to believe every doom-and-gloom general who comes calling with a ten billion dollar end-all-and-be-all weapon-system blueprint in his pocket? Christ almighty, the best work you've done for me has been turning that kind away at the door. Now you want me to start believing that self-serving whining and cringing.''

''I want you to come to grips with the fact that Mongoose is going to start a war we're not ready to fight.''

''Now, I don't know what you mean by that,'' Robinson said, settling back in his chair.

''I mean there's no follow-up. What happens after the Q-plane repaves Red Square? Four hundred million people are not going to just throw their hands in the air and say, 'Oh, well, you win, good game.' You've got no plan—''

''Nonsense,'' Robinson said. ''Half the Pentagon does nothing but plan, and the other half wargames the plans. Thunderbolt. ABC 123. Charioteer. Omega. Are they just paper, or are they real?''

''They weren't drawn up for this. Not for fighting a knife-in-the-back sneak attack.''

Robinson rested his elbows on the armrests and folded his hands at his waist. ''There's a copy of Thunderbolt in the comcom trailer. Would you like to reread it? It's remarkably neutral on the subject of how and why war starts. But I will concede one omission. None of the planning teams had the advantage of assuming the war would start with Moscow destroyed and the Soviet civilian and military leadership eliminated.''

''Peter—I don't think you understand. If even one Russian missile wing or one Red SSBN smokes its birds, there's going to be a lot of dying. You can't shrug that off. These are our people we're talking about.''

"The war will already be over," Robinson said quietly.

"Oh, that'll be spendid comfort to the millions who're going to do the dying. Go on television while the birds are in the air and tell them to be proud while they're frying, that we won."

Robinson's face wore a solemn frown. "The tree of liberty must be refreshed."

"What?"

"Jefferson. 'The tree of liberty must be refreshed from time to time with the blood of patriots.' Funny how much wisdom we've forgotten, isn't it?" Robinson said. "Something I don't understand happened along the way to here, something that made us too reluctant to spill our own blood, made us willing to surrender anything to avoid it."

"The 'something' that happened was called Hiroshima."

"It's just another weapon, Gregory. It's not the devil's spawn."

"It's a hell of an incentive to keep the peace."

"Peace," Robinson repeated. His head lolled back against the chair until he was looking up into the cabin's rafters. "There's been more fighting about that than almost anything you can name. Do you know, Gregory, there's a very simple reason why peace on earth is a pipe dream. Peace has the disadvantage of freezing the status quo, and there'll always be individuals, groups, nations who find the status quo unacceptable. This time, it's us."

O'Neill had never expected to hear it said so plainly, confessed to so proudly. "Our own survivors will come for you," O'Neill said quietly. "They'll hold you to account for starting the war that killed their sons and mothers."

"They'll never know," Robinson said with calm certainty. "We'll pull together, and we'll build together, and we'll go on."

"I wanted to believe that you just didn't see where this could lead," O'Neill said slowly. "But you do. And you're willing to do it anyway."

"Did you think this was a casual decision, a whim you could turn me from with a few words and a dramatic entrance? I know, Gregory. I've never deceived myself about what could happen."

"Or questioned your right to decide this for all of us."

"There's no reason to question it. What are governments and Presidents for, Gregory? Should farmers and steelworkers vote on defense policy? Should we conduct foreign policy by plebiscite, commission the FNS to take a poll on every crisis?"

"You can at least poll your own advisors. You haven't even convened the NSC on this."

"I have polled my advisors, as many as considerations of security will allow. You're alone in objecting. I've listened to your objections, Gregory. You have to grant me that. You've been able to speak freely, and I have listened. But I'm not obliged to agree."

"What about the Tank? Are you saying the Joint Chiefs are with you on this?"

"The Joint Chiefs gave the only assent they needed to when they signed off on Thunderbolt," Robinson said with a shrug. "Every one of those war plans says, 'If you need us, this is what we can do.' It's not the Chiefs' place to judge the need."

Grim-faced, O'Neill shook his head. "I can tell you that they do think about things like that. They don't stop being citizens when they become soldiers."

"I'm only interested in what they have to say as soldiers," Robinson said.

O'Neill leaped to his feet. "For the love of God. You're not the fucking king of America," he shouted. "You can't do this. You just can't do this."

But Robinson did not so much as flinch. "There's something I want you to think about before you mount your high horse and ride away: Mongoose will go on with you or without you," he said evenly. "So you can resign to salve your conscience, if you have to. You can also stay in good conscience, knowing that your leaving would make no difference. The only positive option you have is to stay and help make it work, and by that minimize the price of change."

When had it gotten away from him? Or had it never been his at all? O'Neill had never felt more powerless. Reason was his weapon, his tool. Robinson had taken it from him and shattered it on a stone of conflicting convictions. "I don't think I can stay," he said.

Robinson nodded, unsurprised. "It's just as well, I suppose. Alpha List is very long. Albert will be glad to hear he can pare a few names from it. You had your kids on it, too, didn't you, Gregory?"

Staring, mouth agape. "You bastard."

"Did you expect to keep the privileges of office after you abandoned the responsibilities?" Robinson asked. "If I were you, I'd sell the house. Washington might not be a good place to be."

His legs weak, O'Neill collapsed back into the cushions. His mouth opened, but no words came.

"You see, Gregory, I never wanted to be king. I can do

everything that needs doing as President,'' Robinson said, his soft words a hammer. "The world is going to change, Gregory. And I'm the catalyst.''

O'Neill's voice was a croak. "How can you be so sure? How can you take such a chance?''

"Wars are conducted between governments, not peoples. And I'm stronger than they are. They've lost the fire. Look at how quickly they caved in. There hasn't been a Red sub inside the line for ten days. I tell you, Mongoose *will* break them.''

"It was just one incident. They had nothing to gain in forcing the issue—''

"If they still had the fire, they would have fought us for pride, for principle.''

Eyes downcast, O'Neill said nothing, locked in silent struggle with himself. *I could make the choice for myself. And Ellen would stand with me, I know she would. But David, and Sara, and Mark, their families—they're the only ones I can save. The only ones. And the only way I can save them is to stay. Oh, God—why do you test me like this?*

"Gregory, I have no intention of being rash,'' Robinson said, as though to soothe him. "We'll take their measure again, I promise you. But I can tell you now what will happen. They'll back down. They'll blink. And when they do, we'll know they're ours.'' He paused, waiting for a response that didn't come. "You're going to stay on.''

O'Neill slowly raised his head to meet Robinson's eyes. "Yes.''

With a satisfied nod, Robinson came to his feet. "I'll call your taxi.''

Rodman joined Robinson at the door of the cabin to watch as the helicopter collected the Secretary of Defense from the end of the pier and roared skyward.

"Well?'' Robinson asked.

"The chain is five links long. From a couple of two-stripers at the weapons depot on up through the base commander to General Matson.''

"Blaze Matson? The SAC commander?''

"He's the one who tipped O'Neill.''

"Damn,'' Robinson said, and spat into the snow. "All right. Here's how it has to be: court-martial for the two-stripers and lock 'em up till this is over. Transfer the base commander to Thule or some other godforsaken hole. Matson—it's about time for Matson to retire. Suggest it to him.''

"They were just doing their jobs.''

"And somebody wasn't. Who fucked this up, Bill? Who handled the procurement?"

Rodman swallowed. "Ken Andrews, from CIA. He was the man on the scene."

Black light flared in Robinson's eyes. "Kendrew again? Goddammit, I thought we told Madison to lose him."

"He was dropped off the tactical team," Rodman said. "He's been a golden boy for them. Madison must have thought that was enough."

"It isn't."

"Peter, I don't think Andrews is at fault here."

"No? Who is?"

"You are."

"Oh?"

"If we'd done this from the top down, we could have done it cleanly. But you wanted to work around O'Neill." He paused and looked skyward. The helicopter was a black speck in the distance. "At least we won't have that problem anymore."

"O'Neill's staying," Robinson said.

Rodman stared. "Whose idea was that?"

"Mine."

"He's the one you ought to be locking away."

"I found his soft spot. He's under control."

"I want a piece of him."

Robinson looked at Rodman's swollen face and grinned crookedly. "He did catch you a good one."

"The ice did most of this," Rodman scowled.

"And you ten years younger than him. I'm disappointed, Bill."

"I just don't see why you want to take him with us. Why you think you can trust him."

"I didn't say I trusted the son of a bitch," Robinson said, shaking his head. "We're going to isolate him. Complete freeze-out."

"He won't take it."

"He will," Robinson said. "As for taking him with us—we won't. You said you wanted a piece of him?"

"I do."

"Then I'll let you tell Tackett. I want O'Neill's counterpart in Blue killed. Some way that'll put his face in every newspaper. So there'll be no place for him on the other side."

Rodman nodded. "That's better," he said. "Consider it done."

• • •

As the helicopter carried him away from Black Duck Lake, shame like he had never known before seeped through O'Neill like slow poison, a spreading stain. How cheaply we can sell ourselves, he thought bitterly. A few lives close at hand for a million faceless strangers.

He stared out the window and for the first time in his life thought of suicide, of evading the accounting. But death would bring its own accounting, one which he now had reason to fear. And Robinson would keep no bargain with a dead man.

He would live, though life promised to be joyless. He would live, the waiting consuming him, the guilt tormenting him, until Robinson's wave of change had swept across the world. With luck, or a merciful God, the wave would drag them both under.

MEDIA WATCH Hot List for February 6, 1978

TM

BOOKS, NONFICTION

This Week	Last Week	
1	2	**THE CURRENCY OF REASON** by Dr. David Romanczk (Straus) A noted psychologist offers his prescription for "nonmaterial enrichment."
2	4	**HOLISTIC HEALTH** by Mary Richard Dunn (Dell) A survey of Asian, African, and native American concepts of the body, illness, and death.
3	—	**THE STARS OUR DESTINATION** by M. A. Banks (UN Press) The UN Space Authority's official history of humankind's first twenty years in space.
4	—	**POWER EATING** by Christopher Bell (Today) Recipes and menus for "makers, shakers, dreamers, doers, and anyone seeking self-maximization."
5	1	**WITCH OF THE WEST,** by Samantha Gaddis (Berkley) A Los Angeles socialite details her thirty-year involvement with the Old Religion.

Heating Up: NEVER AGAIN!: *The Case for Internationalism* by Senator Ryan Cripps; THE NEW ANARCHISTS by Ramon Juarez Cuartero.

CHAPTER 14

The First Casualty of War

Bloomington, Indiana, Alternity Blue

"Oh, look at the line," Shan said breathlessly, clinging to Wallace's elbow as they rounded the corner into a flurry of snow.

Wallace looked. The theater ticket office looked like a bank teller under siege on Black Tuesday. "If we run, I think we can beat that couple across the street."

"Let's," she said.

Gloved hand in gloved hand, they splashed through the slush to the opposite sidewalk and the end of the line.

"I want to pay for mine," she said.

"Not necessary."

"I have a job, you know."

"That's just my own money coming back at me."

"I don't mean the shop. Flower arranging. Three days a week."

He shook his head: "Florist, the shop, classes—do you ever sleep?"

"You left out the Songsisters."

"I didn't know about them."

"It's a community choral club. Tuesday and Thursday nights."

"Anything else?"

"Mmm—not right now. You changed the subject."

"Did I?"

"The shop actually made a profit last month. That's mad money. And the concert would have been free."

227

"Forget it."

She was persistent. "Then I'll pay for the calories after."

"If it's important to you."

"It is," she said. "Have you ever been to the Princess before?"

"No," Wallace said, looking up. From the outside, the New Princess Theater looked like any vaudeville-era small-town movie palace Wallace had ever seen. Its carved-stone facade rose high enough to promise a balcony inside, and the huge thrust marquee shielded several dozen ticket-buyers from the fat, wet flakes of snow cascading down through the yellow halos of the streetlamps.

"There was a theater a lot like this in Richmond," he said. "Every now and then the whole family used to go across the county to see a movie, as a special treat. Birthdays, mostly."

"What did you see?"

"I can't really remember," Wallace said. But he did. *Invaders. The Wind in the Willows.* Dean Martin and Jerry Lewis in *Just My Luck.* Richard Thomas facing those snarling range hogs in *Old Yeller,* a sight that had given him nightmares for several days thereafter. The thriller *Train from Berlin.* No titles, he thought. It's okay if I don't give titles.

"I remember the last time we did it, though," he said. "It was my thirteenth birthday. Mom thought we were going to see a nice safe patriotic movie, but she got surprised. There was a scene in a sleeper car on a train, between the American agent—a strong, silent type—and the German girl who'd helped him get back the lost files."

"Hmmm—blonde, long-haired, fresh-faced, improbably gifted—"

He grinned. "I remember being impressed, anyway. Things got kind of heated. They didn't really show you anything, just sounds and words in a dark room. But Mom grabbed me by the hand and dragged me out. Dad and Brian—my older brother—stayed and watched the rest of the movie."

"Thus jumbling the moral message."

"Thus starting one of the few really ugly arguments I ever saw my parents have, in the car on the way home. Brian and I sat in the back wondering if we were going to end up as tree food."

She laughed sympathetically. "Do you go to movies much?"

"Not very often." He tried to remember. Discounting an eye-opening visit to a smoker house in New Jersey during a Red run, the last time had been a month or two after he and Ruthann moved to Boston. They had thought Katie would sleep through it, but she had talked and squirmed throughout, and as a bonus befouled her diaper twice. Wallace could not remember anything of the film itself.

"This is awfully nice of you," she said. "I've been wanting to see this one since I first heard about it, before Christmas."

"You're easy to be nice to." God—did I really say that?

He had called with an offer to take her to a coffeehouse concert on campus, and she had countered with the suggestion of *The Jeweled Dagger*. Wallace was content for her to choose, would have acceded to any suggestion so long as he could share her company. He was happy enough that she had consented to see him again.

Their first meeting had evolved into something resembling a date. She had played him one song after another on the shop's hi-fi, bubbling over with the honest enthusiasms of someone sharing something she loved. He had bought two cartridges for the Magic and two discs, though he had nothing to play them on. The evening ended with talk of hometowns and childhoods over coffee in the Traveler's Club Restaurant.

But that had been two weeks ago, two frustrating weeks during which his duties either tied him to Indianapolis or took him away to even more distant places. He sent her two silly cards at the shop, called her from a motel room in Kansas City and talked for an hour at the Guard's expense. It was not enough, not nearly. He yearned to be as powerful a presence in her life, her thoughts, as she was in his.

The theater was more than half-full by the time they reached the aisles. No theater Wallace had ever been in had had a pitch as severe or a screen as large as the curved blue-lit expanse filling the entire front wall of the theater. On the screen, shimmering letters sliding through the spectrum read "MagiCine— The Ultimate Film Experience."

"Where?" he asked. "Down front where everyone else seems to be?"

She shook her head. "The effect is just as good back here," she said. "And I'd rather sit in one of the doubles. They're more comfortable."

"Lead on."

Following her, he found that the top half-dozen rows were composed of benchlike double-wide seats, with no chaperoning armrest to come between a couple sitting together. Gloves came off, coats were folded over backrests. He sat far to the left, giving her the choice to sit close or far away. She settled near, but not touching. They were like two magnets teetering on the edge, locked to each other but still separate.

When the lights went down, Rayne reached for her hand. Her fingers were strong, her skin warm. The answering, accepting pressure of her touch was electrifying. He traced slow teasing circles on her palm with the soft pad of his thumb. She squeezed his hand and then withdrew her own. It was postponement, not rejection. A gentle "not now."

The screen went black, and music began—a solo cello, plucked, joined soon by a bass flute. Words, stark white print, came up slowly from the black and then vanished again. He could not sever his link with her enough to read them. He heard her gentle breathing as a song among a thousand hushed sounds, felt her heat beside him, her wholeness overlapping his.

Then the first image flashed onto the huge screen, a sticklike corpse burned to faceless anonymity, and he forgot that she was there.

The audience filed out largely in silence, the few combative voices counterpoint to the hushed conversations and head shakes.

I can't let her see, Wallace thought frantically as the overhead lights brightened and the screen went to blue. *I can't let her know. Jesus! Three words. That's all they said about Norfolk during orientation.* "A nuclear accident." *A nuclear accident. Jesus.*

Only slowly did he realize that there were others in the same state, rooted in their seats, still staring blankly at the screen. He looked at Shan. Her cheeks were wet with tears, but her lips held a small, poignant smile.

"Are you all right?" he asked.

She nodded wordlessly and wiped the moisture away with both hands. "I was hoping—I don't know, I felt—she felt right. Diana, I mean. I can see—I'm sorry." She twisted in her seat, turning away from the screen and toward him. "I'm not quite collected yet. Are *you* all right?"

He took a deep breath. "Not quite. How many theaters are there like this?" Protective camouflage.

"This was your first MagiCine?"

He nodded, his lips twisting into a wry smile. "Started out with a good one."

She let out a breath as though it had been trapped inside her for minutes. "Except this one you can't walk out and say 'It's just a movie.' "

"No," he said. "I didn't know."

"Know what?"

230

"I never really knew what the bombs could do. What it meant—Norfolk. It was just a word."

She smiled, and the fingers of one hand grazed the nape of his neck. "Not your fault. You were—what, nine?"

A quick mental calculation. "Eight."

"And I was ten," she said, her eyes softening. "More than anything, I remember the way my parents acted. I'd never seen my father so angry or my mother so sad. I didn't really understand why. I thought it was me, that I'd done something."

He felt like a fraud. "A lot to take on yourself."

"I had a good fifth-grade teacher. She helped a lot of us. We sat in a circle and she told us what had happened." Her eyes were downcast. "Told us plainly, something my parents didn't seem able to do. They thought they could protect us. But we needed to know. About the people who were dead and how the city was gone. Norfolk was something ugly from the adult world pushing into our world. Mrs. Lilley, she let us be adult long enough to start to understand it."

He took both her hands in his and squeezed them, and she raised her eyes and smiled. The conversation was closing down into a trap, an invitation for him to impale himself on his own fraudulent inventions. The longer they sat there, the greater the danger would be. He nodded toward the theater ushers, moving through the rows collecting trash. "I guess they'd appreciate it if we left."

"I guess they would."

They gathered up their coats and started up the aisle. Near the top, something glinted on the carpet ahead of them: a new penny, face down. Wallace bent over and turned the coin face up, but left it there when he took Shan's hand to lead her on.

"Why did you do that?" she asked, holding back.

"If you find a penny heads up, it's lucky."

"So they say."

"So, when you find a penny face down, turn it over and leave it for someone else to find."

Her face brightened. Her eyes held a quiet delight. "What a wonderful thought."

He smiled back, but inside there was sadness. A wonderful thought, yes—one I learned from you, years ago in another place, and you years before that from your grandfather. Except it wasn't you, after all, was it? How much are you like her, Shan Two? How much of a fool am I?

"We'd said something about calories," he said to have some-

231

thing to say. "What about the Oaken Bucket, down the block? Didn't you say the food was good there?"

"I don't think I'm up to Sully's."

He held the exit open for her. "Is it too expensive? You don't *have* to pay."

She frowned. "The truth is, I'm not very hungry. Too much going around in my head."

The snow had stopped and the skies cleared, leaving an inch-thick film of soft, cold down that sparkled in the light like the scattered stars overhead. "A drink, then. There must be some-place on the Square."

She looked away, down the quiet street. "I think what I'd like is to go walking with you for awhile. Would that be all right? Maybe down to campus to sit by the observatory and look at the sky."

"If that's what you want."

She sighed. "What I'd really like is to go out to Yellowwood Forest and walk in the woods. I'd like to get away from all these walls and stop seeing Norfolk."

"How far is it?"

"Oh, it's too far. Ten miles. Maybe fifteen. It takes me more than an hour by bike in the summer."

"Let's go."

"What?"

"It's not summer, and you're not riding a bike. Let's go."

"Are you sure?"

He drew her to him and kissed her forehead softly. "I'm sure."

By the time they reached the park, a gibbous moon had climbed above the horizon to paint the new snow in cold light. They left the Magic in the road by the locked gate and crossed the drift-covered parking lot to where the black trunks of trees formed a surreal colonnade.

The forest was quiet save for the squeak of snow underfoot. Shan, too, was quiet, turned inside herself, and Wallace did not intrude. Her steps were unhurried, but purposeful, as though she were retracing her way to a familiar place. He dropped back and let her lead, granting her the privacy she seemed to want.

Where the trees thinned on the bank of a small frozen stream, Shan ran ahead to throw her arms around the massive gnarled and scarred trunk of a full-crowned arboreal giant. As Wallace drew nearer, she turned, resting her back against the scaly bark.

Three feet above her head, the lowest limbs reached outward like sheltering arms.

"Isn't this a wonderful tree?" she asked.

He stepped up and ran a hand over the fissured surface of an old burl, legacy of a past infection. "It's got character."

"I call it the grandmother tree," she said. "It's a white oak, like most of these. They can live seven hundred years. Can you imagine what that would be like? Seven hundred years standing here and watching the world."

"I wonder how old this one is?"

"Two hundred—three hundred years. It was already old when this land belonged to the Algonkin and the Iroquois. When the whole state was oak-hickory forest as far as you could see, before the French started cutting trees to build their forts and their fires. Do you see how the younger trees seem to give it room, out of respect? They're her children and grandchildren. She's proud of them—they're protective of her. This is a good place to grow old."

"Nothing like this in Chicago," Wallace said, remembering her mother's words.

"No," she said. "There are white-tailed deer in this forest, did you know? I fell asleep here once, and when I woke up there was a beautiful buck with a broken antler standing on the bank, drinking."

Snow melted by his own body heat was saturating his socks, but his feet were becoming too cold-numbed to notice. "It's peaceful here. Calming. I can see why you wanted to come here, after that movie."

"It's a little piece of the world that never changes. At least not on the time scale of one person. You have to have some place you can go that feels like home."

He shivered. "I know."

"Where is it for you? Where do you go?"

Shaking his head, he admitted, "I haven't found it yet."

Her smile was one of sympathy. "If you'd like, you can borrow mine until you do," she said, spreading her hands wide in an echo of the spreading limbs overhead.

"Thank you."

She came forward a step to hug him. "Thank you—for bringing me here."

"My pleasure."

She twisted and looked upward into the web of branches. "I just needed to remind myself that it was here."

"Feeling better?"

"Yes. I'm all right now."

"Then I guess it's time to take you home."

"No," she said, reaching for his hand. "I think it's time I took you home."

Where Shan lived had been a polite secret between them. She had not offered the information, allowing him to pick her up at the shop because it was "convenient." He had not volunteered that he already knew she lived upstairs, in an apartment on the second floor.

The apartment was a long wood-floored room with a brass bed at one end and a porcelain stove at the other—a railroad flat without the partitioning walls. As he removed his coat and stepped out of his wet shoes, she turned on a warm yellow lamp, then retreated toward the bed. He followed, the uncertainties he had accumulated during the drive back vanishing.

Her blouse was unbuttoned by the time he reached her, and he slipped it off her shoulders, bending his head to kiss the bare skin before discarding the garment carelessly on the floor. She reached for his belt, and it became a playful race, each undressing the other with eager curiosity. Clothing littered the rug, his mixed with hers.

When she stood nude before him, he naked before her, a tremor of uncertainty ran through his body, the newness suddenly threatening. She had had other lovers before him. Would he know how to touch her, how to please her? The anxiety must have shown on his face, for she came to him with a searing kiss, all hungry lips and teasing tongue.

"Touch me," she whispered.

Heat drove away the wisps of fear, unleashed passions old and new. She chased a cat off the flowered comforter and drew him down with her onto the bed. Guiding his hands, whispering urgent invitations, she did not merely accept his passion, but answered it. She did not merely yield, but welcomed him, closing a circle around them both that shut out all thoughts of past and future.

Her hands coaxed, stroked, teased. His hands explored the lushness of her body, the soft fullness of breast and buttock. He nibbled the soft skin below her ear, she the crinkled nub of his nipple, an unfamiliar but electric sensation. Kneeling facing each other, they traded long, slow kisses and intimate touches, she curling soft fingers around his hardness, he parting slick silky lips with a gentle probing touch. They clung together on a rising spiral of energy, learning the secrets that new lovers give shyly to each other.

And at the peak of the spiral she lay back and pulled him down on top of her, opening to him and guiding him inside, moving with him and against him, her little cries and his grunting moans the orchestration of their wordless oneness.

It was not poetry, it was not romance. It was fire and fury, matter and antimatter. It was sexual hunger, obsession, compulsion, the full surrender of self to sensation. It was soaring, transcendent flight.

And when the gasping, shivery break came—his first, knotted liquid, hers soon after, grasping, gasping—it was not an ending, but only a pause. For the burning had lit a greater fire that could not be quenched in one night or a hundred. Lying in her encircling arms and holding her in his was at once a very old and a very new feeling.

This is the place, he thought, though he could not have whispered it to her without his voice breaking. This is the place that feels like home.

Washington, D.C., Alternity Blue

A tenth of a mile from the South Portico to the fence at E Street. A tenth of a mile back. In a heavy coat, with an eager full-grown Gordon setter pulling on its leash to hurry him along, that was enough to clear Daniel Brandenburg's sinuses and loosen sleep-tightened joints.

The sunlight on the snow-covered south grounds of the White House was brilliant, almost blinding. A circular depression marked the location of the fountain pool. Above the denuded trees of the Ellipse rose the obelisk of the Washington Monument, stark and hard-edged. On the horizon, between a gap in the trees, gleamed the rounded dome and pillars of the Jefferson Memorial.

Halfway to the fence, Brandenburg heard footsteps behind him, and stopped and turned. A stocky man with short oily-black hair was hurrying down the machine-plowed path toward him. As Brandenburg surmised, it was Richard Bayshore, the director of the National Information Agency. Bayshore had called early that morning for a breakfast appointment, and then missed it.

"Sorry I'm late, Mr. President," the newcomer said. "There was an accident on the Rochambeau Bridge, and I got hung up in traffic."

"Don't fret about it, Richard," said Brandenburg, resuming walking. "I assumed you were late for good cause."

"I'll be happy when they finish boring the tunnels," Bayshore said, alluding to the plans to link major federal buildings with a network of underground rubber-and-rail shuttle lines.

"In the meantime, you could learn how to ski," Brandenburg said. "What did you want to see me about, Richard?"

"Did you watch the news this morning?"

"I did."

"Did you happen to catch the item about that ugly business last night in Dayton?"

"The murder?"

"Yes."

"Grisly business, murdering a man in front of his wife."

"There's more to it than that. We've joined the investigation, along with the FBI."

"Oh?" They had reached the farthest point of the U-shaped path, and Brandenburg raised his hand to wave to the several dozen shivering, frost-breathing tourists waiting beyond the fence for a glimpse of him.

"Half of them are probably Secret Service agents," Bayshore observed.

"Almost certainly," Brandenburg said. He knelt and released the catch on the dog's leash, freeing him to dash forward into the deep snow. "Air Force man. Is that why we're interested?"

"Partly. The victim's name was Gregory K. O'Neill. He was an Air Force colonel assigned to Wright-Patterson as a logistics officer."

"Was he involved in anything sensitive?"

"Not particularly. He was a solid, low-profile career officer with nothing out of the mainstream in his jacket or his job."

"So why are we interested?"

"Because the whole business doesn't add up. About seven o'clock last night, an hour before O'Neill was due home, a man breaks into the house and takes the colonel's wife prisoner. He ties Mrs. O'Neill to a chair in the living room, but otherwise doesn't touch her."

"Not a rapist."

"Or even an opportunist. He doesn't talk to her. He doesn't search the house, he doesn't go through her purse. He just sits behind her, out of sight, and waits."

Brandenburg whistled, and the black-furred setter came bounding back. "For the husband."

"Yep. O'Neill comes in the side door, calls for his wife,

236

comes into the living room, and our visitor shoots him four times. He then puts a noose around O'Neill's neck, hangs him from the banister—the living room has a sixteen-foot ceiling and a balcony off the bedrooms. And he writes DEATH TO THE ENEMIES OF PEACE on the wall. I have pictures of all this up at the House, if you need to see it.''

The dog back on its leash, the two men started back toward the White House. "This message—in blood?''

"Nothing so crude. Red ink marker. Brought it with him, took it with him.''

" 'Death to the Enemies of Peace.' I didn't hear anything about that on the news.''

"Because we have Mrs. O'Neill and the press doesn't,'' said Bayshore. "Everything that was released came through the Dayton police, who're helping us. The TV reports were edited to avoid the writing.''

"And then he leaves, with the wife alive.''

"After leaning over her and whispering, 'This is just the beginning,' or something to that effect.''

Brandenburg grunted. "I guess I know why we're interested. Any leads at all on the shooter?''

"No. He was a pro, Mr. President. He didn't leave forensics anything to play with.''

"He left a witness.''

"Just another puzzle. Like I said, it doesn't add up. None of the internationalist groups have any history of violence.''

"A solo crazy?''

"Or a new player.'' They had reached the portico, and both men stamped snow-coated shoes on the concrete. "I want to put this out to the network,'' Bayshore said. "You know I need your approval to activate the Volunteer Watch—the alerts go out over your name.''

"Nationwide?''

"Regions 1 and 3, for now. Everything east of the Mississippi except the Deep South. A top-down alert, very quiet. Nothing on the open media.''

Brandenburg sighed. "You know how I feel about your citizen spies.''

"Yep. It keeps me from asking most of the times I want to.''

With a reluctant nod, Brandenburg said, "All right. Anything else?''

"You might want to give up these walks for a while.''

Brandenburg shook his head. "Richard, the day the President can't go for a walk in his own backyard, the country's too far gone to be worth saving."

Washington, D.C., The Home Alternity

The messenger entered only one step, then saluted. "The car is ready, Mr. President."

"Thank you," Robinson said, rising from the couch. "Let's go," he said to the two men waiting with him.

William Rodman turned from the window, scowling, his hands stuffed into his pants pockets. "Don't do this, Peter. You're not going to get anything out of Somerset."

"There seems to me to be little chance the Prime Minister will change his mind," Ernest Clifton added, struggling into his coat. "It's quite possible that protest will simply open a breach between Washington and London."

Robinson was already at the door. "Open a breach, E.C.? You're not reading this right. The breach exists. It opened the moment Somerset sat down to write me that letter. Now, come or stay, the both of you—but don't tell me not to go."

Frowning, Rodman shook his head. "I'm coming," he said.

Clifton silently fell in behind, following the others out the South Portico to the idling limousine, which was sandwiched between two armored escort cars. Two Secret Service marksmen armed with M-5 rifles and armored against the night cold occupied the bird's nest on the lead vehicle.

This is so foolish, Clifton thought as he climbed into the limousine. The others made room for him on the broad back seat. Where is Gregory? He should be here. He could make the President listen. Running to the British embassy at midnight. Betraying weakness through empty anger.

The car started forward. Foolishness. Where is O'Neill? Where is Robinson's conscience?

As the motorcade growled its way up Massachusetts Avenue toward the embassy, Clifton replayed recent history in his mind, seeking release from his own conscience for what was about to happen.

The seventh government of the Sixth Republic of France had disintegrated three weeks ago, the opening act of a crisis which nearly brought down the republic as well. Pushed to the wall by a struggling economy and governmental deficits, President Louis

Ribaud had moved to protect the economic interests whose strength had carried him to office.

Ribaud's "shock therapy" program imposed 100 percent "temporary" tariffs on all imports from Germany and Italy, France's two largest trading partners, and selected imports from Belgium, Spain, and Great Britain. He clearly had hoped that the emphasis on "temporary" would stave off retaliation, and as far as the minor trading partners were concerned he succeeded.

But after less than a day's consideration, Germany and Italy had placed "temporary" 100 percent "equity taxes" on all imports from France, and Ribaud's program began to unravel. There were general strikes in Paris and Lyon, and in Aude and Bourgogne angry vintners, who depended on exports for their margin of profit, spilled wine casks in the streets in protest.

Ribaud stood firm in public while privately going hat in hand to the German and Italian presidents, pleading for a regional economic summit meeting. Probably at Moscow's direction, his pleas were refused. That was when the bankers and merchants cut Ribaud loose and began looking for a new champion.

With key supporters of the President conspicuously absent, a motion of censure had been raised in the National Assembly. Ribaud ordered the Assembly to dissolve. To enforce the point, he sent troops to surround the Palais-Bourbon, ostensibly to protect it from rioters. Defying the order and the troops, the Assembly remained in session and passed the motion of censure.

A full-blown constitutional crisis was finally averted when Ribaud, either patriot or realist, stepped aside. Which left Denis Gaschet, the Prime Minister and leader of the Parti Communiste Français, as Acting President. France had "fallen" to the Communists without a shot.

It was exactly the sort of situation Somerset had anticipated. It was exactly the sort of situation which should have prompted him to play his Weasel card. Robinson and his inner circle waited expectantly, then wonderingly, finally impatiently for the announcement. But there was only silence from Somerset until the letter, routed through Ambassador Taskins and relayed to Washington in code.

The key paragraph was brief: "As the French situation has resolved itself without immediate danger, your security guarantees are no longer required. I respectfully request that all personnel on loan be recalled within sixty days."

Translation: Thanks for the safety net, but you can have your missiles back now.

Robinson had been enraged, the more so after Somerset refused his call. No guarantees of the integrity of communications, London said. Risk of exposure of sensitive information. Confidence only in lines from the embassy. Snubs and insults.

Like dominos falling, click, click, click, from Ribaud's miscalculation to Somerset's betrayal. Nothing that could have been done. Nothing to do but admit they'd been skillfully outmaneuvered and walk away. Except that Robinson was a brawler, not a diplomat, and the graceful face-saving retreat was not in his repertoire.

The caravan slowed to make the turn into the embassy drive. Ah, Gregory, Chifton sighed. It doesn't matter. Enjoy, wherever you are. There's probably nothing you could have done.

The communications technician wore a British Navy uniform and a supercilious expression. "I should caution you, sir, to be judicious in your language. Although we have considerable confidence in the Maskit coder, there are no guarantees that the Soviets will not intercept your conversation."

"I hope they do," Robinson said. "Now, place the goddamned call."

The technician stiffened, taken aback. "The connection is already made," he said. "It's part of the verification process. Just pick up the receiver."

"Then get the hell out of here." Robinson waited until the technician completed a huffy departure, then turned to his companions. "No interruptions," he said. "If you have something to say I'll hear it afterward."

Rodman nodded, and Clifton quickly said, "Of course, Mr. President."

Turning back to the table, Robinson picked up the phone. "This is President Robinson."

"Yes," said a voice. "This is David Somerset."

"I want to know if I'm reading between the lines right," Robinson said. "Are you asking me to pull the Weasels out?"

"Weren't you warned about this line, Mr. President?"

"Answer the goddamned question."

"Very well. Yes, I'm asking you to take the Weasels out. They're no longer of any use."

"Christ reborn, the whole reason you asked for more was you were afraid the French would end up on Moscow's tit. Now they are, and you say they're of no use? My intelligence people tell me the French military has at least three hundred nuclear warheads. Those are Communist warheads now, twenty miles away from you. And you tell me you're not worried."

"I was never afraid of the French," Somerset said easily. "I have at times been concerned about my own people. But it's been quieter on the back benches than I feared might be the case. The truth is that the French look rather foolish from here, not at all threatening. The whole matter has been taken rather as a comedy."

"I take it you're laughing, too."

"The Communists are in power, true enough. Likely they'll stay there. But France is not a Communist state. More to the point, it is not a Soviet client. Nor do I see any prospect that it will soon become one. A French Communist is as independent-minded as a French Socialist. I'm confident they'll refuse the tit."

"What makes you so damned sure?"

They could almost hear Somerset's smile. "Because they already have."

"What?"

"I can't discuss my sources, you understand," Somerset said. "But Gaschet was approached by Soviet officials last Thursday. They offered hard currency loans and an agreement to double purchases of French wine, wheat, and automobiles by the Red bloc."

"Son of a bitch—"

"Even though what they offered would go a long way toward solving his immediate problems, Gaschet told them the French would do for themselves, thank you very much. So you see, either he'll succeed and retain France's independence, or his government will fall and a centrist take power, to the same effect."

Robinson scowled. "This is a side issue," he said. "You wanted to look strong when France went Communist. Fine. I understand the political game. But the Weasels aren't targeted on Paris. They're targeted on Murmansk and Leningrad and Odessa. How about facing up to the real threat, Prime Minister?"

"We have no quarrel with the Soviet Union."

The stupidity of the statement galled Robinson. "Are you a Communist yourself, then?" he sniped. "I'd heard they were strong in British Labour."

"Shit," said Rodman under his breath. Clifton groaned.

"Thank you for not disappointing me," Somerset said. "You're every bit the ass I was told to expect."

"So you don't bother to deny it."

"No, I don't. Because I don't bother to deny idiotic blather," Somerset snapped. "You bloody yabbo, we deal with Communists every day. You've been hiding behind that wall so long you haven't the first idea what's on the other side.''

"The Reds have enough weapons to smash your entire island into sand—"

"But why would they? Really, Peter. What would they have to gain? Nothing. They have no need of more land—they're facing a hundred-year task to develop what they already own. And anything else we have or make they can buy from us at a fair price. We have differences, many more than a few. I wouldn't call them friends. But neither can I call them enemies.''

"I can't believe that you intend to make that kind of bar-stool liberal thinking the basis of policy. Don't be naive, Somerset. Anytime the other bastard is stronger than you are, you've got to be careful.''

"I am being careful. That's why I want the Weasels gone.''

"You asked for them, goddamn it! You let us think you understood the strategic issues.''

"I understand *our* strategic interests. And our interests demand that those missiles go back to your side of the Atlantic.''

"They're no goddamned use over here unless we go to war with fucking Greenland.''

"That's none of our concern. Put them in Alaska and invade Kamchatka.''

"You used us, you bastard.''

"Yes. A payback, Mr. President, for the high-handed way you and my predecessor used us. For your arrogance in trying to draw us into your little feud. Sixty days.''

"Sell us the oil platforms," Robinson said on sudden impulse. "We'll move everything offshore.''

"No.''

"Look, there has to be some reasonable middle ground here—"

"There is none. You can take them out, or you can watch us drop them into the sea. Sixty days.''

Indianapolis, *Alternity Blue*

The sound of a key in the lock announced the return of Wallace's roommate. Fowler had a sack of groceries in his arm and a dusting of melting snow decorating his knit cap and coat.

"How'd it go?" Wallace asked, looking up from the notes and photos arrayed around him on the living room floor.

Fowler tossed Wallace a keyring in a looping arc. "I tried three different stores, including one in Millersville as large as a

General Supply back home. It had everything you could want if you were cooking Spanish or Ukrainian. But the fish was all frozen, the only seaweed was in the aquarium supplies, and they had never heard of Chocos.''

Fowler had been moaning about the chocolate-glazed cinnamon-filled pastries for weeks. "I hadn't either, and we call the same world home. Don't make yourself crazy. Bring some back next time you rotate Home."

"That's not funny. I'm not going to break quarantine."

"I guess you'll just have to adjust," Wallace said with a shrug. "I've had frozen fish. It's not that bad."

"I don't trust frozen food," Fowler grumped, stepping past Wallace's scattered work en route to the kitchen. "It's just a way of passing off food that didn't sell five minutes before it spoils."

"I don't think that's how they do it."

"Why not? No one in their right mind would pick frozen over fresh. Anyway, thanks for the use of the car."

Smiling to himself, Wallace returned to his work. "How long is it until your next pink card?"

"Three weeks. Why?"

"I just want to know how long I'm going to have to listen to you complaining about Choco deprivation."

"Oh," Fowler said, folding the empty sack and tucking it under the sink. "Well, as far as that goes, I think you need to get Home, too," he volunteered.

Wallace looked up. "What do you mean?"

"Just that if you were working as much as you say you are, you wouldn't need to be catching up on your paperwork the few nights you are here—like now."

"Oh."

"Not to mention the stupid smile you wear on your face when you are here."

The stupid smile appeared on cue. "What do you think it all means?"

"I think it means you're bending the fraternization rules," Fowler said crossly. "Don't tell me, because I'm not asking. But just because I don't go out doesn't mean I don't know anything. Some of the reports that come across my desk would pass for pornography on the other side of the gate."

"Some of what you watch on that television would, too."

"I'm not watching for myself," said Fowler. "I'm trying to assemble a picture for the Guard. This world offends everything we know about how people should live. The things women here do—the things they allow—I would never have believed it. The

243

women who've been seduced by the pills and the propaganda, running away from their parents and running out on their husbands.

"A woman can divorce her husband here for no reason—incredible! They take men's jobs and ape men's roles and suddenly they're as shallow and selfish as the worst of us. Sluts. Seducers. Marriage doesn't mean anything to them, motherhood doesn't mean anything to them, morality doesn't mean anything to them."

Wallace had experience with Fowler's little sermons, and he had learned the best way to shorten them was to say little or nothing. But this time the attack seemed personal.

"There's some special women, too," he said, knowing he should remain silent. "There's women that can fill a house with music and show you ways of thinking about the world that you never dreamed of. There's women who have so much love and joy inside them that one smile, one look can make you feel like your life has started over again."

Fowler stared for a moment, then came and sat on the chair opposite Wallace. "The worst I thought was that you were slopping the whores on Central Avenue or trolling Michigan Street for students. But that's not what this is, is it."

"Who are you asking for? Yourself or the Guard?"

The analyst squirmed uncomfortably. "Myself."

"Are you going to report me to Frederick?"

"I don't want to get you in trouble. But I don't want to see you get yourself in trouble, either."

Sighing, Wallace leaned back against the front of the couch. "I already am," he said.

"Not yet. Nobody knows. Just stop seeing her."

Wallace shook his head. "Did you ever know someone who made the rest of the world go away for you? So that it was just you and her, and nothing else was real."

"Don't try to tell me you love her. God in heaven, you can't be that stupid."

Bristling, Wallace said nothing.

"How long has this been going on? A month?"

"About," he said gruffly.

"Then you don't love her," Fowler said firmly. "Are you slopping her?"

"Christ almighty, Gary," Wallace snapped. "Is that the only word you know for it? Is that what you call it when you get romantic with your wife?"

"That's the right word when there's no ring," he said stiffly.

"When you touch somebody—when it's right—" He caught

244

himself and started again. "Shan brings everything she is to her lovemaking. She gives it time, and love, and thought, and energy. She's so different from—Look, it's not like what you're saying at all."

"You don't love her," Fowler said. "Women use sex as a trap. They make you call those feelings love, make you think you have to have her, when all you have to have is friction."

"This isn't like that," Wallace said, shaking his head. "And besides—I loved her before I met her."

"What are you talking about?"

"She's Common World."

Fowler stared. "Somebody you knew back Home?"

"My might-have-been. The person I'd think about on those nights when you're lying wide awake in bed at two in the morning. Think about and wonder if she ever thought of me. Doesn't everybody have one?"

"Sweet Baby Jesus—Ray, how could you be so stupid?"

"I don't know," he said. He walked to the frosty window and stared out. "This picture of her in my mind," he said slowly. "It's part what she was and part what she is, all mixed in together so I can hardly tell which is which. And there's all these old feelings that never went anywhere working with everything that's so good about being with her."

"You've got to break it off."

"Arens had a girlfriend. He was even trying to get her pregnant. Nobody cared. We make our own rules. That's what he said. What business is it of Frederick's? Why should he care?"

"Forget Frederick," Fowler said. "Forget the Guard. Forget frat rules and quarantine. You're married, Ray. That's for keeps."

"A life sentence? The way they do it here makes more sense to me, Gary. You don't have to spend all those years pretending."

"You're making excuses that even you don't believe. You know it's wrong. Just a moment ago, you stopped yourself from comparing them. You won't let yourself think thoughts like 'Shan's a better ride,' because you know how unfair it is."

Wallace turned away from the glass. "There's no way Ruthann will ever know. It stays on this side of the gate. It has to."

"It only stays here if you stay here. Don't you know that you'll be comparing them, every minute? Ruthann could fail a test she didn't even know she was taking."

"I wouldn't do that."

"Yes, you will. It has to end, Ray. It has to."

"Is that a threat?"

"I don't believe in what you're doing. It's wrong—for you,

245

for the Guard, for that little girl you claim you love." Fowler took a deep breath. "Ray, I know. *I know*. I made a . . . a mistake, three years ago, with that kind of woman. I know. Please—open your eyes. You know I'm right."

"Are you going to report me? Tell Ruthann?"

Fowler folded his arms across his chest as he considered an answer. "No," he said finally. "But if you keep this up, I'm not going to have to. End it. You've got to end it."

Wallace turned back to the window. "I know," he said. "I just don't know if I can."

"You can."

He shook his head. "You don't know what it's like to fly."

Never Again

EXTENSION OF
REMARKS

OF

HON. RYAN
JACOB CRIPPS

OF PENNSYLVANIA

IN THE SENATE OF THE
UNITED STATES

*Tuesday,
September 12, 1961*

MR. CRIPPS: Mr. President, I am honored to introduce to the Senate for its consideration S.B. 141, the Common Security Act of 1961.

There may be no legislation this century which less needs introduction and explanation. S.B. 141 has already attracted seventy co-sponsors, and the companion bill, which is to be introduced this morning in the House by Thomas Kuchel of California, has over three hundred. If only its sponsors vote in favor, the Common Security Act will carry resoundingly. President Dirksen has already announced that he will sign it into law.

But it would be a mistake for us to simply let the rising tide of support sweep us forward to a pro forma approval. For the historical record alone, we are obliged to spell out clearly and carefully what we mean to and why we mean to do it.

The black scar of Norfolk will be a long time healing. So many of us lost family or friends. We all lost, in great measure, our innocence.

But the tragedy of Norfolk is compounded by the knowledge that it could have been avoided. Over the last three months, the stories have come out, one after another: The bartender who laughed off a bragging customer. The neighbor who wondered at the late meetings in an upstairs apartment. The librarian who researched odd questions for a cardholder named Diana Harris.

Again and again, we have heard the plaint: If only we'd known what to watch for. If only we'd known who to tell.

When I was a boy in Pittsburgh, my neighborhood was victimized by daytime burglars and nighttime muggers. The police did what they could, but they could not be everywhere. They needed help to do their job. My parents and my friends' parents and our neighbors pulled together to organize a neighborhood sentry program, an alliance of people who cared, protecting the homes and lives they cared about.

And together, we made our neighborhood a safe place, a happy place again. Not by taking to the streets with guns. Not by usurping the role of professional lawmen. Our weapons were our eyes and our ears. Our strength was our sense of community. And we made a difference.

In a real sense, this nation is one neighborhood. We have the same problems my old neighborhood had—invaded by lawlessness, assaulted by the ruthless and the selfish. The wolves of crime and subversion prey on us, one at a time, taking advantage of our inattention and isolation.

But we have the same weapons, the same strengths my old neighborhood had, if only we can mobilize them. Our eyes and ears. Our sense of community. We must become partners in our own protection, assets instead of victims. If we do, we can preserve this neighborhood, this nation.

The scale of the task is daunting. But sociologists tell us that any one of us is no more than four handshakes away from any other. Or, to put it another way, each of us knows the entire population of the nation through a chain of acquaintances no longer than five links long.

Within this network of relationships are all our friends, families, colleagues and co-workers. Hiding there, too, are our enemies, the real enemies of America. If we know what to look for—if we know who to tell—we can find them, and we can stop them.

Just as we could have found Diana Harris and her fellow conspirators and stopped them. Remembering Norfolk, I want to call this the "Never Again" Bill. For the key feature of the Common Security Act is the creation of a nationwide citizens' reporting network, to be known as the President's Volunteer Watch.

In high school civics classes and community education programs across the nation, we will teach our people what to look for. And from the graduates of these classes we will draw the membership of the Volunteer Watch, a million Americans mobilized in the service of America. In the defense of freedom.

Volunteers all.

Patriots all.

They are asking us what they can do to help. This bill is their answer.

CHAPTER 15

Spies and Scholars

Boston, The Home Alternity

Rayne Wallace was not surprised to find the woman manning gate control was a stranger. True, when he was running, coming through the gate every day, he had known all the gatekeepers by name and they had known him on sight.

But much could change when six weeks passed between crossings, and, besides, there were many new faces in the Tower these days. The expansion in Blue had had a powerful ripple effect, with hundreds of people changing jobs and new bodies coming on board to fill the vacancies at the lowest levels. As one veteran runner had dourly observed, "The place is being run by the B team."

It seemed that way to Wallace, in any case. Even if some of the new faces were pleasant to look at. "Rayne Wallace, 21618, Blue," he said. "Standard furlough."

The dark-haired gate controller dutifully flipped through her file. "Nothing on your card."

That was no surprise, either. Operations no longer had the manpower to debrief every returning agent. It seemed sloppy, compared to the way things had been done in the past. But the Guard was changing.

"Do you want to schedule a return?" the controller went on.

"They're doing that up here now?"

"The assignment desk was getting swamped handling the busywork and the runners both," she said, looking up. "And you haven't answered my question."

Busywork. "Let's."

"Plus seven?"

"Plus seven."

"I'll put you down for 10:45."

Wallace nodded. "See you Sunday."

The gremlins of change had had their day in the change-out room as well, Wallace discovered. Gone were the waist-high privacy walls, banished to make way for new ranks of lockers. Gone were the individual chairs with valets conveniently mounted on the back, replaced by long benches more suited to the narrower aisles. The changes made the CO feel more like a crowded locker room than a gentlemen's club.

There were a dozen or more Guardsmen in the CO, despite the hour and the day. Ignoring them and the noise they were generating, Wallace threaded his way through to his locker. The lock dial spun, the door fell open, and he began to strip off his transit clothes. His face wore a distracted, almost vacant expression that belied the turbulent feelings within.

It was his second full-length visit home. The first had been even more disastrous than his brief appearance before Thanksgiving. He had come in on New Year's Day, and within an hour Ruthann had angrily excoriated him for his absence during both Thanksgiving and Christmas. He had tried not to answer back in kind.

But when she sent Katie to retrieve the presents given her in his name—"Why don't you show your father what he got you for Christmas," in a savagely sarcastic voice—all good intentions evaporated, and he found himself sliding down into the muck of charge and countercharge, accusation and evasion, anger and tears.

Everything he had said had been the truth. That she was using Katie to get back at him. That there wouldn't have been any money for presents—and, truly, as he saw later, it had been the richest Christmas they'd known together—without his job. That other Guard wives managed to cope with their husbands' absence without creating a family crisis.

And everything he had said needed saying. But somewhere in the middle of it, Ruthann stopped listening. And when he was done, she had nothing to say, then or for the next six days. Nothing more than the minimum requirements of politeness. You want a wife who never complains? she was saying. I'll go you one better and give you a wife that never speaks.

For half that time, he cherished the silence. But presently the distance between them began to prey on him. It was not the way they had been, not the way he wanted them to be. There was a wall between them in bed, a mountain between them out of it. Neither of them dared to climb to the top, for fear of finding themselves alone there.

And so they circled each other, never touching. In pure self-defense, he had spent most of the last two days with Jason March, fleeing from a frost so deep and hard that it promised to kill any living thing upon which it settled. He wanted no repeat of that.

Wallace scooped his jewelry out of the cupped hollow on the top shelf of the locker. There were only two pieces. The first was a silver confirmation cross on a time-tarnished chain, more a family memento than religious symbol—an expensive gift from his grandmother. It had become a lesson in the value of things when he lost it playing army in the cornfields. A nighttime search by flashlight, his father, brother, and himself walking parallel rows, had revealed its glint and restored it to him.

The other piece was his wedding ring, a thick band of gold-plated metal holding a fragmentary chip of diamond. He slipped it on, forcing it past the knot of his knuckle, wondering at how strange its weight and hardness felt there after just five weeks with the finger naked.

Since joining the Guard, he had had the ring on and off so often that any symbolism of permanence or unity had been lost. This last time the ring had come off, it seemed as though he had also lost the substance. Or why else had what happened with Shan been so easy, with the guilt only coming later, and most of that only when he failed so miserably in trying to explain himself to Fowler?

He wanted to believe that the temptation of a second chance with Shan, the easy pleasure they had found in each other's company and each other's arms, was something that existed outside his troubles with Ruthann, that they did not touch each other, that they were not cause and effect, effect and cause. Even wanting to believe it, it was difficult to believe. Conscience pricked at the bubble of illusion.

And yet, in fulfillment of what he had told Fowler, he had not broken it off. True, he had stopped himself from calling or writing through the ten days between that first morning after and his appointment at the gate, a breach of etiquette which might in itself be enough to accomplish the break. But to say, "I'm sorry, this was a mistake"—to himself, much less to Shan—that had been beyond him.

Now restored to home, however briefly, he hoped to find the strength for such confessions. It was one of many hopes, sharp and turbulent within him yet beyond his capacity to articulate, for these seven days. There was a place within him that was hurting, and a place within him that was needful—for silent forgiveness for what he had done, for reasons to turn away from what he might yet do.

If only Ruthann could provide.

Within the Guard no job was held in lower esteem than that of property master—almost inevitably, since the domain of the propmaster was dotted with the likes of washing machines, sewing needles, and dirty laundry.

The propmaster's most visible task was to maintain the inventory of basic gate-safe clothing—blue pullover shirt, drawstring slacks, and hand-sewn slipover shoes—which could be assembled into transit kits for use by ferrymen and outstation staff. For the runners, the propmaster's designers and seamstresses created individual wardrobes appropriate to their covers and clearances. Toward that end, the propmaster was expected to be the authoritative voice on fashion and fad in the various alternities.

To make things worse, Operations had long used the PMO as a dumping ground for washouts and discipline cases. Virtually every male among the propmaster's contingent of sixty fell into one of those two categories, meaning a Guardsman could look across the counter and confidently feel superior to the man on the other side. The nicknames bestowed on the PMO betrayed the contempt. Regardless of gender, the propmaster was "Mom"; the clerks "checkgirls" or just "girls."

But "Mom and her girls" had ways of extracting their revenge. The clerks were frequently surly, the counter line inevitably slow, and the transit kits randomly dotted with missized and even misassembled clothing. New runners learned quickly that to surrender part of their wardrobe to a checkgirl for maintenance was to risk its disappearance or destruction.

Wallace had not dealt with the propmaster's office on a regular basis for nearly a year, but he had not forgotten what to expect. He stood in line with the same sort of resigned patience seen on the faces of supplicants awaiting their audience in a post office or vehicle registration bureau. His transit kit was rolled up in a ball under one arm; it had done double duty as home-sitting clothes on the other side and was long overdue for an appointment with soap and water.

True to form, the clerk took nearly twenty minutes to dispose

252

of the three ferrymen who had been in line when Wallace arrived. When his turn at the counter finally came, Wallace placed the bundle of clothing on the wood sill and waited for the clerk to look up.

"Drop." Wallace said finally.

"I need a number."

"I said a drop, not a swap."

"I still need a number."

"21618."

"And a name."

"Wallace."

The clerk looked up, and Wallace recognized him as a former runner. "Tough business, huh?"

"What?"

"Hasn't anybody told you yet?"

"Told me what?"

"Shit," the clerk said. "About your buddy."

"Who? Jason?"

"I guess they didn't tell you." The semipermanent sneer faded from the clerk's face. "He came up missing. On a run to Kiev, is what I heard."

Wallace stared. The words seemed to glance off some inner shield, leaving no trace on his emotions except a scorched surprise.

"He was your buddy, wasn't he?" the clerk prompted.

"Are you sure it was Jason March?"

"I'm sure. I knew him too, y'know. A little too impressed with himself, but a right guy. Yeah, I'm sure. Jason March. What a fucked operation, huh? Somebody should have told you."

A knot of ache and nausea was growing cancerlike behind Wallace's ribs. "Yeah," he said. "You got this?"

The clerk collected the roll of clothing. "I've got it."

Nodding numbly, Wallace left the counter. Upstairs, in the dispatch superintendent's offices, he found Deborah King at a desk. "Tell me about Jason," he said hoarsely.

She looked up from her work, and the empathy in her eyes struck a killing blow to Wallace's self-control. "Come on," she said, reading his pain. "Let's go up to the grill."

Mercifully, the windows of the tenth-floor Tower cafeteria looked out on the Charles River and not inward to the gate house. They sat at a hideaway table, under an American Pride mural depicting a smoking tractor engulfed by wheat fields. He sat facing the corner, she in the corner facing him.

"There's hardly anything to tell," she said slowly. "You know that. He was outbound to Black and never came through."

"When?"

"Thursday. The 21:20 slot. I'm sorry, Rayne. It's a shame."

"You bastards, he wanted out. If you'd let him out he'd still be alive."

She sighed. "We can't have singles working long-term on the other side."

"We've got them in Red."

"Nobody's happy about that."

"Why not?"

"You really need an answer?"

"I do."

She glanced past him briefly, then answered in a lowered voice. "Because Operations is afraid of defections."

"Damn it, Jason was as solid as they come."

"You put a man or a woman out there alone for six months and they might find reasons not to come back."

"Being married's no insurance against that," he said bitterly.

Her eyebrow arched in curiosity. "Operations has to draw the line somewhere. Jason got a pass just making it to runner as a single."

"Because he had what you wanted. Because you needed him. But you didn't care about what he needed."

"He was doing his job, Rayne. Solid, like you said he was. There's nothing wrong with the way he died."

"You don't know how he died," he said hotly. "Nobody does, because the blinders are on. You think maybe this'll put enough names on the memorial for somebody to start asking some questions?"

She sat back uncomfortably. "I don't know what you mean."

"The hell you don't. There's something in there, between the gates. Everybody knows it. Jason saw it late last year."

"He didn't report it."

"Because everybody knows that those kind of reports get you put out on the street with a psych release. Because everybody knows Operations doesn't want to hear it. We don't count for much up in the penthouse, do we?"

"The Guard is a combat unit. That's why you get paid what you do. You want to know what our casualty rate is? One death in every two thousand transits. That's acceptable risk, Rayne."

254

"Yeah? How come it's always the guys with nothing to lose who decide what's acceptable?"

Annoyance flashed briefly across her face. Then she reached across the table and squeezed his hand. "Go home to Ruthann," she said, standing. "She'll help you through this."

"How?" he asked, looking up at her helplessly. "I can't tell her enough to make her understand. Am I supposed to make up a story about how he died?"

"I'm sorry," she said. "This is all I can do."

He was silent for a moment. "You could—"

"No. Don't ask," she said, cutting him off. "That won't help you. Go home to Ruthann."

"You stupid bitch," he said, shaking his head in frustration. "I was going to say you could find out about his family."

"Were you?" she asked, skeptical. "All right. I'll see. But I don't see the sense. You can't go knock on their door and say, 'Mr. and Mrs. March, I was with your son in the Guard.'"

"I know that," he said, furiously blinking back phantom tears. "But just because you're ready to forget him doesn't mean that I have to."

Sunday was a family day, and the quad was appropriately quiet. "Annie?" Wallace called hopefully, pocketing the key and pushing the door open. "Katie-cat, Daddy's home."

There was no answer. He checked his watch. Church was over; he wondered where else they could be. Dropping his coat on the couch, he walked slowly through the apartment. A doll rested by the television and two of Katie's picture books lay on the coffee table, but with those exceptions the rooms were clean and tidy—the products of Saturday chores, enduring into Sunday.

His work schedule was still hanging on the front of the refrigerator, though nearly lost under later additions to the family bulletin board. You knew I was coming, he thought. Is that why you're not here? He saw that neither mail nor newspapers were awaiting him in their accustomed places.

What did you do, Annie? Run home to Hagerstown? I've tried that. It doesn't work.

All the places that he might have expected to find a note—kitchen counter, dresser, the pillows of their neatly made bed—he found nothing. Wallace stood for a long minute in front of the closet, trying to decide which, if any, of her clothes were missing. His memory was not equal to the task, even without the several new garments to confuse him.

Think, think. Out of habit, he had checked the mailbox on the way in. Empty. Friday is mail day. So she's been here sometime in the last two days. Belatedly, he thought of the Spirit and hurried back to the bulletin board and the rotation schedule. In the box for Sunday, February 12 was the name FINCH. *She doesn't have the car.*

He went to the bathroom to splash water on his face and found the towels damp. *She was here this morning. You're being silly,* he told himself, and went out into the quad to knock on Rebecca's door. She opened the door only a few inches when she answered.

"Hello, Rayne. Back for a while?" Her smile seemed forced.

"Yeah. I was wondering if you'd have any idea where Annie is."

"Did you check at the clinic?"

"The clinic?" Among the facilities in the Block core was an eighteen-bed three-doctor Federal Health Clinic—more insurance against the war the Block was supposed to survive. "What would she be doing there? Is Katie sick?"

"Katie's in with my daughter, napping—"

"Katie's here?"

Rebecca allowed the door to open another foot. "I told her she ought to tell you," she said, frowning. "Annie's working at the clinic."

"Working!"

"As a nurse's aide. Try to understand. She really needed to get out of the apartment, Rayne," Rebecca said earnestly.

"Why do you think I won't understand? What's she been telling you? I wish she was here instead of there, sure. I haven't seen her for five weeks. But if she wants to put in a few hours of volunteer work now and then, that doesn't bother me. It's not doing Katie any harm, after all. When did Annie say she'd be back for her?"

Rebecca looked inexplicably nonplussed. "Six."

"That long?"

"Rayne, Katie spends Saturday, Sunday, and two nights a week here."

"Why?"

A frown. "Maybe you'd better go up and see Annie."

"Maybe I'd better."

They caught sight of each other at opposite end of the clinic's main corridor. There was no hug. Her hands were clasped in front of her and fluttering nervously. His hands were jammed flat-palmed in his back pockets.

256

"Hi, Annie."

"So you are here."

Her tone was a needle. "You had the schedule. You should have known I'd be home today."

"I didn't think I should count on that."

"What, so you didn't even tell Katie? You want me to be some sort of surprise visitor?"

The hands fluttered, but the gaze was cool and steady. "I can only talk for a few minutes. They left me a long list of things to do."

"What's this all about? Rebecca said Katie's there half the week."

"I'm working C shifts until there's an opening on A."

He shook his head sharply. "Your job is taking care of Katie."

"That's your job, too. So where are you?"

"You know where I am. Earning a living for the family."

She tucked her hands under her elbows, against her side, as though to smother and still them. "I don't have the first idea where you are," she said. "I don't know where you go or what you do. You tell me I'm not supposed to ask, it's important, official, like I'm not good enough or smart enough to know. I'm just supposed to carry the load and wait, and jump up and smile when you walk through the door."

"I never—"

She took a step toward him. "Well, to me you're just away, and do you know what? It's getting to where I don't hardly miss you. In fact, it's getting hard to see what spaces you used to fill. And I found something else out. There are more ways of feeling good than getting one of your little pats on the head. They say I'm doing a good job here, and I get checks with my own name on them, and both of those things feel just fine."

"I thought you were volunteering, to get out of the apartment for a few hours—"

"Why? Because you didn't think anyone would want to pay me?"

He did not have the energy to answer or even parry her challenges. "You're getting ready to do without me."

The hands had climbed all the way to her shoulders, wrapping her in a self-hug. "I can't depend on somebody who's not here."

A voice inside Wallace was screaming, Who is this person? Who is this stranger who looks like Annie? He gaped, blinked, opened his mouth and heard himself say, "Neither can I." Felt

257

his feet carry him out of the clinic and toward the exit doors and the transit stop beyond. Wished that he could make the clock jump forward a week to his next date with the gate.

And understood that Shan, strange and wonderful Shan, real or shadow, was all that stood between him and being completely alone.

Washington, D.C., The Home Alternity

Ellen O'Neill did not notice when her husband left their brass-railed blanket-heaped bed. But stirring in her sleep in the silent hours between midnight and dawn, she became aware of the empty space beside her and came fully awake. The glowing hands of the alarm marked the time as a few minutes after two.

Sitting up, she listened for a moment for telltale sounds from the bathroom adjacent or the kitchen below. Hearing none, she threw back the covers and went looking. Collar and tags jingled at the foot of the bed as their terrier raised his head in sleepy curiosity.

"Stay, Roscoe," she whispered as she glided out of the room. Seeing the wisdom of that suggestion, Roscoe obeyed.

She found Gregory in the darkened living room, sitting sideways in his robe on the couch. "Honey? What's wrong?"

He looked up, then made room for her beside him on the edge of the couch. "I'm trying to find a way to undo a mistake," he said softly.

"Can I help?"

"You can hug me."

Though he accepted her embrace gratefully, as a child accepts the hug of a mother, he remained distant. Something had taken him far away, and his body jangled with the rawness of the pain which had driven him into retreat.

Wrestling demons. That was how she thought of such episodes. There had been few of them in recent years, far fewer than suffered by the earnest and troubled young man she had married twenty-six years ago.

She waited, knowing that if he chose to share more, he would do so without prodding.

"There is an imperative in the blood," he said slowly, "which compels a parent to save the life of his child at any price, even his own life. Look at our values of noble sacrifice. The woman who goes back into a burning building for her baby. The man who dives into the surf to save a son being dragged out to sea by the rip current.''

"We make heroes of them, even if they fail," she said.

He nodded, sought a hand to hold. "And we judge them hard if they stand by and do nothing, if they let the baby burn, watch the boy drown. I wonder how God judges them, whether the dictates of biology mean as much to Him as to us."

"Parents are charged with caring for their children," she said. "Maybe part of the charge is in our genes."

"Perhaps," he said. "But is it an absolute? Should a parent steal to feed a hungry child, lie or cheat to protect a defenseless child?"

"Are you asking the parent, or God? The parent would say yes. I would say yes. I would have done that for David, or Sara, or Mark. You would have, too."

"Yes," he said. "It amounts to risking your soul, instead of your life, for your child. God would put the sin on one side of the ledger and the good on the other."

"The good would count for more, I think."

"But what if a man could save his own children's lives by accepting the deaths of other children as the price? How does that one sit on the scales?"

"Is that what you've done?"

He drew her close, until his arms enclosed her and her head rested on his shoulder. "I went along with something I didn't believe in, to protect us and ours."

She drew back from him, alarmed. "Went along with who? Who threatened us? Please tell me that you're not compromised—"

His expression soured. "Would that be worse? Do you really think patriotism is a higher value? No, don't answer. These children we'd do anything to save, we proudly send them off to die as soldiers. So we must think country counts for more than family. Though I don't think that's what Jesus had in mind when he said 'Render unto Caesar . . .' " He smiled sadly. "No, Ellen. I'm not compromised—not in the way you're thinking."

"Then I don't understand—"

"The government that compromised me is our own. The man I went along with is the President."

"This is scaring me, Gregory."

He brushed her cheek with his curled fingers. "It scares me, too, sweetheart."

"Is there going to be a war? Is that what you're talking about?"

"Yes. I thought I would be able to make myself heard. But he's slammed the door on me. He doesn't want to hear 'No.'"

"Then there doesn't have to be a war," she said.

"No."

She returned to his shoulder and the comforting embrace of his arms. "It's all right to put our family first. But you can't stop there," she said finally. "You can't stand and watch while other parents' babies burn."

"I know," he said. "That's why I'm sitting here in the middle of the night. Trying to find a way back in."

"Isn't there anyone else who feels the same as you? Someone who's still on the inside?"

He was a long time in answering. "I don't know," he said dolefully. "I just don't know."

Bethel, Virginia, The Home Alternity

The woman's body carried a hundred marks from its encounters with whip and needle, flame and blade. Cigarette burns decorated the curves of her breasts and the soft roundness of her belly. She wore Endicott's initials carved into her right buttock and the bruise shadow of his hands on her throat. Welts of varying vintage were everywhere, from pale scars to the neat crisscross pattern of bright red ridges across the backs of her thighs from that night's session in the basement bedroom.

It was harder to find marks on her spirit. Like Scheherezade, Rachel seemed to believe she had struck a bargain that would keep her alive, buying the next day with her nightly screams. She no longer believed he would kill her, he thought. She was wrong, of course. He would kill her, in time.

But even he was surprised at how long he had kept her, how he had broken all his own rules with her. Even to taking her into his own bed. She lay naked atop the blankets, an ankle chain securing her to the footboard, her folded arms her only pillow. Sleeping peacefully, the sleep of the exhausted, the cleansed. He had made her life simple as a child's.

In return, she stole his sleep from him and made his life ever more complex. She had learned not to lecture him, not to argue with him, not to whine or fight, but still she found ways to manipulate him. Give me beautiful marks, she had begged tonight, and he had, with the care of an artist working a canvas. As if what she wanted mattered. As if she mattered. Everything she said, everything she did, plucked at the knots which held his selfness together.

The closer she came to unraveling them, the more cruelly he punished her. He had nothing to explain, no one to account to, and he would not let her make him think otherwise. The two worst beatings he had given her, savage mindless maulings that had left her half-dead, followed the time she forgave him and the time she gave him permission. There was nothing to forgive, and he did not need or want her permission.

And yet she worked on him, always holding that one little piece of herself back, watching him and keeping silent secrets. She was changing him, and he did not understand how. He had made love to her and even given her pleasure. Another rule broken, another mistake. A repeated mistake. He knew he should kill her now, before her web was complete and he was helpless. And knew he would not, not yet.

Not until he had pierced that final veil. Not until he knew what it was she knew about him.

Washington, D.C., The Home Alternity

The meeting in the White House Situation Room had been originally scheduled for 1:00 P.M., postponed until 4:00 and again until 7:00. It had finally convened at 10:00 with one of the principals absent.

All the trouble had begun when the British Airways plane from Glasgow carrying a CIA courier had been diverted by mechanical trouble to Halifax, Nova Scotia. When it became clear that the delay was going to be a lengthy one, a two-seat jet trainer was dispatched from the Air Force station at Bucks Harbor, Maine, to pick up the courier and ferry him to Washington.

Madison had gone personally to Bolling Air Force Base, on the Potomac, to await its arrival. In his absence, Admiral Fisch, the Chief of Naval Operations, took center stage to address the group.

Fisch was a round-shouldered, chain-smoking, bulgy-cheeked veteran of the surface fleet—captain of a cruiser in the Pacific War and a task force commander during the Cuban intervention. His uniform was stretched tight at the buttons, and he walked with a rolling gait which made it seem as though he had never quite regained his land legs.

But Fisch spoke simply and authoritatively, a businessman in the business of war. "Mr. President, I was asked to brief you on our ability to carry out a peacetime attrition campaign against the Soviet submarine forces operating in international waters off our coasts," he said, standing in front of a wall covered with maps.

"That's correct, Admiral," said Robinson.

"Before we discuss tactics, I want to make sure you understand some of the conditions under which our ASW forces will be operating. With your permission—"

"Go ahead."

Fisch nodded to his tactical aide. "Wally?"

Slender and hoarse-voiced, the aide stepped forward. "Mr. President, the Foxtrot-class vessels are fuel-cell-powered and very quiet—they emit less than one milliwatt of broadband acoustic energy when underway. Cyclops has to pick that up against an ambient noise background caused by ocean turbulence, vessels and storms up to several hundred miles away, surface waves, even sea life."

"Whales," Clifton remarked. "Amazing sounds."

"Many smaller animals, too, sir, even certain species of shrimp. Cyclops's East Coast ASW element alone includes nearly twenty thousand hydrophones—between ten and twenty per nautical mile—connected to twelve shore stations, each of which directs fire control for six to twelve Javelin batteries. Even with all that hardware, detection is often marginal, especially on the outer shelf where the subs are now operating."

The aide turned to the map behind him. "This is a composite plot of contacts in Sector Five for the twelve hours ending midnight yesterday. Sector Five extends roughly from the Delaware Bay to Cape Hatteras, North Carolina. The blue tracks are confirmed sub movements; the red tracks are guesstimates. As you can see, even when a Foxtrot is on the move we lose contact periodically."

Robinson leaned forward. "Am I reading this correctly, that there were five subs in the sector?"

"Five confirmed, sir. There are other contacts which may or may not have been subs. They do a lot of station-keeping, and there are shadow zones and submarine canyons to hide in. You could have a big sixteen-tube Hotel-class sub sitting on the bottom anywhere along here," he said, pointing, "and Cyclops would never know. That's where the coast patrol and the ASW aircraft come in, trying to fill the gap with sonar and magnetic detection."

Robinson was growing impatient with the detail. "So it's not easy to find them. Obviously you can, or that map would be blank. So why is any of this relevant?"

"I wanted to address one other matter," the aide said, hurrying his words. "The subs can take active countermeasures if there's reason to believe they're under attack or likely to be under attack. Obviously, any system as sensitive as Cyclops can be jammed rather easily. Also, the Foxtrots have long-run decoy torpedoes which carry recordings of sub noises. They have growlers which can be towed—"

"Enough," Robinson said irritably. "Admiral, maybe you can answer the question your aide ignored. Why is any of this relevant? I didn't ask you to make me an antisubmarine warfare expert."

"No, sir," Fisch said, coming forward as the aide retreated to a chair. "It matters because it affects the tactics we choose to use and the chances of success."

"Let's talk about that, then," Rodman said.

"Gladly," said Fisch. "We have four ASW platforms available to us—the Javelins, the Rogers-class destroyer escorts, the P-5 patrol plane, and the Sea Devil helicopter. Of the four, the only one which satisfies the requirements of a program of deliberate accidental incidents are the missiles. They're quick-hitters, which gives us a reasonable chance of cloaking the truth of the event."

"That seems simple enough. If we go forward, that's the way we'll go," Robinson said. "What's all the fuss about? Or was your aide just trying to show me what a good student he was at the Naval War College?"

"Wally was doing what I asked him to," Fisch said. "For all the reasons he outlined, the chances of success are no better than one in five for a single missile against a single target, or three in five for a salvo. The Javelin carries an acoustic homing torpedo, and the moment it hits the water all the boards on that sub are going to light up. If we miss, there'll be no second chances and no 'accident' cover. He'll have the spoofers and jammers on, and the first chance he gets the wire will go up for a bulletin to Moscow."

Though the news was discouraging, Robinson showed no sign of distress. "The truth is, Admiral, I want Moscow to know. This isn't a military operation so much as a diplomatic one. I have a card I want to play, and I can't do it until they raise the stakes. So tell me, isn't there some way to make a sure kill?"

The tactical aide and the Admiral exchanged glances. "Depth charge," the aide said tentatively.

"No," the Admiral said, shaking his head.

Robinson pounced. "What does he mean, depth charge?"

263

"Mr. President, I don't think—" Fisch started.

"Don't say no to me. You—Wally—explain," Robinson said sharply.

Whipsawed between two superiors, the aide drew a deep breath and let it out slowly. "The Javelin can deliver either a torpedo or a nuclear depth charge. The DC makes very little noise on entry, no noise on the way down—"

"And a hell of a lot of noise when it goes off," the Admiral said. "Kondratyeva will never let you get away with nuking one of his subs, Mr. President. I know you haven't asked for my opinion of the consequences of this kind of operation—"

"That's right, Admiral," Robinson said. "I haven't. And please don't offer one. You're not fully in the picture on this."

But the Admiral had a bit of bulldog in him. "Mr. President, is Secretary O'Neill in the picture? It seems to me that he ought to be involved in this decision."

Rodman intercepted the question. "The Secretary has been consulted," he said. "He is fully informed."

The arrival at that moment of Dennis Madison precluded any further explanations. Madison carried a slim briefcase in his right hand, a cup of coffee in his right. "Got it," he said simply.

"Good," Robinson said. "Admiral, what are the odds of success with the depth charge?"

"Maybe eighty percent," Fisch said reluctantly.

"Thank you, Admiral. That'll be all for now."

While the Admiral and his aide reluctantly gathered up their maps and exited, the four remaining men gathered around one end of the elongated octagonal table. "Did you have a chance to look at it?" Robinson asked when they were alone.

"Just a minute or two, in the car on the way up from Bolling," Madison said, unlatching the case. "But it was enough. You were right, Mr. President. The British have A-bombs of their own, at least a hundred warheads and maybe twice that."

"I knew it," Robinson said with grim triumph. "Sons of bitches, I knew it."

"I would never have believed it," Clifton said, shaking his head. "They've been in violation of their bilateral treaty all along."

"It's the only thing that made sense," Robinson said. "I never did think Somerset would do all this, take that kind of risk, just to twit us. Especially walking into the situation cold. Not unless he knew that they were already in violation."

"It does seem that their threshold resistance should have been higher," Clifton agreed. "I am astonished, I truly am."

"He used us pretty good," Rodman said. "Used us to protect his own hole card."

"Just so," Robinson said.

"What's the delivery platform?" Rodman asked Madison. "You can't tell me they've managed to hide silos or a bomber fleet for twenty-five years."

"No doubt they hid a submarine in Loch Ness or something equally outrageous," Clifton said under his breath.

"French-built cruise missiles," Madison answered. "Air-launched from a Wasp interceptor."

"What was the price of the intelligence?" Rodman wanted to know.

"High. We had to kill one and buy a couple."

Nodding, Rodman turned to Robinson. "This is what we wanted, Peter. It's all fallen in place."

"Yes," the President said. "Yes. We can take care of our British problem, and at the same time take the measure of the Kremlin. Bill, will you see that our people in England receive instructions to sit tight and leave the missiles in place?"

"I will. What about Fisch?"

Robinson's eyes were thoughtful. "I'll tell the Admiral myself."

Bloomington, Alternity Blue

January was usually the coldest month in Indiana, but this year someone had forgotten to tell the Elemental Engineers. The pattern of bitterly cold days and even colder clear-skied nights which had settled on the state just before Wallace left had held through to his return. Three weeks into February, the wind whipping around the corner of the Five Friends building had as much bite as any yet that season.

The back stairs to Shan's second-floor apartment reminded him of the apartment in Richmond. The moment he noticed the resemblance, he pushed it out of his mind. He did not want to think about Ruthann or anything connected to her. He did not want to live in what felt like the past.

The wind blew tiny ice crystals off the roof and railings and into Wallace's face as he climbed in the dark. There was no light at the top except for a faint glow from a curtained window. Shivering in a sudden gust of arctic air, he pulled back the screen door and knocked heavily on the windowless wooden door.

A few moments later, the overhead light came on and a face

peeked briefly out through the curtains. The door opened to reveal Shan, barefoot and wearing a flowing caftan and an expression which was less than fully welcoming.

"Hi," he said. "Can I come in?"

"I don't know," she said. "I was beginning to think I was wrong about you."

"The apology is short, but the explanation takes a while," he said, showing a sheepish smile. "I don't mind doing them here if your feet are up to it."

Her face warmed slightly. "I don't think they are," she said, stepping back to admit him. "I can always throw you out when you're done."

An open book and a cup of steaming tea marked the chair where Shan had been seated. Pharaoh, the big gray-furred cat, was curled up in the warm depression she had left in the cushions. Wallace dropped his coat on the edge of the bed and tried to cover the flat, square package which he had been concealing under it in the same motion, but without success.

"Is that part of the apology?"

"No," he said. "Just a late Valentine's Day present. It needs to warm up."

"Mmm, frozen chocolate," she said. "My dentist will be doubly fond of you."

"Not chocolate. Too predictable."

"That *is* one of the seven deadly sins, being predictable." She reclaimed her chair from Pharaoh, gathering him up and offering him the hollow of her crosslegged lap when she was settled. In true cat fashion, he disdained the substitution and leapt off. "What happened, Rayne? Why didn't I hear from you?"

He knew already that she would let him keep secrets, but she would not let him lie. "I was going to try to convince you that I've just been busy, traveling," he said, looking down at the floor, avoiding her eyes. "That's even partly true. This whole last week, I couldn't have reached you, no matter how much I wanted to."

Having waited long enough to consider it his idea, Pharaoh jumped lightly up onto Shan's lap. "But you didn't want to."

"Shan—you made me feel wonderful. Here, and here," he said, tapping his temple and the middle of his chest in turn.

A mischievous smile fought its way onto her face. "Nowhere else?"

"All right," he said, patting the bed. "Here, too."

"Thank you. I didn't want to think I'd read everything wrong."

"You didn't read any of it wrong," he said. "Being with you—it kind of lights me up inside."

"But—" she prompted.

He answered haltingly, partly a struggle to edit his thoughts, partly a struggle to understand them. "But the only long-term . . . relationship . . . I've ever had, just blew up in my face. As special as what happened between you and me was, when I got away from here I got scared. I don't—trust—my feelings. My judgment."

"Are you afraid of being hurt?"

He looked up from the floor. "Maybe more of hurting you."

"That's not for you to worry about," she said, scratching Pharaoh between the ears. "The risk is mine. The decision is mine. And I thought it was a good risk." She smiled, and it was like a flower opening to the sun. "I guess I still do."

"Shan—I've never done this before."

Again the twinkle. "It didn't seem that way to me."

"I mean this is special for me—this feeling. You're the only one I've ever wanted to break the rules for."

The cat's deep-throated purring was audible across the room. "Will you talk to me next time? When you're thinking about things you don't think you can tell me, or you don't want to admit to yourself? Instead of disappearing inside yourself?"

"I'll try," he said. *I want to, anyway—*

"Then apology accepted," she said. "Is that chocolate warmed up yet?"

He brought her the package and sat on the floor at her feet, watching her face expectantly as she dissected it. He was not disappointed. As the wrappings fell away, her expression moved from anticipation to surprise to open-eyed wonder. She turned it over in her hands twice before looking down at him for explanation.

"Something wrong?"

"This is a Judy Collins album."

He nodded. "You don't have it, I hope."

The ten-inch-square cover bore a photograph of an antique scale against a white background and the title *Not Legal For Trade*.

"I've never even heard of it," she said wonderingly. "I don't know a single one of these songs."

"They're good songs. Play it."

"You don't understand," she said. "I know everything she's ever recorded. She has been my favorite for ten years."

"Then I surprised you. Good. That's what I wanted."

267

"But I've never seen a record like this. It's not an LP, it's not a single. It's in between."

Wallace had been prepared for the question. "It's a private release. A proof-of-concept pressing. They were going to test-market them and changed their mind."

"How did you get it?"

Images of the truth flashed through his mind. Smuggling it into the Tower under his coat. Taping it to his abdomen to get it past the gatekeeper. His heart racing and his palms sweating every second, every step. Jumping at voices. "I asked around. I have a lot of friends."

She hugged it to her chest possessively. "I guess that means you *were* thinking of me."

"Every day."

"I want to play it."

"I want you to."

She climbed out of the chair, chasing Pharaoh for a second time. Halfway to the stereo, she turned and looked back at him. "If I let you stay, does that mean I won't hear from you for another two weeks?"

"You'll hear from me. Promise."

"Then get your wet coat off my bed and onto a peg, all right? And maybe stack up the pillows so we have somewhere to sit together." She took a half-step farther, then added, "I need to go downstairs and make sure the shop is locked up properly."

She was gone several minutes, but he thought nothing of it until the morning, until the three men approached him as he stood by the Magic fumbling for his key. One flashed a badge and said, "Rayne Wallace?"

"Yes—"

"I'm John Krill of the NIA. Would you come with us, please?"

Too surprised to resist, Wallace allowed them to lead him to a waiting van. But when he looked back at the shop and saw Shan watching from an upstairs window, he found no surprise on her face—only a touch of shame in the moment before she turned away.

"THE NETTLE ON THE ROSE"

Music and lyrics by

KATHLEEN RICHARDS

I heard you calling
From the darkness 'cross the way
Dying in the endless empty days
I had no answer
To the question never named
Listening for the song that never came

In isolation
Wrapped in darkness in my room
Crying in a secret silent tomb
If I could reach you
Hear the music in your heart
Could I understand your gentle art?

The price of fear is loneliness
The secret no one knows
The price of life is dying
The demon in the garden, the nettle on the rose

In desperation
I reach outward for rebirth
Measuring in courage my own worth
And still you're calling
I might answer you today
And share your quiet prison if I may

CHAPTER 16

A Practical Palace

Boston, The Home Alternity

The day was dawning gray and gloomy by the time Albert Tackett slewed the big Pontiac up the slushy ramp of the Tower garage. But neither the weather nor being awakened at five could dampen his spirits. Overnight, a cracker team had made a breakthrough into a new alternity, now designated Orange. Important as that event was, it was even more important that Alternity Orange had a domestic gate—a Catholic seminary near metropolitan Detroit.

Tackett waved off the surprised ramp attendant and steered for his reserved space adjacent to the executive entrance. Before the engine had stopped dieseling, a coatless Bret Monaghan was standing beside the car.

"Morning, Albert," the deputy director said as Tackett opened the door to climb out. "That was good time."

"I broke several speed limits, including one shaving," Tackett said, fingering the fresh scab on his jaw. "Are things rolling?"

They started toward the doors, walking briskly. "Finally," Monaghan said. "Been a while since we've had to do this. I'd almost forgotten the drill."

"I guess that's why we write things down."

A pair of elevators were just inside the entrance, and the two men halted there. "I guess. I've got eight of the best DA's sequestered in the committee room with the doc kit. Good materials, textbook snatch—newspaper, news magazine, alma-

270

nac, money sample. They should have a first cut profile ready within an hour—"

"Can you tell me anything yet?"

"Not much. I've had my hands full running around drafting bodies and getting them on-task, and haven't had a chance to look in. I do know Orange's on the same time track as us, just like the others. Harper—Will Harper, that's the cracker that made the return run—said it looks a lot like Blue. The President's a Georgian named Carter. The Yankees beat the Dodgers in the Series. That's all you hear at this point. Trivia."

Tackett nodded as they boarded the elevator. "Go on. You were saying—"

"Malcolm is assembling a skeleton staff for Section Orange, and the other Section supervisors should get their transfer lists by the end of the day. Documentation of the route is finished, and Harper is doing a tutor run right now with a training specialist."

"What's the gate status?"

"We're holding everything across the board until we have at least three T-runs in, just to be safe. All the stationmasters have been notified."

"Sounds like you've spent your time well."

"Everybody's pulling," Monaghan said. "This has put a little crackle back in the air around here."

The elevator opened, and they turned down the hall toward the committee room. "I'm going to want to sit in awhile and get a look at the doc kit myself," Tackett said. "Can you keep the wheels turning by yourself for a little longer?"

Monaghan nodded affirmatively. "Sure. The next thing up is to put together another scratch analysis team to work the materials Harper brings back from the T-run. I can do the call-ins."

They had reached the closed door. "I'm going to want to see Malcolm and the sec supers before they start putting meat on that skeleton," Tackett said.

"I'll schedule it. Probably about eleven, if that's enough time."

"I just want to get my hands a little dirty."

"You'll be hip deep in ten minutes and you know it," Monaghan said. "But before you do, something came in late last night from Blue that needs your attention."

Tackett released the doorknob. "Which is?"

"Matt Kelly in Blue is reporting one of the new moles as a possible over-the-hill." He reached inside his coat and pulled out a sheet of paper folded once lengthwise.

"Son of a bitch," Tackett said, taking the report. "Wallace. One of the new kids. You screened those, didn't you?"

"Yeah. I missed this one, Al. I'm sorry."

Shaking his head, Tackett handed the paper back. "I hate it when one of our people goes bad. Not your fault, Bret. This is what I was trying to warn the President about. When you make the schedule God, standards slip—they have to. I expected something like this. To be honest, I'm surprised it took this long."

"Wallace's roommate says he's gotten himself mixed up with a local."

"What else?" Tackett said disgustedly. "There's no dumber animal on earth than a man with a hard-on."

"How do you want to deal with this?"

"I don't."

"Do you want him brought back?"

"What for? The Guard's got no use for a turncoat."

"Matt's been screaming about discipline. Maybe Wallace could make a useful object lesson."

Tackett's mouth puckered as though he had just bitten into a lemon. "Administrative reviews, Guard court, investigations— just what we need right now," he said. "We've got our hands full and so do they. Let's keep it simple. Tell him we want the kid found, but we don't want him back. His people will get the message."

Fairfax, Virginia, Alternity Blue

Looking like the keep of a neo-modern concrete castle, the headquarters building of the National Information Agency rose from the center of a sixty-acre park and forest campus. The tall, narrow windows were tucked into sheltering embrasures, and there was no ground-level entrance—the snaking two-lane main drive dove underground as it approached the east face of the eight-story structure. Antennae of assorted shapes and sizes decorated both the roof and the ridgeline of the grassy hill to the south.

Inside, Director Richard Bayshore oversaw a kingdom whose knights bore titles such as General Analyst, Sociometric Division and Report Correlator, Volunteer Watch. The weapons in his armory were the sociograph and the flagged rumor, the telephone and the computer. Four subterranean chambers held racks of cartridge files representing nearly forty million people, information captured through a fifteen-year campaign.

And now, for the first time in Bayshore's memory, the castle also held a flesh-and-blood prisoner.

The man who claimed to be Ray Wallach had arrived that morning in the custody of two Region 3 warders. The vol who had reported him had arrived just minutes ago, in the company of Region 3 coordinator Willa Stanton. Bayshore joined up with Stanton in the anteroom to the evidence lab.

"Willa," he said, offering his hand to the round-faced woman. "Sounds like you've come up with a real head-scratcher."

"Better you should go bald than me," she said, patting her thinning silver hair.

"I get paid for it," he agreed. "Where's the vol?"

"Shan's downstairs. Your personnel director is arranging local housing for her."

"And the record?"

Stanton inclined her head toward the closed door to the lab. "Inside."

"Let's have a look."

The record and its jacket were lying side by side on a lint-free pad under a stereoscopic camera. The technician who had been preparing them stepped back to allow Bayshore near.

"We dubbed a cartridge of the music and photographed the cover when we had it in Chicago," Stanton volunteered, "just in case something happened on the way here."

"Looks like it stayed in the dryer too long," Bayshore said. "Ten-inch disc?"

"Yep."

"What have you found out?"

"It's still a cipher, just as Shan said it was. It doesn't exist."

"Don't tell me that. The damn thing is here."

"What would you call it? The label doesn't exist. The format doesn't exist anymore, not even as a novelty. RCA was the last one pressing this size, and they gave it up twenty years ago. And none of the songs has been copyrighted or listed with the performance payments registry."

Bayshore frowned and picked up the album to look at the back. "I'd say it doesn't exist, I guess. What about some of these names? You've got musicians, songwriters—"

Stanton nodded. "Our office didn't have the time or resources to run them all down. We did some quick checks. The American Federation of Musicians came up with one match, on the bass player—Leitch. But they have him registered as a keyboardist, and there's no studio work on his gig sheet."

"This is not what I want to hear," Bayshore said gruffly replacing the album.

"You haven't heard the best one. We flew a cartridge out to Denver to play for Collins, the putative performer. This is a quote—'It sounds a lot like me. If I had a sister, that might be her. But it isn't me, and there isn't a song she does I'd want in my repertoire.' "

With a sigh and a disgusted shake of the head, Bayshore turned from the camera table and walked out of the lab. "What the hell is going on here, Willa?" he fumed in the anteroom. "That thing is like—like a perfect counterfeit nine-dollar bill. It's absolutely perfect, and absolutely wrong."

"I don't have any answers, Rich. If I did, I'd have slept better last night."

Bayshore folded his arms across his chest. "Do you know what else?" he asked, shaking a finger in the air. "That damned thing doesn't look like it was put together on a kitchen table. When I look at it I see fifty of 'em stacked up in a box. Do you know what I mean? I'd like to get someone who knows something about record manufacturing in to look at it."

"Some of us were wondering about some sort of knock-off coming in from overseas. A lot of consumer products get counterfeited by the sweatshops in Sao Paulo and Shanghai."

"No," he said grumpily, shaking his head. "I wish I could believe that, but no. They wouldn't pick Judy Collins, for one thing. They'd be knocking off Tin Whistle or Voyage or someone like that. Besides, this isn't a counterfeit. It's more like—a dummy. Like a movie prop."

"Maybe it is one."

The director's face brightened fractionally.

"Or maybe it's a joke."

Bayshore grunted. "Maybe. I think I'll go see if Mr. Wallace will explain the punch line."

"It'd be the first helpful thing he's said since we picked him up," Stanton said.

"So I hear," he said, sighing. "This is queer as hell, Willa. But it shouldn't worry me. I can't see the threat."

"But it does worry you."

"Yes," he admitted. "It does."

Eyes closed and holding his head in his hands, Rayne Wallace sat swiveling slowly from side to side in the big chair. He had done it their way this time. Charlie Adams' way. *Next time, stay put and let us handle the problem.* Except before they could find

274

him, almost before he could be missed, he had been whisked away to this place.

The plane ride. He still felt weak, and remembering why made it worse. The thundering take-off had been overwhelming—the roaring engines behind them, the thumping of the tires on the pavement beneath them, the airport flashing by on either side. He endured it by going rigid, steel fingers gouging the armrests.

Then came the big banking turn as the jet climbed away from the airport. He looked out. More properly, looked down. Saw with sudden clarity that the plane was an eggshell hanging in midair from a fragile string. A string he could neither see nor trust. Seconds later he threw up on the window.

Twice more his control was to fail him, the first in turbulence over Ohio, the second during the landing approach, dry aching heaves that took the place of tears. The smell was still in his nostrils, though they had allowed him a shower and provided new clothes after landing.

Stay put. He had no choice now. He had to hope that the Section could trail him. That they would even make the effort. *They would have missed me just a couple hours after I was snatched, when I missed the procedures seminar on Monday morning. But they were too slow. No—I made it too hard.*

He wished he had told Fowler more. How would they even know where to start? His travel logs were full of lies. It was beyond hoping that these NIA types would have left the Magic parked across from the shop to be found. Had he told Fowler that Shan was Common World? Maybe that would be enough. *Enough to send them out to question Ruthann about my old flames. Almost better to leave me here than to rescue me to face that.*

Thinking of Ruthann made him feel lost. Thinking of Shan set his empty stomach churning. Her betrayal, so coldly calculated. *Stay the night, darling—so they'll know where to find you in the morning. Like a fucking whore. Like a total stranger.*

The sounds of someone entering the room brought Wallace's head up and eyes open. The newcomer was a short, wide-shouldered man with shiny black hair and a measuring gaze.

"My name is Bayshore, Richard Bayshore," he said, advancing to the opposite edge of the table. "Would you rather I called you Ray, or Rayne? It doesn't matter to me, since I know neither one is your real name."

"It doesn't matter to me, either," Wallace said. His paper-thin cover was in shreds, and he had long ago wearied of defending it. You can only fool a fool, and his captors were dangerously smart. He was entangled with the Blue intelligence community like Br'er Rabbit with the Tar Baby, and there was nothing he could do to get himself free. "I've been called both."

"So I hear," Bayshore said, pulling a chair back and sitting down. "Ray, I'm hoping that you'll give me a boost on a couple of little puzzles that are bothering me—"

"I don't do crosswords."

"I need to know who you are, and what you're doing here."

"You brought me here. If my being here bothers you, you can always send me back."

Bayshore showed a hint of a tolerant smile. "That might actually be in the picture, Ray, if you'd be more helpful. When you lie to us, or just turn to stone, it's hard not to think that you're hiding something we really ought to know."

There was no point in embracing the hope of freedom; he could never tell them enough to satisfy them. "I can't help what you think."

"Not true, Ray," Bayshore said, leaning back in his chair and dropping his folded hands into his lap. "I'd love to hear something from you that proved out to be true. Nothing has so far. Nothing you told us—nothing you told Shan."

Wallace looked away, trying to hide the anger and the hurt under an ambiguous scowl. The bitch. The goddamned whore. Why did you do this to me, Shan? Why did you have to do this?

"Something wrong, Ray?"

"No," he said curtly.

"I'm glad. If I were sitting where you are, I might be feeling a little hung out, a little short of friends."

The man sitting across the table suddenly felt dangerous to Wallace. "Why don t you leave me alone?" he flared. "I'm not going to answer any more damned questions. I don't have anything new to tell you."

"You don't mind if I say my piece, do you?" Bayshore said, his patient voice and presumptuous familiarity unchanged. "I have a feeling that you're a stranger here. So much of a stranger that you don't even realize how much you stand out."

"I don't even know where 'here' is, so you're probably right. How about sharing the secret?"

"Do you remember your school pictures, Ray? Standing in line in the gym, waiting for your teacher to comb your hair? Downstairs we have something called an image indexer. It contains photos of everyone who's gone to school anywhere in this country in the last ten years, and a lot of other people besides. Like everyone who gets an entry visa. Do you remember being fingerprinted when you got your driver's license? We have a

276

computerized gadget that catalogs the fingerprints of everyone in the country who holds a driver's license.''

Wallace looked up. "What, a stamp collection wasn't enough for you?"

Bayshore chuckled under his breath. "It might surprise you to hear it only takes ten minutes to do a look-up. But you're not going to be the least bit surprised to hear that you're not in either system. Your license is a forgery, and I'm half-tempted to say that you are, too."

"Say what you like." *This wasn't supposed to happen. Goddamn it, they didn't train me for this—*

"I don't like it, Ray. Don't make that mistake. I wouldn't have cared whether you were king of the prom or king of the pack, so long as we'd found you. But we've been to Wayne County. We've checked every Wallace or Wallach family, and a few other things, too. They don't know you. In fact, as near as we can tell the only person in the county who does know you is a certain state trooper. You probably remember meeting him."

He paused, but Wallace answered only with sullen silence.

"You do, I see," Bayshore went on. "Do you understand why this business bothers me, Ray? Do you see why I can't even think about letting you leave here until I know who you are?"

"I have nothing to say."

Bayshore nodded absently. "Yeah. So you've said. I guess you think you've got friends out there who are going to be able to do something for you. Or maybe you're just protecting them. But I don't think you're going to be able to do that. Somebody leased that car for you, and I guess I don't take it too seriously that she reported it stolen this morning. Not when we know you were driving it a month ago."

It was a jolt to hear that the Section wasn't supporting his cover, and Wallace scrambled for plausible explanations which would not mean they'd cut him free. *They must think I skipped,* he decided. *They want the police to help them find me.* Though it meant they did not know where he was, at least it meant they wanted to know.

"I had a fight with my boss," Wallace said offhandedly. "She was jealous, you know?"

"Of Shan," Bayshore prompted.

"Yeah."

"Which I guess explains using a different name with her."

"Right. That's why." Maybe the cover was salvageable, after all.

"But it doesn't explain why you used a phony name for work,

277

too, or why your real one didn't come up out of the indexer. And it doesn't help explain that oddball record album. You want to tell me about that?''

Wallace slumped back in his chair. ''No.''

''You want us to ask your boss—former boss, now, I guess—you want us to ask her about it?''

''No,'' Wallace blurted. ''I mean, she wouldn't know anything.''

''Maybe you just don't want her to know anything,'' Bayshore said. ''I get a picture that says you're not at the center of this. Forged license—dummy product—you didn't do those yourself. I see some saltbacks, brought over the border, maybe from Canada, to run bogus goods for somebody. Is that where we should look for your family, Canada?''

''I don't have anything to say,'' he said, wrapping his arms around himself.

''We can protect you, Ray. Even get you back home safe when it's all done.''

I wish, Wallace thought plaintively. *I wish you could.*

''Get fucked,'' he muttered.

''Very kind of you,'' Bayshore said, pushing back from the table and standing. ''But I have other business to see to first. Just remember, Ray—you're all alone in this because you want to be. If you decide you want to change that, tell the warder you want to see me.''

Wallace stared at his feet, which were propped on the seat of the chair beside him, and said nothing. He sensed, rather than saw, Bayshore turn away from the table and head for the door. Drawing a deep breath, Wallace used it to clear the poisons trapped in his lungs during the long tense minutes of the interview. *Let go. It's over*, he told himself. *No more picking and probing.*

But even as Wallace was relaxing, Bayshore whirled, two steps from the door, and barked one last question. ''Ray—why was Gregory O'Neill murdered?''

Wallace's head came up. ''He was?''

Inexplicably, Bayshore smiled slightly. ''Thank you, Ray,'' he said. And then he was gone.

Releasing an animal cry of frustration, Wallace came flying up out of his chair, fists clenched, body jangling. He did not know what it meant for O'Neill to be dead. He did not even understand exactly what he had given away. He only knew that Bayshore's smile meant that he had given away too much.

• • •

278

Bayshore leaned over Willa Stanton's shoulder as they watched the replay of the interview together. "There. Right there," he said. "How did you read that? Surprise or confusion?"

She considered. "Both. Surprise first."

"Which means—"

"I'd say he knew the name, but he didn't know about the murder."

Nodding, Bayshore straightened up. "That's how I read it."

"I don't understand—"

"How many people knew O'Neill before his death hit the papers?"

"Maybe it's a different O'Neill," she pointed out.

"Maybe," Bayshore said. "But I don t think so. I told you this worried me. Now I think I know why." He clapped her on the shoulders. "We're going to have to get you back home."

Stanton remained dubious. "If he'd been part of some sort of conspiracy to kill Colonel O'Neill, wouldn't he have known the job was done?" she asked, twisting in the chair to look back at him.

"Doesn't matter," he said, shaking his head. "Willa, there's something I learned thirty years ago when I was a green-as-grass just-off-the-boat OSS agent: The world is not tidy. There's always some detail that doesn't fit the picture you're building. Sometimes you have to ignore them and just go on building."

He shook a finger in the direction of the room where Wallace was under guard. "He's connected somehow with the O'Neill murder. They've got the same smell. I just don't quite know what the smell is yet."

The Pentagon, The Home Alternity

A fierce sun enveloped in a halo of white fire dominated the cloudless morning sky over Washington. Long-banked snowdrifts were sagging, and streets and driveways running with the melt. The sunlight loosened coat collars, bared heads, and thawed smiles.

Inside Gregory O'Neill's E-ring office, the intense sunlight streaming through the windows transformed a portion of the carpet from cocoa to tan and splashed jewel-bright reflections from the steel window frames across the ceiling.

O'Neill sat in a comfortable chair just outside the glare, balancing a thick pressboard binder on his lap. Between the covers of the binder was the thousand-page report of the Defense

Procurement Office auditor on the Barracuda-class SSK hunter-killer program, delivered to him just that morning.

Compared to the almost uniformly upbeat missives originating from the shipyards in Groton and Camden, it was a joyless document. The auditor foresaw another fifteen percent cost overrun and a further three- to five-month slippage in the delivery schedule for the first of the three hulls already laid. More than thirty instances of mismanagement, substandard construction, and design blunders leading to expensive change orders had surfaced during the investigation.

What made it more frustrating was that O'Neill had seen it coming. Looking at the troubled histories of the Rogers-class DE's and the carrier *Liberty*, O'Neill had lobbied for the Barracuda class to be built in the Navy's own yards in Philadelphia and Boston, under contract management.

The suggestion was doomed by the high front-end cost of bringing the Navy's facilities up to grade. But now he was left with little leverage against the contractor, giant New York Shipbuilding Co. O'Neill wondered if the Justice Department would conscience a threat to nationalize the company and replace the top management with DPO staff.

His ruminations were interrupted by his secretary entering the office. "Gregory—I just got a call from the gate. The President is in the building. I don't know why we didn't get any notice."

He nodded absently. "Thank you, Marilee."

"Do you want me to try to find out why he's here? I have a contact or two on the White House staff—"

"No," O'Neill said, turning the page. "That's not necessary."

"You can't let him treat you this way," she said with motherly insistence. "People had to know he was coming. They must have been told to black us out or we'd have heard. You have to defend your turf."

He looked up and smiled ruefully at her. "When the President starts talking to the generals directly, a Secretary of Defense doesn't have much turf left to stand on. It's all right, Marilee."

"But—"

"You are a treasure, my lady, and your loyalty means a lot to me. But the fact is my role has been redefined." He hefted the report. "This is my turf now—budget, readiness, procurement. The President has reserved policy to himself. Let it go."

"Yes, sir," she said unhappily.

Smiling, he sought his place in the volume. But instead of the door closing, he heard an "Oh!" of surprise.

"Secretary O'Neill?" she said. "The President is here."

O'Neill set aside the binder and rose uncertainly from his chair as Robinson entered.

"Gregory," Robinson said, offering a hand.

O'Neill took the hand. "It's good to see you, Mr. President, if something of a surprise."

"I want you to come up to the War Room, Gregory. There's going to be a bit of excitement this morning, and I want you to be there."

"You don't mean—"

"Mongoose?" the President interrupted, fingering the model of the B-55 which stood on a pedestal near the door. "No, I made you a promise, a promise that we'd test the Russians first."

"You made your plans without me. I don't see why you need me now."

"I don't *need* you, Gregory," the President said. "But I would hope you're open to discovering you're wrong. This is for you, Gregory. Come and learn."

To judge by the activity in the War Room, the Joint Chiefs had been expecting Robinson, O'Neill thought. Several senior officers—including Admiral Rogers, the new Chief of Naval Operations—were gathered at the War Room's huge main table. A dozen or so aides and advisors had taken positions on the risers along the west wall.

Staff officers and noncoms manned the consoles and telephones connecting the room with the major commands or stood by one of the teleprinters where routine reports from the various intelligence bodies were received.

General Rauche, the Chairman of the Joint Chiefs, came out of a small cluster of uniforms to greet O'Neill and Robinson. "Mr. President," he said, stopping two steps short and saluting. The arm came down, and he nodded in O'Neill's direction. "Mr. Secretary."

"Good morning, General," Robinson said. "How do we stand?"

"We just received the latest sitsum from Reykjavik. There's nothing unusual in the Soviet alert status, no short-term increase in signal traffic, no cryptographic change. Several Russian second-echelon divisions are conducting a fairly major exercise in the Rhine highlands, but there's no reason to think that that's anything more than routine training. Atlantic Fleet intelligence shows only routine traffic out of the Soviet naval centers at Kola and Tanninn. In a word, things are quiet."

Robinson had continued walking as he listened, and now he stopped before the floor-to-ceiling electronic maps on the east wall and looked up. "And what about our side?"

"We are at Defcon 1, high readiness. There's been some intermittent land-line trouble in the net between here and our Central American bases, probably related to a minor earthquake overnight in Mexico. But we still have high-band clear-channel radio to both G2 Cristobal and G2 Mazatlan."

"Is Molink hot?" Robinson asked, referring to the direct Washingon-Moscow cable. The Molink teleprinters, manned around the clock by Russian linguists on the Joint Chiefs staff, were located in a smaller room adjacent to the War Room.

"It is."

"What about the film teams?"

"Photo recon aircraft with long-range optics are flying the ASW routes in place of the P-5s all up and down the coast. The nearest one will get an alert in code three minutes before we smoke the bird. We have at least a fifty percent chance of getting good film."

"And FNS is standing by?"

"Yes."

"I want to see the bulletin."

With a gesture, the General called an officer down out of the tiered seats. "Show the President the draft news release," he told the new arrival.

The young public affairs officer dug into a folder and came up with a sheet of paper. "Yes, sir. You'll see it's all ready except for the dateline. All we have to do is fill in the location and dictate it. It'll go out immediately on radio and TV. I also have drafts of the first two updates."

O'Neill shouldered forward. "Do you have a draft that starts 'Southeastern Cities Destroyed in Soviet Reprisal'?"

"Sir?"

"Maybe you'd better get to work on one," O'Neill said coldly.

"Sir?"

Shaking his head and smiling, Robinson handed the paper back to the PAO. "Never mind," he said. "The Secretary was making a joke. General, do you know any operational or tactical reason not to go ahead?"

"No, Mr. President."

"I was not making a joke," O'Neill said stiffly.

Robinson ignored him. "Then let's pick a target."

As the General turned and gave an order to one of the technicians, O'Neill realized that the room had grown very quiet. Then the center third of the display mutated into a map of the East Coast and the Atlantic Shelf.

It was the Cyclops plot, the closest thing to magic O'Neill had ever seen—a real-time presentation of twenty thousand data points, distilled down to an assortment of oblong blips in black, red, and blue. The overlapping semicircles showing the Javelin batteries and their zones of coverage gave the coastline a lace-edged look.

"The black markers are private and commercial traffic, the blue our naval forces, the red known Soviet vessels," the General said. "Most of those are submarines."

Robinson scanned slowly up and down the map. "What's your recommendation?"

The General turned to the tactical aide at the Cyclops console. "Lieutenant Russell?"

"Best on the map is S-16, there off the Florida coast," the aide said, twisting in his chair. "Fifteen miles out, forty fathoms down, and nowhere to hide. We've had a real good track on that one for more than a week. She seems to have a bad bearing somewhere in the power train, possibly in the primary turbine—been noisy as hell. She's been trying to use a shadow zone landward of the Florida current, but we can still hear her. Soviet Fleet Operations probably has a replacement already on the way."

"Surface traffic?" the General asked.

"Weather's been spotty, so almost none. One fishing trawler six miles out, won't get more than a good bouncing. Oh, and there's a good, solid fifteen-knot westerly to blow any fallout out to sea."

"Is this the one?" Robinson asked, pointing to a red marker off the tip of Florida.

"Yes, sir."

Robinson turned his head so that he could look directly at O'Neill when he spoke. "General, I want that sub destroyed."

The General's orders were simple and brisk. "Mr. Walsh, alert recon 12. Lt. Russell, transmit the go orders." He turned back, mouth puckered in thought. "I suspect they'll hear this on the beach in Miami, Mr. President."

Gazing up at the map expectantly, Robinson nodded. "I'll be disappointed if it's not heard a lot farther away than that."

Blake Plateau, The Atlantic Shelf, The Home Alternity

Like a great gray whale, the elint picket submarine D-57 nosed slowly through the cold green waters, its briskly turning twin screws barely holding their own against the eight-knot current. The teardrop hull resonated with D-57's high-pitched whale song, being sung by a progressively disintegrating ring bearing on the vessel's primary generator.

On the choppy white-capped surface some forty fathoms above, a passive antenna buoy bobbed at the end of a slender tether. Invisible to sonar, the buoy's three-meter whip collected radio energies ranging from the chirp of the navigation light at Key Biscayne to the chatter of air traffic control at Homestead Air Force Base.

Inside D-57, Captain Andrei Sorkin moved from compartment to compartment, observing the first shift at their stations, trying at once to measure and lift their spirits. The measuring was an easier task than the uplifting; there was a weariness in the men's voices, a sluggishness to their movements. It was a disease to which Sorkin himself was hardly immune. After nearly three months on station, his friendly jokes were flat, his fatherly admonitions old and familiar, even to himself.

He blamed Fleet Operations as much as himself for conditions aboard. Unlike the big blue-water ballistic-missile boats, D-57 was cramped and noisy, burdened with a grab bag of missions. Mines aft, missiles amidships, torpedoes forward, radio electronics everywhere—all stole space from the ninety-man crew. There was little room for physical activity, none at all for luxuries. Only structured, meaningful activity could fight the lethargy and indifference of a long deployment.

The games of hide-and-seek with the American coastal fleet, the simulated attacks and mine-laying drills, the shadowing exercises, had provided welcome challenge and variety. Predictably, morale had plummeted since the picket fleet had been ordered to withdraw beyond the twelve-mile limit. Here, they had only the rare encounter with a patrol plane to break the monotony.

Last night's bloody fistfight between two second-shift seaman engineers was only the most overt sign that crew fatigue was becoming critical. Sorkin feared his crew was coming apart. Of late, even the nagging mechanical problems aboard seemed calculated to aggravate the problem—the foul-tasting rust which had appeared in the drinking water, the generator which sang at a pitch that drilled into the skull.

Sorkin entered BCh-4, the communications hut, and settled in an empty chair. The problem with BCh-4 was in many ways the most acute, for their work was the most unrelentingly routine. In recent days an ensign had found the chief operator tapping his foot to music broadcast by American radio stations, and Sorkin himself had found an operator asleep on his watch.

"*V more kak doma, da?*" he said with a forced smile that no one answered. "At home in the sea, yes?"

Three miles west of the submarine and four thousand feet above the water, a slender metal arrow reached the apogee of its graceful ballistic journey. The furious white-smoke trail of the solid-fuel rockets thinned as the second stage burned out, and three explosive bolts fired to separate the spent cylinder from its stubby payload. A halo of small vanes opened at the base of the depth bomb, imparting spin that at once stabilized and slowed the projectile.

"Everything is quiet, Captain," the senior specialist said dutifully. "Even the American pilots seem bored today. There has been little idle talk among them."

Like a gleaming stone thrown by a playful child, the depth bomb fell toward the sea. The splash of its impact sent water twenty feet in the air. The force of impact armed the hydrostatic trigger and snapped the stabilizing vanes flat. The canister sank swiftly, trailing a fine veil of bubbles.

"Splash transient, Captain," the hydrophone operator called out.

"Our dolphin companions are back," Sorkin said over his folded hands.

"No, Captain—"

Three hundred feet below the surface, the electrical current created by the pressure of the sea against a tiny crystal reached a threshold, freeing far larger currents to pour through the depth bomb's network of circuits. Shaped explosive charges fired in synchrony, slamming fragments of enriched plutonium together. In one infinite instant of time, neutrons flew like the devil's fireflies, shattering atoms and freeing their deadly energies.

Around the starlike fireball, an expanding bubble of super-heated gases and furious radiation violently displaced millions of tons of water. The surface of the sea roiled and lifted up in a great dome, pierced by ferocious jets of steam.

Caught on the fringe of the bubble, D-57 was shoved sideways and upward as though by a great hand. Plates twisted, welds tore open and bulkheads crumpled, opening dozens of leaks through which poured poisonous steam instead of cold brine. As the pressure inside the submarine soared, eardrums burst, blood ran. The air was like fire, scalding skin and lungs.

But there was no time to scream. The fireball was dying, the bubble collapsing, and the water which had been displaced came crashing back to fill the vacuum. Swept along, tumbling, like a fragile shell before a breaking wave, D-57 was cast against a wall of blue-green steel and, torn by forces beyond its builders' conception, vanished.

The Pentagon, The Home Alternity

Waiting had worn thin, and the excitement of the successful attack had long dissipated. Robinson drummed his fingers impatiently on the table. "What time is it over there?"

"It's 7:35 P.M. in Moscow," Rauche said.

"What do you think?"

"It's been less than an hour. I'd say they're still trying to figure out what happened."

"You said they monitor the FNS. They must have heard the bulletins."

Rauche nodded. "They're probably trying to get independent confirmation."

"Here it comes!" someone cried as a printer started to chatter.

But it was not Molink, which had gone silent minutes after the submarine was destroyed. Instead, noise came from the Fleet intelligence link. A waiting technician tore off the paper and ran it to the main table. "Sir, the Soviet Atlantic Command has gone on war alert."

"Shit." Three voices said the word at once.

"Here we go," another voice said ominously.

"Bogeys dropping off the board," the Cyclops operator sang out. "Everybody's cutting loose the buoys and going deep."

"We'd better go to Defcon 2," Rauche said, his expression grim. "Mr. President, this is a soft target. You should go. Your helicopter is waiting at the river entrance."

"Tell 'em to turn off the engines," Robinson said as he came up out of his chair. "I want to talk to Kondratyeva. If he won't call us, we'll call him."

O'Neill leaped up to block his path. "What are you gonna say now? 'Excuse me, I seem to have stepped on one of your little submarines—' "

"Shut up, Gregory," Robinson said, brushing past. A Molink translator came running up with a tablet. "No. The hell with the codes and ciphers. I said I want to *talk* to him. Point me to the right phone and get him on the other end."

"Here, Mr. President," a technician called. "We're requesting the Premier. Stand by for the green light."

Standing beside the radiophone console, Robinson smiled and flashed his eyebrows. "I do hope our friend Somerset is listening in."

"He probably will be," the CIA director said.

"Green light, Mr. President. They must have been expecting us."

"You bet they were," Robinson said, lifting the receiver. "Mr. Premier."

The voice on the other end of the line was terse, the words clipped. "Mr. President. Apologies are not enough. You have destroyed the very foundation of international trust with your gangsterism—"

In the background, the printers were all chattering, the gallery was hushed.

"I didn't call to apologize," Robinson snapped. "Our intelligence shows you at a war alert. Your ships are acting in a hostile and provocative manner—"

"We did not initiate the 'hostilities,'" Kondratyeva growled. "You brazenly destroy a harmless reconnaisance submarine and dare accuse us of provocation. We will answer your brutality, Mr. President, and teach you the lesson of your blindness—"

"If you find one of our submarines inside Russian territorial waters, you're welcome to do your best to destroy it," Robinson said. "But if you order so much as one missile launched toward the United States or one American naval vessel attacked, before you can start your celebration you'll find the Kremlin coming down around your ears—"

"Empty threats will not deter us from defending the free oceans and avenging our dead. I, too, have intelligence reports. Your bombers are hours from our borders."

"If you underestimate me, Mr. Premier, it'll be the last mistake you make," Robinson said. "That's no empty threat."

"Send your planes. Long before they reach our border justice will have been served on the murderers, and when the planes arrive we will shoot them down."

"Mr. Premier, you have been misled by your intelligence bureau. I have a squadron of nuclear-tipped missiles sited within a fifteen-minute flight time of where you're standing—"

"Somerset is screaming right now," O'Neill said under his breath to Rauche.

287

"Liar. Lies will not deter us."

Robinson turned to the Army Chief. "Targets. Name some targets." When the Army Chief stared mutely, Robinson called to the room at large. "Quickly. Name some targets the Weasels can reach."

A young lieutenant at one of the consoles was the first to find his voice. "Ports and naval facilities at Murmansk, Tallinn, Gdansk, Odessa. Steel plants in the Ukraine—"

Others joined in. "The command centers at Kiev, Kharkov, Gorki," Rauche said.

"The Central Industrial Power System."

"Refineries. Rybinsk. Cherepovets."

Robinson repeated the names into the phone. "Are you ready to risk all that? Or do you think you can shoot down our missiles, too?"

"I do not believe these missiles exist," Kondratyeva said coldly. "We will not be taken in by your bluff—"

"Watch your radar screens, Mr. Premier. Watch your screens and see what a bluff looks like." Robinson put down the phone and pointed to the Army Chief. "I want a Weasel launched. Now!"

"Mr. President, we have to go to Defcon 3," Rauche pleaded.

"If we launch a missile now their whole Atlantic fleet is going to empty its silos," O'Neill said angrily. "Back off, Peter. You've pushed it too far."

"I know what I'm doing," Robinson said. "Target it toward Greenland, anywhere away from the Reds—but make sure they have a good look at it."

"Sir—"

"Now, you bastard!"

The Army Chief blanched. "Yes, sir."

Moscow, The Home Alternity

Kondratyeva turned slowly from the command display, from the bright green line extending from northern Scotland to the mid-Atlantic north of the Azores, from the track of the American missile. His cold eyes fixed on the director of the GRU.

"Explain this!" he bellowed. "How can this be!"

"Premier, I will not deny the facts," the harried man said. "But they could not have introduced these weapons in squadron strength without our knowledge."

"Why not? If one, why not a hundred?" Kondratyeva roared. "Now what am I to do?"

The Chief of Naval Operations stepped forward. "Even if they number a hundred, it is only a fraction of what we have at sea. Robinson will not dare to use them. We must answer what they have done."

"He dares anything," Kondratyeva said. "He is unpredictable, uncontrolled."

"He will not risk the destruction of his country over the destruction of one city, one air base," the Minister of Strategic Rocket Forces importuned.

"And how do you evaluate what we risk, Vladimir? What is the accuracy of these new missiles, their power? How many will fall to our defenses, and how many will die where the defenses fail? Geidar, tell me what we risk."

"That will take time," Voenushkin said in a small voice.

"Yes," Kondratyeva said. "But you ask me to risk those uncounted lives for a hundred men and one submarine, for pride. You ask me to trust the restraint of a man who has shown no restraint. You, whose failure has placed on our very doorstep a threat you cannot even gauge for me."

"What are you going to do?"

The Premier threw his hands in the air in disgust and frustration. "What have you left for me to do?"

The Pentagon, The Home Alternity

The bell chimed, the printer clattered, and talking ceased. The officer standing by the machine tore the sheet from the guides and read it aloud.

"The alert has been canceled," he said. "The Russian fleet is standing down." He looked up from the paper and grinned. "They blinked."

As the gallery burst into applause, a triumphant smile came onto Robinson's lips. He stood and clapped O'Neill firmly on one shoulder. "That, Gregory, is how you beard a bear."

O'Neill said nothing.

"Mr. President? Do you want to talk to Somerset now?" the Chairman asked. "He's hotter than a hornet."

Robinson laughed. "I do *not* want," he said. "I want lunch. General Rauche, can a civilized plate be had anywhere in this monstrosity?"

The General's face was still touched by a mixture of awe, respect, and relief. "You've heard of the Chiefs' chef, I see. I'll show you the way."

File No. I80351 **STANDARD CANDIDATE
EVALUATION FORM
NATIONAL RESOURCE CENTER**

CANDIDATE: Wallace, Rayne Alan

<u>Ok</u> Birthdate: 8-29-1952   Birthplace: Richmond, Indiana

<u>Ok</u> Married: 6-12-1971 to Ruthann Rhea King

<u>+</u>   Children: Katherine Jean, b. 1-15-1972

CREDENTIALS REVIEW:

<u>Ok</u> Highest Education: Hagerstown Consolidated High School

<u>Ok</u> Graduate? <u>1970</u> Rank: 103/268 IQ: 108 (1969)

<u>Ok</u> Brasson National Assay: 41.4 (2nd quartile)

<u>+</u>   NSA Attitudinal Assay: L Scale—91 M Scale—93

<u>+</u>   Interest Groups: <u>y</u> Youth Defense Reserve <u>3</u> yr.

                     ___ Youth Service Corps   ___ yr.

                     <u>y</u> Tomorrow Camp   <u>2</u> yr.

INTERVIEW:

In standard exercises, candidate demonstrated average-to-good verbal facility, good-to-very-good memory skills, very good visual recognition/discrimination. Personality integration fair, resilience high. Adaptability appears high, but eagerness for acceptance poss. masked accurate reading. Negatives: lacks clear sense of his own limitations._____

_____

_____

SUMMARY:

Candidate is highly motivated due to present financial pressures. History indicates high loyalty, diligence; average intelligence, limited introspection. Exit options minimal. YDR captain describes cand. as follower, not leader. Family climate positive toward national service. Not qualifiable as field agent, but should be a reliable courier._____

_____

_____

Recommendation: Reject _____

                Accept for: Group M _____ Group A _____

                        Group R <u>X</u> ____

RECRUITER: M. Hirsch

CHAPTER 17

Mist on the Mountain

Bloomington, Indiana, Alternity Blue

No doubt Wallace believed he had been discreet, Donald Arens thought as he rounded the corner of the alley.

True, Wallace had left no addresses on scraps of paper, had paid cash wherever possible. But the signs he did leave were nearly as easy to follow. A theater ticket stub recovered from Wallace's apartment, a first name provided by his roommate, and a telephone number gleaned from the station's massive billing had been enough to bring Arens to Morton Street and the back stairs of Five Friends.

The neighborhood was agreeably deserted. Counting Shan's, there were less than a half-dozen second-story apartments scattered along the block. It was nearly midnight, and curtains were drawn against drafts and streetlamps. The sidewalks were empty, and the streets nearly so.

But no amount of stealth could make Arens' approach up the sagging wooden stairs a silent one. He almost wished Wallace would hear him coming and run, and thus restore a little challenge to the chase.

Arens knew that was too much to hope for. Wallace had already demonstrated his weakness by allowing himself to be controlled by his cupidity. Instead of running or fighting, he would whine and wheedle and whimper that what he did wasn't so terribly wrong. You understand, he would plead, you especially have to understand.

Arens understood, and his contempt for Wallace flowed from

the understanding. Putting a woman above the Guard, particularly a woman from this world, was unforgivable stupidity. Nothing a woman can give a man is worth his loyalty. And only a fool would allow a woman to control him with love or sex.

A short, plain-faced woman wearing flower-print flannel pajamas answered his knock. *You sold yourself cheaply, to boot,* Arens thought as he looked at her. "Hi," he said, flashing a smile. "I'm looking for Ray Wallach. Is he here?"

The woman stiffened and peered at him closely. "I'm sorry," she said. "I'm afraid you have the wrong address."

"You're Shan, aren't you? I'm sure this is the address he gave me."

"I'm sorry," she said, and started to close the door.

Turning sideways, he drove the door open with his shoulder, knocking the woman backward into the little utility room. She retreated before him, her face showing fear, but not panic. "Ray?" he called. "You'd better come talk to me."

"I told you there's no one here."

"Then tell me where he is."

"I'm just housesitting. I don't know who Shan sees or where they might be."

"I don't believe you," he said simply.

Whether because she sensed the far wall uncomfortably close behind her or merely in defiance, she stopped retreating and stood her ground. "It's the truth."

"Then call her," he said. "You know where she is, call her."

"I can't," she said. "I don't know where she is."

"I do," he said. "Right here. Right in front of me."

A skittering sound behind him spun Arens around and brought the pistol out of his right coat pocket. It was a cat, a gray blur diving for a hiding place beneath the bed. Arens made no effort to halt the reflex that the noise had begun. The silenced pistol hiccoughed, and the cat squalled and skidded into a heaving, jerking lump of bloody fur.

He had thought to intimidate her, to push her past fear into a submissive panic. Instead, the woman bolted while his back was turned, lunging toward a closed door on the opposite side of the room. Surprise rooted him long enough for her to take three, four, five steps and actually touch the doorknob.

But before she could open the door, he launched himself at her, tackling her with enough force to carry them both hard to the wall and then to the floor. When she continued to fight him, clawing at his face and struggling beneath his weight, he brought the pistol whipping across her face, opening a long scarlet gouge in her cheek.

That had the desired effect. Her body went stiff, and she stared up at him wide-eyed and white-skinned.

"Don't try that again," he said. "I've got no reason not to kill you, too."

She shook her head jerkily.

"Let's drop the nonsense. You know who I'm here for."

She nodded, tentatively.

"He's not here. That much is clear. Do you know where he is?"

"I don't know. I really don't know. Please don't hit me again."

"Is he coming back?"

She swallowed. "Yes."

"When?"

"I'm . . . I'm not sure."

He sat back, straddling her hips.

"How long has he been gone?"

"Uh—two days?"

"What's the last time he called?"

"He hasn't called—"

Cold trail, Arens thought. *Good for you, Rayne. You're already running. Maybe this will be entertaining after all.* With a casual motion, he returned the pistol to his pocket. "While we're waiting, maybe you can show me what Ray got so excited over," he said, seizing a handful of fabric.

"No—"

With a powerful jerk, he tore her pajama top open to the waist. Her breasts were full, soft, and pale, with a fine tracery of blue veins. He looked up from them too late to see her glance sideways past him into the room. But he did not miss the hopeful look in her eyes, or the shadow of the man standing two steps from them and holding a blue-steel revolver trained on Arens' head.

"John Krill, NIA," the man said. "Hands in the air, stand up very slowly, and face the wall. You're under arrest."

Sweet fuckin' redbait, Arens thought disgustedly as he complied. *Only a fool—*

With a grunt, Albert Tackett dropped the paper on his desk and rubbed his eyes tiredly. "So what do you think?"

The two senior aides exchanged glances. Barbara Adams spoke first. "I don't think there's any question that there's more to Wallace's disappearance than a fling with this Shan Scott."

"Couldn't he be responsible for this?"

"Arens was one of the best icemen working Blue," Bret Monaghan said gruffly. "A special projects type. No way does a scruff like Wallace take him."

Dropping into his seat, Tackett raised an eyebrow and asked, "What are we looking at, then, Bret?"

Monaghan considered his answer carefully before speaking. "Wallace and Arens were both plucked clean. The woman has disappeared. The police throw their hands up on the cars and the people both. I'm thinking we've gotten ourselves crossthreaded with the gray men—domestic security."

"How?" Tackett demanded. "How'd it happen?"

"We've had to raise our profile for Rathole," Adams said. "And it just takes that one dumb move that attracts official attention, and then they're into us."

"Like the O'Neill business," Tackett said glumly, slumping back in his chair.

"That wasn't your call," Adams said.

"It should have been," Monaghan said. "That should have gotten a harder look, President or no."

Adams said, "It doesn't have to have been O'Neill. We sent a lot of raw meat over there to get the work done. Like Wallace. Brains aren't at the top of the list when we recruit runners, after all."

"Or directors, it seems," the Director said acidly. "So, who do you think's got him? Local blueshirts? Or feds?"

"It looks now like Wallace's girlfriend was a Volunteer Watch cell leader," Adams said.

Monaghan nodded. "NIA or FBI, would be my guess."

"Which means federal detention, a safe house who knows where. It's not going to be easy to get at them," said Tackett. "But we have to, don't we."

"We have to do more than that," Monaghan said. "We're wide open. I'm concerned that we could lose the gate house."

"Yes," Tackett acknowledged. "So what's the answer?"

"Cut back. Get those kids out of there and send everybody else to ground. Keep it very simple, very clean, and very quiet until we can recover Wallace and Arens and assess the damage. Maybe in six months, nine months we can start to ramp up again.''

"Barbara?"

"I'm afraid I agree," Adams said quietly.

"That kills Rathole," Tackett pointed out.

"Every cloud has a silver lining," was Monaghan's acerbic reply. "Rathole's not what we're here for, Albert. I won't miss it.''

"We're here to do what the President asks us to do," Tackett said. "Not to dictate to him."

"We can't do magic," Monaghan said. "If we're not careful with this, we'll lose a lot more than Rathole.''

Adams offered, "If we're successful in getting control of the gate in Orange, we can use some of the excess manpower there. The early indications are that Orange would make an even better hideaway than Blue. Things are wide open there.''

"But it'd be a year before operations in Orange could support anything this size," Tackett mused.

"At least," Adams agreed.

"All right," Tackett said. "Leave me."

When they were gone, he escaped from behind his desk and walked to the inner windows to look down at the Cambridge. Too much to control, he thought. Too much to understand. It's not the hole in Alice's hedge, beyond which anything can happen. There are limits, Peter. Please understand that there are limits—

Reluctantly, he turned away and walked back to his desk. There are times when direct access to the President is no advantage, he thought as he waited for the White House operator to route the call.

He was kept waiting barely a minute. "Good morning, Albert," said a cheerful Robinson.

"Provisionally, Mr. President. You might want to withhold final judgment on that for a little while yet.''

"Don't be cute with me, Albert. What's going on?''

"Mr. President, we have a problem with Rathole—''

"You know my answer on that. Fix it.''

"We've lost some personnel. We're in danger of exposure. We're going to have to pull back and go slow.''

"Stop right there," Robinson said. "You're telling me things I don't want to hear.''

"We've lost a mole and an iceman. There's a good chance that they're in the hands of the Blue intelligence community.''

"So what's the danger?" Robinson demanded irritably. "They aren't going to talk, are they? Or are you telling me they went over the wall?"

"I'm not greatly concerned about them talking," Tackett patiently explained. "I am concerned about having our whole operation come into focus under their microscope. We can't take the scrutiny, Mr. President."

"I thought the secret of these operations was that our agents were untraceable. Even if these traitors are talking, who's going to believe them? Look for them in the sanitoriums, not the prisons."

"We are going to try to get them back," Tackett said, his own irritation on the rise. "But as I said, these two men are not the issue. What matters is that they've sensitized the immune system. We brush up against it again anywhere in the near term and we're likely to get clobbered. And the first priority has to be protecting the gate house."

"Near term—what does that mean? A week? A month?"

"Six months at the inside. Mr. President, this new alternity we're opening up—it's got excellent potential. The delay could be a blessing if it puts us in a better place."

"Wheels are turning, Albert. I can't wait six months."

"This particular wheel is about to fall off the wagon, sir."

Robinson said crossly, "You told me you'd be there for me, Albert. You told me I could count on you. You need more security over there, borrow some grunts and goons from one of the services."

Tackett sighed. "You don't understand. We could have ten thousand soldiers there. It doesn't matter. Once they find us, the operation is dead."

"Then make sure they don't find you," Robinson said curtly. "But hold that goddamned door open." And then the line went dead.

Tackett slammed the receiver down into the cradle. "Son of a bitch," he growled. "Bret! Get in here."

Several seconds later, the deputy director ambled into the office with a bemused smile on his face. "No sale, I take it."

"The President was adamant. He wouldn't agree to any change or delay in Rathole."

"Too bad."

"Yes. Bret, I'm trying to think if we ever talked about a contingency plan for abandoning a gate house and destroying it once we're gone."

"Burning the bridges behind us? No."

"Maybe we ought to."

Monaghan squinted in Tackett's direction. "I don't think we even know what would happen to the gate if we did."

"Then we ought to try to find out," he said. Elbows propped on the armrests and hands steepled in front of his mouth, Tackett rocked slowly in his chair. "We'll have to do what we can to keep the lid on. If worse comes to worst, we may have to abandon the gate house. And I don't intend to see us leave it intact for them to play with."

Fairfax Co., Virginia, Alternity Blue

By Wallace's count, he had been a prisoner for nine days.

The word arrest had never been used, and in some ways he felt almost like a guest. His hosts had gone to some trouble to make him at least physically comfortable, moving him late in the second day from the little room with the air mattress and chemical toilet to what looked like it might have been an executive office. The room had been stripped to the walls, but they had provided a real bed that did not go flat in the middle of the night, and there was a connected bathroom with a tiny shower stall.

In other ways, Wallace was beginning to feel like a specimen. After the third day, Bayshore stopped coming, and those who replaced him stopped trying to question him. But they kept coming, someone every day, sometimes a woman, sometimes a man. For each different person there was a different pretext— more photographs, blood samples, throat scrapings, a hair cutting. Today it had been a dentist to look at his teeth.

Ten, fifteen, twenty minutes they would spend with him, superficially friendly but saying nothing except what was required by the task that had brought them there. And then they would go, leaving him alone again. All the interruptions in a day added up to less than an hour. The rest of the time he was alone.

It seemed as if they were hoping that isolation would drive him to open up to them, to be so desperate for company that he would blurt out something they would find valuable or interesting. He already looked up hopefully at the sound of the door opening. One day—not soon, but one day—he might be restless enough in his captivity for it to happen.

Filling the idle time was a continuing burden. He exercised. He masturbated. He napped. He pried the buttons out of the mattress and invented games to play with them. He painted toothpaste pictures on the vanity mirror. He pulled up one corner

297

of the carpet and started unraveling the pile from the backing. And always, he wondered what was happening beyond the walls.

It was clear that they still did not know what to make of him. He understood that he was in limbo, that once a decision was made he would be taken somewhere else, perhaps to be discarded, perhaps to be leaned on. He was eager for that decision, even for real prison, so long as it would give the Section a breath of a chance to find him. Which is why when the door opened and Bayshore entered, Wallace could not help but feel cheered.

"Hello, Ray," his visitor said. "I hope you've been doing all right here."

"I'm okay so long as I have something destructive to do," Wallace said, with a nod toward the tangle of rug yarn in the corner.

"Glad we were able to accommodate," Bayshore said with a lazy smile. "I need you to come with me for a little while, Ray."

"Now?"

"Please."

No guards fell in to escort them. The two of them walked alone together, down a corridor, across a small lounge, into an elevator. Along the way there were people, voices, laughter, and Wallace was nearly overwhelmed by that which he hadn't thought he had been missing.

The quiet of Bayshore's office presented itself as a refuge. But after the sterility of Wallace's cell suite, even the ordinary accoutrements of the room presented themselves as an almost painful sensory richness.

"Have a seat, Ray," Bayshore invited.

Still disoriented, Wallace felt for a chair and lowered himself into it.

"You've managed to stay pretty calm about being here, Ray," Bayshore said. "Most of us figure you've been trying to wait it out until your friends find you."

"I'm still not going to tell you anything."

"I understand, Ray. I brought you up here because I have something to tell you. Someone came looking for you a couple of days ago."

Wallace tried and failed to look disinterested. "So?"

With an almost casual motion, Bayshore retrieved a photograph from a stack of papers to his right and slid it across the desk. It was a head-and-shoulders mug shot of Donald Arens. Despite the implication, Wallace's spirits lifted. "Ugly fellow."

"To answer the question you won't ask, no, he's not here.

Mr. Arens is in the Indianapolis city jail, under arrest for simple assault, sexual assault, forced entry, and weapons violations."

"Why do I care?"

"You're not the poker player you think you are, Ray. I have no doubt that you know him. And I know it'll be no surprise to you that he comes up as a nonperson, just like you."

"I guess your records aren't as complete as you thought."

"Aren't you curious to know why your friend's in jail?"

"He's not my friend—"

"Don't insult my intelligence, Ray. Don't deny the obvious."

"Don't insult mine," Wallace snapped. "I'm not stupid. I know why he's in jail."

"Oh?"

"Sure. Sucker bait. Now that you know who came after me, you want to see who comes for him."

"True enough. But I was talking about how we came to pick him up."

"You run things here. You can make up any reason you want. I don't even know why you picked me up."

"Don't you?" Bayshore asked lightly, but did not wait for an answer. "We had a vol housesitting for Shan and her place wired, just in case someone started to wonder where you'd gotten to," Bayshore said, reaching for the intercom. "Myra, would you ask Donna to come in?"

A moment later the door opened, and a short round-bodied woman entered. Her right eye was shadowed by purple bruises, and a string of tiny black stitches closed a long gash across her cheek. "Ray, this is Donna. She was in Shan's apartment when your friend showed up."

Wallace squirmed and avoided the woman's gaze. "So you say."

"Your friend thought Donna *was* Shan, and that she knew where you were. When she told him the truth—that she wasn't, and she didn't—he started to work her over. Thanks to the wire, we got someone there before it got any worse."

This time Wallace could find nothing to say.

Bayshore dug in a desk drawer. "I can't tell you how glad I am you know Arens. I'm assuming it means that you know his voice." He set a small cart player on the surface between them and pressed the play button.

The recording was almost too clear to be credible as a remote recording off a wire. But there was no doubt that it was Arens' voice. Wallace listened to the encounter with ever-growing discomfort. At the sound of a shot and an animal cry of pain, he started. "What was that?"

"Your friend shooting the cat."

"He killed Pharaoh?"

"Is that a surprise?" Bayshore asked.

"It's stupid," Wallace muttered. "He didn't have to do that."

Talking, he had lost the thread of what was happening in the far-away room captured on the cartridge. "Could you play that part back?" he said suddenly.

Bayshore wordlessly complied. It was Arens' voice, calm and cold.

"Don't do that again," the recorded Arens said. "I've got no reason not to kill you, too."

He wanted to ask to hear it again, wanted a reason to deny or disbelieve it. Glancing sideways, he saw that Donna's face was pale, that she was struggling not to cry. "Is that you? Is that real?" he asked.

She nodded, and the tears broke through, tears of shame and humiliation, of a painful memory relived.

"Thank you, Donna," Bayshore said gently. "You can go." He waited until the door closed behind her, then turned his gaze on Wallace. "What's it mean, Ray?"

The words did not come easily. "I . . . I should have—" He stopped, swallowed, and started again. "Rayne," he said, his eyes downcast but his voice a little stronger. "My name is Rayne. R-a-y-n-e."

Bayshore nodded, but said nothing.

"They told me to sit tight. They'd take care of it." He looked up and met Bayshore's eyes. "You shouldn't have done that to Donna. You shouldn't have made her hear that."

"You had to know she was real," Bayshore said simply.

"Yeah," Wallace said, and shook his head. "I can't believe he killed Pharaoh. Isn't that the height? He comes to kill me and I'm getting exercised about the cat."

"Do you want to tell me what this is all about, Rayne?"

Wallace bit his lip, then nodded almost imperceptibly. "Yeah," he said. "I think I do." He hesitated. "I don't know where to start."

Bayshore reached for the machine on the desk and touched the controls. "Why don't you tell me about the record. Start there."

Sipping coffee from a huge ceramic mug, Bayshore listened patiently for almost an hour, the cart player dutifully capturing every word. It took that long to sketch even a skeletal explanation of the record, of Shan, of Wallace/Wallach.

Even as he offered them, Wallace felt his explanations to be painfully disjointed and full of digressions which were themselves incomplete. And he seemed to be talking more about himself than about anything Bayshore would be concerned with. But Bayshore did not seem to mind. He made no effort to steer Wallace toward or away from any subject, contenting himself with occasional questions highlighting or clarifying something Wallace had already said.

"Is any of this helping?" Wallace asked finally. "Is any of it making sense? For that matter, do you *believe* any of it?"

"The picture is coming together—slowly," Bayshore admitted. "But I do believe you. Would you mind if I asked someone else to join us?"

"Are you going to make me repeat it all?"

"No. Just put a bookmark in your brain until I get back."

In five minutes, he returned with a white-haired black man and a matronly woman. After introductions—the man was something that sounded like "ethnologist," the woman a counterterrorism specialist—they settled into empty seats to listen.

By the end of the afternoon, there were a total of nine people in the room, two sitting crosslegged on the floor. They were an attentive audience, and he told them everything he thought they could want to know. He had few names to give them, and only three addresses—the gate house, the satellite station, and his apartment. But he detailed the organization of the station, the financial and operational structure, the roles of the analyst, the iceman, the mole.

From time to time, he saw flickers of doubt and skepticism on some of their faces, a raised eyebrow, a sidewise glance, a curled lip. But he was not challenged or questioned, not interrogated at all. They wanted to hear his story, and he told it as well as he could.

The one exception, the time he seemed to disappoint them was at the end, when the counterterrorism expert asked about O'Neill.

"Gregory O'Neill is the Secretary of Defense," Wallace said. "I can't think why the Guard would kill his counterpart."

"But you would if there was a reason."

Wallace shrugged. "It's something an iceman could do."

"Someone like Arens."

"Yeah."

"What about you?" the woman pressed. "Would you have done it if there was a reason?"

"I wasn't trained for that kind of work."

"Did you ever kill anyone?"

"Once," he said, meeting her hard look without flinching. "A badge that was trying to keep me from getting Home."

Bayshore stepped in to end the exchange. "It's almost seven o'clock, and it's a mystery to me that Rayne has any voice left. Lot of people here with growling stomachs, too. Let's—ah, let's call it a night."

"Fine by me," Wallace said.

"Rayne, it's going to be a day or two before we can get you out of here into someplace both safer and more comfortable. What can we get you to get you through?"

Wallace stood, stretching protesting muscles. "Music. I'd really like to hear some music."

"What kind?"

"Any kind."

"We'll get you a player and some carts," Bayshore promised.

"Any chance for company? Other than a guard?"

"That's a little tougher. We're going to leave somebody with you, just for our own peace of mind. But your door will be open, and I'll try to see that it's someone with a personality."

"Thanks. And dinner," he added. "One of those growling stomachs is mine."

"Myra, my secretary, will take care of you."

"Okay." He turned toward the door, then stopped and turned back. "Good night."

"Good night, Rayne."

He half-expected them not to keep their promises, but they did. The door was unlocked. The guard, wearing neither uniform nor weapon, showed up with a portable television and a sense of humor. And by the time he was ready to turn out the lights, he had music, a half-dozen recordings to fill the room with melody, harmony, and rhythm, to take him away on a quiet ride to the most peaceful sleep of his captivity.

When the prisoner was gone, there was an outburst of long-suppressed snickers and snide comments. But there was a nervous quality to the ridicule, as though no one was quite confident enough to pronounce the story a lie.

The ethnologist expressed it more openly. "Rich, in eight years here, I've been called out on reports of UFO sightings, satanic sex rings, cursed houses, mind-control drugs in drinking water, and minotaurs in the Jersey wetlands. I've listened to the nicest, most earnest people you've ever seen tell the wildest stories you can imagine. I've listened to sad people desperate for attention and wild-eyed psychopaths rounding up converts. But I've never had a chill run down my back like I did listening to that boy.''

"Come on, Malcolm," someone scoffed. "You don't mean to say you believe all this."

Rummaging in his jacket pocket for a lighter, the ethnologist nodded gravely. "I always thought that if I stayed in this job long enough, I'd run into a story that was crazy *and* true. This feels like the one. You saw him. He didn't proselytize, like so many of them do. He was glad to tell us, but he didn't worry about whether we believed him. He didn't need us to validate what he knows is the truth. Did anybody see it any differently?"

No one raised a voice of dissent.

"I have as much trouble with magic mazes and alternate worlds as anyone here," Bayshore said at last. "Frankly, I don't think I can judge those claims except on the basis of prejudice and emotion, and I'm fighting myself to withhold judgment until someone with better tools has a chance to look at it."

"Amen," someone muttered.

"But Rayne also made a lot of claims that can be checked right here, in our 'alternity,' on this side of his so-called gate," Bayshore added. "Let's get our people out on the street and check them. Then maybe we'll have a better idea what to make of Rayne Wallace, and what we need to do about what we heard today."

Boston, The Home Alternity

A courtesy visit, the Secretary's traveling secretary had called it. Secretary O'Neill is in Boston on an inspection tour of military facilities, he had said. Would Director Tackett be available to receive the Secretary for private, casual discussion?

It was the kind of dodge a friend might have used to say, Let's get together for a beer and gossip. But O'Neill was practically a stranger. They came from different worlds—O'Neill a mix of Ivy League theorist and pennypinching business manager, Tackett all learn-by-doing street fighter. They reigned over distinct fiefdoms, brought together only rarely at the table of the king.

A courtesy visit, they called it. And as a courtesy, Tackett had agreed, but not without wondering the real reason. Did O'Neill know about his Blue counterpart? But there was no way he could have known. Was it Alpha List and Rathole? Technically O'Neill was still part of both. But if he asked to tour the gate house, to know the details of the gate, the courtesies would end. Tackett would have to say no.

O'Neill did not keep him wondering long. As soon as they were alone in the suite's comfortable lounge, O'Neill turned to him and asked, "Are your offices monitored in any way?"

Tackett was taken aback. "No."

"Do you sweep for outside bugs?"

"Every day."

"Are you sure?"

"What makes you think my office might be wired?" Tackett asked with annoyance. "Is yours?"

He was stunned when O'Neill said, "Yes."

"What?"

"I've been watched for months. I'm followed wherever I go. My office, my home, and my car have all been bugged. "

"Have you reported it to the FBI?"

"Enough times to discover there's no point. The FBI takes them out, the NSA puts them back."

Tackett stared. "Let me get this straight—you claim you're under survellience by our guys?"

"Yes," O'Neill said.

"Do you have any proof? I find that difficult to believe—spying on the Secretary of Defense. Who'd order such a thing?"

"The President," O'Neill said.

"Come on."

"It's no secret to you that I'm on the outside."

"I know that there've been some hard feelings," Tackett acknowledged.

"This whole inspection tour was put together to get me here, with you. I've been bused around to five Air Force bases in four states, Camp Edwards, and the Navy shipyard over at Charleston, all so people wouldn't scratch their heads and wonder what the Secretary of Defense wanted with the Director of the National Information Agency."

"What *do* you want?"

"Your help."

The two men sat in chairs only a yard apart, but there was an ever-widening gulf between them. Tackett listened with growing incredulity as O'Neill related his versions of the *Marjorie* incident and the sinking of the D-57. Eventually his resistance to what he was hearing reached the point where he could not listen any more.

"Mr. Secretary, I know the President hates the Russians and

the status quo. I know that he is committed to a shift in the balance of power. But I just can't credit the kind of recklessness you're accusing him of."

O'Neill did not flinch. "You were there when he turned the CIA loose. You heard him say he was going to turn up the heat."

"Are you saying we actually went out and nuked a Red boat outside the limit just to see what the Russians would do?"

"Yes."

"How do you know that?"

"I was there. He picked the target himself. There must have been thirty witnesses. Everybody knew the target was out beyond the twelve-mile limit."

"And the Joint Chiefs stood by for this?"

"General Rauche dragged his feet a little beforehand. But afterward, he was just like the rest of them. They cheered, Albert. They stood up and cheered like they were at a football game and Robinson had just run back the opening kickoff."

"Gregory—" Tackett stopped and sighed. "For the sake of argument, let's say it happened the way you and Pravda claim. It's done. He got away with it. What's to be done about it now?"

"It's not done," O'Neill said, shaking his head. "It's only the beginning. Two months ago the CIA brought Robinson a proposal to mock up a VC-24 like a Tu-85, fly it to Moscow, and drop a bomb on the Kremlin—"

Wheels are turning, the President had said. "Dennis flies a lot of oddball ideas," Tackett said, uncomfortable with the memory.

"This time he had a sympathetic audience. The President gave him the go-ahead, behind my back. I found out when Blaze Matson called to ask what the CIA wanted with a Mark XII Super—that's the biggest in our arsenal. One had been pulled from inventory at Wurtsmith and transferred to a special unit at Westover."

"Westover—that's near Springfield."

"Yes. A transport wing base. Lots of VC-24s available."

"Didn't Matson just retire?"

"He was forced out. He thinks I was responsible, in fact," O'Neill said. "Albert, I went to Westover Thursday. *The Q-plane is gone.* No one will tell me where it is. No one will even admit it was ever there. The base commander lied to me, to my face."

Wheels are turning— "Have you asked Robinson about this?"

O'Neill shook his head. "It's too late. They've already built a wall around him."

"What are you talking about?"

"Robinson doesn't take my calls, and Rodman won't let me in to see him. That's why I need your help, Albert. Someone has to make the President take a second look at this. It has to be someone he trusts, someone who still has access to him."

"Who else knows?"

"Clifton—"

"What does he say?"

"Clifton's gone to jelly. He saw what happened to me. He won't stand up to Robinson."

"Who else?"

"Rodman. Madison, of course."

"The Vice-President?"

"No."

"So this hasn't been run past the National Security Council."

"No. It's all back-room, back-door. A lot of other people know parts of it. I don't know if any others understand what it means."

Tackett scowled. "How could I explain knowing, then? How could I even raise the question with the President?"

"Rathole is your entry point," O'Neill said. "You're part of this, Albert. You're driving the getaway car."

The picture O'Neill painted—Robinson as gangster—caused Tackett's resistance to stiffen. "He's the President, Gregory. I just don't know what I can do."

"How can you let this happen?" he asked, his expression exquisitely pained.

"How do you know it will?"

The Secretary stood and fired what he no doubt meant as an angry parting shot. "Because no one who can stop it has the nerve to act."

Anger begat anger. "What have you done, except crawl around looking for someone else to do it for you?" Tackett demanded, coming to his feet. "Have you gone to the Hill? Talked to the independent papers? All it will take is a little sunlight and this melts away."

"I don't think my keepers will allow either of those conversations to take place," O'Neill said darkly. "But when I run out of time or options, I'll have to try."

"When do you run out of time?"

"When they call for Asylum," O'Neill said. "Then it'll be too late."

One day turned to two, and two to four. To Rayne Wallace's surprise, they were quiet days, with even fewer interruptions than before, and no note-taking, fire-breathing interrogators. In some ways, he felt as though he had merely been transferred to a larger cell.

During the day, he watched television and played cards with his warden. After hours, he ran the empty halls for exercise, listened to his growing library of music, and wondered if he had been used.

But at noon on the fourth day, Rayne Wallace looked up from his bed and his newspaper to find Bayshore standing in the doorway.

"Moving day," Bayshore said, tossing him a soft-sided roll bag. "Pack your things."

Wallace caught the bag in one hand and swung himself to a seated position. "Where to?"

"Safe house. Pennsylvania."

"What took so long?"

Bayshore shrugged. "We had to see if you were telling the truth."

"I thought you said you believed me," Wallace said, crossing the room to where his modest inventory of clothing was arrayed on the shelves of a bookcase.

"There are degrees of belief."

Wallace pushed a handful of music carts into the bag beside the clothing and laid the player atop it. "What degree are you at now?" he asked, looking up quizzically.

"Off the scale," Bayshore said with a grunt. "I have to tell you what's been going on this morning. We've sent three closed vans out of here since eight this morning. Every one of them has been followed."

"By the Guard? They know I'm here?"

"They may just be hoping. Anyway, we're going to take you out of here by whirlybird."

Wallace zipped the bag closed. "I'll get sick again," he warned.

"If that's the worst that happens, I'll be happy. I trust your people don't have any jet fighters or antiaircraft missiles."

"Not that I know of."

"Hope you're right," Bayshore said heartily. "Ready?"

Wallace swallowed hard. "Ready."

• • •

Waiting in the tunnel for the helicopter, Wallace was surprised to find the world outside surprisingly springlike. The trees were still bare, but the snows had vanished to reveal a matted carpet of grass, and the air carried the promise of warmer days.

"What's the date?" Wallace asked Bayshore.

"March 14."

"What happened to winter?"

"Groundhog gave us a break. We've hit fifty a couple of days already. Buds are popping out. Might see crocuses in another week or so if this keeps up."

"Bird over the boundary," the guard called to them from the guardhouse.

Waving his acknowledgment, Bayshore led Wallace forward to the mouth of the tunnel. The blue and white twin-rotor helicopter came in low from the west, ground-skimming and tree-hopping. As delicate as a hovering hummingbird, it settled on the drive in front of them.

"Come on," Bayshore said, ducking his head and trotting forward.

Wallace followed on his heels, painfully aware of the intermeshing rotors thrashing the air over his head. Bayshore held open the door of the small rear cabin, then nimbly climbed in after, slamming the door shut and much of the noise out. While Wallace was still fumbling with the seat harness, the machine rose up from the pavement and skidded off toward the east at treetop level.

The helicopter was worse than the plane had been. Wallace succeeded in controlling his stomach, but failed to keep the stress of the struggle off his face.

"I take it people don't fly often where you come from," Bayshore said.

Tight-lipped, Wallace shook his head.

"Would it help if you knew these were practically crashproof?"

"How?"

"The drive train has a centrifugal clutch. If the engine quits, the rotors will freewheel—like a maple seed. We might hit hard enough to bounce, but not to break."

It helped, though Wallace could have done without the final speculation. "About the only flying back home is military or government," he said. "Regular folks take the interurbans. Trains. When they travel at all."

Bayshore said, "Which isn't often?"

"No. The first long trip I took was moving from Indiana to Boston when I joined the Guard—"

• • •

Talking helped more. Almost before Wallace realized it, the helicopter was whisking them a thousand feet above the rust-tinged soil and yellow winter wheat of Pennsylvania farms, above wooded valleys gouged by quiet streams. They flashed over an automated highway clinging to the side of one of the long fold ridges, over black iron trestles carrying old roads and rails across narrow gorges. Dense gray clouds formed a solid blanket overhead.

Forty minutes after leaving Fairfax, the helicopter crossed over one last humpbacked ridge and then began to descend toward the gently undulating lowland. Wallace peered forward through the bubblelike front canopy and tried to pick out their destination from among the scattered farms.

The pilot finally brought them to earth on a rolling meadow by a green-roofed two-story brick farmhouse. Boasting twin chimneys and a wooden porch that ran the full width between them, the house was encircled by low hedges in front and mature trees in back. A few hundred feet away was a battered red barn with an overthrust second story. Downslope in the meadow was a banked pond, the product of some past farmer's ambition.

Bag in hand, Wallace was the first out, grateful to have solid ground underfoot again. When Bayshore joined him, they started the long walk up to the house. The sound of the helicopter had drawn a trio of people out of the house, two of whom started down the walk to meet them.

"Company?" Wallace asked.

"Eh? No, not yet. Oh, we'll be bringing some people in to talk to you. One or two will probably move in for the duration," Bayshore said. "But the two you don't know are staff here."

Wallace took a second look at the woman who had hung back on the porch, and this time realized who she was. "You didn't say *she* was going to be here."

Bayshore shrugged. "You didn't ask."

"Does she have to be?"

"Yes. She's part of this."

The two walking parties met, and Wallace nodded through introductions to the house manager and the security chief, all the time looking past them to Shan on the porch. The anger of the first days was refreshed by the sight of her. But so were other memories, and he could not resolve the conflict.

When the quartet filed back toward the house, Wallace trailed behind, wrestling with his ambivalence. He mounted the three porch steps slowly, pausing as he reached the top.

"Hello, Rayne," she said.

Anger won. He continued past her without a word.

Wallace ignored or avoided Shan for the better part of two hours, retreating to his second-story room and into his music when Bayshore was called away to the basement communications center. But he could not forget that she was there, could not stop the thoughts tumbling head-and-tail after each other in his mind.

Even hiding behind the closed door of his room, he felt her presence in the house, felt it as both magnet and barb. His failure to shut her out was at first an irritation, then an annoyance, finally an obsession that drove him to throw his legs over the side of the bed and leave his room in search of her.

He found her on the porch, sitting crosslegged in a gently swinging basket chair suspended from the porch rafters. She was sad and silent, gazing out at the meadow and the gray skies. The boards groaned under his feet, but she did not seem to know he was there until he spoke.

"I need to talk to you," he said.

She turned her head to look up at him. "All right," she said.

"Not here. Let's go for a walk."

Nodding, she uncrossed her legs and eased herself out of the chair. "I'll tell security."

While Shan was in the house, Wallace stood on the porch steps and studied the sky. The unbroken blanket of clouds was grayer and lower, rain-laden and threatening.

"Okay," she said, rejoining him. "Tom will alert the perimeter patrols."

"You've been here a while," he observed. "You know all the rules."

They started down the walk, side by side but not touching.

"I've been here for a week," she said. "Since the trouble at my apartment." She paused. "They told me that you knew him."

"He was my roommate for awhile," Wallace said. "He let me think he was a friend. Just like you did."

After that, they walked in silence for a time. The ground was soft underfoot, the air heavy with moisture. He waited, expecting an answer, an apology, even acknowledgment.

Finally he stopped short and seized her wrist to turn her toward him. "Why?" he demanded. "Why did you do it?"

With her free hand, she plucked at the viselike hand imprisoning her. "You're hurting me—"

"Damn it, answer me!" he shouted, grabbing her other wrist and shaking her. "Why did you have to do this? Why did you do this to me?"

"I didn't know—what you were. That's what you do when there's something you don't understand. I didn't know they would take you away like that."

In a single sudden motion, he pushed her away and released her. "I showed you what I was. I showed you everything I was."

"I know," she said. "That's why I let you stay. Not to keep you there for them. Because I know that part of you, I knew I was safe with you."

"Then why?" he raged. "Why be afraid of me at the same time?"

"If you were from here, you'd understand," she said. "It's not just a duty. It's something you do because you care. I was ten, Rayne. Even the movie couldn't teach you what it meant to us."

"I broke the rules for you," he said hoarsely, the words stumbling out. "I risked—I gave up—and then you put them first. I felt so . . . so close . . . to you. I would have done anything—"

She took a step toward him. "And I wouldn't."

"No."

"I couldn't. Not yet. Not this soon. The closeness is real, Rayne. Was real. But you don't let go of everything for it—"

He closed his eyes and shivered. "You do when you wait so long for it," he whispered. "You do when it feels like your last chance."

Her gentle voice reached into the place where he was hiding. "Who am I in your reality, Rayne?"

His laugh was brittle, bitter. "Someone I loved."

Just then it began to rain, fat soaking drops that slapped against the grass and splattered on bare skin. "Come on," she said, taking his hand. "Run."

They ran for the barn, the closest structure. The skies opened just as they reached the shelter of the overhanging second story. The tangy odors of silage and moldy hay assaulted Wallace with ancient memories and associations.

Shan clung to his hand and stood close to him. "I'm not her," she said softly.

311

"No," he said. "But the two of you are—it's like you're one person in my mind."

"I know," she said. "You didn't say if she loved you."

"I never knew," he said, looking away. "We didn't have a chance to be anything."

The rain was rattling against the hollow shell of the barn, and a gust of water-laden wind drove them a step closer to the back wall and to each other.

"Rayne, I'm not her," she said. "I can't be her for you. But the person I am, this different person—I love you. And I'm sorry—for what I did and for what it did to you. And for what it did to us."

The regret in her eyes was real, the hard edge of his anger gone. He opened his arms to her, and they clung together in an embrace that changed slowly from simple reassurance to something which felt like renewal, like reunion.

include "Chromagraph" (elegy for brass choir), "Ruminations" (tone poem for chamber orchestra and electric ensemble), and the choral song cycle "An Exultation of Larks." In 1976, after the premiere of his controversial atonal symphony *Life −1*, Edelman resigned his post with the New Orleans Symphony Orchestra to accept a chair with the North Texas State University School of Music.

BIOGRAPHICAL/CRITICAL SOURCES:
"Full Critical: The Genius of Erik Edelman," *Symphony*, March, 1969
New Grove Dictionary of Music and Musicians, 1974

EDEN, Warren D(avid), physicist.
PERSONAL: born San Diego, May 12, 1938; s. William Kenneth and Jo Anne (Zane) Eden; m. Barbara Lee Newman June 26, 1965; 2 child., Mark David and Krystal Lynn; div. Oct. 7, 1969.

EDUCATION: BS in physics, U. Cal. San Diego, 1953; MS in physics, Stanford U., 1955; MS in astronomy, Stanford U., 1956, PhD in astrophysics, U. Cal. Berkeley, 1959.

AWARDS: Bohr Medal (American Chemical Society), 1961; Draper Medal (National Academy of Sciences), 1964; honorary doctorate, Princeton University, 1968; Gold Medal (Royal Astronomical Society), 1968; Charles Vernon Boys Prize (London Institute of Physics), 1968; Nobel Prize in Physics, 1969.

BIOGRAPHY: Possibly America's best-known, most-honored, and least-understood contemporary scientist, Warren D. Eden has in the first twenty years of his career made fundamental contributions to the disparate disciplines of physical chemistry, theoretical physics, and cosmology. His theory of synthetic elementalism revolutionized the study of high-energy particle physics and earned him international recognition. In recent years, Eden has devoted himself to the advocacy of his controversial cosmological system, known as "random structuralism," or, more popularly, the "wild-card model."

Eden was a child prodigy, reading at age two and solving differential equations at age seven. One of the youngest doctoral candidates in the history of the University of California, Eden drew attention

CHAPTER 18

The Odd Perfect Number

Washington, D.C., The Home Alternity

The visitor's part was ruler-straight, his cheeks freshly shaven, his teeth white and straight. His Capitol pass dangled from a tailored mouse-gray suit, and he wore a Cornell class ring on his right hand.

For all of those reasons, Walter Endicott distrusted the man on sight.

He knew the kind, had seen too many of them across his desk. Smooth-speaking advocates who tried to disguise the narrow interests they represented behind impassioned platitudes on public welfare, who cultivated an image of affluence and influence but came into the office with empty wallets and promises.

They didn't understand that real power came in through side doors and made its needs known in private. They didn't understand that the currency of the Capitol was mutual consideration. And they did not understand that he did not need them.

But he still received a trickle of supplicants, some few out of self-indulgence or idle curiosity, the larger fraction as favors to those to whom he was beholden. The visitor, a Rembert Wilkins from the International Commodities Exchange, belonged to the latter group. The majority leader, in whose state Wilkins' firm was based, had asked Endicott to give him a hearing.

"I'd suggest you get right to the point, Mr. Wilkins," Endicott said. "Fifteen minutes go by in a hurry."

"As you wish, Senator," Wilkins said, opening his briefcase. "If you prefer bluntness, I'll be blunt. My firm trades in agricultural products, minerals—and information. I have a number of questions to ask you. Before I ask them, I want to give you a reason to answer.''

Wilkins drew a small tape-tied portfolio from the briefcase and handed it to Endicott. For a moment, Endicott wondered if he had misjudged the visitor. Most bribes were not so nakedly offered. They came disguised as honorariums, campaign contributions, consulting fees, gifts.

But the envelope contained a surprise. Instead of a bundle of cash, Endicott found a bundle of photos showing him with Rachel in the woods behind his house. Rachel nude, bound standing between two trees, barefoot in the snow. The photos were sharp enough to show both his features and the whip marks on her frost-white skin clearly. A few long shots showed a recognizable portion of his house.

Endicott remembered the occasion but not the date. *Was that three weeks ago, four?* "I have better," he said offhandedly, sliding the envelope back across the desk.

"I don't think you can afford to be casual about these, Senator," Wilkins said, leaving the envelope where it rested.

Rocking back in his chair, Endicott said, "Well, since you're looking out for my welfare, why don't you explain real clearly what you think I ought to do."

"You have a great deal to lose, Senator Endicott. Your position, your reputation. Your wife Grace. Your freedom. Kidnapping—torture—murder—those are the credentials of a psychopath, not a U.S. senator."

"Kidnapping? Murder? I see two adults playing a game. Perhaps a minority interest, but no felony."

"I don't think you would enjoy trying to make that case in public, Senator," Wilkins said. "And you know very well the skeletons your house conceals—as do some of those you've invited to share in your game. They will tell what they know, if we ask. But I didn't come here to threaten you—"

"No?"

"No. If I reward you for your help only by allowing you to keep what's already yours, then I'm no better than a thief. We're prepared to give good value for what we receive."

Turning to his briefcase a second time, the visitor pushed a small binder across the desk. Endicott found its several pages filled with photographs of women—Oriental, African, Nordic, many beautiful, most voluptuous, all strangers. He leafed through the binder slowly.

"Answer my questions, and any one of them can be delivered

to your front door by tomorrow night, yours without conditions or restrictions," Wilkins said. "Work with us, and eventually you can have all of them, or others more to your taste."

"I see you're not quite the moralist, after all."

"A pragmatist will grow fat while a moralist starves," Wilkins said. "I have reason to think that you're a pragmatist, Senator."

"What are you after?"

"As I said, information. About the National Resource Center. About the gate, the Guard, and Rathole."

Though Endicott's poker face never showed the faintest tremor, behind the mask he was reeling from the shock. Even the questions denoted a breach in secrecy so serious that Endicott had trouble crediting it. It was easier to think that this was Tackett's doing, a little buddy-fuck meant to cost him the President's confidence. "Who wants to know?"

"Does it matter?"

"Yeah. Who's your client? Who's buying?"

"I don't see that you should entangle yourself with my business dealings."

"I asked you a question. If you don't have an answer, we're done talking. Who's buying?"

Wilkins frowned. "A foreign interest."

"Who?"

"That should be enough."

"Who?"

The frown deepened. "A friendly power."

It felt like an evasion. "If you want the truth from me, you'd better give me the same."

For a long moment, the two men tried to stare each other down. "A Mr. K is the principal buyer," Wilkins said finally.

Kondratyeva? "Jesus Christ, Wilkins, you're one of us."

"I said I was a pragmatist. Just as you are."

Only fools left their guns hidden in drawers. Endicott's four-shot pistol rested in an open soft-sided sleeve in the well of the desk, out of sight but close to hand. He did not need to worry that Wilkins was armed; the wand-carrying guards at the entrance were very thorough.

"You don't know me very well," Endicott said, sitting forward and reaching for the pistol. "No woman's worth that much."

"I didn't want to insult you with money. But we would consider sweetening the offer—"

Tackett or the Russians, it did not matter. The same message

316

needed to be sent. Endicott leaned back until his hands cleared the desk, then raised the pistol and smoothly squeezed the trigger twice. The pistol sounded like a cap gun, but the bullets left Wilkins slumping slack-jawed in his chair, fast-flowing blood darkening the fine fabrics of his shirt and coat.

The office door flew open, and his secretary rushed in, stopping short when she saw Wilkins.

"Senator—"

"It's all right, Jo," Endicott said, gathering in the tie envelope. She gaped disbelievingly. "You shot him?"

"We still execute spies. I just saved us the cost of his trial."

"I'll . . . I'll call security—"

"No. Get the FBI for me, Counterintelligence Division. Then I want you to leave and lock the door after yourself. Nothing should be touched until they get here."

"Are you sure?"

"Please."

He held the line until he heard her leave, then hung up on the puzzled FBI agent. It took five minutes to make sure that neither the briefcase nor Wilkins' clothing contained anything that would not bear scrutiny. Then he placed his own call.

"This is Walter," he said. "Peter, we have a problem."

Somerset County, Pennsylvania, Alternity Blue

Richard Bayshore looked up from the clipboard at the sound of footsteps on the porch.

"Where have you two been?" he asked as Wallace and Shan entered. "No, don't tell me, I don't want to know. But for future reference, please be informed that rain does *not* wash straw out of a sweater."

Wallace flashed a guilty smile as he looked down at his clothing. Shan's smile was the kind that went with childish secrets.

"You remember Malcolm Davis?" Bayshore continued, inclining his head toward the ethnologist seated across the table.

"Sure. From headquarters. Look, I'm sorry—"

Bayshore held up his hand. "It's just as well you took the opportunity. I don't know the next time you're going to get a free moment. There's a lot of work ahead."

"I understand."

"We need to decide what to do about the Guard's incursion. But that's almost secondary. We need to find out everything we can about how the world you come from is different from ours. I hope that will help us figure out why it's different.''

"You'll be ahead of me if you do," Wallace said.

"What did they tell you when you became part of the Guard?" Davis asked.

"I can't say they tried to explain it. They took me through the gate, showed me another alternity. Made me understand that we had to control the gates, control the maze, to protect ourselves."

"But didn't you wonder?" Davis pressed.

"When you see it right in front of your face, you don't wonder. You just accept that this is the way the world is."

"But why should it start being that way in our lifetimes?" asked Davis.

"I don't know."

Wallace looked uncomfortable, as though he were failing an oral exam, prompting Bayshore to intervene. "Malcolm's got a list here of more kinds of experts than I knew existed," he said lightly, hefting the clipboard. "Frankly, I don't know what questions to ask you. I'm bringing these people here to pull things out of your head."

"I'll do my best to help."

"I know you will. I want you to know what to expect. There'll be some people coming in yet tonight, and we'll start first thing tomorrow, eight to noon and one to six. By the end of the day, you're going to think you've been wrung out by a three-hundred-pound washerwoman."

Grinning, Wallace said, "I can take it. Bring her on."

"Malcolm and I and someone you'll meet tomorrow, a man named Warren Eden, will sit in on everything. After dinner we'll roundtable, the three of us, to talk through the day's sessions and figure out what we learned. I'd like to have you part of that, too. Both of you, actually."

Shan nodded. "Are you going to have enough bunk space for everyone?"

"It might get to where it's a bit crowded around the sinks in the mornings," Bayshore allowed.

"Rayne and I will only need one room," she said, taking his arm. "If that's all right."

Wallace looked startled.

"I've got no problems about it," Bayshore said. "Except if I send you two upstairs to change and move your stuff, I want you back this century. We need to get started tonight."

"Promise." She tugged at Wallace's arm and led him away.

As the sound of their footsteps in the hallway above receded toward the far end of the house, Davis grunted. "I'm impressed," he said. "Just as you wanted it. How did you know?"

Bayshore rose from the couch to walk to the window. "Necessity, not sagacity," he said, peering out. "We had to help him find a better reason to help us than being afraid of his own people. That wouldn't have lasted long."

"Did you tell her that's what you wanted from her?"

"It wasn't her that I was worried about," Bayshore said. "You finished at the Waterford safe house?"

Davis nodded. "I am."

"And?"

"As might be expected, Messrs. Robinson, Barstow, and Tackett are all thoroughly confused by having been spirited away to a cabin in the woods to be given a cultural litmus test."

"And the test showed—"

"They're ours. A Chicago banker, a Stanford English prof, and a Boston drunk, just as advertised. Are you going to hold them?"

"Yes," Bayshore said.

"What on earth do you want them for?"

"I don't want them. I just want to make sure that no one who does can find them."

Through an endless rainy night, members of Bayshore's study team continued to arrive. Lying wide awake in the dark with Shan sleeping peacefully beside him, Wallace heard another helicopter and at least three cars.

Shan's body was warm against him, and the rich scents of their lovemaking lingered, trapped in the blankets, but those were minor distractions. He knew he should sleep, knew a restless night would dull his wits, but he could not turn off his brain.

It was Davis who had pushed Wallace to consider matters which he had always found more convenient to ignore. The mysteries were for the men upstairs. Even among themselves, even in private, runners avoided such questions.

The gates *were*. You used them. You learned the routes and how to read the changes. You didn't waste time wondering why. The only exception was the Shadow. A brush with that silent gatekeeper made runners mumble in their beer about devils. But even that was pointless, for there were no answers. As far as Operations was concerned, there weren't even any questions.

In truth, Davis' vision of multiple worlds was foreign to the experience of the runner. The Cairo of Alternity White was more real to Wallace than the Cairo of Home, which he had never seen. With no two gates located in parallel cities, the maze seemed less a link between different realities than a shortcut around a single world. Not until his visit to Hagerstown had Wallace confronted the differences between the alternities—and he had shrunk from the encounter.

Now Davis and Bayshore and the parade of nighttime arrivals would expect him to confront Hagerstown again. Without understanding how that threatened him. Without knowing themselves the terrible emptiness of being a stranger, an outcast, a nonperson in a familiar land.

Nor would they ever know, even if he could somehow take them on a tour through all the alternities. They were Common World, all of them, cats with nine lives, or ninety. His grasp on life was frailer than theirs, his existence more tenuous. A candle flame, quivering in the breeze. That was all he was.

An elemental truth, learned by asking dangerous questions. Foolish questions. Foolish questions with the power to keep his eyes wide open in the dark, the power to deny him the sleep his body craved.

The morning session began with a pinch-faced linguist quizzing Wallace about a lengthy list of words gleaned from transcripts of earlier interviews. He wanted to know what the words meant, but also when Wallace had first heard each one, where he had heard it, what kind of people used it.

And when the list was done, there was another list, even longer, ferreting for words which hadn't come up. What do you call a lumpy white cheese? Is this a common, a median, or a boulevard? What does the water come out of at a sink?

Before Wallace could find out why any of that mattered, the seat where the linguist had sat was being warmed by a jet-eyed political historian. At her request, Wallace flawlessly backtracked through the modern presidents—Robinson, Robinson again, Rockefeller, Vandenberg, Douglas, Stevenson. That took them back to 1956.

But all he could remember of Stevenson's predecessor was that he had succeeded someone who died in office. Yes, he remembered Roosevelt. Something about the war. And Truman sounded familiar. 1952? No, not Eisenhower. That wasn't the name. Scott Lucas? Never heard of him. Millard Tydings? What kind of name was that for a President?

Outside the presidential arena, Wallace could name one of Indiana's two senators, the current mayor of Boston, the premier of the Soviet Union, and very little more. That was not nearly enough to satisfy the historian, who expressed her frustration over his head shakes and "I don't knows" with sighs and tightlipped frowns.

"Mr. Bayshore, I can't make a picture out of this," she pronounced finally. "He's politically ignorant. He simply doesn't know enough."

"You're out of line, Doctor—" Bayshore began.

"No, that's all right," Wallace said, interrupting. "I have a friend—I used to have a friend—who said you can only vote for who the parties put up, and they put up who they want, not who you want. That the Republicans and the Democrats have it worked out to take turns at the top and make sure no one else gets there. He said he would never vote, because none of them are any better or any worse than the rest."

"Sometimes it looks that way here, too," Davis said with a smile.

Wallace continued, "Well, I voted the one time I was able to, and I voted for President Robinson. But the truth is I didn't know much about him, and I still don't. His name was at the top of the right column. But that's not the whole story, because there were fifty names underneath his that I knew even less about, and I voted for them, too. So I guess I am ignorant, like she said. Ask your next question."

The afternoon session went better, Wallace thought. The technologist, round-shouldered and chipmunk-cheeked, seemed delighted with Wallace's descriptions of electric runabouts, thermostat-controlled showers, and the weaponry he had seen at Fort Harrison, Camp Atterbury, and the Jefferson Proving Ground. He was curious about everything from kitchen appliances (conventional) to computers (rare).

When did your family get its first television? (When I was seven.) Were records always ten inches across? (No, most of his father's records were the old style, larger and thicker.) What were women's stockings made of? (Silk, and almost no one could afford them.) These were questions Wallace could answer.

He had a little more trouble with the questions from a Dr. Jo Anderson, though not because he didn't know the answers. The thirtyish woman was introduced to him as a human counselor, a title which did nothing to prepare him for her questions. She had a little list of inquiries which the linguist had overlooked, which ran him through such delicacies as charlies, pump boys, street sweet, parting the petals, riding lessons, and zipper queen.

Then things got personal. When did he first have sex? How

many partners had he had? Had he had anal intercourse, performed cunnilingus, received fellatio? Had he had any homosexual experiences? Where did he obtain his contraceptives? Had he ever contracted a venereal disease, and who did he report it to?

Shan's presence was partly responsible for Wallace's discomfort, and she read him well enough to realize that fact. After the first half-dozen questions, she tried to excuse herself. But Dr. Anderson called her back.

"No, please, I'll need your input as well."

"Me?"

"I'm interested in knowing what differences you perceived between Rayne and your other partners—"

"Jesus Christ," Wallace snapped. "If I started asking how long it's been since you ran wet for somebody, whether you like a long ride or a hard one, you wouldn't tell me. What gives?"

"We don't consider basic human functions state secrets, if that's what you mean. Healthy adjustment—"

. "Fuck that," Wallace said. "Could someone explain to me why this matters?"

"I'd like someone to explain it to me, too," Bayshore said, looking to Davis.

"Sexual mores are critical factors in the social construct," the ethnologist said, frowning. "Sexual competition drives economic systems. Sexual selection determines value systems. The energy's there. You have to look at how it's channeled, dammed, diverted. You have to know where it goes. Believe me, it's not voyeurism."

"Then ask him what he knows, not what he's done," Bayshore said gruffly. "That's the only way you're going to get anything useful out of a sample of one."

Dr. Anderson tried to mount a protest. "We need hard data, objective facts, not guesses and impressions. An individual knows his own experiences—"

Bayshore raised his hands. "That's it. Thank you, Dr. Anderson. Malcolm, who's next?"

I like this man, Wallace thought as the counselor gathered up her papers in stony silence. *Not a friend, perhaps, but at least an ally—*

"You can't fool me," Shan said, leaning close and whispering. "You just didn't want me to hear about your other women."

"That's right," he said. "Rich, how about a break? The washerwoman's starting to wear me down."

Bayshore nodded. "Ten minutes, everyone. Malcolm, why don't you try to find out what's keeping Dr. Eden?"

• • •

With Bayshore exercising a firmer hand over the proceedings, they managed to squeeze three more interviewers into the afternoon session—a business historian, a specialist in geopolitics from the Department of State, and an epidemiologist.

Wallace told the historian about Columbia bicycles and Federal Foods, the State analyst about the consolidation of Germany and the '59 Egyptian war, the epidemiologist about the Guinea grunge and the hepatitis scares. All three seemed more understanding of his lapses than their predecessors.

And all three focused more sharply on the chronology of the stories they were hearing. What's the earliest you heard of X? How far back did Y happen? When did Z disappear? The same theme recurred when the core group gathered in the parlor after dinner for the roundtable.

"I'm going to be heretical. I'm starting to think the details don't matter," Davis pronounced.

Bayshore shot a questioning glance to the other end of the couch. "We spent a good nine and a half hours on details today because you said they were important."

"They were. I think they've already told us all they can."

"Which is what?" Wallace asked.

"Confirmation of the basic fact we had already." He uncoiled a finger in Shan's direction. "You were born when?"

"June 2, 1951."

"And you, Rayne?"

"August 29, 1952."

"A matter of fifteen months between them. And yet she belongs to the Common World, and he doesn't. Whatever happened, happened then, during that fifteen-month span. When she was conceived, there was one world. When he was conceived, there were many. One root stock, divided into many branches. The way it looks to me right now, at the moment of the Split everything that followed was randomized, right down to the level of which spermatazoan nailed which egg. Every alternity is another roll of the dice."

"Then why are they so alike?" Shan asked. "I didn't hear anything today that couldn't have happened here or been created here."

"There's an underlying symmetry," Davis acknowledged, "but that's to be expected. There's a limited determinism at work, a certain momentum in human affairs that creates high-order probabilities and weighs against certain other events or turns."

"A limited determinism," Bayshore echoed.

323

"Yes. The initial differences were small, trivial even—but the alternities have continued to diverge over time. Now, almost three decades later, they're more or less independent, children of a common parent, each following its own pattern. Language, customs, politics, geopolitics, mores, technology—they've all diverged. By now something approaching half the population of each alternity is unique to that alternity."

Bayshore sighed and covered his mouth with steepled hands. "Christ, I knew I didn't want this job," he said tiredly. "So you're saying the Split didn't happen suddenly."

"It could have happened suddenly. It just wasn't dramatic, and there's no point in working Rayne over in a quest for the exact moment," Davis said. "It's either right there in our history, too, or it passed without any notice at all."

"What about the reason?" Shan asked. "Is that there in our history?"

Davis surprised them all by shrugging and saying, "Who says that there is a reason?"

Bayshore nearly jumped out of his seat. "Sweet Norfolk, Malcolm—"

"Maybe Rayne is right," Davis said. "Maybe this is just the way things are."

"You don't believe that. You didn't believe it when he said it."

Instantly, the ethnologist's body language went from open to closed. "What do you want me to say? That it's a fucking miracle? That God got good enough at the game that he decided to play on more than one board at a time? What good does that do?"

Leaning toward Davis, Bayshore reached for his shoulder. "Malcolm, I've got to report to the President on this. I need to know why this happened."

Pulling away to avoid the touch, Malcolm left his seat and retreated to the parlor's wide entry arch. "I don't *want* to know, if you want the truth," he said.

Bayshore grunted and slumped against the back of the couch. "Yeah. I understand that, all right." He blew a breath into a cupped hand and looked toward Wallace and Shan. "Either of you any braver?"

It was Shan who spoke. "I've been thinking that we're never going to know why, even if we find out when," she said slowly. "It's like . . . like someone called our name just as we were about to step out in the street in front of a car. Whatever was about to happen, didn't. There's no way to get the number of the car that didn't hit us."

Bayshore nodded thoughtfully. "I can almost live with that. Except I want to go on and ask 'how?' and 'who?' And questions like that are just going to keep Mrs. Bayshore's boy awake at night."

"There's something else to think about, too," Shan said. "However and whyever it happened, whatever force was responsible—is the Split reversible? Are the alternities going to converge again?"

"How can they?" Davis said contemptuously, taking a step back into the room. "Think of our extra two billion, and the next alternity's two billion, and the next, and the next—"

Shan said, "Maybe it will be gradual. The same child born simultaneously in two or more alternities—then another—"

Sitting forward, Bayshore rested his chin on folded hands. "Or perhaps time isn't moving at all. Maybe we're on some sort of spur. Like a roller-coaster loop-the-loop, carrying us around in a circle back to the moment of the Split."

"That doesn't make any sense," Davis said scornfully.

"It makes as much sense as any of this," Bayshore snapped. "It's clean and simple, at least. I'm just trying to get rid of the problem of the extra people."

"By discarding them?" Wallace said.

"Nothing personal."

"But plenty egocentric," Shan said harshly. "The Chosen People of a capricious God—"

"I was just thinking out loud," he said defensively. "What I want is for Dr. Eden to come tell us this is just a bit of trickery on the part of Mama Nature, so we can put the who's and why's to rest."

"You lack a sufficiently paranoid imagination, Rich," Davis said quietly.

"What do you mean?"

Davis hooked his interlocked hands behind his neck. "We don't really know what Rayne and his people were doing here. Maybe they came here to disrupt us, to cripple us. I'm not saying Rayne knows the answer. But his bosses do."

"What are you talking about?"

"Don't you see? It's entirely possible that all the different alternities are in competition with each other—a competition that only one can win. That somewhere, sometime, a champion will be crowned to carry forward."

"Crowned or chosen?"

He shrugged. "Your choice. A philosophical preference."

"And the rest? What about the other alternities? What about the losers?"

The ethnologist's voice was hoarse. "Gone, like we were never here."

Bethel, Virginia, The Home Alternity

Endicott bound Rachel to the standing frame before he said good-bye. Naked, her limbs splayed in an X, she was open to him, and he caressed her lovingly, knowingly, until her body shuddered and strained at the cords which held her. He brought her fragrant wetness to her lips with his fingers, then seized her mouth in a burning, tongue-raping kiss.

When he stepped back, somehow she knew. "Is tonight the night?" she asked.

He had intended not to tell her, but he could not lie to her. "Yes."

"You're going to kill me."

It was easier for her to say than for him to acknowledge. A nod was all he could manage as he felt in the pocket of his robe for the little ring.

"I thought that was gone from you," she said, her voice breaking the smallest bit. "I thought that we'd put that—anger to rest. I thought I could tell—"

"Not anger. Never anger," he said. Within the privacy of his pocket, he slid the ring on the middle finger, then rotated it so that the soft bulge was turned inward, toward the palm. "Not then. Not now. This is—necessity."

He stepped forward and caressed her cheek gently with his right hand. She did not flinch. Her eyes, empty of light but for the brightness of tears, fixed on his.

Necessity. Not because he was afraid—but because conformity was the price of protection, for himself, for the initiative. Because Madison had decreed, and Robinson concurred. Keep a tidy house, Walter, they had said. This incident is closed, but we can afford no others. In critical times there must be caution. So for caution, he would kill her.

"Please don't—"

"Your victory is that I wish there was no need," he whispered. "My gift is a death without pain. Madison promised me that."

Rachel made a plaintive sound which was both protest and surrender and looked away, down toward the floor.

Cradling her head in his hands, Endicott kissed her forehead tenderly. Then his hands moved lightly, the left downward to her neck, the right lifting her chin so that he could kiss her lips. She accepted the kiss, and he pressed the ring hard against the side of her throat. The tiny needle pierced its protective shroud and stabbed into soft skin, discharging its minute toxic burden.

He felt her body twitch in surprise. Then Rachel broke the kiss, pulling her head back. "No. Oh, no," she said. A faint tremor ran through her body, a cold shiver felt within. Short seconds later, her body sagged against the ropes, her eyes closing as in sleep.

His own eyes wet with tears, Endicott kissed her forehead one last time, then cut her down with care. He did not have words for what he was feeling, could not imagine that words existed equal to the confused torrent.

But when the body was gone, entrusted to Evan's custody, Endicott took ax and crowbar to the room's damning furnishings with a terrible violence that was all too familiar.

Somerset County, Pennsylvania, Alternity Blue

It did not take long for everyone in the safe house to learn that Richard Bayshore was having a bad day. The night had passed without any sign of Warren Eden, and Wallace and Shan came down from their room for breakfast to find Bayshore and Davis locked in a shouting match.

"Chess? He's playing a goddamned game of chess?" Bayshore bellowed.

"What do you want me to do, send the Marines in to kidnap him? You know what Eden's like."

"He's missed a whole day of sessions. If he's not on the plane soon, he'll miss another."

"We've faxed transcripts of everything we did yesterday to him through the Sacramento office. He says he'll have them read before he gets here."

"And when is that gonna be?"

"I understand he's up two pawns."

Bayshore threw his hands in the air and stalked out.

"Rich has a lot of pressure on him," Davis said apologetically to Wallace. "He'll pull things together."

"That was this Dr. Eden you were talking about?"

"Yes."

"What's going on?" Shan asked. "Doesn't he understand how important this is? Or doesn't he believe it?"

"Oh, he understands. He takes it seriously. He called me this morning at five A.M. to give me a twenty-minute critique of our roundtable last night. Listen, this is a man who thinks so fast that I can hardly hold a real-time conversation with him. It took me an hour after I hung up to pick through what was backed up in my buffer. We're not likely to leave him behind."

"It being five A.M. might have had something to do with your trouble," Shan said.

"Charitable child," Davis said with a smile. "Look, there's fresh corn muffins and orange juice in the kitchen. Better grab something before the thunder lizard returns."

Through most of the morning session, Bayshore's impatience was evident but not intrusive. He held his tongue as a substitute human counselor picked up where the banished Dr. Adamson had left off, even forgetting his pique long enough to join the conversation when the subject turned to sex laws.

"Do you mean if two couples get together some Saturday night and swap partners, you've got four criminals?" he asked, incredulous.

"I know things are looser here—"

"How would anyone find out? It's not like you have to apply for a permit to have sex, is it?"

"Gossip gets around. A wife might report her husband. Prostitutes talk to stay out of jail. Mostly it's when there's some kind of disease or a baby for proof."

"So at least they don't go breaking down doors to see who's sleeping with whom," Shan said, relieved.

"They're just trying to protect families."

"Great way to help," Bayshore said. "Throw mom or dad in jail."

Wallace grew defensive. "Not jail. There's weekend work camps for all kinds of little offenses. There was a guy on our street who got caught who ended up on a crew repainting the fire house."

"Not that bad an idea, actually," Davis said thoughtfully. "If family integrity is at the top of your list, that's not such a bad way to go."

After the sexologist came a cultural anthropologist, who also came through unscathed despite substantial overlap with her immediate predecessor. Dating habits. Social legislation. Family migration. Marriage and divorce.

It was when the team of two educators attempted to put Wallace through a multidisciplinary assessment that Bayshore finally blew up.

"No, no, no, no," Bayshore said, slapping the tabletop for punctuation. "We had enough of this yesterday. You aren't going to know what his wrong answers mean. There's more than enough people right here who couldn't tell you half that stuff. Let's at least focus on what he does know and build from there."

"Rich, this is worth doing, believe me—"

"I want somebody who knows something he knows," Bayshore said stubbornly. "Get me a—what do you know?" he asked, turning to Wallace. "What're your hobbies?"

"Uh . . . baseball. Music—"

"So get a sportswriter in here. Get somebody from Hot List magazine."

"Certainly. Let's turn this into a trivia contest."

"At least we can deal with something concrete."

"I told you last night that details don't matter. We're trying to get the broader picture—"

"Then ask him about the other alternities. He's been to—what, three of them?"

Wallace nodded.

"I'm trying to keep the process orderly, the most familiar first—" Davis began.

Bayshore shot up out of his seat and smashed his clipboard down on the desk with a clatter. "Goddamn it, can't anyone do what I ask them to?" he demanded. In the stunned silence that followed, he stomped out of the room. A moment later the front door slammed.

Wallace and Shan found each other's hand beneath the edge of the table and flashed smiles that were not half as reassuring as they were meant to be. The two educators sat wide-eyed and petrified. Davis just shook his head slowly back and forth.

"This is not like him," he said, tight-lipped. "He's losing it, and things are falling apart." Davis fixed his gaze on Wallace. "Nothing personal, son, but I wish to God I'd never heard of you."

Davis glanced down at the binder propped open on his lap and flipped backward to a divider. "All right," he said, wearily rubbing his forehead with the fingertips of one hand. "Tell us what you can about Alternity Red."

• • •

Bayshore had still not returned by midafternoon, when the helicopter bearing Warren Eden lighted on the meadow.

Wallace and Shan came out on the porch to watch, curious for their first glimpse of their notorious visitor. Davis ran out to the meadow to attend to protocol. But Eden did not stand on protocol. Before Davis was halfway to the aircraft, Eden was out and walking upslope toward the house.

A slender six feet tall, Eden wore a shapeless gray-green overcoat, a dark-green scarf around his throat, wrinkled blue jeans, white sneakers. His hair was a gray and white lion's mane, combed straight back from a broad smooth forehead, blowing in the rotor downwash. A short black-streaked beard sprouting from his jawline made him look gnomelike despite his height.

"Do geniuses have to look scruffy?" Wallace asked. "Is it part of the rules, or something?"

Shan gave him an elbow in the ribs. "You're terrible."

"I thought he was supposed to be this young wunderkind. He looks older than my dad."

"I've seen pictures of him. I guess he went gray in his twenties."

"Too much heat under the hood," Wallace gibed.

Shan frowned instead of laughing. "You'd better get those out of your system before he gets up here."

"I'm trying."

"Inferiority complex?"

"Maybe a little. I never met a genius before."

"Don't meet one now. Meet a person."

Moving with long easy strides, Eden swept through the gap between the hedges and up the stairs to the porch. He almost walked past Wallace and Shan, then hesitated and looked sideways at them.

"You're the fellow responsible for all the fuss?"

"I'm Rayne Wallace."

The newcomer gestured toward the door, inviting them back inside. "I'm Warren Eden. Let's talk."

Alone among those who had made the pilgrimage to the safe house, Eden took no notes as he listened to Wallace's stories. He sat in his chair in an almost meditative state, his eyes and mind alert, his body at rest. His apparent inner peace seemed to exude a calming influence on everyone, and the air of panic which had seized the house earlier in the day melted away.

Wallace felt the change inside himself with wonder. He did

330

not understand it, but the man seemed to have a tangible presence which extended beyond his physical body, almost as if he was radiating some sort of energy to the room.

It was nothing as shallow as charisma, nothing as simple as authority. Though Eden said or did nothing overt to accomplish it, from the moment he arrived he was in control. Even Bayshore bowed to it. When he finally returned, half an hour after Eden arrived, he slipped wordlessly into an empty chair, content to be a spectator.

Long before that, Wallace's anxieties had been allayed. In the last thirty-six hours, he had been quizzed, interrogated, interviewed, cross-examined, and scrutinized. He had feared that facing Eden would feel like the worst moments of that experience times a hundred—his credibility disputed, his inadequacies revealed.

But Eden's voice lacked any note of challenge or skepticism. Before Wallace had spoken a word, he knew that Eden would believe him.

"I've seen photographs of the Indianapolis gate house," Eden said. "Please tell me about the others. What are they like? Tell me about each one."

"The Yellow gate is in England, in a ruined castle. Dunstanburgh, on a hill overlooking the North Sea."

"Massive stone," Eden said. "Masonry, like the Scottish Rite Cathedral."

"Yes."

"How much of it stands?"

"The keep. The gate house. Some of the perimeter wall."

"Where do you find the gate?"

"Inside one of the buildings. Usually the keep."

"Always inside?"

"Always—"

"Talk me through a transit. Tell me what you perceive."

"When you come through the gate, there's a junction—"

"How many branches are there?"

"Three. Almost always three."

"Close your eyes and see them. Point. Show me."

"There. There. And there."

"Where are we going?"

"Red. It's the simplest of the routes—"

"You say you can feel the gate. What does it feel like?"

"Like being tickled from the inside. A crawly sensation when you get close. When I first pick it up, it seems more like I hear

331

it. But not with my ears. I can cover my ears with my hands and I hear it just the same."

"Is the pitch high or low?"

"It's not so much a pitch as a . . . a smear of sound. But it goes higher as you get closer. Until you can't hear it anymore. Then you start to feel it. That's how you can track the gate down in a big gate station, like the Bellevue Strat."

"Can everyone hear it?"

"They have to train you. Some can't learn to pick it out of the background. I heard it right away—"

"Do you breathe while you're in the maze?"

"I never stopped to notice—"

"Suppose you walk through the Boston gate at noon. What time is it when you come through at Dunstanburgh?"

"Later."

"How much later?"

"If you go through in the afternoon, it'll be dark there."

"England is five hours ahead of us, sun time. But that's not what I was asking. How long does a transit take?"

"Oh. A minute—five minutes. It seems longer."

"Is it ever?"

"There were stories about a cracker that got lost and was in the maze for three hours. Oh—"

"Problem?"

"I guess we do breathe in there—"

"And the policeman simply disappeared?"

"Like he was eaten up by the maze—"

"Tell me about the Shadow—"

The clearing skies over the safe house were dissolving to a violet-black by the time Eden said, "Thank you, Rayne. I have no more questions." He looked at Bayshore. "You're the project coordinator?"

"I'm Richard Bayshore," was the answer.

"When can I have access to the Indianapolis site?"

"We haven't made a decision about what action to take there."

Gracile and expressionless, Eden rose from his chair. "When do you expect to make a decision?"

"The President wants to hear more from us before scheduling an action caucus."

"I see."

"Is there a problem?"

"No," the scientist said, collecting his coat and scarf. "You have a room for me?"

Davis answered, "The first door on the left, upstairs. Your bag is there."

"Thank you," he said, and turned to leave.

"Wait a minute," Wallace said, jumping to his feet. "Aren't you going to tell us what you think?"

Eden looked back. "I'd like some time to assemble those thoughts. Besides, you realize that without access to the Indianapolis site, anything I might say would be provisional."

"Understood," Bayshore said, also rising. "But I think everyone here would like to hear at least your general impressions."

Frowning, Eden looked down at the carpet as he considered. "At this point, there's only one observation I feel confident enough to share," he said. His head came up and his eyes found Bayshore's. "With apologies, Director, I must tell you that questions of who and why remain in order."

"Why is that?"

"Because this is not a natural phenomenon. We *are* dealing with an artifact."

BROADCAST TRANSCRIPT

Program Title: D.C.
Broadcast Date: May 12, 1977

[ ] VIDEO: Studio / POKE: Capitol Building /
GRAPHIC: "Black Budget"
ANTHONY GREEN[1]: This morning in the House, more
questions about the Pentagon's rumored secret
quick-strike commando force, Group 10. During
routine budget mark-up hearings in a House
appropriations committee, Representative John
Simpson[2] of Minnesota charged that a requested
eighteen percent increase in the Pentagon's secret
operations appropriation, or "black budget,"
would be used to create and fund Group 10.

[ ] VIDEO: Committee chamber / GRAPHIC: This
Morning
SIMPSON: Director, I would like to know how much
of Line 900 is earmarked for Group 10?

[ ] GRAPHIC: Bernard Wills[3], OMB
WILLS: As you know full well, Mr. Simpson, I
cannot comment on any Line 900 appropriations.
SIMPSON: Are you denying that Group 10 is being
funded out of the black budget?
WILLS: I have nothing to say on the subject
whatsoever. The Secretary of Defense spoke to
the Joint Committee concerning classified
operations three weeks ago. I have nothing to
add to what he said.

[ ] GRAPHIC: Rep. John Simpson
SIMPSON: You known damned well, Director, that
his testimony was in closed session, off the
public record. I happen to think that the American
people have a right to know what the President
wants with a back-door black-coat guerrilla
army.
WILLS: I can safely say the President neither has
nor wants a force such as you describe.

[ ] VIDEO: Studio / POKE: Pentagon / GRAPHIC:
"Group 10?"
GREEN: Despite denials from the Pentagon and the
White House, Simpson's charges are being
taken seriously in D.C. A former member of the
Joint Committee on Intelligence and Military
Affairs under past Democratic administrations,
Simpson is considered a leading congressional
expert on defense matters.

---

[1] Substitute anchor for D.C.; an employee of DuMont
affiliate KYW-TV in Philadelphia
[2] Democrat from Minnesota's 5th District
(Minneapolis); first elected 1960
[3] Director of the Office of Management and Budget;
appointed Jan. 27, 1977 by President Daniel
Brandenburg

CHAPTER 19

Rats in the Rafters

Somerset County, Pennsylvania, Alternity Blue

Swaddled in a light blanket stolen from their bed, Wallace and Shan huddled together on the porch roof and surveyed the night skies over the safe house.

"This is the best time of year," Shan said raptly. "With the Winter Hexagon still above the horizon, but the nights warm enough to let you enjoy it. We'll have perfect seeing until the moon rises."

Wallace shook his head. "Of everything that's strange here, the hardest thing to accept is that there's people actually living on the moon. And the pictures of the earth from space—"

She nodded and squeezed his hand. "If we're out long enough, we might see one of the SA stations."

"You can see them? How long is long enough?"

"S-1—that's the big equatorial station—goes over every ninety minutes. Or we might get lucky and catch S-2, the polar station."

Wallace snuggled closer. "I hope one goes over before Eden's ready and they call us back downstairs," he said.

"It's not much to see," she warned. "Just a light crossing the sky."

"I don't care." He craned his head and looked up toward the zenith. "They all have names, don't they? I don't know anything about the stars."

"Then let me teach you something," she said. "There—see that very bright star just above the trees?"

"I see it."

"That's Sirius, the Dog Star. It's the brightest star in the sky, at any season."

"Why the Dog Star?"

"It's in the constellation Canis Major—the Big Dog."

"What was that thing you said earlier? The Winter Hexagon?"

Five minutes later, he had memorized the names of the bright stars marking out a great figure enclosing a third of the sky—Sirius, Procyon, Pollux and Castor, Capella, Aldebaran, Rigel. The names were just sounds to him, the stars just points of light of subtly different colors. But the circumstance and the company made it special, and he tried to stretch himself and see the skies as Shan did.

"Until yesterday, I didn't realize how beautiful this part of the country was," he said. "We came through on the train when we left Indiana for Boston, but it was nighttime. I slept most of the way between Pittsburgh and Philadelphia."

Shan rested her head on his shoulder. "I've always liked the Appalachians better than the Rockies. The Rockies are beautiful the way ice is beautiful—stark and sculpted and cold. These mountains are full of life."

"I've never seen the Rocky Mountains," he said forlornly.

She reached up and kissed his cheek. "We'll put it on the list of things to do together."

"Yeah," he said without conviction.

"Did I say something wrong?"

Pulling her closer, Wallace said, "I just can't think about that kind of thing. All I can handle is where I am right now. I can't think about the future."

"What about the past?"

"I can't think about that, either."

They held each other, the contact between their bodies a fragile bridge between minds a thousand miles apart in thought. A meteor streaked across the sky overhead, unnoticed.

At last, Shan broke the silence. "I wish you'd talk about her," she said gently.

He shook his head wordlessly.

"You're trying to pretend you didn't have a life there," she said. "I know that's not true. You don't have to protect me. You're married. You have a daughter—"

"She was such a charmer on that train," he said, giving voice to the memories which had occupied him. "A year and a half old and so full of smiles and hugs. She'd hold whole conversations with you, her half all nonsense except for a real word every now and then to make you wonder. We could have adopted her out a

337

half-dozen times, the way she made friends all through the car. She'd sit on Ruthann's lap and look out the window at the scenery racing past and say—"

A strangled sound of anguish scalded Wallace's throat like molten metal. He shook himself as though shaking free from an invisible hand and tried to finish the thought. "And she'd say 'Bye, tree'—'Bye, house'—"

The breach tore wide open. Wallace dropped his head to his drawn-up knees and began to cry, great noisy sobs that racked his body as he fought them and failed. Shan's arms were tight around him, but he barely knew she was there.

"God, I miss her," he moaned, his words muffled against his crossed arms. "I miss my little girl."

Washington, D.C., The Home Alternity

Wearing her worry on her face, Ellen O'Neill entered the study where her husband was reading. "Gregory?"

He looked up and saw immediately the tightness around her mouth, the clouded eyes. "What's wrong?" he said as he rose from the chair.

"I don't know," she said. "There are three men at the door. Two are soldiers. The other showed me Secret Service ID and said I should tell you 'maison de sante.' That means asylum, doesn't it?"

O'Neill's mouth was suddenly dry. "Yes. It's the code phrase for an Alpha List evacuation."

"Oh, God."

He reached for her hand. "Don't panic yet. Asylum is a low-urgency plan—precautionary, phased, core group first," he said, knowing it was false assurance. With its assortment of illness/vacation/speaking-tour cover stories for top officials, Asylum was exactly the kind of evacuation which would precede a preemptive strike.

Not surprisingly, she, too, knew his words were counterfeit. "What's going on, Gregory? Is it what you were afraid of?"

"I think so."

"Can't you do anything?"

He reached for the phone. "I'm going to try. Please cover for me. I'll be down as soon as I can."

The number he began dialing was one he had never used before, but he knew it as well as his own. It belonged to John Rasten, senior Washington correspondent for the *New York Times*, a man whose name rarely came up in White House conversations without epithets attached. O'Neill had committed it to memory the day after his disappointing meeting with Albert Tackett.

In the two weeks since, O'Neill had wrestled daily with the question of whether to use it. Twice he had gotten as far as dialing the area prefix before changing his mind.

It was not time, he had told himself. Reading rumors and clues like tea leaves in a fortune-teller's cup, he had found reason for hope. The Q-plane was still missing, but Kondratyeva's blistering letter of protest had virtually silenced the gloating and cheerleading over the D-57 incident.

In the sternest possible language, Kondratyeva had warned Robinson to "keep your place or be put in it." The text contemptuously referred to the Weasel squadrons as "trivial irrelevancies" and made no demand for their removal.

The explanation for that surprise was embodied in an astonishing attachment—seventy-five pages apparently drawn directly from working Soviet military plans. A list of nearly three thousand American military sites, industrial centers, and other targets, along with the number and size of missiles and bombs allocated to them. *See what* you *risk*, the list said.

O'Neill could imagine the vehemence with which Soviet strategists had resisted releasing the target list. But there was little in the list that American analysts had not guessed at, and it was a masterful psychological stroke, a daring exercise in diplomacy and statecraft. It had had a chilling effect in the E ring, along the Bradley Corridor.

But not, it now seemed, where it most needed to—in the Oval Office.

The phone clicked and hummed. "Rasten residence," said a woman s voice, thin and tired.

"John Rasten, please."

"Who's calling?"

"This is Secretary—"

That was as far as O'Neill got before the connection was abruptly broken. He dialed again immediately, only to hear the grating sound of a busy signal.

His wife's voice outside the door alerted him to replace the receiver. A moment later a black-suited man preceded Ellen into the room. "Secretary O'Neill, I'm agent Ken Andrews, Secret Service."

O'Neill fixed the stranger with a frosty gaze. "I asked you to wait downstairs."

"Yes, sir. I was concerned that there might be some problem.

339

Under the circumstances, I thought caution more important than etiquette."

"What exactly are the circumstances, Mr. Andrews? Do you have a sitsum for me?"

"I understand that briefing material will be available at the assembly point."

O'Neill gazed steadily into the younger man's eyes, looking for confirmation. "Yes. Well, as you see, there is no problem. If you'll excuse me, I need to pack."

"With all respect, sir, there's no need. Your go bag will be sufficient for the interim," Andrews said, referring to the prepacked suitcase in the bottom of the big closet.

It was no mystery that Andrews knew he had one; any top official who might be called to travel on short notice did. In any event, Alpha List had been warned to plan ahead. "It won't be sufficient for Mrs. O'Neill."

"Having you both leave abruptly could arouse curiosity, Mr. Secretary. My instructions are for Corporal King to stay with Mrs. O'Neill. Another agent will come in the morning for her. She'll have plenty of time, sir."

It was then that O'Neill knew that Andrews was no Secret Service agent, knew that even if he managed to be alone that Rasten's line would always be busy to his call. With a growing sense of futility and desperation, he measured himself against the younger, stronger, and highly wary visitor.

Andrews caught the appraising look and knew its meaning. "We need to be very careful, Mr. Secretary. If Mrs. O'Neill could get your bag, please—"

His wife was sensitive to the shifting undercurrent, the unspoken tension, but without understanding. "Gregory—"

"Go ahead, Ellen. Please get my go bag."

"What's going on, Gregory?"

"Things may be—more serious than I thought," he said, his gaze never leaving Andrews. "Please."

She brought him the bag and an anxiety-laced kiss. "Are you all right?" she whispered.

"Try not to worry," he said, taking the bag from her hand. He kissed her forehead tenderly. "I love you."

Andrews watched the exchange with voyeuristic zeal. "If you could, Mr. Secretary—" he said, stepping back from the door.

O'Neill nodded mutely and led the way downstairs and out into the yard. His wife was halted by the soldiers at the front door, and he waved a final good-bye before climbing into the back seat of the dark blue sedan.

340

"Where are you taking me?" he asked as the vehicle bumped its way down the tree-lined drive.

"The Minnesota retreat."

"Will the President be there?"

"No. You're in quarantine, Mr. Secretary. President's orders."

"What's going to happen to my wife?"

"House arrest. A guarantee against your good behavior. There will be no more calls, Mr. Secretary."

O'Neill slumped back against the seat cushions and looked out the window. "No," he said. "No more calls."

Somerset County, Pennsylvania, Alternity Blue

In the week since Eden had come to the safe house, Rayne Wallace had lost the thread of what was happening around him. The daily sessions continued, but at a less frenetic level—four or five hours a day instead of eight or nine—and without the participation of either Eden or, most days, Bayshore.

Eden was in near-isolation working on the alternity puzzle, emerging only to consult with another specialist by phone or to ask for more of the paper, clay, and wooden sticks he was evidently using to build models. As far as Wallace knew, Eden was still refusing to voice any further conclusions or speculations.

Bayshore's focus had returned to Indianapolis and the Guard's network there. Apparently NIA and FBI agents under his direction were blanketing the station staff, though still on a hands-off basis. The mole-bait had not been taken, and Arens had been moved from city jail to another safe house, from which he had already attempted two escapes.

Even Shan excused herself from the sessions more often than not, for which Wallace did not blame her. The ego value of having an eager audience for his every utterance had faded, and he was often bored himself. And the lighter schedule meant he had more unpressured hours with her, hours which passed in an easy haze of stargazing and lovemaking and watching spring erupt in full flower in the meadow.

If not for Davis, patient and persistent, the interview schedule would probably have been dropped completely. The ethnologist was determined to document every conceivable aspect of Wallace's life and experience. Wallace did not understand where the drive came from, what made his visit to the smoker house in Red or the time the grain elevator in Connorsville blew up like a bomb matters of interest.

Already Davis knew enough about him to write a biography so detailed that not even his mother would be able to endure reading it. Wallace had even found himself talking about Ruthann with Davis and a sympathetic "interpersonal auditor." He remembered some of his answers with discomfort.

"Did you love her or not?" they had asked.

"I loved her."

"What changed? What was missing? Did you tell her what you wanted?"

"I didn't know what to ask for," he confessed forlornly. "I didn't pay enough attention when I had it."

The driveway and the makeshift helipad were as busy as ever, the morning confusion in the kitchen and bathrooms as great, the traffic through the basement communications center as relentless. But Wallace could no longer see where all the activity pointed. Nor was it clear whose work was controlling the pace—Eden's, Bayshore's, or even Davis'.

He did not want to think about the future, but it was becoming harder every day to live in the present. Without direction, he could neither mourn nor plan. He was at once happier and more miserable than he could remember being, at once flying and crawling through the slime, his joy married to his pain in a way that made it impossible to let go of either.

Rudderless, he drifted through the hours, taking his direction from those around him. It was easy, but it was also empty. He knew that somehow he had to seize a goal, choose a direction. But the shattering truth was that at that moment, he could not even say what sort of choices he hoped to be offered.

If he was to have any choices at all.

Boston, The Home Alternity

The first wave of Alpha List evacuees began arriving at the Tower at six in the morning.

These were the elite, Robinson's top appointees and friends—the Attorney General, the President's counsel, Senator Endicott, and others of equal stature. It was as important to conceal their presence in Boston as it was their absence from their home cities. After Endicott's encounter with a Soviet asset, no one doubted that the Tower was under close scrutiny.

So the evacuees arrived invisibly, anonymously, riding the company vans and even the flesh-haulers, concealed among the mass of regular Tower staffers. Children and a few of the most recognizable adults came in under darkness, huddled on the back floors of private cars driven by Guard managers and executives—Tackett chauffered the Secretary of State to the Tower in just that fashion. The children loved it, the adults hated it.

As they trickled in, most were escorted to the ninth floor. The analysts' cubicles there had been stripped of furniture, numbered, and supplied with pillows and air mattresses to create a makeshift dormitory.

Once there, the waiting began. Several mattresses were soon being used for naps, and the stacks of magazines and the stocks of food available from the accommodations team were in heavy demand. The children played in the aisles, while the adults stood in groups of three and four, wondering in worried tones just what crisis had brought them there.

In his thirty-sixth floor suite, Albert Tackett was entertaining the same question. Notice of the Asylum alert had come on the quiet, via a messenger from the Pentagon's civil defense office, which was responsible for the logistics. There were no explanations included with the notice, only a final hoolist and a timetable.

Other than an unannounced drill, Tackett could only think of one fact or rumor to account for the move: the threat of an imminent reprisal for the sinking of D-57. If that were the case, military facilities everywhere would be on alert, under lockdown rules, but the aide Tackett sent on a manufactured errand to the Navy yard had no trouble getting in.

That report so troubled Tackett that he had risked a call to a family friend who lived near Hanscomb Air Force Base, just outside Lexington. No, she told him, looking out the window. The planes are just where they always are. Everything's quiet.

Tackett viewed that as the worst possible news, for it fit Secretary O'Neill's paranoid scenario for a sneak surgical strike on Moscow. The discrepant factor was the timing. The date O'Neill had given for the next session of the Supreme Soviet was weeks away, and it would be nearly impossible to conceal Asylum that long.

But there was a window of uncertainty in that analysis, for the newest entries in his foreign-papers clip file on the Soviet Union were ten days old. There could have been some change that would put O'Neill's scenario back on track.

The logical next step was to talk to O'Neill again—except the Secretary was not on the Boston hoolist. Considering recent history, that was only a minor surprise. But it was a major inconvenience. The blackout rules for Asylum ruled out any calls to Washington, much less the kind of conversation Tackett needed to have.

Years of experience had taught Tackett the value and necessity of using back doors and open windows. But it was starting to look like the only way on this one was the front door—and Peter Robinson had the key.

Robinson and William Rodman arrived together at the Tower shortly after ten, in the back of a food service delivery truck. Just then, Tackett was huddling with Monaghan on the timing of the recall from Red that was to precede the mass transit, and so did not meet the truck. The President's insistence on putting in an appearance on the ninth floor delayed their meeting still further.

But a few minutes shy of eleven found them finally face to face in Tackett's suite. "How's everything running, Albert?"

"We're doing our best under the circumstances," Tackett said. "The circumstances are not the best. We're also a bit hungry for explanations. What's going on out there?"

"There's pieces moving all over the board, Albert," Robinson said, digging in his sweater pocket for a cigarette. "Two Russian subs are sniffing up Task Force 21 in the Atlantic—the carrier *Kearsarge* and its escorts. There've been three peeper overflights of the Panama Canal and our Venezuelan oil fields in the last twenty-four hours. And there's a Russian air-amphibious division on maneuvers in the Bering Strait, thirty minutes from our facilities at Cape Prince. Something's going to break loose real soon."

There was nothing in what Robinson said that Tackett could either refute or affirm. "So you think that Kondratyeva's planning to spank us."

"I don't think he'll settle for making us wet our pants, do you?" Robinson said. "I have to listen to Rauche and his people. They think the psychology's right. Mr. K's been forced to call a special plenary session of the Central Committee to bolster his position after the D-57 fiasco. It'd be a hell of a coup if he could walk into the Grand Palace tomorrow and tell them a revenge raid destroyed the Canal locks or sank the *Kearsarge*, eh?"

Tackett's blood ran cold as he listened. A meeting of the Central Committee, with the top military brass there to testify. That's the missing piece in your nightmare, Gregory, he thought. Served up to order by Peter Robinson.

But still Tackett resisted believing. Robinson's story *was* plausible. Moscow's response to date had been puzzlingly mild. Tackett had heard about the "death letter," but a tongue-lashing, however pointed, however earnest, hardly seemed enough. Some sort of selective, eye-for-an-eye response, even a measured escalation, was entirely credible.

"Where is Secretary O'Neill? I noticed his name wasn't on the list," Tackett said.

"Gregory chose to stay in Washington, at the National Command Center. He'll be my eyes there."

"I would have thought he'd send his family along, at least," Tackett said, still probing.

"My understanding is that Ellen decided to wait with the flash plane at Bolling. The same with the Vice President and his family," Rodman said. "Very courageous."

"General Rauche wasn't on the list, either."

"The chiefs will go to the Rock," Rodman said.

It made sense for the Pentagon brass to relocate to the alternate command center buried in the Catoctins. But a skeptical inner voice offered Tackett another explanation. They're not in on it, he thought. They're in the dark. It's all been arranged by Robinson, Madison—and me.

Robinson seemed bored, though not annoyed, by the conversation. "What's the status of operations in Blue? I trust you've got your problems under control."

"Hardly. We still haven't recovered our agents, the Volunteer Watch is still under alert, and the gate house is almost certainly being watched. I'm not convinced we can support Rathole at this time."

But the President did not seem to hear him. "What's the head count for the Blue station?"

"Four shy of two hundred."

Robinson frowned and shook his head. "I was hoping for five hundred, between Alpha List and your people. But we'll do what we need to with any number, so long as they're loyal."

It was all Tackett could do to keep from staring open-mouthed. He heard in Robinson's words a confession, confirmation of O'Neill's nightmare, validation of his own worst fears.

Rodman was frowning with disapproval, as though he too had noted Robinson's indiscretion. "You have Defnet access here?"

It took Tackett a moment to realize the question was meant for him. "Yes."

"We've been out of contact with Washington for nearly an hour," Rodman prompted Robinson.

"Yes," the President said. "If you'd excuse us, Albert—"

That quickly, Tackett found himself ushered out of his own office. It can't be true, he told himself as he hastened down two floors to the Tower's communications center. I've got to be reading this wrong.

The cork-floored rack-filled room was manned by a single technician, who blinked in surprise at seeing Tackett there.

"Director?"

"Are any of my office lines active?"

"Yes, sir."

"Who are they talking to?"

"I don't know, sir."

"Can you put that line on a set of phones for me?"

"Yes—"

"Do it. Then get out of here."

"Sir, this room's supposed to be staffed around the clock—"

"*I'm* here, aren't I?" growled Tackett. "Do it."

Somerset County, Pennsylvania, Alternity Blue

Unlikely as it seemed, the newest arrival at the safe house was being treated with even more deference than Warren Eden had enjoyed. But then, after all, he was the President.

Wallace did not know which of the day's surprises had brought Brandenburg there—Eden's casual lunchtime announcement that he had solved the structure of the maze or the disquieting news that large numbers of Guard agents were returning to Indianapolis and reporting to the gate house. He knew only that as the principals gathered in the dining room for the action caucus, there was an urgency and a tension in the air which he had not seen before.

Eden claimed the floor first. "This was an interesting problem," he said, and there were chuckles at the understatement. "The solutions are even more interesting. They're also a bit abstruse. I know that no one in this room is a physicist or mathematician. I suspect that's to your advantage. It's certainly to mine. A room full of physicists would be positive they know why what I'm going to say can't be so, and the proofs are not yet compelling.

"I said several days ago that this was an artifact. That remains my conclusion. Specifically, I would describe it as a forced macro-uncertainty, an artificially created quantum bubble supporting mirror pockets of shaped spacetime."

As brows furrowed and eyes glazed, Eden stalwartly continued. "I will try to explain that. For more than twenty years, we physicists have been arguing over the implications of certain experiments in subatomic structure and behavior, whether they mean that alternate universes are required or merely possible. I myself have wasted the last dozen years modeling the possible creation of fundamentally different universes at what cosmologists call Time Zero."

"Wasted? Clearly, they *are* possible," Davis said.

"Yes—but," Eden said. "The key experiments which led to the debate were conducted with high-energy cyclotrons and accelerators built in the 1940s and later. All of the most important work took place after the Split."

"Experimental error," Davis said suddenly. "Systematic experimental error."

Eden nodded. "The results were influenced by the fact that they took place inside this bubble. We were describing the local case, not the general case. I don't know what rules hold outside." He smiled. "Some of us would welcome a more orderly Universe."

"But inside the bubble, at least, this kind of thing can happen," Bayshore said.

"Not by itself. Not without a hyperdimensional structure like the maze."

"A structure made of what?" asked Wallace.

Shrugging, Eden said, "Out of what is—matter-energy and the five forces through which it interacts."

He reached into his pocket and produced a many-creased flat paper disc. He laid it on the table, and when he released it, the disc popped up into a many-sided three-dimensional figure. "I've been playing with some geometries, treating the entire complex as a kind of macromolecule, considering the junctions in terms of bond angles. This is the one that makes the most sense."

"Isn't that a dodecahedron?" Shan said.

"Yes. The most complex of the Platonic solids. But don't look at the faces. Look at the edges and vertices. The edges are the force channels, and the vertices are the junctions. Imagine each alternity as a sphere connected to a single vertex at a single point."

"The gate," Wallace and Davis said in concert.

"More exactly, the gate house," Eden said. "Functionally, the gate houses are a combination of anchor and fulcrum. The key characteristics they have in common are relative physical prominence and non conductive mass. That argues for them serving both as both antennas and insulators."

347

Shan asked, "Insulators?"

"A tremendous amount of energy is being poured into keeping the alternities apart. It's that energy which makes the gate 'sing' to the runners, that 'grounds' through metallic objects brought into the maze."

"So when I make a transit," Wallace said slowly, "I'm moving along these force channels."

"Yes," Eden said, folding his arms and leaning forward to rest them on the table. "But the fact that transits are possible is probably an incidental consequence of the structure. The energy apparently is carried along the force channel in such a way as to create a neutral zone, just as the charge on a cylinder resides on its outer surface."

"We're just rats in the rafters?" Wallace asked.

"Essentially."

"How can they survive in there?" Shan asked.

"I suspect that air molecules cross over through the gates at random, because of the pressure differential—nature abhors, and all that. Speculation only."

"Antennas, insulators—but not doorways," Davis said. "Am I reading the implications correctly?"

"I believe so. The entire structure seems designed to perform a balancing act—binding the alternities together, and at the same time isolating them from each other."

"There's no reason to think the gate houses were put there for our use," Davis pressed.

Eden nodded. "The gate houses are fully justified by their structural functions."

Brandenburg had picked up the dodecahedron and was turning it over in his hands. "In this model, Dr. Eden, there would be more than seven alternities, would there not?"

"The most likely number is twenty," Eden said. "Push the model out to four dimensions, creating a hyperdodecahedron—which I am inclined to do, in fact—and the number soars."

Bayshore looked stunned. "Twenty universes—"

"Oh, no. Not universes. The Split was not a Time Zero event," Eden said, shaking his head vigorously.

"Meaning?"

"That this is a local phenomenon. The radius of each pocket may be no greater than a few hundred astronomical units, enough to enclose the solar system and little more—a very minor irregularity on the cosmic scale. It's not that each alternity includes the whole universe—rather that the greater part not included is sensible from here. I don't know how the rest of the universe perceives *us*. From their vantage point, we may simply have disappeared.''

Returning the model to the table, Brandenburg pressed his palms together and touched his fingertips to his chin. ''Archimedes spoke of moving the Earth if only he had a place to stand. It seems the builders of this structure found that place.''

''Yes.''

''Who do you think they were?''

''That question I have no answer for.''

The President nodded acceptingly and did not pursue it. ''You spoke of a balancing act. What would be the consequences if the balance were upset?''

Pursing his lips, Eden considered. ''Less energy in the core structure and the alternities likely collapse back into a single identity. More energy and—'' He shrugged. ''Perhaps an alternity would go flying off into spacetime like a car broken free from a spinning carnival ride. Or rather two, in complementary pairs, to preserve quantum mechanical symmetry. It would be nice if we could keep a few principles of physics intact—''

Throughout the action caucus, Rayne Wallace had been doing his best to fight past the foreign words and wrestle with the foreign ideas. He had persevered, but the fight had left him weakened and his sensibilities bruised. He suspected that everyone in the room, Shan included, understood what was going on more clearly than he did. So when he heard the question which had been consuming him passed over so casually, he rebelled.

''But why?'' he blurted out. ''Why did it happen? I'm tired of half-answers, goddamn it.''

Eden stopped in midsentence. ''What?''

''Why did they do this to us? For God's sake, why is there only one of me and twenty of you?''

There was a moment of surprised silence.

''None of us knows, Rayne,'' Davis said, looking down the table. ''That's the plain truth. There are no seers or prophets in this room. Even half-answers are more than we had a right to expect.''

''That's not good enough,'' was Wallace's grim reply.

''I'm not satisfied with it, either,'' Davis said. ''But, look—is it any more a mystery that many worlds exist than that one does?''

Shan answered for Wallace. ''No, not if they've existed ever since Dr. Eden's Time Zero. But when they show up suddenly at zero plus five billion years, it *is* a different question. Doesn't anyone have any ideas?''

Surprisingly, it was Brandenburg who stepped to the fore to answer. "Dr. Eden spoke of the theoretical context for his contribution," he said slowly. "The rest of the answer may lie in the historical context. How much do you know about the time into which you were born, Miss Scott?''

"Not enough to see what you see.''

"I am something of a student of history, Miss Scott," he said. "And I have the advantage of having lived through those years. Let me try to paint you a picture of the world before the Split.

"What I remember most of all is the fear and the ferment of the post war years. By 1950 the Soviet Union had tested its own fission bomb, and the U.S. was beginning a crash program to build a fusion weapon. Real estate ads offered homes 'a safe fifty-eight miles from Washington.' The first round of McCarthy hearings, about Communists in the State Department, were in full swing. Truman was under constant attack for being soft on communism.''

"Wrongly," Davis opined.

"Your opinion. It did look like we were trying to give Europe to the Russians, the Marshall Plan notwithstanding," said Brandenburg. "We had demobilized so quickly that there were a hundred and seventy-five Russian divisions facing no more than fifteen Allied divisions, some of which were armed with fifty-year-old Italian rifles. We had put dozens of ships into mothballs, junked thousands of aircraft.

"Then in June the Korean War started, and we jumped in with both boots, perhaps in part to prove Truman's manhood. But the pressure kept coming, and so did the problems. In the span of one week that November, Truman survived an assassination attempt, lost two key allies—Tydings and Lucas—in the Senate elections, and learned that the Chinese had entered the war on the side of the North Koreans.''

"My mother was already pregnant with me by then," Shan realized aloud.

Brandenburg nodded. "The last moments of the Common World. At Thanksgiving MacArthur was still talking about having the boys home by Christmas. Over the next three weeks, the Chinese handed us the worst military defeat of our history, routing a 300,000-man army, and Truman started talking out loud about using the bomb. On Christmas Day, he declared a state of national emergency and ordered the military to call a million veterans back to active duty.''

"Jesus," Wallace said. "I'm amazed you got through it."

"That's your history, too," Brandenburg said. "I remember Tydings saying it would be a miracle if the U.S. and Russia avoided war. Well, perhaps it was." He looked around the table. "Of all the times in our history when we might have used a helping hand, I would point to that one as when we were most needy."

Bayshore pounced. "Why? The U.S. and the USSR didn't have more than fifty atomic bombs between them in 1950," he said skeptically. "No intercontinental missiles. No megaton-yield H-bombs. No hair-trigger warning systems. We were in more danger in 1960 than 1950."

"Oh, I concede that there have been crises since then where more was at stake," Brandenburg said agreeably. "But 1950 was the beginning of the new era of superpower nuclear conflict. It was a cusp—the last time we still had a real choice about which direction we were going to take. If the Split had come in 1960—even our 1960, much less Mr. Wallace's—the odds would have been against any alternity surviving the next thirty years. We barely got through Norfolk without calling down the fire ourselves."

Bayshore was still resisting. "You're saying that some power took pity on us and gave us a few extra chances to survive?"

"I am content with that answer. You're free to find your own."

The director's mouth twisted into a wry expression. "No slight intended to my gathered friends, but what makes us worth all that trouble?"

"We're not in a position to judge how much 'trouble' it was," Eden said.

"Or to judge worth, for that matter," Shan interjected.

Eden continued, "To an intelligence capable of such instrumentalities, it may have been no more trouble than snipping off the terminal bud of a growing plant to encourage it to branch."

"They're not miracles to God, in other words."

"If you wish."

Bayshore looked from face to face in search of an ally. He found expressions ranging from somber to numb. "All right." he said resignedly. "All these ifs and maybes make fine dinner conversation, but we have a problem right here. What do we do about Indianapolis?"

"We take the gate house away from them," Davis said simply.

"Yes," Brandenburg agreed. "But that's not enough."

"No?"

351

"Dr. Eden expressed a belief that the channels were not meant to function as bridges. I agree. This gift only works if each alternity believes that it's the only one, and acts accordingly. We have to think that we only get one chance. Otherwise we might take risks we have no right taking."

"That particular cat's out of the bag," Wallace said. "We know. You know. You can't undo that. Besides, we're not your enemies. We're more like brothers."

Brandenburg stiffened. "It seems to me that you and your people chose the sides."

"We should work together. We believe in the same things—"

"Not from the evidence I've seen."

Wallace patiently tried to explain. "You don't understand where the Russians have us. You could be the difference. You could help us push them back."

"Why would we want to?" Brandenburg asked coldly. He turned to Eden. "Doctor, what happens if the cathedral is destroyed?"

"I couldn't hazard a guess. Not without more than second-hand data and blue-sky models."

Brandenburg closed his notebook. "Yes. That's fair," he said. "First things first. Mr. Bayshore, it's time to move on the gate. How long before Group 10 can be ready?"

"They'll be in position for tonight, if we need them," he said, then added a warning. "There may not be many of the Guard left to round up by then. Unless they're stacking them three deep inside, it looks like they've got some sort of move of their own underway."

"That doesn't matter," Brandenburg said. "I want the gate in our hands by morning."

Bayshore nodded and stood. "Yes, sir. Dr. Eden, Rayne— grab your things. You, too, Shan," he added in an obvious afterthought. "The Indianapolis Express leaves in ten minutes."

TARGETING SUMMARY, VMF NORTHERN FLEET, ATLANTIC GROUP
Mixed Counterforce and Countervalue (General Plan SD)

Target Description	Location	No.	Yield
Philadelphia Metropolitan (continued)			
Sun Shipbuilding	Chester	1	20 KT
Boeing Corp. (aircraft)	Essington	1	20 KT
U.S. Steel Works (steel mill)	Fairless Hills	1	10 KT
General Electric (indust. elec.)	King of Prussia	1	10 KT
Westinghouse (indust. elec.)	Lester	1	10 KT
Delaware River Complex	Philadelphia		
International airport		7	115 KT
Atlantic Richfield Co. (oil refinery)			
Naval shipyard			
Marine freight terminal			
Naval supply depot	Philadelphia	1	10 KT
SKF Industries Plant #1 (bearings)	Philadelphia	1	10 KT
Naval air station	Willow Grove	1	35 KT

New Jersey

(see also New York Metropolitan)

Target Description	Location	No.	Yield
Monsanto (chemicals)	Bridgeport	1	10 KT
New York Shipbuilding Co.	Camden	1	20 KT
General Aniline Works (elec. comp.)	Grasseli	1	10 KT
RCA (electronic components)	Harrison	1	20 KT
Naval air station	Lakehurst	2	40 KT
Javelin missile battery #16	Longport	1	10 KT
RCA Missile & Surface Radar Div.	Moorestown	2	30 KT
Naval air station	Pomona	1	20 KT
Javelin missile battery #17	Stone Harbor	1	10 KT
Bendix Corp. (aircraft components)	Teterboro	1	20 KT
State capital	Trenton	1	10 KT
McGuire air base: Ft. Dix army base	Wrightstown	3	60 KT
Coast Guard antisubmarine C&C	West Cape May	2	40 KT

- -

CHAPTER 20

Moins Cinq

Boston, The Home Alternity

Long before the Asylum evacuation was called, Walter Endicott knew what he wanted from the Tower.

It had been a long road back to Boston. The planning and scheming that had returned him at long last to this place had begun years earlier. It was he who had placed the idea of leaving this alternity in Robinson's mind, he who had pointed out what a loyal fifth column might achieve in the service of its commander.

Endicott remembered the conversation, in an Atlantic City hotel room, three weeks after the election. "Best of all is to rule in heaven, don't you think?" he had said to the President that day. "There are better places than this, Peter. Why not pick one and take it for our own? Why scratch and fight for table scraps here?"

Robinson had said little at the time, but it was barely the dawn of his presidency. The lessons of the limits of power, the weight of the chains forged out of past mistakes, had yet to be learned.

Soon enough Endicott began to see signs that his suggestion had been taken to heart. The Guard growing like a wild weed, to serve the king in his new kingdom. A new emphasis on first-strike weapons, so that there might be a dramatic exit. Rathole, by which the king's favored courtiers might blindly accompany him on his journey.

I die and am born again, exalted. I shall not want.

The flaw, annoying and aggrieving, was that Robinson had transmuted the "we" into an "I." Like a parasitic playwright,

Robinson had taken Endicott's idea and built it into a powerful script in which he was the only actor of substance. Endicott's sole thanks was to be written in as a supporting role.

Though Endicott remained first among the courtiers, true power-sharing eluded him. Blinded by the courtesies and the other symbols of status, Endicott learned too late that Robinson never truly consulted others in his decisions, never suffered the insecurities which would lead him to meaningfully solicit opinions and advice.

But in seeming to, Robinson had a powerful tool for collecting information and controlling people. And Endicott had been one of those controlled—with comforts and confidences, garnished with an illusion of responsibility. *I need a friend in the Senate, someone I can count on*— But it could have just as easily been another.

Outwardly gracious, Endicott had never crossed Robinson on any matter of substance. He carefully negotiated the traps laid for him by those who coveted what they wrongly thought he had. And he bode his time with stoic patience, waiting for the right moment to introduce a bit of anarchy into the play.

And now that moment had arrived. There are many worlds, Endicott thought. I will find a new one.

Tackett's gnomes tried to make Endicott a prisoner of the ninth floor, locked up in storage with the round-faced men and thick-lipped boys, the wire-haired wives waiting uncomfortably in line for the toilet. The gnomes took him for one of them, one of the bleating sheep herded to Boston with no more grasp of events than an animal on its way to be butchered.

To be lumped with them was an insult, but Endicott could not concern himself with insults. To be penned with them was a straight-jacket, a strangling hand on his throat. But the gnome supervising the warren had already gone deaf to special pleadings long before Endicott arrived.

"I'm sorry, Senator. I can't allow any green badges to leave the floor without word from above."

"I'm sorry, Senator. Yes, the director is in the building, but he's not available."

"I'm sorry, Senator. I don't know where to reach the President."

Then Robinson made a brief visit to the ninth floor to lance the boil of anxiety which had been growing all day. Looking composed and almost cheerful, the President climbed atop a desk to address the evacuees.

"I know you all have questions which aren't being answered," he said in a voice that carried to the far corners of the room. "I'm afraid that all of us upstairs have been too busy doing to do much explaining. I can tell you that the Soviet Union has not backed down from its threatening posture, but neither have they launched any attacks on our forces.

"We're ready to defend ourselves and to respond to any hostilities, though I hope we won't need to. But if fighting does come, I promise that you and your families will be safe. Please continue to cooperate with the NRC staff, as you already have so magnificently. Your prayers and your patience are both invaluable to me in this crisis."

Endicott fought his way forward to catch the President by the elbow before he could exit the room.

"A minute," he insisted. "We need to talk."

"Of course," Robinson said, leading him through the checkpoint and into the corridor outside. "What is it, Walter?"

"I gave you all this," he said in a harsh whisper. "Everything that's about to be. The Tower wouldn't be here if it wasn't for me. I don't like being locked up here like a stranger and a security risk. There aren't any secrets that need to be kept from me."

The President distractedly agreed. "Get the Senator a visitor's pass," he told the gnome at the checkpoint.

"Yes, Mr. President."

"Unrestricted," Endicott said helpfully.

"Sir, there's no such thing as an unrestricted guest pass," the gnome said. "We just don't let people roam free here. Except for you, of course," he amended hastily.

"If you can make one exception, you can make two."

The gnome squirmed, discomfited. "Sir, all visitors must be escorted. That's SOP here."

"Then get the Senator a pass *and* an escort, and custom will be served." Robinson turned to Endicott. "I know you understand, Walter, that I've got my hands full—"

"Oh, I understand, Peter." The blue and white visitor's badge now dangling from his lapel just below the green Alpha List badge was all he had needed from Robinson. "I won't be underfoot."

"Thank you."

With an acknowledging salute, the President boarded an elevator and left. Endicott waited for his escort, gloating at the gnome who had earlier refused him. Warm bodies were apparently in short supply, for it took nearly ten minutes to produce one. But when he finally arrived, the escort gnome proved more astute than the guard gnome had been.

"I know you," he said, recognition dawning in his eyes. "You're the one that shot that Russian spy. I saw you on the news, didn't I?"

"That's right," Endicott said, pleased at being recognized. A little innocent awe and deference would be useful in the hours to come. "What's your name?"

"Edwards, sir. White Section. Where can I take you, Senator?"

"You have a cafeteria here?"

"Yes, sir."

"What's the chance of the coffee being any better than the poison they're serving in there?" he asked, jerking a thumb in the direction of the warren.

"Not good, sir. But I know a department on the sixth floor that has a supply of Columbian and a black-water wizard named Angelica. We can probably boost you something potable there."

Endicott worked the younger man for nearly an hour, sharing stories of Washington and of the President, drawing him out about the Tower, binding him in a conspiracy of confidences. Not until he knew he would not be refused did he voice his real interest.

"I'd like to see the Cambridge," he said, pushing his empty cup across the cafeteria table. "I'd like to see the gate house."

"Well, sure," Edwards began. "There's a lot of offices above the fifteenth floor with windows on the atrium—"

"I've seen it from there," Endicott said. "I mean the way the runners see it. Ground level, from the atrium floor."

Edwards looked at his watch. "It's almost four," he said. "The pre-evac withdrawals from Blue should be finishing up. It's been hectic down there, but I guess we can get you a peek." He shrugged. "Sure. This might be as good a time as any."

The three monitors working gate control looked like they had been under siege. Voices were hoarse, patience short, and the countertop looked like a battlefield. Several inbound runners were waiting in a ragged line for clearance, check-in, or directions. Other runners waited restlessly in the chute, using their transit bags as seats or pillows.

"Donnie, this is Senator Endicott," Edwards said, approaching the counter from the side. "I'm going to take him inside for a few minutes."

"Don't gaff me. I haven't got the time," the monitor gnome grumped without raising his head.

357

"No gaff. The President gave specific orders for me to take him where he wants to go, and he wants to see the gate house."

Wearing an expression that said, why-are-you-doing-this-to-me, the gnome looked up and locked a querying gaze on Endicott. The gaze took in the dual badges, then shifted focus to Edwards. "The middle of the craziest day we've ever had and you're giving tours?"

"This is Senator *Endicott*," Edwards repeated in a tone that Endicott found pleasing. "Just tell the snipers we're coming and buzz us through, all right?"

The monitor gnome sighed and surrendered. "Keep it short, will you?"

"The snipers?" Endicott asked.

"You'll see."

Endicott did. Bathed in light from a hundred floodlamps and the afternoon sun reflecting down from overhead, the Cambridge stood like the dark kernel of a great towering crystal in the center of a magnificent rectangular atrium. Sixty feet up the inner walls, in the glare zone beneath four of the clusters of lamps, were pairs of armored security nests. Their overlapping fields of fire blanketed the entire open zone surrounding the gate house.

"How do they know not to shoot?" Endicott asked, squinting in a vain attempt to see how many marksmen occupied each nest.

"See there, at the front door?" Endicott looked and saw a black waist-high pedestal. "Everyone coming back has to stop there and dial their transit code. If it's not a valid code—"

"I get the picture," Endicott said. "Do you have this kind of security at every gate house?"

"Oh, no. This is special. We've got to treat this one like a border checkpoint. We have to be careful who we let in. The outbound traffic can't hurt us."

"Can we go inside? I'd like to see the gate itself. You can see it, can't you?"

"In the dark. But there's a special forces team monitoring the gate. I don't think they're going to let us in."

"Let's try, can we?"

There were two sentry gnomes in the brightly lit focus room, crouching behind portable trifold shields positioned fifteen feet from and facing a blank wall, sentries at an invisible door. Endicott allowed Edwards to precede him into the room, then

358

edged to one side until his escort's body was between him and the more distant of the two sentries.

"Corporal, this is Senator Endicott with me," Edwards was saying. "The President wanted him to have a tour. How long until we get outbounds, so he can get a peek at the gate?"

Both sentries glanced Endicott's way, then turned their attention back to the gate. Discipline, Endicott thought. Albert did a good job with discipline.

"Soon," the sentry gnome replied. "But not soon enough. I've got the wanders from staring at nothing for three hours. I don't know what the old man is so nervous about today. You couldn't squeeze an extra body through unless it was on somebody's shoulders."

Edwards laughed.

Three, Endicott thought. More than I'd expected. More than I hoped for. But it has to be now.

The gun felt larger in his hand than it had in the pocket of his suit jacket. He pointed it at the middle of the nearer sentry's back and fired twice. The wet slapping sounds of the bullets' passage though the sentry's body were almost lost in the echoes which bounced around the bare-walled room. His body twitching, the sentry toppled forward to the floor.

Edwards' head whipped around in surprise. Behind him, the second sentry was rising from his crouch, trying to see what was happening, starting to push Edwards out of the way. But before the corporal could turn his weapon on Endicott, the Senator's little revolver spoke again. Seconds later, the corporal was on his back in a pool of blood, sucking air raspily through his chest.

"Jesus Christ," Edwards breathed, backing toward the wall.

The revolver held two more bullets. The first missed, vanishing through the gate without ever marking the wall. The second caught Edwards in the hip and took him to the floor, where he lay writhing while Endicott calmly reloaded. Endicott said nothing to him before he silenced the screaming with a bullet to the head.

He did not allow himself to think or feel, only to do. Methodically, he discarded watch and ring, shed belt and slacks to reveal a pair of cotton drawstring warm-up pants. He threw his jacket and tie aside, then cupped his hands in the blood pooling on the floor and smeared his remaining clothes with the crimson stain. *There's been fighting in the Tower—I was the last one out—*

Last of all, Endicott tossed aside the revolver, dropping it on Edwards' corpse. For the briefest moment, he stopped and surveyed the carnage—three shattered bodies, endless blood. How many of these phantoms, these aliens, have I killed? He was jarred to find he had almost lost track. Eight. No, nine. Mustn't forget the first. Can't forget killing myself.

Cleaner hands next time, he vowed silently. I'll let others do the killing the next time. That's what separates Presidents from mobsters, after all.

Then he walked toward the wall, through the gate, and out of the world to which he had never meant to come.

It had been so long that the sensations were almost new, the shuddery tingling in his limbs, the coursing energies flowing like water over skin dead to sensation, the sightless images pouring directly into his brain. Endicott laughed in the soundless corridors in celebration of his victory.

See what I am, Peter! he cried, lingering at the junction. See all the choices I have! I give you one world, a token for your hospitality. Scratch, you silly bastard, scratch and fight for your empty words, your shallow ideals. You'd have been better to stay in bed with Janice than to rise up to hatch your plots and plan your quests.

Ah, Peter, you simple fool, you never learned the secret. Wait until your new world becomes real and your real world moves out of reach. Then you'll see that none of it matters to God. Then you'll see that *we* are God. So easy. Too easy!

He chose a corridor at random and fought his way upward to it, seeing it as a well to be climbed, a journey from the darkness into daylight. His hands grasped, feet slipped and found purchase in nothingness. Upward he rose, the substance of the maze a channel for his will, the challenge a harmonic with his intent. His body grew light, floating, drawn upward as much as driven.

Then the light above him vanished as though the corridor had closed, and Endicott was suddenly touched by awe. A gatekeeper for the gate. A cruel and lovely joke. He continued on, borne toward the new presence by currents in the very substance of the corridor. It was no mere runner that awaited him, no accident of transit. This one was one with the maze. This one embodied all the powers of the maze, and something more besides.

Liar, he cried. Cheat. Oh, yes, now, you demon trickster, now you come to ask an accounting. Silken whore. Who are you to judge me? Thief and liar. Mother-raping murderer, you kill millions. I defy you. I defy you. You judge me for being like you, for learning your rules and playing the game too well. I know you, coward! I know you. Come for me, then, you bastard god—

Then they touched, and Endicott screamed. He felt the cold dispassion, the inexorable power, the inevitability of his own destruction. For one brief moment, he merged with the other, before his will was drained and his essence dissipated like a handful of salt in the sea.

And in that one frozen instant he saw with the demon's eyes, saw the twinkling worlds like beads on a string, the whirling stars marching in soundless synchrony, the many-folded fabric of Time shot through with threads of gold, saw the pattern and the purpose, the patient handiwork, the intricate design.

It was too late to recant, too late even to understand. There was time only to know that it was beautiful and that his death would erase a blemish on its sculpted face.

Lexington, Massachusetts, The Home Alternity

Margaret Mills was accustomed to looking out her bedroom window, beyond her backyard, beyond the gleaming outer fences of Hanscomb Air Force Base, and seeing the slump-winged tanker aircraft arrayed on the parking apron. She was accustomed to the deep-throated roar of a takeoff, rattling the house windows a dozen times a day.

But never in the eleven years she had lived there, never in the five years since the big planes had replaced the mosquitolike fighters, had she seen and heard anything like what was before her now. Ever since Albert Tackett's curious call that afternoon, she had been drawn again and again to the window, wondering what he had thought might be happening at the base. At last she knew.

The base was lit up like a Christmas display, every spotlight and floodlight ablaze. Trucks scurried everywhere, and men ran instead of walked. It seemed as though every aircraft was in motion, creeping along the taxiways, queueing up for the runways. She stood at the window with the telephone receiver at her ear, barely able to hear the ringing over the thunderous rumbling of a hundred idling jet engines. Their smoky exhaust formed a haze over the base, blowing eastward like an oily fog rolling off a concrete sea.

Margaret did not know where the planes were headed. Neither did she understand just what they would do there. But she was a pilot's widow, and she felt the urgency of their departure as a shadow on the night—and feared both for them and for herself.

"Answer, Albert," she said anxiously. "Answer, Marian," she pleaded. "Please be home to tell me how foolish I am—"

At the end of the runway, a pale-bellied tanker lurched forward, its screaming engines a sharper note against the unrelenting background tumult as it rolled ever faster along the concrete ribbon. Trailing four twisted tendrils of smoke, it strained upward into the darkening sky, hurrying to a distant rendezvous.

Stubbornly, desperately, she let the phone ring until after the last plane was gone, though she knew the phone was ringing in an empty house. When the futility overtook her and she hung up at last, there was not even enough feeling left inside her to allow her to cry.

Boston, The Home Alternity

The skies outside Tackett's office were as dark as the tone of the meeting taking place inside.

"I have to tell you, I feel betrayed," Robinson pronounced in a stentorian voice. "Betrayed by Senator Endicott, and betrayed by you, too, Albert."

Tackett grunted in indignant surprise. "Me?"

"There's no excuse for this kind of screw-up. Three dead in a shootout, an evacuee lost, a violation of the gate house, of the gate itself—carelessness, that's the only explanation. Carelessness and incompetence. Your internal security stinks, Director. Why were there only two sentries at the gate? Why was there no metal detector to catch the gun?"

If he had been huddled privately with Robinson, Tackett would have pointedly reminded him of his contribution to the fiasco. With Monaghan and Rodman for an audience, Tackett made an effort to cloak his rebuke.

"Senator Endicott was a highly motivated individual with special knowledge of the gate house," Tackett said. "No one else on the evac list could have done what he did."

"You want me to write it off as an aberration, an exception—"

"Mr. President, there was nothing wrong with our security at the gate house. We think of the Cambridge as our back door, and we keep it locked up tight. The problem was this morning I had to throw the front door wide open. I've got a hundred and sixty security breaches camped out on the ninth floor. I assure you they don't usually get in that easily."

"You knew they were coming. You should have made better provisions for internal security—"

Tackett fumed. *It would help if you wouldn't sabotage the ones we do have, you son of a bitch—*

"—I assume you've already taken steps?"

Monaghan answered, "I've placed a Special Forces team on each floor, in the main corridor."

"Fine." Robinson glanced at Tackett and thought better of voicing his next thought. "To other matters. Just before coming in here, I received a discouraging report. One of our patrol planes has disappeared off Puget Sound. It may have been shot down by a missile from the Russian sub it was tracking. And according to a CIA intercept, civil defense 'drills' have been scheduled for tomorrow morning in Moscow and several other major Russian cities—that's the middle of the night here."

That conformed in every detail to what Tackett had heard on the recordings being made for him in the signal shack. But it did not explain why so far none of the conversations captured had been between the President and his Secretary of Defense. Robinson had talked to Rauche, to other members of the Joint Chiefs, to Madison, to the head of the FNS—but not to O'Neill, the man he had proclaimed would be his eyes in Washington.

"It's starting to look more and more like there'll be fighting," Robinson was saying. "In all good conscience, I don't think that we can sit still and let ourselves be caught here. Starting at midnight, I want Alpha List moved to Alternity Blue."

And you're number one through the gate, Tackett thought. He made one more attempt to catch Robinson in a lie. "Mr. President, does the Secretary of Defense agree with that evaluation?"

But there must have been something in the way he asked it that betrayed his suspicion, for Robinson answered the accusation behind the question. "I don't know, Albert," he said somberly. "The fact is that, at the moment, I'm without Gregory's counsel. I'm sorry to have to tell you that the Secretary suffered a stroke overnight."

A lie to cover another lie, Tackett thought bitterly. O'Neill had anticipated his own disappearance, just as he had predicted everything else. Wheels were turning—the great steel wheels of a war juggernaut hurtling out of control.

"He's in Georgetown University Hospital, under wraps, very weak," Robinson continued. "Bill thought we should try to conceal from the other side the fact that we're without him. I suppose I carried the deception further than strictly necessary. My apologies, Albert."

"We can't have the Russians thinking we're weak, Albert," Rodman said. "You understand that."

"Yes," Tackett managed to say.

"We just need to hold together, all of us," Robinson said, backing away toward the door. "We'll come through this, Albert, and we'll be stronger for it."

He nodded, not trusting his voice. Thoughts in turmoil, he sat woodenly in his chair as Robinson and Rodman retreated from the room. Would it be such a tragic thing if Moscow were transformed into radioactive sludge? And after so many years of playing by pragmatic rules, why should covert action—even on this scale—suddenly make him queasy? How much did it matter who threw the first punch, after all?

Slowly, his thinking crystallized. It did matter, somehow. There was something cowardly about throwing a rock at a bully and then running to your mother's skirts. Even if you took a beating, you had to stand your ground and finish what you started. Honor. There was a question of honor involved.

It mattered, too, because Rathole had perverted the organization he had worked so hard to build. Everything the Guard was, everything they had done, had been done to strengthen and secure, not an individual, not a government, but a country, a people, a tradition. Yet Robinson had coopted the Guard into helping him endanger what they previously had struggled to protect.

Monaghan was eyeing Tackett with a troubled gaze. "Is something wrong?"

"Yes," Tackett said. "Something's very wrong. We've been badly used, Bret. And I've been trying too hard not to see it."

"Oh." There was a pregnant pause. "Do you mind letting me in on it?"

"Do you mind being shot for treason?"

Monaghan blanched momentarily, then moved closer. "What's going on, Albert?"

"I'm serious. In a showdown between the President and me, which side do you want to be on?"

Monaghan crossed his arms over his chest. "Albert, I've got a lot of friends who aren't going to get anywhere near that gate tonight. I'm scared to death for them. If you're talking about something that might save their lives, I want a piece of it. What do you want me to do?"

Tackett looked up with grateful eyes. "Help me stop a plane."

• • •

364

The senior communications specialist was playing cribbage with one of his technicians when Tackett appeared in the communications center. Tackett chased the technician away and dragged the comspec into the privacy of a glass-walled booth.

"We're going to find out how good you are, Zack," Tackett said."

"What do you need, Director?"

"I need to talk to Europe."

"That's easy. We've got international access through the transatlantic phone cables."

"That'd have to be patched through a local switching center, right?"

"Well, sure."

"That's no good, then. This has got to go through. I need something that can't be jammed or cut off."

"Then there isn't any way."

"There has to be."

"The only medium with no middlemen is radio. We've got shortwave, because of Defnet—five thousand watts worth. We can flood any channel from 3 megahertz to 30. It's a long bounce, but they'll hear us all the way to the Ukraine. But radio can always be jammed. And if you're looking for something private, look somewhere else."

"Who listens? Do you know who's on what channel, worldwide?"

"Not every little one-watt transceiver. But we've got a directory of the major players. This building is a hell of an antenna. We do a lot of listening when we have the time. Who do we want to talk to?"

"The Kremlin. The Soviet high command. Any military units that could relay a message to them. Their Atlantic task force, whatever."

He whistled. "I didn't think we were going to get directly involved in that."

"We need to, now."

The comspec's jaw dropped. "Son of a bitch. Did they knock out Washington?"

"Not yet," Tackett said. "And if you do your job, maybe they won't have to. Do you know the Soviet frequencies?"

"Sure. They're in the book."

He reached in his pocket. "I want this message to go out immediately, repeated at one minute intervals," he said, unfolding a half-sheet of paper and handing it over. "Notify me immediately if there's any response or acknowledgment."

Blinking, the young man looked up from the paper. "Are you sure about this, sir?"

"Yes. Will you know if you're being jammed?"

Zack nodded, swallowing hard.

"I'll want to know about that, too. As soon as I'm gone, Special Forces is going to seal off this floor. I want this place locked up tight. No one gets in or out. Ditto for traffic. Everything incoming is embargoed, starting now. Nothing interferes with this, do you understand?"

"Yes—"

"Then move, boy, move. It's getting late in the day."

The Baltic Sea, The Home—Alternity

Thirty thousand feet above the choppy waters of the Baltic, the modified VC-24 bearing the bomb in its belly bored on through the darkness toward Moscow.

Its pilot, an eleven-year CIA veteran named David Matthews, used a light touch on the controls to keep the heavily laden plane in the center of its invisible lane in the sky. The copilot, as fluent in Russian as he was in the workings of their four-engined metal condor, quietly monitored the radio while idly scanning the blackness below for the running lights of freighters and fishing boats.

They had every reason to think that the hard part was over. It had been almost two hours since the switch had been made, in the cloud-shrouded skies over the Norwegian Sea. Approaching from the southwest, flying a mere hundred feet off the water, they had seen the Soviet airliner go down, a fiery ball falling ten thousand feet through the blackness to the sea.

How many other eyes also saw it and knew it for what it was, they had no way of knowing. Nor could they know if the key British air traffic control center had experienced the brief power failure intended for it, blinding controllers to the switch. They could only do their part: switch to the destroyed plane's frequencies, activate their identification transponder, climb to altitude, and hope.

The first hour had been the most tense. By the time they reached the Norwegian coast, they were beginning to feel confident enough to flash smiles and thumbs-up signals across the cockpit. They acquired Copenhagen air control, were handed over to Leningrad, all without incident. Ten minutes ago, the lights of Stockholm, looking like a carnival in the night, had slipped by just to the south.

Then, without warning, the copilot sat up suddenly and grabbed for a clipboard. One hand clamped the headset cup to his ear, closing out the noise of the cabin, while with the other hand he wrote furiously on the blank page.

"What's going on?" asked Matthews.

The copilot shook him off, continuing to write. When he was done, he snapped the pencil back into its holder and stared at what he had written. "This just came over the Soviet A channel," he said. " 'To General Secretary Kondratyeva, Minister of Defense Pokryshkin, Commander in Chief of the Voyska Protivovozdushnoy Oborony Strany, units of the Soviet military everywhere: Warning. A United States military aircraft disguised as a Soviet commercial transport will attempt to detonate a thermonuclear bomb over Moscow—' There, it's starting again, plug in, you can hear it yourself."

Reaching out with his left hand, Matthews complied. He heard, "—will attempt to detonate a thermonuclear bomb over Moscow. This plane may already be in the air, following a direct commercial route from a West European city, with a scheduled arrival at a Moscow airport at or near 8 A.M. Moscow time. This is an unauthorized mission. Do not delay. Locate, intercept, and destroy this aircraft immediately."

"Jesus Christ," the pilot breathed.

"I don't believe it. They sold us out," the copilot said, still staring. "What the hell do we do now?"

Matthews glanced down at his flight plan. "We keep going."

"An hour and twenty minutes to go. We'll never get there. We'll never even get to the border. Do you know how many fighters there are at Tallinn? How many SAMs between here and Moscow?"

"I don't care," the pilot said firmly. "We keep going. You didn't expect to live forever, did you? We're supposed to deliver this package to the Kremlin. And it's going to take a missile or a recall in God's own voice to stop us."

Boston, The Home Alternity

The clock on the etagere read 11:15 when Tackett walked into his office without knocking, Monaghan and the commander of Guard Special Forces trailing in his wake. They found Rodman alone there. The chief of staff jumped up from his chair and scowled at the intrusion. "What's going on, gentlemen?"

"Where's the President?" Tackett asked.

"Down the hall, with Janice and the family, preparing for the move."

"You'd better go get him," Tackett said.

"Why? What's happening?"

"Just get him."

By the time Rodman returned with Robinson, Tackett had cleared his desk of foreign matter and reclaimed it as his own. Neither the act nor the symbolism escaped notice.

"What's going on here, Albert?" Robinson asked darkly. "Shouldn't you be downstairs making sure that everything's in order?"

"There isn't going to be a move, Mr. President." Tackett said, meeting his gaze squarely.

"What are you talking about?"

"It's very simple. No one is going through the gate. No one. Not you, not me, not those people on the ninth floor. We're not going to drive your getaway car—sir."

"Now, just a goddamned minute," Rodman snapped. "This is the President, goddamn you. You can't do this."

"I already have," Tackett said, settling into his chair. "This isn't the White House, Bill. These are my people. There's a hundred soldiers guarding the gate house—on your advice. Communications are locked up—you can't make so much as a lunch reservation without my permission. I say there's not going to be a move, and I can make it stick, believe me."

"You don't understand what you're doing," Robinson said, a red flush climbing his neck. "You little bastard, you're fucking with our lives. You in a hurry to die, old man? You want to stay here and be part of tomorrow's sunset?"

Tackett glanced across at the clock. "It's eleven twenty-five. I figure that gives you at least a half an hour to stop anything you feel you need to stop. You were going to wait around to make sure that it came off, weren't you? I don't think you would have wanted to miss your moment."

Understanding dawned in Robinson's eyes.

"Yes, I know about the plane," Tackett added. "Secretary O'Neill told me. Which reminds me—where is he, really? Dead, or just tucked away somewhere?"

"He should be dead," Rodman muttered. "I should have killed the sonofabitch."

A hard ugly look had taken over Robinson's features. "I'm not going to stop a damned thing," he said. "How do you like that, old man? We'll stay here together and watch it all happen.

How many bombs do you think they'll drop on Boston? Half a dozen at least, wouldn't you say? You little shit, you can't stop anything. You can't save anything. All you can do is kill more people. You think I'm afraid to face what I've done? By dawn either we'll both be dead, or I'll be the President who chopped the Reds off at the knees. You lose both ways, asshole."

Tackett's expression never changed. "I was hoping for better from you, Mr. President. I'm glad I didn't count on it. Maybe I'd better let you talk to General Rauche, so you can see where you really stand."

Moscow, The Home Alternity

Kondratyeva was shaving in the shower when the telephone rang. It was a surprise to be called out of the shower by his wife, still more of a surprise to hear the note of hysteria in Marshal Zaitsev's voice. Kondratyeva stood dripping, the receiver smeared with shaving cream, as the Commander of the National Air Defense Forces poured out his improbable tale.

"No. No, Evgeny," Kondratyeva said when at last he had an opening. "I do not understand it. A trick, certainly, but in which hand? No, the risk is too great." He sighed. "On my authority. Yes, all of them. Bring them all down."

Like a giant hand snatching gnats from the air, the Soviet air defense system awoke, reached out, and swept the skies clear— swiftly, efficiently, and indiscriminately.

The first to fall victim was a two-hundred seat Turkish airliner flying from Istanbul to Odessa. Struck by a missile fired from a Russian frigate cruising the Black Sea, it broke up into a rain of charred fragments which fell to the surface and vanished.

Less than a minute later, a Polish Tupelev-94 with sixty-one passengers aboard was intercepted by two PVO jet fighters just west of Minsk. Each launched a single heat-seeking rocket. One rocket malfunctioned, but the second crawled up the exhaust of the airliner's tail-mounted engines and exploded, sending a ball of flame forward through the cabin.

In the Warsaw military district, confused air controllers warned targets off even as others vectored fighters in. Flight 201 from Munich, forty-five minutes behind the Tupelev on the same route, tried to turn and run from a pair of Polish Air Force interceptors. An air-to-air missile sawed the right wing off, sending 117 passengers and crew earthward in a death spin.

The carnage reached from the Barents to the Adriatic. Ground fire from a Yugoslav air defense unit claimed an Aeroflot plane inbound from Rome. An overzealous Frontal Aviation pilot downed a military transport three minutes after it had taken off from Arkhangelsk.

High above the island of Saaremaa, off the eastern coast of Estonia, David Matthews was alone at the controls of the VC-24. His copilot lay dead in the aisle behind the command seats, his flight suit dark with the blood still seeping from the bullet hole in his back. The great bomb was armed now, over his copilot's objections.

Raw sunlight flooded the cockpit, for the aircraft was flying directly toward the sun, now just rising above the horizon. There was much frantic chatter on the radio in Russian, but Matthews could decipher none of it. It did not matter. He knew he was going to die. But he knew, too, that the pilot, the gunner, the artilleryman who eventually killed him would die, too.

An alarm squalled in the cockpit, and Matthews pushed the plane over in a dive. He did not hope to outrun the air-to-air missiles whose targeting radar had triggered the alarm—they were hundreds of miles per hour faster than his craft. He hoped only to gain a few more seconds, to carry his cargo another mile or two closer to Soviet soil. He would not reach Moscow. But he might reach Riga.

A second alarm, pitched higher and trilling faster, joined the first. Matthews did not wait for the automatic relay linked to the alarms to do its job. He reached out, twisted the black key, and pushed.

Instantly, a malevolent sun appeared in the gray skies over the Gulf of Riga, its light purple at first, then blindingly bluewhite, starkly etching each line on the surface of the world for a hundred miles in every direction.

Like a hungry child, the new star grew, even as its cataclysmic birth cries hammered at the sea and the land. And masked within the fireball's swollen heart, seared by the light, shattered by the sound, two fragile aircraft, hunter and hunted, were transformed into an evanescent haze of disassociated atoms, contaminating the purity of the nuclear fire.

Indianapolis, Alternity Blue

Like voyeurs for violence, Wallace and Shan each claimed a pair of binoculars and a west-facing window to watch the assault on the gate house. From the top-floor offices of the Federal Building, they had an almost unobstructed view diagonally across grassy Memorial Plaza at the fortresslike cathedral one block away.

Bayshore had an even better view. He was on the Federal Building's roof with a nightscope, radio, and the Group 10 commander, a silver-haired lieutenant colonel named Fletcher. But Bayshore and Fletcher were as much spectators as Wallace and Shan, for operational control had already passed to the unit leaders in the streets.

Only Eden did not seem interested in what was about to happen, possibly because he was already looking past that event. He sat across the room from the windows, notepad on his crossed knees, designing what he described as "chemical instrumentation" for his eventual forays beyond the gate.

Through the first hour of the flight from Pennsylvania, Eden had lobbied Bayshore for permission to enter the maze as soon as the cathedral had been secured. Wallace had volunteered to escort him, but Bayshore had flatly refused both the request and the offer.

"I'm not going to risk the only man who knows how to play the game and the only man who has a chance to figure out the rules," Bayshore had said. "So if either of you thinks he's getting near that gate tonight, you'd better revise your thinking."

So Eden pored over his papers as Wallace peered through his binoculars and wondered if anyone he knew was about to die.

The first subtle sign of the assault was the disappearance of all traffic on Meridian Street as the assault zone was quietly cordoned off. Then, at eight minutes past midnight, the cathedral and the eight blocks which surrounded it were suddenly plunged into darkness. Street lights and business signs went dark, buildings turned to shadowy cubes and columns.

Darkness reigned for barely more than a minute. One after another, brilliant, blinding shafts of light stabbed down from the sky toward the cathedral as a quartet of helicopters bearing armored floodlamps made their appearance.

Seconds later, from the plaza on the east, the parking lots on the north and west, the roof of the commercial building to the south, gas-masked commandos fired a salvo of rifle-launched suppression grenades. The cathedral's small upper-story windows frustrated some of the marksmen, the canisters going wide or high and striking the stone walls instead, spewing their potent mix of blinding, stomach-knotting gases on the manicured lawn.

But enough rounds found their mark. The ornate Gothic windows of the bell spire shattered and collapsed inward. Each of the three-story towers at the corners of the building took multiple canisters, until so much gas was escaping through the broken windows that it seemed the building was on fire.

"How well armed do you think they are?" Shan asked.

Wallace shook his head. "I don't think they ever dreamed of coming up against something like this."

A squat armored personnel carrier on tracks raced down Meridian Street, pivoted, and raced up the front steps to batter down the great mahogany doors under the entry arch. The rear doors of the vehicle sprang open, and black-uniformed commandos with breathers and stubby automatic weapons poured out and into the building.

After that, there was little but noise to tell Wallace and Shan what was happening—a rattle of small-arms fire, the pop of a pistol, the *krumph* of a suppression grenade, the thrum of the nearest helicopter hovering in the sky.

At one point, a handful of station personnel fled to the cathedral's roof and took refuge behind the decorative stonework of the mock parapets, from which they fired down at the assault troops deployed around the building.

But a helicopter gunship quickly moved in and peppered their hiding place with machine-gun fire. Shan turned away from the sight; Wallace did not, but his body went rigid, and the acids of guilt seared his throat.

That was the last outward sign of resistance. Shortly after, Bayshore and Fletcher returned from the roof.

"It's ours," Bayshore said jubilantly.

Fletcher elaborated. "It looks like there were only twenty or twenty-five people inside, and most of them were disabled by the DM gas. The operation at the satellite station house went even smoother—we picked up another fifteen or so there without firing a shot."

"What now?" Shan asked.

"We're going over to the cathedral," Bayshore said, standing with arms akimbo. "Rayne, I need you to come along and show us what's what."

Wallace shook his head stiffly. "No."

"Pardon?"

"You got what you wanted from me. You even managed to close my eyes to what you were making me into. We call it a traitor where I come from."

"You did the right thing," Bayshore said.

"Yeah? It sure doesn't feel like it."

"They turned their backs on you when you were still playing by the rules."

"Maybe they did," Wallace said. "That still doesn't mean I'm ready to see them lined up in rows, ready for the engraver." He reached for Shan's hand. "Come on. We're getting out of here."

As they moved toward the door, Shan looked back over her shoulder at Bayshore, as though expecting a protest. But Bayshore made no move to stop them.

"I can call down to the entrance checkpoint and have them held," Fletcher said when they were gone.

"No," Bayshore said, shaking his head. "He'll be back." He shrugged. "Where else can he go?"

Boston, The Home Alternity

General Rauche's strong voice boomed from the speakerphone, carrying the unhappy news to each listener's ears. "We're getting hammered in the Atlantic. Task Force 21, near the Greenland-Iceland gap, has taken the worst of it. The carrier *Kearsarge* has been sunk. The cruiser *Collins* is sinking. A fleet oiler is burning. Three patrol planes down. They'd been shadowing us, so it was easy for them to hit quickly."

"What about the ICBMs?"

"Still no reports of launches, but I frankly don't know what they're waiting for."

"And our missiles?"

"Targets programmed according to Thunderbolt, ready to launch on your order, sir," Rauche said. "Sir, I consider the Weasel squadron extremely exposed. In my opinion, the situation is use-them-or-lose-them."

"Peter, we need breathing space. Request a cease-fire," Rodman urged.

"There were a thousand sailors on the *Kearsarge*," Robinson said stiffly.

"There's a thousand people right here in this building, and they're still alive," Tackett said. "Bill is right. Ask for a cease fire. For God's sake, you might even apologize. Offer to pay reparations."

"Reparations? They're sinking our ships, killing our sailors—"

"For crying out loud, you tried to nuke Moscow," Monaghan snapped. "What do you expect them to do?"

"The war's already started, goddamn you. What do you want *me* to do? We're not walking away."

"No, someone's going to have to carry us—if there's anyone around to do it."

Rauche interrupted the squabbling. "Something off Molink, Mr. President. I'm reading this verbatim: 'To Peter Robinson, President, United States of America. At 1:00 A.M. Washington time, or immediately upon evidence of any further threat to the Soviet homeland, all units of the Strategic Rocket Forces and the SSBN fleet of the Soviet Navy will be authorized to proceed with a full retaliatory attack upon the United States.

" 'This attack will proceed unless you immediately agree to and begin to comply with the following demands: One, that the U.S. abandon and destroy all missile launchers sited in Europe. Two, that the U.S. immediately recall and ground all long-range bomber aircraft. Three, that the U.S. immediately withdraw all naval units to American territorial waters—' "

Robinson fairly leaped around the corner of the desk to get at Tackett. "Jesus Mary, Albert, what are you waiting for?" Robinson cried, grabbing Tackett's shirt front with both hands. "Can't you hear? I can't let them do that to us. I've got to go ahead with the war. Which means we've got to get out of here, starting now. We're out of time. Rathole—"

"Rathole is gone," said a new voice. They looked up to see Barbara Adams standing in the doorway. "We've lost the Blue gate house. Some kind of commando team hit it at midnight. We recovered three people, just minutes ago. That looks like all that's coming."

There was an ominous, cornered look in Robinson's eyes. "I won't do it," he said, releasing Tackett's shirt and stepping back.

"You have to."

"It's wrong," he said. "Don't you understand, it's wrong to give them anything. They have too much already. This was supposed to be our century, not theirs. We're the chosen."

Rauche said, "Mr. President, can I remind you that the Soviets have a seven-to-one edge in throwweight, a ten-to-one edge in warheads. Our bombers would be facing a fully alerted and fully functional air defense. This isn't a fight we can win."

Robinson kept shaking his head. "It doesn't have to be Blue. We can go somewhere else. General, can you hear me?"

"Yes, Mr. President."

"Initiate Thunderbolt."

"No!" shouted Monaghan.

"Peter, I'm sorry," Rodman said, as his right hand closed around a bronze statuette on the corner of Tackett's desk. His face grimly determined, he swung the makeshift club upward, catching Robinson full in the throat. The President staggered backward, coughing, and Rodman struck him again, this time a backhanded blow across the side of his head. Robinson dropped to his knees, and the statuette came down once more on the back of his skull.

No one moved or spoke. Shocked and disbelieving stares took the place of words.

Rodman stepped toward the phone, the bloody implement still in his hand. "General Rauche, this is Chief of Staff William Rodman," he said, his voice unsteady. "The President is incapacitated. Since he was not able to give you the authorization countersign, do you agree that his last order is non-operative?"

The general was slow to reply. "Yes," he said finally. "I do agree."

"The Vice-President is now Acting Commander in Chief. You can reach the Vice-President, and the Secretary of Defense, at the President's Minnesota retreat," Rodman continued. "Any further orders should come from them. But in order to be sure that there's enough time for them to be properly briefed on the situation, do you agree that you have sufficient command authority to begin carrying out Secretary Kondratyeva's demands?"

"Yes," said Rauche, sounding relieved. "I'll send an acknowledgment out over the President's name. And I'll begin the recall of our forces immediately."

"Thank you, General," Rodman said, and pressed the button to break the connection. He looked down at Robinson's inert, bloody form, then up at the stunned faces of the others.

"He wouldn't have listened to any of you," Rodman said simply, sadly. Then he walked out of the room, past Adams, and into the corridor. A few seconds later there was a crash of glass.

They found his broken body in the street.

POSTLUDE

The Best of Blessings

In the three weeks since the assault, most of the cathedral's scars had been patched or painted over. The windows had new glass, the entrance new doors, the scorched floors new tile, the stained walls new paint. To Daniel Brandenburg's eyes, it was almost impossible to tell that there had been a battle there.

He was met in the central hall by Bayshore, who guided him to the north turret. There they stood side by side in the darkness and gazed into the pale wondrous glow of the gate.

"Astonishing," Brandenburg breathed. "A door to twenty worlds. I am half-tempted to ask you to take me through to see one."

"I'd be half-tempted to do it, if I could go with you," Bayshore said. "Our probe teams have made sixty-four sorties into the maze for data. But we haven't risked an exit at any other gate, for obvious reasons."

"You've done a good job here, Richard," he said, patting the director's arm.

"We know a lot more than we did. We don't know nearly as much as we should."

Brandenburg nodded. "I accept that," he said. "Do you have any better idea who or what built it?"

"Nothing better than yours, and nothing more concrete," Bayshore said, with a slight shake of the head. "They don't seem to have signed their handiwork."

"What about the Shadow?" asked the President. "You had been hoping that would be part of the answer. What does Dr. Eden call it now?"

" 'The Gatekeeper'," Bayshore said with a soft chuckle. "It seems to be some sort of instrumentality for maintaining the maze. Apparently it travels along the channels in a regular pattern, damping out variations. But Dr. Eden's learned how to 'call' it—it breaks its routine and responds directly to disruptions above a certain magnitude."

"So it *is* intelligent."

"Yes. But not enough to be one of the Builders."

Brandenburg nodded. "So where do we stand, Richard? What's the urgency to your recommendation?"

"We lost a second probe team yesterday. They may have run into a party from Wallace's alternity. We know they're back in the maze."

"How?"

"There've been ten or a dozen sightings. What concerns me more are the two scouts they've sent through our gate. The first surprised us, got back through, though we grabbed the other one. I think this Tackett is going to try to take back the gate house."

"I can't see what use it would be to them."

"I don't think he'll try to hold it. He'll try to destroy it. It won't be that hard, either. Not much more difficult than tossing a bomb through a window and running."

"What happens to the gate if this building is destroyed?"

"Dr. Eden is predicting that the gate would skip to a new focus somewhere else. We've already seen microshifts within the gate house. This would be a macroshift, on a scale ranging anywhere from across the street to across the country. He thinks it's happened already, just in the natural course of urban evolution. Some of the gate houses may be second or third generation."

"Could we find the gate again?"

"Not a tenth as easily as they could," Bayshore said somberly.

"True enough," the President said. He turned away, prompting Bayshore with a touch on the elbow to follow. "But you have something else in mind for them? You think you can cut them loose completely."

"I'm at Dr. Eden's mercy on this, but he says yes."

"Without destroying their world, their reality."

"They'll just be the way we always thought we were—alone."

Brandenburg nodded approvingly. "They deserve a chance to make their own choices about survival," he said. "All right, Richard. I want you to close the door on Rayne's world."

It had taken three phone calls and a visit from a pair of polite but persistent NIA agents to get them there, but Wallace and

Shan were waiting for Bayshore when he returned to his gate house office.

It was the first time he had seen Wallace since the night of the assault on the cathedral. Contrary to prediction, he and Shan had not come back. By morning, they had been halfway to Bloomington, hitching on a robot freighter on the automated. According to the reports which had crossed Bayshore's desk, they had spent the weeks since sharing the apartment above the little store, trying very hard to act and think and live like just another couple in love.

"Hello, Shan," Bayshore said, nodding and flashing a smile. Her eyes held a hint of sadness. "Director."

Bayshore looked across the room to Wallace, standing gazing out the window. There was some intangible difference in him, something that proclaimed him to the eyes as a man, not a youth. "Rayne, I know you didn't want to come back here."

Wallace turned away from the window. "That's right."

"My apologies for insisting. But if you two will follow me, there's something I need to show you."

The floor of the small basement room was nearly filled by the two plaster-white obloids. Wallace and Shan dutifully inspected the man-sized pupae, then looked to Bayshore for explanations.

"We've taken to calling these Dr. Eden's little pills. A joke," he added unnecessarily. "I'd like to remind you of a point the President brought up during our safe house caucus. He said that this gift of many worlds only works if we all think and act as if we're the only one.

"At the time, Rayne, you said something to the effect that the cork was already out of the bottle. Well, we're going to put it back in.

"We can't make your world or our world forget the maze exists. But we can make sure that there's nothing they can do with the knowledge. Inside all that insulation is a metal cylinder wrapped in about eighteen pounds of superfine self-oxidizing explosive enriched with—"

"It's a bomb?" asked Wallace.

"It's a bomb," Bayshore said. "And in about twenty minutes, we're going to blow the gate to Home."

Wallace frowned and reached out to touch the plaster-like surface of the pill. "What's that got to do with me?"

"I need to know which side of the maze you want to be on when it happens."

378

Slowly, Wallace raised his eyes from the pill and looked back at Bayshore. "Are you asking me if I want to go back?"

"Yes."

His eyes clouded by an unreadable emotion, Wallace looked toward Shan.

"Five minutes," Bayshore said, moving toward the door. "That's all I can give you."

Touching his hand, she felt his pain. "It's all right."

He turned away from her and stared at Dr. Eden's little pills, rubbed the sides of his head with his hands. "It's not fair to you," he whispered. "How can I even think about it?"

"There hasn't been a day you haven't thought about it. Did you think you had to tell me for me to know?"

"I never thought I'd have to choose," he said, shaking his head.

"It's an opportunity, not a punishment. Take the life you want."

His hands slid up toward the crown of his skull, fingers raking through his hair. "Why do they have to be so different? Why can't—one choice—have everything?"

"Because sometimes we don't get everything, Rayne," she said, her voice breaking. "Sometimes we just get pieces. Sometimes we get it all, but just for a little while."

Turning back, he seized her by the shoulders. "This—magic. It's real, isn't it?"

Her eyes running with tears, Shan nodded and smiled. "Like knowing each other from another life. Something special."

"I don't know if I'll ever find it again."

Biting her lower lip, she reached out and touched his chest with her fingertips. "It'll be here, whenever you need to touch it. I'm part of you—wherever you are."

"I have to go back," he said, and the words brought his tears, angry, acid.

"I know."

"I've learned everything I can by loving you," he said. "So much, so fast—"

"But now there are things you need to learn by leaving."

A slow nod. "Maybe it's not the world I'd have chosen if I were starting from scratch. It may not even be a world with much of a future. But I have a wife and a child there, and I owe them something. I don't know how much of what I had I can get back. But I can't abandon them to whatever's going to happen. I could never be happy here, wondering."

"I know," she said, coming into his arms one last time in that easy way that said she belonged there. "Just hold me."

• • •

Five bodies and a bomb were a crowd in the little turret room.

"You'll be first through, Rayne," Bayshore said. "But the probe team's going to be right behind you, so don't dawdle. The maze starts eating at that insulation right away, trying to get at the metal."

"I understand."

"You didn't have much warning," Bayshore said. "Was there something you wanted to take back with you?"

Wallace shook his head stiffly. "Everything that's worth taking is inside me. Memories—feelings—songs that'll be playing in my head to drive me crazy." He laughed self-mockingly. "No. Thank you. I'm ready."

"The gate's yours."

He took two steps toward the pulsing halo of light, then stopped an armslength from the wall and turned. "Richard—thank you."

The director nodded. "A full life, Rayne."

Wallace's eyes found Shan. "I love you," he said.

Smiling brightly, she pressed her fingers to the hollow between her breasts. "Remember."

Eyes locked on her face, Wallace retreated to the wall and toppled backward through the gate, taking the light with him.

She cried out, an involuntary protest against the loss and separation, then clapped a hand over her mouth. The brief darkness hid the worst moments of her pain. By the time the gate reappeared, she was bravely holding her head high.

Next through was a ferryman, holding the pill in a bear-hug embrace, followed a minute later by his partner. When the gate reappeared again, Bayshore caught Shan looking wistfully into its depths. "Are you sure that's what you wanted?" he asked gently.

"It's what he wanted."

"You didn't have to give him the choice."

"Yes, I did," she said firmly.

"If you hadn't called me, the issue would never have come up. We've got sixty-six others we didn't send back."

"There wasn't any more Rayne could give you. You didn't need him."

"No." Bayshore regarded her with an affectionate curiosity. "You could have made him stay."

"I know," she said, cheeks wet again. "My gift to him is that I didn't try to."

He crossed his arms over his chest to keep from touching her. "You're a pretty classy woman, Miss Scott."

Her smile was rueful. "I am," she said. "But I'm still going to have to sleep alone tonight. So where's the justice in this world, anyway?"

He laughed sympathetically. "How about some coffee?"

They turned toward the door together. "I think I'll just go now, if that's okay."

"It is."

"Thank you," she said, pausing for one last glance back. "I have—a friend—who lives in Yellowwood Forest. I think I need to go spend some time alone with her."

Bayshore crossed the green expanse of the War Memorial Park to the Federal Building with easy, unhurried strides. For the first time in two months, his duty-bound conscience was satisfied that the urgency was gone.

When he reached the top floor, Bayshore was ushered into the same expansive office from which Wallace and Shan had watched the assault. "It's done, Mr. President."

"The pill worked?"

Bayshore sought a chair. "With surgical precision. Just the right amount of energy in just the right place. We went back for a look as soon as the Gatekeeper would let us near the junction. Wallace's alternity is gone. There's no longer a gate there."

Rubbing his hands slowly together as though warming them by a fire, Brandenburg nodded. "And what of the placebo? Did it also do its job?"

"Everyone who was supposed to see it or hear about it, did."

"The young woman? Shan?"

"Especially her. Two bombs, two gates to close. She believed."

"I'm uncomfortable with this power, Richard," Brandenburg said.

"It was too much to let go of. There's so much more we have to learn."

"I know that," Brandenburg said. "I'm just afraid that we'll repeat their mistakes."

"A second chance. A chance to learn from mistakes. Isn't that what this is all about?"

"So I've said," Brandenburg said, reaching for his pipe. He struck a match, drew the flame deep into the packed bowl, and then blew a perfect smoke ring. "I wonder how the young man made out."

• • •

"Freeze!" the sentry in the focus room shouted.

One step out of the gate, Wallace froze. The sentry's weapon was pointed directly at his belly. "Easy, all right? I'm one of you."

"Try another story. Walk forward now, slowly, away from the gate."

Wallace complied, advancing until he was nose-up against the opposite wall. "I'm Rayne Wallace, runner 21618, assigned to the station in Alternity Blue."

"Now I know you're a liar. Hands behind your head, now. The Blue station's been closed for weeks."

"They don't tell you anything, do they? I just got out of Blue. Why don't you march me over to gate control and let Monaghan or Deb King arbitrate this?"

"You know Monaghan?"

"Christ, yes. Can we get a move on?"

"Well—if you did come back from Blue, there's some people that are going to want—" There was a sudden sizzling in the room. "Jesus Christ, sweet-son-of-Mary—"

Wallace risked twisting his head around to look. He saw the sentry staring with mouth agape at a gate that was shot through with squirming lightning-like discharges. From moment to moment it grew, spreading over the walls and ceiling and floor. Then, with a roaring, whistling sound, a minute black cavity appeared at the center of the gate, and the swirling fingers of energy suddenly leaped across the gap to where the sentry stood.

The sentry screamed, and Wallace ran. He ran out the door and down the corridor toward the stairs, bucking a strong draught, as though the gate were drawing the air from the building. As he reached the stairs, the lights went out. He looked back to see the gate swollen into a seething, crackling ball of energy a hundred feet in diameter.

It was eviscerating the heart of the building, consuming it as the maze had consumed the officer Wallace had brought through the Philadelphia gate. Already the floors above the cavity were beginning to buckle and sag, and still the roaring maw grew. Choking plaster dust filled the stairwell, and the treads danced under his feet.

By the time he reached the first floor, Wallace could feel it pulling at him, trying to drag him back into the maelstrom. The whole building was shaking, creaking, cracking, bowing inward as it tried to obey the call of the insatiable energies within it. Bits of masonry flew through the air, bits of metal glowed with inducted currents. The roaring was of a demon, a monster, caught in cataclysm.

Head ducked low, Wallace ran out the front door of the Cambridge into a hail of glass fragments falling from a hundred windows blown inward by the drop of pressure in the atrium. Behind him the thunder of collapsing walls mixed with a screaming whistle that climbed up through the octaves until it felt as though a dentist's drill were grinding at the inside of his skull.

He flung himself full-length on the ground a few feet short of the door to gate control and covered his head with his arms as fragments of debris rained around him. He fully expected to die.

But then the whistling disappeared into the silence of octaves beyond hearing. The roaring faded to the sound of a soft breeze and was stilled. The cracking and shifting of rubble settling replaced the crackling of the insatiable fingers of electric fire.

Slowly, Wallace lifted his head to look back. The Cambridge was gone. All that remained was a hole heaped with crumbled stone and twisted steel inadequate even to make a skeleton of the structure which had stood there just moments before.

Picking himself up off the ground, he shook bits of glass and plaster from his clothes. The gate control door swung open, and a handful of glassy-eyed Guardsmen emerged into the atrium to stare disbelievingly at the astonishing sight. Wallace walked past them and into gate control, up the runners' chute and out through Guard country toward the Tower's north entrance.

His torn, filthy clothing and dust-filled hair drew stares, but no one stopped him or even spoke to him until he reached the rank of turnstiles spanning the corridor at the security checkpoint. There he was hailed by a sentry, obediently still at his post despite his hunger to know what the tumult inside the Tower had meant.

"Hey, what happened in there? Was there an explosion?" the sentry called from his booth.

"No," Wallace said, pushing through the jaws of a turnstile. "Somebody slammed a door."

"What? Wait, where are you going?"

Wallace just kept walking toward the bright light streaming in from the street beyond.

"Home," he said softly. "I'm going home."

The first casualty when war comes is truth.

> —Hiram Johnson

The tree of liberty must be refreshed from time to time with the blood of patriots and tyrants.

> —Thomas Jefferson

ABOUT THE AUTHOR

Michael P. Kube-McDowell (pronounced cue-bee) has at various times called New Jersey, Indiana, and Michigan home. He holds a master's degree in science education and was honored for teaching excellence by the 1985 White House Commission on Presidential Scholars. Mr. Kube-McDowell's short fiction has been featured in *Analog*, *Isaac Asimov's SF Magazine*, and *The Magazine of Fantasy and Science Fiction*, as well as in the anthologies *After the Flames* and *Perpetual Light*. Three of his stories have been adapted as episodes of the television series *Tales from the Darkside*.

Outside of science fiction, Kube-McDowell is the author of more than 500 nonfiction articles on subjects ranging from space careers to "scientific creationism" to an award-winning four-part series on the state of American education.

Emprise, the critically acclaimed first volume of the "Trigon Disunity" future history was a Philip K. Dick Award finalist. Mr. Kube-McDowell's other books include *Enigma*, *Empery*, and *Isaac Asimov's Robot City: Odyssey*. He is currently at work on a new novel, *The Quiet Pools*, for The Berkley Publishing Group.